A Whip OF Cords

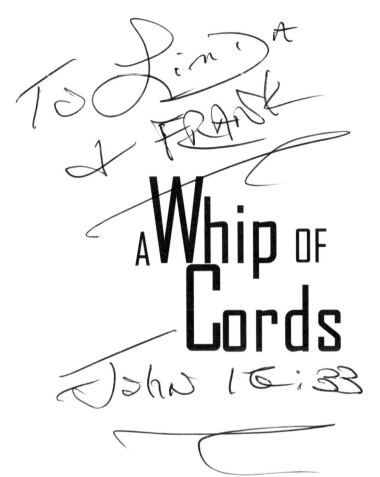

A Whip OF Cords

Walker Buckalew

Fideli Publishing Inc.
WWW.FIDELIPUBLISHING.COM

12   11   10   09   08   07   1   2   3   4   5   6

Library of Congress Control Number:

ISBN: 978-1-962402-70-5 (hardcover)
        978-1-962402-69-9 (paperback)

Copy editing by Frances Archer
Cover art and design by Reel Video & Stills

www.WalkerBuckalew.com

Author's Note

This book may be read separately from the previous books in the Rebecca Series, but new readers may wish to know that it is a sequel to these titles:

- *The Face of the Enemy*

- *By Many or By Few*

- *Such Thy Mercies*

- *Choose You This Day*

- *A Fearful Thing*

The first four novels in the series take place one (fictional) year apart, starting in the late 1970s and continuing into the early 1980s. The fifth novel, *A Fearful Thing*, takes place four years after *Choose You This Day*, and so is placed in summer of 1985. This novel, *A Whip of Cords*, the sixth in the series, follows within just a few (fictional) days of the fifth, and so is also placed in the summer of 1985.

That being the case, the Cold War between the United States and the then-Soviet Union is depicted as being in full swing. The Soviets' notorious intelligence agency, the KGB, is featured prominently throughout. The Prime Minister of the United Kingdom is Margaret Thatcher; consequently, all pronoun references in the novel to "the PM" are feminine.

As for 1985 technology, desktop computers — the precursors of laptops — are found commonly in business and academic settings, but also in many households. Hand-held communication devices are rare and, where found, are large and clumsy in comparison to what they will become. And the internet as a popular means of communication is still on the horizon.

Regular readers of the Rebecca stories are aware that, except where a setting must be fictional (e.g., "The Lodge" near Birmingham, England), real sites, presented fictionally, are used whenever feasible: for example, St. David's Cathedral in Wales in the first novel; Navy-Marine Corps Stadium in Annapolis, Maryland, in the second; the Italian coastal village of Amalfi in the third; Israel's Yad Vashem and Tel Megiddo in the fourth; the Washington, D.C., area in the fifth; and Duxford Royal Air Force Base, near Cambridge, England, in the sixth.

The central character in the series, Rebecca Clark (birth name Manguson), is in her mid-20s in *The Face of the Enemy;* she is 33 in this story. She is single in that first novel, but now is the married mother of four-year-old twins.

In the years between the writing and publication of *Choose You This Day* and *A Fearful Thing,* I completed two novels for young adults: *The Visioners: Into the Wilderness;* and *Visioners2: Into the City.* Both young-adult novels feature Rebecca's twins, Joanna and Samuel, who, in fictional time, have grown from infancy in *Choose You This Day* to early adolescence in the two Visioners stories. A third novel in this series remains on the drawing board at this writing.

Let me add a gratuitous note about style: some foreign words and phrases, such as the Hebrew phrase *Rebekka Yahalomin,* are italicized on first mention, but thereafter are simply worked into the text without having special attention called to them. However, other foreign words or phrases, such as the French word "sans," have become so commonplace in American parlance that they appear in this book without italics or quotation marks. They have been "adopted" into the English language.

And let me add that, if this is your first encounter with Rebecca and her colleagues, I welcome you to their world of intrigue, danger, and, in equal measure, respect for God's creation and for us, its inhabitants.

Walker Buckalew
Greer, SC

"The fear of the Lord
is the beginning of wisdom."

Psalm 111:10

"The word of the Lord was rare in those days;
visions were not widespread."

1 Samuel 3:1

CHAPTER ONE

Thursday, June 13, 1985

EARLY ON A THURSDAY MORNING IN DOWNTOWN LONDON, Graham Roberts-Holm, senior MI6 agent and director of the small MI6 subgroup created to focus on "unexplained and unexplainable" data sources, found himself wrestling with the task of introducing a young colleague to the subgroup's mission. The two were seated opposite each other at a small table in one of the agency's briefing rooms.

Roberts-Holm had just pushed a thick file folder across the table to his mentee. The file was a duplicate of the one Roberts-Holm had open in front of him.

The two were dressed similarly in dark suits, white shirts, dark ties, and black wingtip shoes. MI6 agents referred to this jokingly as the MI6 uniform. The dull, conservative dress code was thought to emphasize the weightiness of the agency's role as the United Kingdom's foreign intelligence agency, never to be confused with MI5, its mere domestic counterpart. MI6 leaders thought of the agency as the model for America's CIA, Israel's Mossad, and the Soviet Union's KGB, among others. Leaders at those agencies would have scoffed at the notion that MI6 was their model, since each of the three regarded themselves as the model for all others.

"First," said Roberts-Holm in his deep, carefully modulated Oxford accent, "you must understand that only our subgroup, which has no official existence whatsoever and thus, no official name, is authorized to investigate and act upon any data coming to our attention from the source."

"The source, sir?" asked the newcomer.

"Yes, the source," replied the senior agent. "Please open your file folder to the first page," he continued. "As you see there, the subject of that entire file is a woman identified as Rebecca Manguson Clark. You may recall her, known then only by her birth name, from her high-profile international tennis ranking of a few years back. She is our paramount source for all 'unexplained and unexplainable' data, the responsibility for which was assigned to this agency subgroup upon its creation in 1980."

The newcomer was thoughtful for several seconds, then asked, "So, she is the 'paramount' source ... does that mean that there are sources for unexplained and unexplainable data other than Ms. Clark?"

"In the several years of our subgroup's existence, there has been none."

"Then why ..."

"We do not want to operate on the assumption that there will be no sources for unexplained and unexplainable data other than this individual. Thus, 'paramount,' implying there may be others."

The mentee nodded thoughtfully.

"For this reason," continued the senior agent, "we have always referred to ourselves, among ourselves, as 'The Rebecca Unit,' and by no other designation. And, I wish to emphasize, that label has no meaning to anyone other than 'Control' — our term for the MI6 director of operations — and perhaps, to the Minister."

"The Prime Minister, sir?"

The senior agent nodded. "Yes, it is indeed she whom I mean to reference. However, you understand, I have no knowledge as to whether or not Control keeps the Minister informed on this topic. The whole subject is regarded with understandable skepticism by many, possibly including the Minister herself."

"Because we cannot prove the validity of the data source."

"Yes."

Roberts-Holm sighed and, uncomfortable as always at this point in explaining his subgroup's mission, forged on.

"Ms. Clark and her family and their associates, some of whom are in the U.S., are themselves quite clear on the ultimate source of the data. If they were writing that word — source — they would capitalize the 's' to indicate their certainty that the data they ... actually 'she,' not 'they' ... receive from time to time … constitute 'divine messages' … messages to be acted upon immediately, because the origin of the messages is the Almighty Himself."

"They think God Himself sends them … sends *her* … these messages?"

The senior agent nodded.

The newcomer was again thoughtful.

"Sir," he asked finally, "do *you* think her messages are from God?"

Roberts-Holm shifted uncomfortably in his chair.

"We have concluded after exhaustive studies — studies you will find described in detail in your file folder — that Ms. Clark's messages come from a source we cannot identify or explain. And, I might add, it was Mossad, not our agency nor the CIA nor, certainly, the KGB … it was Mossad that first concluded Ms. Clark's data source was indeed either supernatural or otherwise completely unexplainable.

"We at MI6 as well as the CIA … and, apparently, the KGB … have accepted Mossad's designation. That designation is a Hebrew phrase, *Rebekka Yahalomin*, meaning 'the Rebecca Communications Unit.'"

Silence, while the newcomer pondered this.

The senior agent decided to continue.

"We do not ask either our own MI6 agents nor agents from CIA nor Mossad whether they believe that the origins of Ms. Clark's data are divine. But all of us intimately involved with Rebekka Yahalomin are in agreement that *something*, from time to time, informs this woman, allowing her to access critically import-ant, threat-specific data that cannot be ignored by the intelligence services. And it is *always … every time* … data that cannot be accessed by any of the rest of us, either 'us,' as individuals, or 'us,' as intelligence services.

"Sometimes Ms. Clark cites an Old Testament verse. I have actually learned it, despite not being a Bible reader myself. It's from the book of First Samuel. 'The word of the Lord was rare in those days. Visions were not widespread.'

"But then, in that same Old Testament chapter, something obviously super-natural takes place."

More silence.

Finally, the newcomer asked again, "But sir, do *you* believe Ms. Clark's mes-sages are indeed from God?"

The senior agent looked hard at the newcomer, frowned his disapproval, and shook his head in impatience.

"Study that file. Make your own inferences. Draw your own conclusions."

The young agent was undeterred, seemingly oblivious to the disapproval.

"But, sir, you have compiled this file. You've been immersed in all these unexplained and unexplainable data for years. You've drawn your own conclusions, I have no doubt. And so, respectfully, sir, I'd like to know, do *you* believe Ms. Clark's messages are from God?"

There was a long pause. The senior agent, no longer scowling his disapproval, appeared to yield to his young colleague's persistence. He first looked vacantly at the ceiling ... then out the window ... then down at the table ... then up at the newcomer.

He cleared his throat.

Then a second time.

Finally, painfully, he extracted an answer from himself. "Well ... umm ... yes ... I tend to think ..."

Throat-clearing noise.

"Yes ... Yes, I must say ..."

Throat-clearing noise yet again.

"Yes ... I suppose I do."

Thursday morning

At almost the same moment, in another section of London, Rebecca Manguson Clark brought the family Volvo to a stop in front of her home, turned off the ignition, and let her head fall back against the headrest. She breathed deeply and smiled. The time was 8:35 a.m. on this warm June Thursday, and she had already completed a 75-minute instructional tennis session for two 15-year-olds at the nearby city courts.

She allowed herself a moment's reflection on the implausibility of sitting safely in the family sedan on a quiet street in metropolitan London, when just days earlier, in the United States, she and her brother had fought with knives and fists for their very lives. She found it almost impossible to place the two things side by side in her mind.

A week previous ... savage violence, deadly weapons, a desperate ocean swim.

Now ... tennis rackets, children, tree-lined neighborhoods.

Rebecca's private devotions and prayers had been completed hours earlier, while it was yet dark, prior to dressing for the tennis lessons she had enjoyed providing for the two adolescents throughout the spring, each of them a child of her husband's work colleagues. She looked gratefully out the car window at her modest home.

She and American Matthew Clark, married now for nearly six years, had moved two years earlier from the barebones flat in which Rebecca had once lived, when still unmarried, with her twin brother, Luke Manguson. She and Matt had researched their first real home with meticulous care and had finally purchased one that would afford separate bedrooms for their rambunctious, growing four-year-old twins, Joanna and Samuel, plus a workroom for Rebecca and Matt, a spacious family room, and a well-constructed fenced backyard in which the twins and their black-and-white border-collie mix, Ginny, also four years old, could play safely.

Now, pushing the recent U.S.-based drama from her mind, Rebecca rose from the right-hand-drive vehicle, walked back to the sedan's boot, then reached inside and hoisted the bulky tennis accoutrement bag from the well. Lifting the bag to her left shoulder by the carrying strap, she strode with her unwieldy impedimenta to the front steps, unlocked the bright blue front door, and stepped inside. She shrugged the bag from her shoulder and onto the floor of the entry hall.

Immediately she found herself laughing softly as she heard the staccato snick-snick of canine toenails coming rapidly her way from the direction of the family room. She stooped to welcome the Border collie she and Matt had rescued when they had moved house. Rebecca gave this uniquely gifted family member a quick scratch behind her soft ears.

Ginny raised her nose and pushed forward to accept the gesture, smiling her border-collie smile and wagging her upward-curling border-collie tail. Yielding to the warm pleasure of the canine greeting, Rebecca dropped to both knees and gratefully welcomed the damp pressure of Ginny's cold nose, as Ginny forcefully nuzzled Rebecca's exercise-hardened abdomen.

Is it truly possible, Rebecca thought to herself, *that just days ago my brother and I fought for our lives on the other side of the Atlantic? Is it truly possible that now I find myself safe in my own home … with my border collie nosing my stomach?*

Of course, she answered, *we knew all the while that if we lived through it all … this was always the outcome … the inevitable outcome …*

Ginny nudged again, bringing Rebecca's attention back to her ear-scratching responsibilities. As she complied with Ginny's unspoken request, Rebecca allowed herself to broaden her "Is it truly possible" question.

Do not our histories always seem cast as inevitable when considered in retrospect … resolutely inevitable? Always appearing, in hindsight, as if things could not possibly have turned out any differently than they have?

Still on her knees, now cupping Ginny's face in her hands, Rebecca closed her eyes and prayed, starting with the five-word "companion prayer" given her by an Episcopal minister during the preceding week's battles in the U.S.

Father, be present, be present … not just in our crisis moments, but in all our moments … in all our moments … be present … be present.

Rebecca opened her eyes, gave Ginny one last scratch, and rose gracefully to her feet. She had no need to use her hands for the maneuver, either for additional push or for balance.

Then, standing, as Ginny rubbed against her knees, she completed the thought.

Inevitability belongs to Almighty God, she reminded herself finally, *not to us … we find inevitability by looking back … God does not have the limitation … the limitation is ours … but for us … what comes next is unknown.*

She continued, now praying again, still standing motionless in the entryway.

I ask again for Your protection this day, Father, for me and for our family, even though, protection from what, I can't know … I can only ask Your presence … I can only ask that You might hold us … each of us … in Your hands this day … Amen.

Rebecca opened her eyes again and smiled down at Ginny, then stooped to give her a kiss on top of her furry border-collie head.

"Good girl, Ginny. Thank you for coming to meet me.

"Where is everybody?"

Having satisfied both herself and Ginny with their morning ritual, and already knowing the answer to her question, *where is everybody?* Rebecca placed her keys and wallet on the shoulder-high knickknack stand that she and Matt had positioned just inside the front door. She, 6 feet tall, had allocated to herself the second shelf from the top. Matt, 6 feet 4 inches, had been awarded the topmost shelf. And Joanna and Samuel had been assigned the lower two shelves for some of their outdoor things: summer hats, rain caps, outdoor toys, illustrated children's books for car rides.

Rebecca, still standing in the entryway, indulged herself one final thought: *Home ... this is home ... this is family ... this is comfort ... this is belonging.* And she prayed yet again: *Thank you, Father. Thank you for all this.*

She then carried the tennis bag to the workroom, paused at the bathroom to splash water on her face, and strode back through the house toward the muffled sounds of her husband animatedly reading to the children from *The Cat in the Hat.* She passed softly, in her athletic, cat-like stride, through the family room. She circled behind the settee on which the children were positioned, riveted by Dr. Suess, and stooped to give a quiet kiss to the crown of each small head. As she did, Ginny, having trailed Rebecca through the house, inserted herself into the space between the twins, both of whom reflexively placed an arm across their border collie's coarse-furred back.

Rebecca continued to the dining room, prepared a glass of juice, and sat quietly at the dining room table. She picked up the morning newspaper, left there by Matt after his 5:30 a.m. breakfast, and turned to the national news section. She rarely read either the international news articles or the editorials, but tried to stay abreast of the goings-on within her "great island."

Near the back of the U.K. news section, she fixed on a small article placed inconspicuously below the fold. Her gray eyes widened as she read.

Falmouth. Cornwall—Fr. Jeremy Donaldson, 41, was found badly beaten last evening in the sanctuary of St. Paul's Anglican Church in downtown Falmouth, following his regular Wednesday evening service. Police report Fr.

Donaldson suffered a severe concussion and a broken jaw, among other, lesser injuries.

Police have no suspects.

Fr. Donaldson has served St. Paul's for six years. His family includes his wife Audrey, who found him unconscious and called police, and two teen-age sons. Mrs. Donaldson stated that she expects her husband to remain in hospital for some time.

Rebecca, a tear starting down the side of her nose, read the notice a second time, dabbed away the tear with a paper napkin from the dispenser on the table, then rose and carried the newspaper into the family room where the children sat absorbed in the rhythm of the Dr. Seuss story. She moved to the settee, gestured to Ginny to get down, and squeezed between her two children in the space Ginny had vacated.

Seconds later, as Matt reached a stopping point, he said, "Okay, you two, you're going to Molly and James's house at lunch time. Go pick out what you want to wear."

The twins, squealing, ran toward their rooms.

"Wash your teeth, dears," called Rebecca, "and after you dress, come back and let us see you."

Their visit would be overnight. This was a somewhat regular occurrence during summer vacation from the Anglican preschool attended by all four of these children, the same preschool in which Rebecca had taught for the past two school years.

As Joanna and Samuel scrambled down the hallway toward their rooms, Rebecca gestured to the newspaper in her lap and asked, "Matt, did you see this piece on the attack on Jeremy Donaldson last evening?"

"What? No, I haven't read that section."

Her voice heavy with bewilderment and sadness, Rebecca read the report to her husband, and they sat staring at each other in disbelief.

"It was just … what? … two months ago," asked Matt, "that Jeremy led that seminar in Oxford on C. S. Lewis's 'Weight of Glory' and several other sermons and essays written by Lewis?"

Rebecca nodded.

"Yes. Mid-April, I think."

She shook her head.

"And poor Audrey will be at such a loss while Jeremy is in hospital ... although the congregation will certainly rally round her and the boys."

She paused, then added, "I just don't understand why anyone would do something like this to Jeremy ... such a sweet, kind person ... and do it in this way, Matt.

"Can you?"

Her husband shook his head, jaw muscles tensing visibly.

"No," he growled.

"Cowards," he muttered.

Thursday, midmorning

Later that same morning, Graham Roberts-Holm and his MI6 protégé met again in their small conference room. The purpose of this session was to allow the newcomer, having completed a thoroughgoing review of the file given him earlier, to listen to a conversation that would involve, at the other end of the line, a member of Rebecca Manguson Clark's inner circle.

In this case, her brother.

The young agent knew this was a magnanimous gesture on the part of his superior. To be granted even a passive role in a conversation with a member of Ms. Clark's group, given the young man's fledgling status with the ultra-secret MI6 Rebecca unit, was extraordinary.

Roberts-Holm pressed the button to engage the speakerphone.

Luke Manguson answered on the first ring from his second-floor office in the downtown building owned and occupied by International Security Perspectives, LLC. ISP had become known during its brief existence as the premier consulting firm for organizational security in the U.K. and much of continental Europe.

"Luke Manguson speaking, sir."

"Luke ... Graham Roberts-Holm here. How are you and the family?"

"We're doing well, Graham. A little excitement for several of us in the U.S. recently, as I'm sure you and your colleagues are aware. You've updated that thick file on Rebekka Yahalomin already, I've no doubt."

Sensing the brief hesitation from Roberts-Holm, Luke corrected himself.

"Oh … sorry, Graham … I should not have spoken the forbidden Hebrew phrase, should I? I should have said 'the Rebecca unit,' right?"

Roberts-Holm laughed good-naturedly.

"Oh, I think *you* are certainly allowed the Hebrew, Luke."

Luke chuckled, then asked, "What's going on at MI6, Graham?"

"First, Luke, let me say that I have you on speaker phone, so that our new man can listen in. That okay?"

"Of course, Graham."

"Well … Luke … as to what's happening here at MI6 … those two assaults in Cornwall and Yorkshire last night did get the attention … not of the agency as a whole, of course … but of our little Rebecca unit."

Luke paused, processing.

"*Two* assaults, Graham? We're only aware of the one in Cornwall."

"Yes, the one in Yorkshire was reported too late for the newspapers, as were the other *four*, which had to be aborted for various reasons. Those reports have come in piecemeal from law enforcement around the country, first to Scotland Yard, then to MI5 and MI6. And I should add that one of the aborted attempts was in Wales."

After another pause, Luke said, "I don't think I understand."

"Information is still being sorted, Luke, but it certainly appears that all six victims — the two actual victims and the four intended victims — were ministers, all of whom had leadership roles at the April conference in Oxford … the one that focused on C. S. Lewis and traditional Christianity."

This news was greeted by prolonged silence at the other end.

Roberts-Holm smiled to his protégé.

"I see you're not eager to comment, Luke."

"Well, Graham … what would I say?"

"Umm … well … you might say that your sister had an unusually instructive dream last night, that she has reported the details to you, and that you are as anxious as ever to report those details to us."

Roberts-Holm and the young agent were greeted by laughter … long and loud.

When the laughter faded, the MI6 operatives waited.

Nothing.

"Luke," continued Roberts-Holm, determined, "I would not have phoned if there were just the one assault that you already knew of. But there were supposed to be *six*."

Roberts-Holm paused, then continued.

"A variety of Christian denominations, Luke, including Roman Catholic … churches located all over England, plus the one in Wales that I mentioned … and the same scenario playing out in both successful assaults … beatings which produced severe concussions, plus numerous lacerations and possible broken bones.

"Thorough beatings … concussions … abrasions … hospitalizations … and there may be more than the two successful ones and the four failures that just have not been reported as yet.

"And *that's* why I've called you, Luke. This is something so finely coordinated and so widespread … and so focused on a particular Christian *perspective* … a perspective featured in that Oxford conference … that it seems to our Rebecca unit that Ms. Clark might well have received something … something we would need to know."

Continued silence on the other end of the line.

Finally, Roberts-Holm said, perhaps a little plaintively, "Luke, surely you can give us something other than peals of laughter or prolonged silence?"

Luke smiled to himself … then spoke … not exactly rudely, but with a certain military brusqueness in his tone.

"No, Graham … as always, if Rebecca receives one of her messages, the fact of that receipt, and whatever details may comprise the message, are closely held within our little group. We let you know only if we deem it necessary and appropriate. But you already knew that. So why this call, sir?"

Roberts-Holm blushed at the implicit reprimand, then answered in a manner consistent with the sudden frost in the conversation.

"Just the fact that these assaults targeted ministers whom we might term 'C. S. Lewis pastors' … advocates for traditional Christianity … each a presenter at the Oxford conference on that very subject …assaults planned to take place at roughly the same moment all over the U.K., and at denominationally diverse churches.

"That's a recipe for the involvement of Ms. Clark's group ... and I consider it my responsibility to make this call and ask the question I've asked you."

Luke nodded to himself.

"Yes, I understand that, certainly ... but I can assure you that at this point I have nothing to offer you on this ... nothing at all."

Roberts-Holm persisted.

"Luke, does that mean your sister has received nothing from her source, or does it mean that she has, but you can't speak about it with me ... yet?"

"You know I can't answer that kind of question, sir. Nor can I answer any other kind of question on this topic. It will always be Rebecca's decision whether or not to engage any outside group. I don't expect that will ever change."

Roberts-Holm took a deep breath, trying to control the frustration surging within him, and knowing that he was the supplicant here, knowing he had no leverage with Rebekka Yahalomin, the Hebrew phrase he often used in his head, but never spoke aloud. He calmed himself and continued.

"I do understand that," he said, "but the fact that your recent contretemps in the U.S. involved the Soviet embassy in Washington, the Russian Mafia in New York, and the KGB ... that makes this the business of MI6, Luke ... and all of that has put our MI6 Rebecca unit on edge. This call represents my effort at due diligence.

"You see what I mean, Luke?"

Luke nodded to himself.

"I do, Graham. Sorry about the laughter. This is not amusing."

"No ... not amusing at all."

"I apologize, Graham. And I will relay to my sister, and to her husband and my wife here at ISP, the nature of your call to me. We'll keep our antennae elevated ... but, as you know, the true initiative in this kind of thing has never lain with Rebekka Yahalomin at all. The true initiative — the ultimate initiative — has always lain where it must ... with the Source."

Luke broke the connection with MI6 and buzzed his ISP colleagues — wife Kory and brother-in-law Matt — asking them to come down one floor to his office as soon as they could free themselves. They each appeared within minutes.

Luke then dialed his sister and pressed his console's speakerphone button.

"Rebecca," he said, "Kory and Matt are here in my office, and the speakerphone is activated. Are you able to talk to us for a few minutes now?"

"Yes, Luke," she answered.

"The children are in back," she continued, "playing with Ginny ... although she has just curled up in the shade and is going to sleep.

"The twins are eager to head for Molly and James's house in an hour or so. I'm watching them through the kitchen window."

Luke proceeded to give her — and Kory and Matt — the substance of Roberts-Holm's phone call.

Then he waited.

After a long silence while his listeners processed the staggering news that at least a half-dozen ministers had been assaulted, or were at least targeted for assault, after their mid-week worship services, Rebecca spoke. Her voice sounded unfamiliar to her brother and sister-in-law — a soft, uncertain, hesitant voice that said simply, "I'm sorry, Luke ... I ... I really can't talk now.

"I'm going to go out back ... with the twins ... Matt, I hope you'll be able to come home soon?"

And she hung up without waiting for a response.

Matt viewed his wife's anxiety-ridden response as a clear call for his immediate assistance. He left his brother- and sister-in-law sitting puzzled in Luke's office while he quickly excused himself. He went to his own office one floor above, picked up his keys and briefcase, and started home.

Meanwhile, Rebecca walked to her back porch, which was an open deck with room for a small table and two chairs. She sat down, smiling at the children, and began to process her brother's call.

She thought about the words Roberts-Holm had reportedly spoken ... assaults or would-be assaults on ministers known to espouse traditional Christianity ... ministers who led sessions at the April conference ... ministers representing a variety of denominations, although with a consistent, traditional Christian *per-spective* ... ministers whose churches are scattered all over England ... their assaults planned to take place at exactly the same time ... thus, precisely coordinated ... the two actual beatings executed with a terrible consistency, so as to produce concussions and other damaging injuries, but not so severe as to cause death ... exactly the sort of thing, Roberts-Holm had emphasized, that Rebekka Yahalomin had been called upon to confront in the past.

Rebecca shook her head quietly, still attending to the twins and to Ginny.

Why do I feel removed from all this? Why am I so unresponsive? Why am I so exhausted at the mere thought of trying to deal with this? And what do Luke and Kory expect of me? And what does MI6 — this Roberts-Holm person — expect of me?

And suddenly she felt answered. There was nothing required of her whatsoever. No matter what expectations MI6 — and her brother and sister-in-law — might have, nothing was required of her beyond what she had just realized. That is, she had already waited several hours, after reading of the assault in Falmouth, without phoning Jeremy Donaldson's wife Audrey. *That* responsibility she understood. *That* she could, and would, do immediately. *That* was her clear obligation and, beyond that, her joy.

Fifteen minutes later, she summoned the twins and Ginny into the house. She gave Joanna and Samuel their late-morning carrot snack, gave Ginny two of her little treat bites, and sent the children off to their rooms for quiet time before they would head for their friends' house. She then returned to the family room with Ginny at her side and picked up her address book to phone Audrey Donaldson.

As she reached for the phone, she glanced out the front window and saw Matt pulling his aging Vauxhall Astra sedan into his parking space just behind her Volvo. She smiled, happy to see her husband and eager to speak with him about her resolution.

The smile faded as she also saw, cruising slowly past Matt's parked Vauxhall, an enormous black Rolls-Royce, its windows heavily tinted, its impressive size and attention-getting cachet starkly out of place in their middle-class neighborhood, a neighborhood comprising only mid-priced family homes and vehicles. She watched the Rolls move to the street corner, stop, and then back up, just as someone might if he were taking careful note of a street address, or perhaps taking photos, or both. The Rolls' occupants made no effort to disguise their intentions.

Matt, focused on getting to Rebecca and completely unaware of the Rolls, stepped out of his Vauxhall and started up the walkway to the front door. Rebecca, instructing Ginny to 'stay,' stepped onto the front porch to greet him, but kept her eyes on the black behemoth, her muscles tensed and ready to tackle her husband to the ground should a tinted window be lowered to expose the muzzle of a gun.

But the Rolls simply stopped, paused, started slowly forward again, moved unhurriedly to the corner, turned, and disappeared from view.

Rebecca took her husband's hand in hers, pulled him inside the front door, and closed the door firmly, locking it behind her. Matt looked at her quizzically.

She took his hand again and led him to the family room, gesturing for him to take a seat in his favorite reading chair. She sat, too, facing him from the settee. Ginny immediately curled up on the floor between them.

Rebecca leaned forward, her face solemn, and described the Rolls and its having rather obviously — even ostentatiously — followed Matt to their home. She emphasized its having insolently backed up, to stop just two car lengths in front of her Volvo, apparently to note their address or to take photos.

Matt's jaw sagged, his eyes wide.

He shook his head in self-disgust.

"I can't believe I did not see that I was being followed, Rebecca," he said ruefully, "especially in a vehicle like that one. Inexcusable.

"I would have led them on a merry chase. I'm supposed to be more aware than that, you know. I'm supposed to check for trailing vehicles as a matter of course.

"We of Rebekka Yahalomin are supposed to be vigilant, Rebecca."

He shook his head again in pained regret.

Ginny looked up at him, concerned by his tone.

Rebecca leaned forward, a slight smile playing across her face, her eyes bright with understanding and gratitude.

"You were focused on getting home to me," she said, her voice gentle, "having heard my pathetic response to Luke's phone call, dear. You wanted to get here fast. And you did.

"And I love you, Matthew Clark."

She rose and stepped to his side, skirting Ginny. She stooped down and kissed him, cradling his head in her hand.

"You're vulnerable when I'm involved," she added, now standing straight and looking down at him.

"Maybe someone hopes to take advantage of that, Matt."

She returned to her seat, bending down to give Ginny a scratch on her way.

"Well," she continued from the settee, "that's just one more thing we'll have to be aware of, dear husband. Don't spend another second with recriminations, Matt. You did what you felt was urgent. You came to me. Fast.

"You love me."

He nodded and smiled at her, but continued to berate himself silently. The room was quiet, husband and wife equally focused on the implications of Matt's having been followed to their home.

Finally, Rebecca said, "Matt, I'm going to phone Audrey Donaldson. I should have phoned her earlier. I don't want to wait. She's my priority for the moment."

"Of course, Rebecca. Of course. Please …"

Rebecca spent 15 minutes on the phone with her friend in Falmouth. Then she broke the connection and turned back to Matt, who had been sitting grimly in his chair, sometimes shaking his head in self-blame at his having been oblivious to the presence of the Rolls-Royce in his rear-view mirrors.

Ginny rose and joined Rebecca on the settee.

"Matt," said Rebecca after several moments, "that phone call from Luke … I know he and Kory must be confused by my absurdly rude response … my non-response, actually … but my reaction was just my mental refusal to entertain the likelihood of our being called upon to wade into something fraught, so soon after we thought we had finished with that kind of thing, at least for a very long time. We've never faced two such things in close succession.

"And Matt, I don't *want* to face this kind of thing … not now.

"You know?"

He nodded.

"I knew that, Rebecca," he said.

"I knew exactly how you were hearing Luke's report of a half-dozen more planned assaults, rather than just the one we learned about from this morning's paper ... the one involving poor Jeremy."

"Yes," she said, "and until I saw that Rolls so brazenly backing up to canvass our house and our vehicles ... I felt not just helpless, but *angry* ... you know ... just angry that we might be ripped away from our quiet home life right now ... so soon.

"When Luke phoned and gave me that summary from the MI6 person, I found I had no interest in thinking about these assaults and would-be assaults. I had no energy for them. Just exhaustion at fighting these kinds of battles ..."

"I know, Rebecca," he said. "I really do know."

She stood and walked to the front window, concentrating. Matt watched her, holding his silence, knowing she would speak again when she had concretized her thoughts. After several moments, she returned to the settee and sat again, her hand automatically going to Ginny's ears.

Then she looked up at her husband, and he sensed something altogether different from the Rebecca he had seen moments before, or the one whose voice he had listened to in Luke's office just a half-hour earlier. He saw instantly that this was the *other* Rebecca Clark.

This was the Rebecca Clark of Rebekka Yahalomin.

"Matt," she said, her voice suddenly hard-edged, "as soon as that Rolls-Royce backed up to study our house and our cars ... so obviously doing a *reconnaissance* on us ... the two pieces of my heart were brought together.

"These global threats to the faith ... these threats we've faced, on and off, for so long ... all the threats finally merged with the one threat that goes straight to my heart ... the threats all dovetailed with a new one ... and that's a threat *to our children.*"

She said this last with anger rising in her voice. Her gray eyes, always her most distinctive physical feature, blazed with a sudden fury known only to mothers of children, and yet universally recognized by those who are not.

A fury recognized in a heartbeat by those who are fathers.

CHAPTER TWO

Thursday, late morning

A HALF-HOUR LATER, MATT CLARK, DRIVING HIS BEAT-UP VAUXHALL, dropped off the twins and their small overnight cases with Dottie — Molly and James's mum. She welcomed Joanna and Samuel at her front door as she waved goodbye to Matt. Meanwhile, Rebecca edged her Volvo through morning traffic to a small shopping area near their residential neighborhood, parked on the street, picked up her shopping lists, and began her rounds.

Rebecca Manguson Clark was now 33, yet she maintained both the queenly beauty and the elegant carriage of her younger days. Six feet in height, with high cheekbones and thick, straight black hair that fell halfway to her waist, she moved with an ever-present suggestion of feline athleticism, an almost otherworldly quietness and calmness that could change in an instant into swift fight-or-flight mode when danger threatened. Especially danger to someone other than herself.

If one faced her up close for the first time, however, neither her willowy height, nor the long, lustrous hair, nor the catlike movements, nor the latent coiled-spring explosiveness were likely to dominate initial impressions. Rather, it would more likely be the deep, penetrating gray eyes and the arresting drama of the facial scar.

The scar, which ran across the right side of Rebecca's face from mouth to ear, traced a shallow V-shape as it traversed her cheek. Five years earlier, a hired assailant in New York City had made the cut when he cruelly slashed her with a

12-inch screwdriver. Once the wound had matured and lost its initial rawness, the residual scar seemed to most observers to make her face simply more interesting, in no way subtracting from its natural feminine elegance.

Wearing now, for her shopping excursion, a white sleeveless cotton top with a simple, dark-blue mid-calf skirt and low-heeled walking shoes, Rebecca, despite the ordinariness of her attire, nevertheless caught the attention of passers-by. There was nothing ordinary about her beauty, her stature, or her presence.

Occasionally, a follower of sports would recognize her from her days as an internationally ranked tennis star. Some would even stop her to ask shyly for an autograph. She always signed carefully in her precise cursive.

God's blessings
Rebecca Manguson Clark

She spent an hour selecting summer clothes for the rapidly growing twins, as well as a few dress shirts and ties for Matt. Upscale dress was required by ISP, the security-service firm that employed her husband, her brother, her sister-in-law as well as Reginald Jones and Horace Chambers, fathers of SallyBelle and Thomas, to whom Rebecca had been providing the tennis lessons for the last several months.

The five colleagues — Matt, Luke, Kory, Reginald, and Horace — had for several years now worked for ISP. The firm had rapidly risen to such pre-eminence that it had, earlier that year, been selected to provide an additional layer of security for the upcoming Wimbledon Championships beyond that normally provided by the All England Lawn Tennis and Croquet Club's own security staff and local law enforcement.

In this summer of 1985, the 99th Wimbledon Championships would be held starting Monday, June 24, and ending Sunday, July 7, conducted as always at the All England Club. While luminaries such as John McEnroe, Ivan Lendl, and Jimmy Connors were expected to dominate the men's side of the tournament, and Martina Navratilova, Chris Evert Lloyd, and Pam Shriver, the women's, rising teen stars such as Boris Becker and Steffi Graf loomed on the horizon, presenting intriguing possibilities of veteran-versus-youth matchups.

On this Thursday morning, June 13, once Rebecca's shopping for Matt and the twins had been completed, she returned to the Volvo and drove several blocks to her preferred grocer. She wanted to select ingredients for lunch, dinner, and breakfast for herself, Matt, Kory — a finicky eater — and Luke. The latter two would be arriving within the hour for what promised to be a full afternoon and evening of discussions about specific aspects of security for the Championships.

Almost a full year earlier, Luke had been placed in charge of a 15-person team selected by ISP's senior executives to work with Wimbledon officials and law enforcement to upgrade all security arrangements for the two-week event.

This included security not just for the athletes themselves and their families, but also for dozens of media personnel and for the thousands of spectators who would flood the grounds and the venues daily. It was a daunting challenge, one that Luke welcomed. He liked being stretched, as his sister knew well.

Luke, Kory, and Matt now formed a small subgroup within the larger, a subgroup charged explicitly with on-site protection for the athletes, both the men and the women. The three had agreed that that day's — and next morning's — deliberations needed to include Rebecca, if she could free herself for the length of time needed.

They wanted her observations for these late-stage discussions due to the extraordinary fact that Rebecca had been a two-time quarterfinalist at Wimbledon when she was in her early mid-20s. With that background, Rebecca was conversant with some aspects of the tournament — especially some of the off-court aspects — that could be known well only by the competitors themselves.

Now Rebecca turned onto her street and pulled to the curb in front of her house for the second time that morning. And as before, she turned off the ignition and let her head fall back against the headrest.

She turned her head and looked toward her house. Her house that she had made warm and inviting on the inside, thanks to her selection and placement of plants and wall hangings. Her house that she had made warm and inviting on the outside, as well, thanks to her dedicated attention to plantings near the street and along the front walkway. And thanks, too, to a fresh coat of exterior paint, a new front door, a new roof, and new shutters.

Her eyes caressed her home. It was modest, but she had made it lovely.

As she opened the sedan's boot to remove the by-now numerous shopping bags filled with clothing and groceries, Matt and Ginny bolted from the front door together and raced down the walkway to help, Ginny easily winning the short sprint. Rebecca waited for the two of them, smiling to see them bounding toward her. She stooped to greet Ginny, then stood to face her husband.

They kissed. A real kiss, never a peck.

They had agreed long before that their kisses were never to become perfunctory. And they were not. Not ever.

"How did you do?" he asked as they turned to collect the shopping bags.

"I think you and the children will be pleased with what I've picked out, but, you know, Matt, with Joanna's little dresses, we can never be quite sure, can we?"

Matt shook his head.

"No, we can't. Don't know where she gets that, do you?"

"Can't imagine, dear."

Luke, Kory, and Matt, in their role as ISP's special sub-committee on security for the Wimbledon athletes, had agreed to meet in Matt and Rebecca's home to make it more convenient for Rebecca to participate as a sort of *pro bono* consultant to the sub-committee. Rebecca, who had retired from the international circuit two years before she met Matt Clark, felt honored by their request to include her in the session, and wanted to give her complete attention to the meeting. That eagerness had driven her decision to arrange for the twins to stay at their friends' home overnight.

It did not occur to Rebecca that *they* might have felt honored that *she* had rearranged her days to join their discussions. She still viewed herself as an ordinary Christian wife, mother, and teacher of young children. Nothing more.

In fewer than 15 minutes, they had sorted the shopping bags and turned swiftly to preparing sandwiches and salads for the 1 p.m. lunch. Ginny, schooled to understand that this was not her treat time, and that her turn would come later, waited in the family room, curled into Matt's reading chair. Just as the sandwich preparations were finished, they all heard a familiar knock on the front door.

"There's Luke," said Rebecca, and trotted to the door to greet her twin, preceded by Ginny, who somehow always knew when her uncle and aunt were knocking. As Rebecca opened the door, Ginny pushed her nose toward Kory's hands, knowing that Kory would drop to her knees, as did Rebecca routinely, welcoming the chance to give border-collie scratches behind the ears.

After affectionate hugs and greetings, hosts to guests, Luke took Kory's and his overnight bags to the guest bedroom, and then the two couples, mindful of the long workday and evening in front of them, seated themselves promptly at the dining table. As they took their seats, Rebecca glanced at the others, the glance reminding her that all four of them carried visible evidence of the battles they had thus far survived.

The left side of her brother's face and neck were pockmarked from a shotgun blast fired at close range into the car in which he and Rebecca had fled along the twisting highway that traced Italy's Amalfi coast, five years before. Only an edge of the shotgun spread had nicked its target, but that had been enough to mark Luke for the rest of his life as a shotgun-blast survivor.

There were not many such.

And Rebecca's husband's left arm and hand were inert and partially atrophied, the arm supported by a cloth sling. The disability was the result of Matt's having thrust himself between Rebecca and the automatic rifle fire that had sought to kill her, more than seven years ago.

And sister-in-law Kory had only partial use of the fingers of her left hand. This was the outcome of a close-quarters struggle, four years ago, against a knife-wielding adversary whom Kory had fought off with her bare hands.

And Rebecca knew, of course, that her own facial scar completed the lunch-table portrait of the danger that was inherent in Rebekka Yahalomin membership.

Now, at the dining room table, Rebecca had no sooner sat down than she rose again and stepped to Matt's side, using her two good hands to prepare his tea for him. He smiled his thank-you to her.

The two of them had quickly become comfortable with that particular public circumstance in which he required her assistance. Either at home or in a restaurant setting, Rebecca would lean over him — actually, lean into him, her face often touching his — and use teaspoon, knife, or fork to prepare anything at his place setting that required the use of two hands.

In public, this conspicuously loving act often led strangers to smile in their direction. In this at-home setting, Luke and Kory barely noticed the gesture. It had become part of the fabric of their lives long before. They simply waited.

Her husband's tea prepared to his liking, Rebecca sat.

Ginny retired once more to the family room.

Matt offered the blessing.

Three of them then tackled their lunch with enthusiasm, the exception being Kory, a dainty eater. While the others took respectable bites out of their sandwiches, she routinely broke off small pieces of hers, seemingly evaluating each bite for its appropriateness. This, too, had become part of the fabric of the foursome's lives, and the others took no notice of Kory's peculiar eating style.

Their families' long-established understanding of family dining, no matter how informal the meal, was never to "talk business" while eating, and so the conversation roamed elsewhere than the Championships and the church assaults. They talked of the children, and they talked of their parents: Rebecca and Luke's parents, in Birmingham; Matt's, in Oakham; and Kory's, in London.

At the completion of the light meal and the clearing of the table, the four sat again and opened the ISP-Wimbledon file folders Luke had brought. Before her brother began the session, Rebecca caught his eye, and he nodded to her.

"I want to apologize to you two," she began, nodding first at Kory and then at her brother, "for my rudeness in response to your phone call this morning. I know you must have felt … dismissed … by my non-response."

"And by my suddenly rushing out of your office, Luke," added Matt.

"Yes," Rebecca continued, "that, too.

"But Matt knew," she continued, "that my strange reaction was a call for help … from him … and he just got in his car and came home. Luke, when you reported what the Roberts-Holm person had said about there being not merely one, but two actual and four planned assaults on Christian ministers, I felt overwhelmed. After what we just faced in the U.S., I didn't want even to *think* about more of the same.

"I simply wanted to be here, with Matt and the twins and Ginny. Just here."

Luke and Kory both stirred to reassure her, but Rebecca raised her hand to stop them. She had more.

"Matt came home hurriedly and was here in minutes … but he inadvertently brought something with him. He brought an enemy."

Luke and Kory's eyes widened in confused surprise.

"He was followed home by an enormous Rolls-Royce that moved slowly past him as he parked his Vauxhall. The Rolls then stopped, reversed, and stopped again almost in front of the house. Its windows were heavily tinted, but we've no doubt they were taking note of our vehicles and of our address ... probably photographing both."

Silence dropped on the foursome as the two guests absorbed the news and while the hosts reexamined the disturbing event. After a moment, Kory spoke.

"And what do you two make of it? What are you going to do?" she said, looking first at Rebecca and then at Matt.

Rebecca glanced to her husband, who wordlessly shook his head.

"We're still processing it, Kory," she said, "and the only thing I know for certain is that the presence of that Rolls-Royce and its reconnaissance of our home changed my heart. In that moment my reluctance to engage some sort of generalized evil disappeared in a flash. Even after all that happened in America earlier this month, if evil now seeks my family ... and, above all, my children ... then I'm ready."

Rebecca nodded to herself, then turned her gray eyes to her brother.

"Now, Luke," she said evenly, "let's have our Wimbledon security conversation. Matt and I will pick up this other topic tonight.

"We'll pray. We'll decide. We'll let you know."

She nodded to her brother with a finality that he recognized from a lifetime of seeing that small, but decisive, nod from her. He knew that there was no point in pursuing anything else at that moment. Just the agenda. He knew his sister would get in touch with him as soon as she and her husband had made decisions.

He sighed.

He glanced around the table and said, "Let's open our file folders."

The session moved swiftly for the four participants. With Rebecca replying at length and in detail to the three ISP professionals' questions, the hours passed so rapidly that, first, Rebecca, and then the others, were surprised to realize that the sunlight from the dining room window had been fading for some time.

Rebecca rose and turned on the room's overhead light. As she resumed her seat, she saw her brother shaking his head in disappointment.

Looking up from his notes, Luke made a sour face and said grumpily, "Well, we haven't got quite as far in this first session as I'd imagined we might, but we need to stop for our workouts and dinner, right?"

Heads nodded. All sat back and stretched in their chairs, then tidied the materials from which they'd been working. Without further conversation, Rebecca and Matt headed for their bedroom to change, while Kory and Luke did the same in the guest bedroom. In just moments all four had descended the stairway to the full-size basement that the builders had included in a postwar era in which bomb shelters were still in the forefront of English families' minds.

In their two years of occupancy, Rebecca and Luke had converted the roughed-out 25-foot-by-65-foot rectangle into a well-appointed workout space. Exercise machines lined one side of the room: a treadmill, two stationary bikes, and several sets of free weights, plus a padded bench and rack for chest presses.

Track lighting was in place down the center of the length of the space, the individual lights arranged alternately to illuminate both sides of the room's width. Non-skid flooring was also in place, along with moisture-absorbing mats under each of the machines and the chest-press bench.

This arrangement left open, along the opposite side of the room, a 10-foot-by-65-foot shaft of completely clear space. This alleyway was equipped only at its opposite ends. At one end there was a thickly padded circular target, 5 feet in diameter. At the end opposite the target, there was a wooden rack specially designed by Luke to hold his sister's array of Barringtons Swords 12-inch competition throwing knives.

On the floor were marks indicating distances of 25, 30, 40, and 50 feet from the target. Rebecca's skill level at 30 feet was by now at championship level, should she ever choose to compete in knife-throwing contests. She was now in the process of increasing her accuracy at the two longer distances of 40 and 50 feet.

Four years previously, after a fourth consecutive summer marked by extreme danger and narrow escapes, Rebecca and Luke had mutually agreed that it was time for her to stop relying on her blazing foot speed and Luke's close-quarters combat experience to extricate themselves and others from physical danger. Luke, highly skilled at hand-to-hand combat from his years as a Royal Navy officer and boarding party leader, urged his sister to develop expertise in competition knife throwing.

She had, since that decision, practiced three or more times a week, year-round, at first under Luke's tutelage, but then solo. The throwing method taught her by Luke was a technically difficult, no-spin, underhand delivery that, once mastered, promoted maximum accuracy and speed-of-flight for the knives. Rebecca's long limbs, sinewy strength, and inbred athleticism were ideally suited to the arcane pursuit.

Until that very month, while on her and Luke's dramatic rescue mission in the U.S., Rebecca had never been called upon to use her knives against flesh and blood. But there, in the process of saving a kidnapped couple from certain execution by KGB agents, she had done so unhesitatingly.

Her single throw had been swift and sure, a non-lethal cast from 30 feet that had sliced through the bicep of the would-be assailant as he prepared to execute the two captives. The 12-inch, razor-sharp knife blade had cut cleanly through the muscle and nerves of the killer's right arm, causing his handgun to fall from his suddenly useless hand. Without Rebecca's intervention the assailant would have been in position to fire one or more rounds into Luke's torso as he charged toward the killer over those same 30 feet of open space.

The KGB agent's shots, had he been able to pull the trigger, would have been fired at point-blank range. But at the instant of Rebecca's knife's impact, the assailant's right arm was rendered inert, the nerve pathways to his hand destroyed. The Glock clattered to the floor two full seconds before Luke thundered into him, driving him to the floor, there to be bound and gagged.

This seconds-long experience rendered worthwhile the hundreds of hours Rebecca had devoted to knife-throwing practice over the years. The awareness that, had she been a second slower, or had her aim been even slightly off, the gunman would have been able to kill Luke, Rebecca, and the two captives, gave renewed weight to the seriousness of the thrice-weekly practice sessions.

The experience also engendered a new consciousness, both in Rebecca and in Luke, that there might be occasions in which 30 feet were not enough. This had driven their mutually agreed upon decision to begin to work toward mastery at 40 and 50 feet, considered to be the maximum accurate knife-throwing distance.

She would tackle the new throwing distance with her customary determination. This activity was not sport for Rebecca.

Now, the foursome worked intently on the machines and in the throwing alley for just over an hour. There was little in the way of conversation. There was just the occasional word of encouragement for each other as they moved briskly through their highly intricate workouts.

Thursday, late evening

Luke adjourned the evening planning session at 10 o'clock, having taken only one break after the late-afternoon workout. That break had been for Rebecca and Matt to speak by telephone to Joanna and Samuel before they went to bed at their friends' house. Good progress had been made in the security-focused discussions, and Luke seemed more satisfied with their work than he had been when they had taken the earlier break for workouts and dinner.

The two couples agreed upon their start time for the next morning and said their good-nights to each other. They retired to the bedrooms.

Rebecca and Matt, however, did not undress. They stood facing each other at the foot of their bed. They smiled at each other, each knowing that they had independently come to conclusions that needed to be articulated, but conclusions that were already known by each of them.

"Matt," she began, "we have to evacuate, and we have to do it tonight."

"Absolutely," he agreed without hesitation. "We've learned never to delay, once a threat has been made clear to us. And now it has."

She nodded, then continued.

"I'll take the twins and Ginny to Birmingham — to the Lodge — tonight," she said. "We should leave within the hour."

"Exactly, Rebecca … and I have been thinking that it would be prudent to leave both our vehicles in front of the house, right where they were when the reconnaissance took place. No need to make clear to an enemy that an evacuation has transpired.

"And I think you should ask Luke to retrieve the nine-passenger from his house. Then you can drive it, with the kids and Ginny, to the Lodge," he continued.

"And with you at the Lodge," he concluded, "there'll be no point at all in having our scheduled planning session here tomorrow morning — with no Rebecca present — and, besides, there is a regular Friday morning meeting at ISP that Kory, Luke, and I will now be able to attend."

"Brilliant!" she replied.

"I love the idea of driving Luke's nine-passenger to the Lodge, Matt. That will make the trip so much easier on the children."

"Yes," said Matt, "and Luke and Kory can take her MG home right now to get Luke's vehicle, and then Kory can follow Luke back from their house to ours, so they can get back home again tonight. That's a lot of back-and-forth, but it works."

Rebecca nodded enthusiastically.

"Perfect, dear," she agreed.

"I'll go interrupt bedtime preparations," she added, "before Kory and Luke are actually in bed."

Matt frowned.

"We're asking a lot of them at the end of a long day, dear."

She shook her head.

"We're on a war footing now, Matt. They already know that."

In minutes, the two couples were ready, and Rebecca had telephoned Dottie to let her know that something had come up, and that the twins would need to go with her to her parents' place near Birmingham, and right away. Matt, she explained, would pick up Joanna and Samuel in 15 minutes.

Luke's vehicle — his pride and joy — was a strange-looking, elongated product called a Five-Door Range Rover. It could be configured to haul a great amount of cargo or to accommodate as many as nine adults in tolerable comfort.

Kory drove herself and her husband home in her diminutive MG, and, as soon as they arrived, they used their battery-driven portable pump to inflate two air mattresses. They placed the inflated mattresses on the floor of the Range Rover, each securely positioned between the first and second, and second and third rows of seats.

They placed two blankets on each mattress.

With the blankets laid out on the mattresses, they nodded to each other with satisfaction, confident that Rebecca and the twins themselves would be happy with the arrangement. And they assumed — correctly — that Rebecca would want Ginny to curl up on the front passenger seat alongside her.

The Lodge, a two-hour-and-thirty-minute drive away from Rebecca's house, was a combination hotel and retreat center that had been operated by Rebecca and Luke's parents, Elisabeth and Jason Manguson, for decades. It was situated on a prominent hill not far from the city of Birmingham. The rambling, three-story structure itself was more than 75 years old, but had been overhauled and refurbished several times over the years. Rebecca and Luke had spent their childhood and adolescence living at the Lodge, and could even recall some of the construction projects, especially the expansion and technological upgrading of its World War II-era bomb shelter.

That shelter had been completely redesigned to serve as a true underground sanctuary, now with two dorm rooms, a small chapel, rest rooms, and a command center. The latter allowed electronic surveillance of the 360-degree perimeter wall which encircled the crest of the hill. The Lodge property extended well beyond that crest and covered densely forested, downward-sloping acreage that allowed vehicular access by means of a winding roadway that led up one side of the hill from a guardhouse. Security personnel staffed the guardhouse 24 hours a day and 365 days a year.

The two couples — Rebecca and Matt, and Kory and Luke — had long ago learned to live in perpetual readiness for fight-or-flight. Go-bags and supplies were always present in their four automobiles' storage compartments, even the tiny MG's.

When they went to bed each night, their specially designed, shoulder-strap-equipped leather satchels were ready to be snatched in seconds in an emergency, each satchel containing money, passports, other official documents, toiletries, and, in the case of Matt, Kory, and Luke, military identification papers that certified them as members of the active reserve forces of the U. S. Navy, in Matt's case, and the Royal Navy, in the case of Kory and Luke.

In addition, each of the four satchels contained weaponry. A military side-arm filled a specially designed interior pocket of the satchels that belonged to the three who were members of their nations' reserve armed forces. In Rebecca's satchel, also in a specially designed interior compartment, were three of her Barringtons Swords 12-inch throwing knives, each encased in its own hard-leather sleeve. Finally, nestled in Luke's oversized satchel, was his unique shoulder holster with its array of knives, tools, ropes, and other accoutrement useful for one who, as a former boarding-party leader for the Royal Navy, much preferred non-lethal weaponry to firearms.

On this night, as Rebecca and Matt prepared for her evacuation, they first brought their go-bags and supplies in from the Volvo and the Vauxhall. Then, while he drove to retrieve the children, Rebecca quietly carried everything onto the back deck, knowing that Luke would pull the Range Rover into the back alley and up to the gate that opened into the Clarks' backyard.

Friday, 1 a.m.

Rebecca arrived at the Lodge's guardhouse an hour after midnight Friday morning. The two on-duty guards knew her by sight, but having not received advance notification of her arrival from her parents … their employers … they did not wave her past the guardhouse until they buzzed the intercom to the Mangusons' bedroom.

Jason, instantly wide awake, answered, asked to speak with his daughter briefly, and awakened Elisabeth. Together they tidied the children's sleeping-and-play room, situated directly across the hall from the room permanently reserved for Rebecca and Matt. Those two rooms were never booked for paying guests of the Lodge.

By the time Rebecca had brought the Rover up the winding drive to the perimeter wall, its gate having been electronically opened from the guardhouse nearly a half-mile distant, her father was waiting at the main door to the Lodge. Knowing that Rebecca would not be arriving unannounced in the middle of the night unless she faced at least a quasi-emergency at home, he gave her only a brief hug and a word of welcome, and the two of them turned efficiently to the unloading process without speaking further.

Details could wait.

"Do you want to put Ginny on the back porch with Max and Margaret, or should she just stay in your room tonight?" asked Jason of his daughter.

"Let's not disturb yours right now, Dad," replied Rebecca. "In the morning, we can re-introduce the dogs to each other."

Ginny, knowing the layout of the Lodge, led the way up the stairs. Jason and Rebecca carried the drowsy children up to their room and tucked them into their beds. Both were immediately fast asleep again. Elisabeth and Ginny stayed with the twins while Jason and Rebecca returned to the Rover to unload Rebecca's go-bag, all-purpose satchel, and the children's luggage.

That done, Jason returned once more to the Rover, drove it to the guest lot, and again climbed the stairs to Rebecca's room where his wife and daughter had just finished making her bed and preparing a pot of tea. They drew three chairs close together, with Ginny curled on the floor in their midst, and sat with their teacups.

The parents waited with a calmness and patience borne of years of faith in the God Whom they worshipped and in Whose hands they rested.

Rebecca began.

"You've read or heard of the Wednesday evening assaults on ministers who led sessions at the April conference in Oxford?"

Both nodded.

Elisabeth replied.

"We know," she said, "about your friend Jeremy Donaldson in Falmouth, and we heard a radio report about another pastor being assaulted ... a Methodist minister in Yorkshire, I believe?"

"Yes, but there is so much more, Mum."

"Luke was contacted this morning," continued Rebecca, "by his friend Graham Roberts-Holm at MI6. He reported to Luke that there had been at least four other similar attacks planned for Wednesday evening on other ministers around the country, but for reasons not yet clear to MI6, those other four assaults were aborted before they could be carried out. The reports trickled into MI6 and other agencies via direct notification by some of the township police departments.

"Mr. Roberts-Holm phoned Luke because, he said, the thing looked so much like previous calls-to-arms to Rebekka Yahalomin. He asked Luke if I had ... you know ... if I had been ... contacted ... if I had received ..."

Her parents nodded.

Jason frowned.

"Surely this Roberts-Holm bloke didn't think we'd actually report any such things to him ... or to anyone at all?"

"Well … Luke called Kory and Matt down to his office this morning — she glanced at her watch — well, technically *yesterday* morning," Rebecca said, "as soon as he got off the phone with Mr. Roberts-Holm. Matt told me that, according to Luke, Mr. Roberts-Holm seemed both discomfited and persistent … both things … and that the conversation eventually turned a little sour, since Luke had to become quite firm."

From this introduction, Rebecca went on to describe the incident at their home, when the Rolls-Royce seemed rather obviously to be conducting reconnaissance. At this news, both parents' demeanor changed instantly from analytical to engaged. Jason noisily put down his teacup and rose to pace the room.

"What's the connection, Rebecca?" he said as he rose.

"Yes," said Elisabeth, "what ties the assaults and would-be assaults on all those poor ministers to you and the Yahalomin? And who on earth is behind all this?

"And what could they possibly want?"

Rebecca smiled.

"Well … we don't really know, Mum," she replied. "We just know that, as Mr. Roberts-Holm said to Luke, these assaults on ministers who had leadership roles in a traditional-Christianity conference do *seem* to be involved in the kind of thing … well … the kind of thing about which I might well have received some … um … news … or instructions … or something … from our Source … but that's all so very speculative.

"What is *not* speculative," she continued, "is the Rolls-Royce following my husband to our home and conducting reconnaissance on us.

"*That* is what led us to get the children out of there, Mum. We wanted the twins to be here … safe … in their own room here in the Lodge. And we did not want to wait even until daybreak to get them here.

"Some things just cannot wait."

Friday, 2 a.m.

As Rebecca spoke these words, her sleeping husband, 100 miles away in their house in urban London, was jolted into wakefulness by the sound of glass shattering somewhere in the house, followed instantly by the whoosh of explosion and the unmistakable sound of flames raging. Fully awake in a fraction of a second, Matt jumped from the bed.

He wore, as usual in summer, a tee-shirt and summer-weight running sweats. One of the many habits Matt had developed during active service in the U.S. military was that he dressed as appropriately for action as he did for bed.

He strode quickly to the wooden clothes valet Luke had painstakingly constructed for him years before, after it finally became obvious to Matt's physicians that his left arm would never recover normal function … perhaps no function at all. Tonight, the clothes valet, cooperatively designed by the two brothers-in-law, had Matt's lightweight red Gore-Tex jacket waiting, the device's arms helpfully holding the jacket open just as a person would do if assisting someone else in getting dressed.

Using his good right hand, Matt steered his inert left hand and arm into the jacket sleeve, then backed into the jacket, turned, and shrugged his right hand and arm into the other sleeve. Stepping away from the valet, he quickly tucked his left hand into a jacket pocket, then pressed the self-fastening Velcro front of the jacket closed. That done, he stepped into his no-tie leather-soled walking shoes and was ready.

Barely 30 seconds had elapsed since the explosion.

Matt hoisted his all-purpose leather satchel, containing passport, cash, sidearm, and other essentials, onto his right shoulder by its long strap. He then grabbed the cloth go-bag from its position next to the clothes valet, walked back to the window, and opened it fully. He dropped the go-bag onto the ground, 5 feet below the window.

Poised to go through the window immediately, he hesitated, then swiftly crossed the bedroom to the doorway and looked down the long hallway toward the family room. He saw what he expected. He saw flames consuming everything in that part of the house, and beginning to spread rapidly in both directions, reaching toward both the back and the front doors of his and Rebecca's thoughtfully furnished home.

He re-crossed the bedroom, and, before going out the window, lifted the satchel's shoulder strap over his head and onto his left shoulder, so that the strap now crossed his chest. The satchel now secure, he pushed his left leg fully out the window, much as a hurdler would do, then bent forward to move his head and shoulders through the window, right leg trailing. Poised briefly on the windowsill, he brought his right leg vigorously through the opening and dropped to the ground.

Matt assumed the perpetrators had vanished as fast as they could, but he nonetheless crept carefully to the corner of the house to see if anyone was in the front yard or in the street. He saw only brake lights flashing on, and then off, as a vehicle paused at the corner before roaring away in the darkness.

He retrieved the go-bag from the ground where it rested, then sprinted across the street to the home of a couple whom he and Rebecca had come to know well in the two years they had been neighbors. He pounded on their front door and shouted their names, purposely waking everyone within earshot. This was not a situation in which neighbors' restful sleep outranked wakeful alertness.

Once inside and on the neighbors' phone, Matt quickly notified the fire department, the police, Rebecca and their parents at the Lodge, and his brother- and sister-in-law. He then returned to his front yard to await the emergency vehicles.

Matt knew that he would be required to make a report of the crime to the police, probably at the precinct office, and that he would then drive his Vauxhall to Kory and Luke's home. He would need to stay at their home for the next several days.

Perhaps longer.

He watched his and Rebecca's home burn furiously and knew that nothing would be left other than the basement workout space and its workout machines and throwing knives. He allowed himself to grow sad, thinking about how much of herself Rebecca had put into making their home a welcoming place for him and the children.

The sadness would linger, he knew, but he also knew that both he and his wife would quickly accept the loss of "things" and would embrace the fact that they and the children and Ginny were safe and secure. They would thank God for that and for their prayerful and timely evacuation.

And they would rebuild.

Just after 5 a.m., Matt drove the Vauxhall away from the precinct station where detectives had interviewed him for more than two hours. He was not surprised to find Kory waiting at the front door of her and Luke's home when he arrived there just before 5:30 a.m. He doubted she had slept at all since his phone call from the neighbors' house. She would have busied herself immediately, preparing the guest room and guest bathroom for him. Like her sister-in-law, Kory was a thoughtful, meticulous hostess.

"Our Friday morning ISP meeting starts at seven-thirty, you know," she said. "You might as well stay up, don't you think? I've got eggs and toast waiting.

"Luke and I just finished."

Matt, grateful, consumed the ample breakfast Kory had prepared, and repaired to the guest room, where he took a long shower and then laid out his clothes from the go-bag he'd rescued from the fire. The go-bag contained no dress shirt or tie, and his brother-in-law's wardrobe was literally a poor fit for Matt, he being 5 inches taller and much longer limbed than Luke.

With his good right hand, he pulled on a pair of freshly washed jeans and a favorite short-sleeved, collared knit shirt. Luke and Kory then helped him fashion a cloth sling for his left arm and hand, and he was ready to go.

Just after seven, as the threesome was preparing to leave for the meeting, using both the Vauxhall and the MG, Luke put in a quick phone call to Graham Roberts-Holm at his house in the London suburbs. The firebombing of Rebecca Clark's home would be something the MI6 Rebecca unit would want to know about immediately.

The call was partly a courtesy on Luke's part. Beyond that, however, he knew that there might come a time when, as had been the case just days before in the U.S., Rebekka Yahalomin would need the assistance of a national intelligence agency … perhaps more than one. There were certain tasks that only agencies of that type could successfully undertake.

So it was that the three sleep-deprived ISP professionals sat down with their colleagues for their routine Friday morning security-group session. Luke, chairing, did not mention the firebombing.

He stayed fully focused on the upcoming Championships.

There was, after all, no obvious connection to be seen, as yet, among the three events … the Wednesday night church assaults, both actual and planned, the Thursday-Friday overnight firebombing of the Clarks' residence, and the great Wimbledon tournament, looming now a mere 10 days away. If the three events were related, evidence of some sort — natural or supernatural — would need somehow to make itself known to Rebekka Yahalomin.

CHAPTER THREE

Friday, 12:30 p.m., England; 7:30 a.m., Washington DC

ON THE OTHER SIDE OF THE ATLANTIC, ANOTHER BREAKFAST OF eggs and toast was being prepared in a Washington, D.C., suburb. The preparer of this U.S. version of eggs and toast was a woman who, to her astonishment, had found herself immersed up to her neck in the Rebekka Yahalomin–driven events that had transpired in her city earlier that month.

Her well-ordered, nicely contained, predictably safe life had been violently turned inside out. She had been swept into a maelstrom of espionage, murder, and, although she had been a practicing Christian since her teen years, a level of divine intervention in human events far beyond anything she had ever imagined.

And, somehow woven into all that, there had come love. She had fallen in love with the man who had served as her clergy-counselor for the two years previous, a man who had, in fact, served as her guide to, and companion throughout, her involvement with the Yahalomin.

Marie Campbell, a widow for a decade, now in her early 30s, was just putting the finishing touches on the breakfast she'd prepared. As she did, her mind flashed, as it had done so often in the last week, to the narrowness of her and her new fiancé's escape from death at the hands of the Soviet KGB.

At the near instant of execution, a 12-inch Barringtons Swords throwing knife had arrowed, seemingly from nowhere, straight into the bicep of the would-be executioner, causing his handgun to fall clattering to the floor. This had given the knife-throwing woman's combat-trained brother sufficient time to hurl himself, leading with his rock-hard shoulder, into the KGB agent, thence to manhandle, bind, and gag him.

Meanwhile, the knife-throwing woman herself had extracted her weapon from the KGB agent's bicep and turned quickly to free Marie and her fiancé from their bindings. This, in turn, had led to their desperate escape from the KGB hideout on the Maryland shores of the Chesapeake Bay.

And now, just days later, Marie Campbell and Jack McGriff continued to reside temporarily in the CIA safe house in Langley, Virginia, just across the Potomac from Washington. Since the conflict's apparent end, they had been busily making preparations for a quiet wedding at their Episcopal church in the city, while looking for a reasonably priced and pet-friendly apartment into which they could move, or, less likely, a house in D.C. which they could afford, as soon as the wedding could take place.

"Penelope," Marie said quietly to her diminutive calico, crouched on the counter while attending helpfully to the odd bit of egg or toast pushed her way, "I'm going to call Jack to come down the hall for breakfast. I'll be right back."

Marie walked to the hallway door, opened it, and called down the corridor in the direction of McGriff's room. She knew that he and she were, at the moment, the only occupants of that hall, and so did not need to moderate her voice.

"Jack," she called, "our breakfast is ready. Can you come?"

And she heard his voice, muffled, through his closed door.

"Be right there, Marie."

She returned to the small kitchen, put the eggs and toast on two U.S. government-supplied plates, got two U.S. government-supplied paper napkins from a drawer, and took the plates and napkins to the tiny drop-leaf table that nestled against the kitchen window. Penelope continued her investigation of the food-preparation surface, purring audibly as she did.

In seconds, McGriff knocked once on Marie's partly open door and entered. He walked briskly to the kitchen, spoke his good morning to Penelope, turned to Marie, and bent down to kiss her as she sat waiting at the table.

He was two years older and at least 100 pounds heavier than she, a disparity he was determined to address. A former small-college football lineman, he had for some time taken note of his gradual weight gain since college days. He had enlisted Marie's help in whittling some of the extra poundage from his large frame.

After Marie's young husband's untimely death, a decade previous, via an accident on his U.S. Navy warship, she had learned to live happily and without regret as a single woman, eventually finding interesting work as an appointment counselor at the Soviet embassy in Washington. Once employed there, she had moved her church affiliation to the downtown Episcopal church in which Jack McGriff happened to serve as the clergy-counselor to the congregation's families. She had soon begun seeing him for twice-monthly counseling sessions, those sessions focused on the fact that she found herself at times embarrassed and confused by her status as an employee of the United States' Cold War enemy.

And, truth be told, she had requested the sessions in part because she had hoped to get to know her church's clergy-counselor somewhat better. When she and he at length agreed that the counseling was no longer necessary, they found in themselves a mutual reluctance to bring the sessions to a close. And he, a lifelong bachelor unpracticed in the art of dating, had finally found the courage to ask her out.

Things had moved fast from that point, not just in their romance, but also in the swirling course of events that had pulled them into Rebekka Yahalomin's orbit. Now, it seemed, those events, incalculable in their possible outcomes, had been brought to a tidy and satisfying close.

Or so they thought.

In addition to preparing for their wedding and searching for a pet-friendly apartment or affordable house to purchase near their church, the couple had begun seriously to entertain the prospect of opening a Washington branch of the Belton and Adelman Detective Agency, a widely respected New York City agency co-owned by Sid Belton, former NYPD detective, and Jaakov Adelman, former Mossad agent. The New York firm's invitation to them was fresh, and clearly a serious one. The parent firm would handle all start-up costs.

As Marie and McGriff's relationship had gradually matured and advanced beyond the counselor-counselee stage, they found they were at least as uncomfortable with McGriff's "other" job, his part-time employment by the CIA, as they were with Marie's work at the Soviet embassy. Like all national intelligence agencies, the CIA dealt fundamentally with deception and, by extension, with calculated violence.

Never mind that McGriff's role was merely as a recruiter of new talent for the agency. He was just as much a part of the CIA mission as if he were working in the field as a counterintelligence agent. No matter what an individual's CIA role might be, he or she would always be an integral part of that mission. The mission might be a national necessity in the contemporary world, but not every individual was suited.

A signal of McGriff's status as a cog in the CIA machinery was the 9mm Beretta that he carried routinely in a CIA-issued shoulder holster. His slightly oversized "priestly sport coat" adequately hid the weapon from casual observation.

McGriff had, with Marie's help, come to understand that he could be at peace with God and with himself only if he resigned from the CIA. And, entirely apart from that, he found, as he considered Belton and Adelman's invitation, that a vocational life with Marie as his partner — while perhaps reducing his role with the church to part-time family counseling only — was an exciting prospect. She had, after all, surprised him, and herself, too, with the coolness and confidence with which she had conducted herself during the tense days of conflict just completed. She had seemed, as McGriff had noted in a recent conversation with her, a "natural."

And detective work, they agreed, was honest. No pretense.

Now seated side-by-side, facing the window, at the small kitchen table in Marie's unit of the Langley safe house, they clasped hands. Then, smiling to each other in the warm comfort of their deepening love, they bowed their heads.

As the informal hostess for the small meal, Marie offered the blessing in her soft voice, saying, "Father, we ask Your blessings on this food, to the nourishment of our bodies, and we ask Your blessings on ourselves, to the furtherance of Your purposes in the world; we ask also that You help us always to be mindful of the needs of others. In the name of Jesus. Amen."

Almost instantaneously, as though it had been waiting politely for Marie to finish her prayer, the wall-mounted telephone rang.

McGriff rose.

"I'll get it, Marie," he said. "I'll ask them to call back later."

He lifted the receiver.

"Jack McGriff speaking."

"Jack? Jaakov Adelman here, calling from New York. I got no answer at your unit, so I asked the switchboard to ring Marie's unit."

McGriff smiled delightedly.

"Jaakov! Great to hear your voice.

"Marie and I were just starting our breakfast … can we call you back when we finish eating?"

"Give me two minutes right now, Jack."

"Sure … two minutes."

"I got a call an hour ago from a man named Graham Roberts-Holm in London. He apologized for phoning me at 6:30 a.m., but he knew I always go to the office early, and, of course, it's midday over there.

"He's with MI6, Jack, and I've known him forever, going back to my days with Mossad. He and I led a couple of inter-agency projects back then.

"He called to tell me … and don't be alarmed when I finish this sentence … everybody's fine … that Rebecca and Matt's home was firebombed last night. She and the children had already evacuated to the Birmingham Lodge, and Matt was sleeping lightly. He grabbed his go-bag and his ready-satchel and went out the window.

"He's bunking temporarily with Kory and Luke."

Adelman paused to let the news sink in.

"Can I keep going, Jack?" he asked thoughtfully.

There was another pause.

Finally, McGriff said simply, "Yes. Go."

"Luke's role at ISP, you'll remember," said Adelman, "entails fairly frequent conversations with MI6, and, mostly as a courtesy, Luke got in touch with Roberts-Holm this morning, at his home on the London outskirts. Luke explained to Graham that Matt had already talked by phone, minutes before, with Rebecca, and she agreed that the 'Rebecca unit' at MI6 should be informed of the attack. Thus, the phone call from Luke to Graham at his home."

Adelman paused again to let McGriff absorb the torrent of information.

Hearing no protest from McGriff, Adelman continued.

"Graham decided to phone me, thinking that we might want to 'activate' the whole Rebekka Yahalomin group. I told him that that sort of thing couldn't be initiated by any of us over here. That's always Rebecca's decision … or hers and her brother's.

"Graham acknowledged, Jack, that his contacting us in the U.S. might be looked upon unfavorably by the Clarks and Mangusons, and he made clear that, as far as he knew, Rebecca had not received anything from the Source, but …"

Adelman's voice trailed off.

McGriff looked toward Marie, his light blue eyes troubled. She rose quickly from the table and came to his side.

He spoke to her, still holding the receiver near his face.

"Rebecca's house was firebombed last night, Marie. She and the children were already at the Lodge. Matt got out okay. He's with Luke and Kory."

Her hand went to her mouth, her brown eyes wide.

McGriff turned back to Adelman.

"Jaakov … what do you want to do?"

"We've been debating that in the hour since I got the call from Roberts-Holm, Jack," replied Adelman. "Sid and I think that we … and you two … should get over there as fast as we can. Just to be there, on-site, to help with whatever may develop. That would be different from 'activating Rebekka Yahalomin,' as MI6 suggested.

"Our going to London or to the Birmingham Lodge would just mean cutting down response time if the rest of us are needed, as we may well be. Sid, as you know, has extensive experience working with Scotland Yard, MI5, and MI6.

"He's a known and highly respected operative over there."

"As are you, Jaakov," inserted McGriff.

Adelman paused, momentarily nonplussed.

"Well …" he said hesitantly. "I suppose … but certainly not at Sid Belton's level, Jack."

"Hm," replied McGriff, disagreeing softly.

Adelman paused, mildly irritated at the interruption.

"Of course," Adelman finally continued, "a decision to 'activate the Yahalomin' would be Rebecca's decision, as it always must be. But we could choose to go there … to be ready … in case she makes that decision. We all know with certainty that, if she does, there will be no time to waste. Sid and I think we should go.

"And we mean now, Jack.

"Today."

Friday, 2 p.m., England; 9 a.m., New York City

Within the hour, Marie Campbell, little Penelope in her carrying crate, and Jack McGriff were on the Washington beltway in McGriff's red Jeep Cherokee, headed for I-95 and New York City. McGriff had swiftly cleared his church calendar for the upcoming week, a week in which only two counseling sessions were scheduled during the early summer lull. And he was not scheduled for worship service leadership at all on either of the two Sundays he guessed he might miss while in England.

Marie, in contrast, was freshly unemployed, having become *persona non grata* at the Soviet embassy, and having grown fond of the idea that her next job could be as McGriff's partner in the soon-to-be-created branch detective agency. As for Penelope, she would be staying in New York with Sid Belton's wife, Dr. Eleanor Chapel, while Belton, Adelman, and the two Washingtonians traveled to England.

Their military sky chariot would be leaving from McGuire Air Force Base, a 90-minute drive from New York City, at 4 p.m. — 1600 hours in military terms — on a Royal Air Force transport plane en route to Brize Norton RAF Base in Oxfordshire, home of the RAF Strategic and Tactical Air Transport Center. Their ticket for these accommodations was Luke Manguson, who was not only a former Royal Navy officer and combat legend, but who had maintained all of his military contacts in the years since his active duty ended. Luke routinely used RAF transport for excursions to foreign destinations in his civilian role as security consultant for ISP. The RAF was always happy to add him to any scheduled flights they had going.

One call from Luke and the American foursome had been booked on the 1600 flight from McGuire to Brize Norton. Jason Manguson, Rebecca and Luke's father, would meet them there in Luke's Land Rover Five-Door, perfect for the job. Given the five-hour time difference and the necessary refueling stop in Newfoundland, the four Americans could expect to arrive at the Birmingham Lodge a few hours after noon on the day following, a Saturday.

They would find that Jason and Elisabeth Manguson had decided to keep the Lodge open for guests, despite the impending crisis. But, in order to gain the necessary space for the Americans, they would prepare the two dormitory rooms in their converted bomb shelter for immediate occupancy. By placing the new arrivals there, the hosts could ensure that the four Americans would not only have satisfactory, if somewhat Spartan, living accommodations, but quick access to the underground command center's advanced telecommunications system.

The three men would occupy one of the two dorm rooms. Marie Campbell would occupy the other. The arrangements appeared serviceable.

Saturday midafternoon, England

The Americans reached the Lodge at 3:30 p.m., local time, on that Saturday. Shortly after, Marie joined Rebecca in the latter's second-floor guest room. Rebecca had left her door open, so that she could see across the hallway to the twins' room. The children were sleeping, having postponed their usual early afternoon nap time, and having had a vigorous hour-plus of chasing, and being chased by, Ginny, their everyday playmate; Max, the Mangusons' enormous-but-gentle German shepherd; and Margaret, their nimble border collie.

The two women sat facing each other next to one of the room's two windows. The other window was encumbered by an air conditioning unit. When visiting her parents, Rebecca rarely turned on the unit, much preferring to open the unobstructed second window to welcome whatever natural air and temperature the day and night might provide. The day was comfortably warm, and both women wore short-sleeved blouses and lightweight slacks with their tennis shoes.

The two were physical contrasts.

Rebecca was impressively tall in the fashion of many of the elite tennis players of the day. At barely 5 foot, 5 inches, Marie was at least 7 inches shorter than Rebecca, with a small woman's frame, small facial features, shoulder-length, wavy brown hair, and sad brown eyes that misled some into thinking, at first, that she was an unhappy person. She was not.

Marie laughed easily and found delight in the small joys of every one of her days. She was, however, still in awe of Rebecca, and often found it enormously difficult to chat normally with her.

After all, Rebecca was not just a well-known athlete. She had been chosen by the Source, Marie knew from first-hand experience, to be a vessel of a kind Marie had never imagined she could encounter in the contemporary world. In fact, Marie viewed Rebecca as somehow misplaced in time.

She was a Biblical figure chosen to receive, at unpredictable intervals, divine messages in a variety of forms. She was alive and well and living the life of a teacher, wife, and mother in the late 20th century, rather than the first, where it seemed to Marie that she actually belonged.

"Tell me, Marie," said Rebecca, having just started their tea, "how are things progressing with Jack. Have you two moved forward with wedding plans?"

Marie smiled.

"You know, Rebecca, the wedding itself is going to be such a simple, uncomplicated affair, with one of Jack's church colleagues presiding and with just a handful of friends in attendance. We're focused really on finding the right apartment or house for us — and Penelope, of course — and on Sidney and Jaakov's invitation to us to set up a branch office in Washington.

"Pretty exciting for us, you know … all three things."

Rebecca nodded her understanding.

"You and I," she said, "have already talked about Jack McGriff as a prospective husband for you, so you know how happy I am about that, Marie, but what about being a principal in a detective agency? Any concerns?"

"Oh, my goodness, yes, Rebecca. I'm terrified.

"But I keep remembering," she continued, "how I was and how I felt … you know … infiltrating the Soviet embassy offices … and facing those horrible KGB people … and how complimentary and understanding all of you were about how I had done. And I think that … well … I really can do those kinds of things, if I have to …"

Rebecca nodded her endorsement.

"And?" she said.

"And … Sidney and Jaakov … and Jack, too, tell me that most detective work is not nearly so exciting, and certainly not as dangerous, as the things I so recently did back in Washington. It's mainly … 'sleuthing' … they insist … you know, looking at evidence and talking to people and assembling patterns …

"And Sidney was even kind enough to point out that he has been able to be 'effective' — that's his modest word choice — despite the fact that his injuries, old and new, have left him hobbled and dependent on a walking cane just to get around. He noted that I was … let's see … he said I was 'young and spry' and would be better than he is … at some things … and that I shouldn't worry at all …"

She smiled at the memory of Belton's kindness and encouragement.

"And," she added, "all said and done, Rebecca, I just think it is something I ought to experience. I do think I might prove to be good at it."

"In addition," said Rebecca quickly, "you'd have no internal conflicts bubbling up of the sort you had, working for the Soviets."

Marie laughed.

"Ugh," she said. "That nagged at me every day, Rebecca. And that's what Jack and I worked on in counseling for almost two years."

"Yes," replied Rebecca, "and those two years of getting to know each other in that counseling context is why you're not really worried about marriage itself, right? You've told me you liked marriage to your first husband, prior to the tragedy, and so your real question, when we talked, was about marriage to this *particular* man."

"Right!" Marie exclaimed excitedly. "And I agreed with you when we talked that … well … first and foremost, Jack is a believer … and … I especially liked this … you noted that he is a 'grown-up' who will not need to be *mothered* by me, as his wife. We have a grown-up relationship now, and we should expect to have a grown-up relationship as husband and wife.

"I'm just excited by everything, Rebecca."

Suddenly Marie's face fell.

"But I'm so unhappy about your home, Rebecca."

Rebecca nodded somberly.

"Yes … we really don't know what to make of that. These recent events are not obviously related to each other. The Wednesday evening assaults on ministers all over England … only one of whom we knew well … and the attack on our home … one which presumably hoped to kill all four of us … five, counting

Ginny, as we certainly do … it's hard to understand how those things fit together. But I have a feeling, Marie, that we're going to find out."

Saturday evening

After dinner, Rebecca made long-distance phone calls to her two teen protégés in London, SallyBelle Jones and Thomas Chambers. She explained to them that she would not be able to meet them for their early morning tennis sessions and wished them well in their hoped-for selection as BBGs for the Championships.

The commonly used, Wimbledon-specific acronym stood for "Ball Boys and Girls." Each spring some one thousand young people engaged in fierce competition to be among the roughly 250 selected for the coveted role at the great tournament. To serve as a BBG at Wimbledon was to undertake a contradiction: that is, to become an integral participant in the world-famous tournament, but to do so in such a way that virtually no one would notice their presence. Only when a BBG made an obvious faux pas would anyone actually attend to them.

When Rebecca spoke that evening with her two charges, they each told her nervously that the final selection would be Monday morning, and that thereafter, if they were selected, they might not be free in any case to continue their lessons with her. The chosen 250 would be given an exacting schedule for the final week of preparation, and they could not know in advance what that schedule would be.

Rebecca assured them she would include them in her morning prayers.

Next morning traced the usual Sunday routine at the Lodge. Elisabeth and Jason Manguson hosted a short, early-morning worship service in the ground-floor library, open to all hotel guests, after which the small kitchen staff prepared a light breakfast. The afternoon was given over to quiet walks around the property's perimeter wall, reading in the library and on the grounds, and conversation. The handful of children usually present on any weekend played outside in the fine weather, accompanied nearly always by their canine hosts.

Late that Sunday night, not long before midnight, Rebecca's mother came softly into her room and placed her hand on her sleeping daughter's shoulder.

"Rebecca, dear," said Elisabeth softly, "so sorry to wake you, but we're going to hold an emergency meeting at midnight in the command center of the underground. It's about eleven-thirty now."

Rebecca sat up quickly. "Are the children ..."

"The twins are asleep, dear. I just checked. But I think we'll want to take them down to the underground and put them to bed in Marie's dorm room while the meeting goes on. It could be lengthy. Don't you think?"

Rebecca agreed immediately and, minutes before Sunday midnight, she and her mother carried the children to the underground and tucked them into separate beds in the women's dorm room. They waited to hear the sleep-breathing of the children, then, leaving their door ajar, crossed the hall to the command center.

They left the command center's door open.

Jason Manguson presided and began with a prayer that God would be with them during their deliberations. He looked at the assembled group, seated around him on folding chairs. The group numbered six, not counting Jason himself: his wife, his daughter, and the four arrivals from the U.S., none of whom had had to be awakened for the session. The Americans' body clocks understood the time to be 7 p.m.

Most had tea or coffee cups in their hands or placed on the several small tables scattered around and between the chairs. Only the three Mangusons knew the reason for the emergency meeting.

Jason began.

"I received a call an hour ago from our son in London. Luke had just spoken by phone with Graham Roberts-Holm, an officer with MI6, and the chair of a small MI6 sub-committee that informally calls itself 'the Rebecca unit.' Roberts-Holm told Luke that he had been receiving reports since about 9 p.m. of another wave of assaults on ministers around England, again following their evening church services ... and, this time, at least one in Scotland ... a preliminary total of six *more* beatings, and, as far as he knew at the time, each of the ministers were among those present at the spring conference in Oxford on traditional Christianity.

"Unlike the case last Wednesday, all six of these were successful, and reports indicate that all six pastors are in hospital or on their way there.

"Obviously, the MI6 interest in our group is centered on Rebecca herself, due to previous instances in which Rebecca's visitations had international implications, and, thus, implications for MI6. Their Rebecca unit is understandably obsessed with the question of whether or not she has had special insights, clues, data … the sort of thing that might help them understand what is happening.

"And not just *what* is happening. Obsessed equally with their need to get a sense of *who* is behind all this. I think it's fair to say that Luke works hard to remain civil in the face of Roberts-Holm's persistence … trying to emphasize, as Luke always does, what MI6 already knows … that the initiative does not lie with Rebecca, nor, indeed, with any of us who have been graced with the Hebrew label for our group.

"It doesn't work that way.

"Nonetheless," continued Jason, "I've called this meeting to bring you four Americans up to date on everything that has transpired thus far, and to invite us to take an hour or so to brainstorm contingencies. Among those contingencies, for example, would be deciding to operate exclusively from the Lodge, if we are called into action, or, alternatively, electing to move to London for the duration of the crisis. And, if the latter, deciding whether we should all go to the city, or some stay here."

Jason paused, thinking over what he had said.

Satisfied, he continued.

"If there is anything we have learned for certain over the years, it is that, if we are called upon to act, not a single hour can be wasted. We need to prepare now, insofar as we can, for whatever may present itself to us."

With that introduction, a productive hour was spent in discussion. Once in agreement that all that could be done had been done, the members moved to their quarters, the American men to the men's dorm room, Marie to the women's, and Jason and Elisabeth to their own rooms upstairs in the Lodge proper. Rebecca elected to stay in Marie's dorm room with the children, in the underground, since that would allow the soundly sleeping twins to remain undisturbed.

Monday, 3 a.m.

Rebecca, Marie, and the children were sleeping soundly in the wee hours of the morning when Rebecca was nudged awake by a familiar sensation. The sensation originated in her sleeping mind and was primarily visual, interrupting a dreamless slumber with a point of light.

She sat up quickly in her bed and alerted herself to observe whatever sensations might be presented, so that no detail would be forgotten later. Almost immediately, as the vision developed, she began to perspire, her body suddenly heated from a Source other than her own nerves and muscles.

The point of light quickly expanded to form a broad canvas on which two images presented themselves in sequence, one after the other. The first, covering the entire envisioned canvas, presented itself as a nondescript, unadorned, unpainted structure seemingly designed to be as uninteresting as possible. Its function was not evident, but its sheer mass was impressive. It appeared to be a mountainous concrete building that simply sat still, in her mind's eye, immobile and massive.

But as the dreamed image continued to present itself to the dreamer, Rebecca became aware she was to understand that this was something more than a mere building of indeterminate purpose. Whatever its function, that function was to be understood by her, the dreamer, as dramatically sinister.

The structure seemed, from her vantage, senseless … that is, inert. And yet it somehow conveyed threat. It somehow bespoke danger. It somehow communicated the promise of mayhem to any who might be so foolish as to approach it.

And that first image persisted while the second presented itself.

The second image gradually took over the foreground for which the concrete mass now served as background. That second image formed a face. Masculine. Impassive. Bespectacled. Bearded. Rugged. Hairline receding. Forehead jutting prominently over widely spaced black eyes, the forehead's prominence emphasized by eyebrows that formed a single length of neatly trimmed, midnight black facial hair.

Rebecca sat waiting as the vision lingered, stationary, during which time she continued to focus on every detail. Finally, the image began to change … a new feature materialized … a hand, indistinct … the man's own hand, holding an implement, still indistinct … perhaps a phone, but one that suggested a weapon of immense power

In just seconds, the vision faded into nothingness and Rebecca was left alone, breathing deeply from the exhausting effort, perspiration now soaking her bedclothes. She knew from long experience that she must not give in to sleep until she had reported every detail to a receptive listener. For the first time, that first listener would be someone other than her husband or her brother.

She struggled to her feet, moved quietly around the twins' beds, and lay down heavily across the foot of Marie's. Rebecca placed her hand on Marie's feet, which lay under the lightweight summer sheet, and squeezed once to rouse her friend as gently as possible. Marie, at first foggy from sleep, pushed herself to a sitting position and saw Rebecca's face in the dim light provided by two small nightlights positioned along the baseboards on two sides of the dorm room.

Marie was momentarily disoriented by Rebecca's appearance, for one side of her face was covered by a cascade of her own dark tresses falling in a disorganized curtain and covering the facial scar which marked her as Rebecca. Her skin glistened with perspiration. Her breathing was labored.

Fully awake in seconds, Marie understood in a flash what was happening. She had been warned that this was Rebecca's usual condition at the conclusion of a visitation. She had also been told of the importance of Rebecca's immediately relating the details of a vision to a receptive listener.

And Marie saw that, in this case, that receptive listener could only be her.

She pushed aside the anxiety that rose from this realization and steeled herself to fulfill the unsought role. She whispered to herself Jack McGriff's companion prayer, one that Rebecca herself now used often.

Father, be present … be present …

She nodded to Rebecca in the faint light.

"Ready, Rebecca."

Rebecca began, her voice soft and husky with sleep. She spoke the entire vision without pause, then asked Marie to repeat the description back to her.

Marie did.

Rebecca thanked her, stood carefully, and moved unsteadily back to her bed. In seconds she fell into a deep sleep.

This time, her sleep was uninterrupted.

Monday, 7 a.m.

Early that Monday, when Elisabeth Manguson glided into Marie and Rebecca's underground dorm room, the twins were just stirring. Marie was fully dressed and ready for the day. Each of the women lifted a child and silently carried them out of the room, leaving Rebecca sleeping soundly.

Mid-morning, the paying guests of the Lodge, as well as the new visitors from London, New York, and Washington, having breakfasted, Rebekka Yahalomin assembled once more in the underground command center. Jason Manguson bade everyone good morning, led the group in a short prayer for God's guidance in the upcoming discussion, and announced that Rebecca had experienced a visitation within hours of the conclusion of their midnight session.

He turned to his daughter.

"Rebecca? Please …"

Rebecca explained that she had slept in the women's dorm room with the children and, since Marie had been sleeping there, as well, the requisite first report of the dream had been given to Marie.

"Marie," said Rebecca, "please interrupt whenever you hear something that does not correspond exactly to what I said to you in the wee hours. That includes, of course, any omissions I might inadvertently make.

"Yes?"

"Yes. I'll do my best, Rebecca."

The two women went carefully through the dream once without entertaining questions, and then a second time with questions invited. The discussion focused for some time on the mysterious concrete structure and the sense of threat that was communicated to the dreamer while the structure was present in her mind.

Then a more general discussion followed regarding next steps. At length, Sid Belton made the definitive set of observations.

"Sounds t 'me we gotta get down t' London," offered Belton in his inimitable Brooklynese. "From what I've just heard ya' say, nobody here at th' Lodge has seen any piece of Mrs Clark's dream. Right?

"That structure she dreamed … an' that face … they aren't here anywhere. None of th' guests look anything like that guy, right?

"An' nothin' here looks anything like that building. Right?

"We gotta get goin' t' th' city. Right?

"We gotta give ourselves a chance t' find the things in th' dream.

"Know what I mean? Hm?

"Know what I mean?"

Within the hour, Rebecca had said her good-byes to the twins, to her parents — each of them holding one of the children — and to the disappointed Ginny. The Land Rover Five-Door had been loaded with luggage and with the four Americans. She had phoned her brother at ISP, briefly described her dream, and been assured by Luke that the company's fifth-floor guest rooms would be ready for the Americans by the time they could arrive, expected to be shortly after noon.

Rebecca would reside with her husband at Luke and Kory's home.

Monday early afternoon

Rebecca checked the Rover Five-Door into the ISP parking lot in London, its guards having been told by Luke to expect his vehicle and five occupants. Luke, Matt, and Kory were all waiting at the rear entrance to the ISP building, and quickly moved into the parking lot to help with the luggage, an unnecessary step, given how light the group traveled, but a courtesy the Americans noted and appreciated.

While the Americans took their luggage to their fifth-floor rooms, escorted by Luke and Kory, Rebecca and Matt stopped at his office, so that Rebecca could phone one of her tennis protégés, teenager SallyBelle Jones. The two, Rebecca and SallyBelle, had grown close during the spring months, not only because of their regular early-morning tennis instruction sessions, but because the youngster also served as a babysitter for Joanna and Samuel whenever the Clarks needed her.

This had offered numerous opportunities for the development of an informal counseling relationship, with SallyBelle eagerly soaking up any bits of life-perspective Rebecca had been willing to share with her. Over the months, Rebecca found herself viewing these sessions as preparation for what her hoped-for mother-and-children relationships might become a decade later, when Joanna and Samuel would reach a comparable stage of adolescence.

"SallyBelle?" said Rebecca when the youngster came on the line. "Rebecca Clark here. Tell me!"

"Yes!" cried the girl. "Yes! I just got the call! And so did Thomas! We were both picked! Can you believe it?"

In the brief conversation, the youngster explained that the chosen BBGs would continue to practice that week, not at the All England Lawn Tennis and Croquet Club where the Championships would actually be held, but at the entirely separate venue where the qualifying tournament would be held, starting the next day. In the qualifying tournament, as Rebecca knew well, having played in that tournament as a rising teen star, each competitor needed to win through three rounds to earn one of 16 Championship Main Draw places for each of the qualifying men, and another 16 Main Draw places for each of the qualifying women.

The 32 "qualifiers," as they were called, were then scheduled into the Championship tournament itself, competing against the best-known and most accomplished tennis players in the world. Qualifiers rarely advanced to later rounds, but the concept of making Wimbledon available to players other than the established elite added a touch of openness to the tournament that would otherwise be missing.

Rebecca offered to be available to drive SallyBelle to or from either venue on any of the days when the youngster's parents might not be able to. SallyBelle quickly accepted the offer and promised to phone Rebecca at Kory and Luke's home that evening to give her the detailed schedule for that week. Rebecca had already made arrangements to ride with Kory in the MG to retrieve her Volvo later that day.

Rebecca also hoped to be able, while at her fire-destroyed home, to access the basement workout space so that she might collect her throwing knives, since she now had only the three that were secure in her ready-satchel, plus the three that Luke kept in his basement for his own throwing sessions. Practicing in Luke's basement with only six knives was going to be less efficient and more time-consuming, even with her brother helping to retrieve them after each round of throws. But she doubted — correctly, as it turned out — that she would be allowed to set foot on her property at all. She expected it to be marked off as a crime scene for some time.

After speaking with SallyBelle from Matt's office, Rebecca climbed one of the stairways with Matt to the third floor ISP conference room, arriving just before the Americans, who had taken a few minutes to freshen up in their fifth-floor guestrooms. Luke and Kory were already there, and a light lunch, prepared by the ISP kitchen staff, awaited them all. The group chatted contentedly over their sandwiches, glad to be together once more.

Once lunch was finished and the room tidied, they took their places at the conference table. Luke, as chair of the ISP sub-committee on athletes' security at the Championships, chaired informally.

Monday, 1:30 p.m.

"Let me focus first on our ISP subgroup's responsibility, security for the athletes at the Championships' venue, starting next Monday. We have two fresh pieces of material from which to work. First, my sister's dream, given her in the small hours of this morning — a report which we have all heard in varying degrees of detail, and which we will want to go over again in this meeting — and second, a disturbing note delivered to my office by courier less than an hour ago.

"Rebecca and Marie," he continued, "since Kory, Matt and I have heard only a brief summary of your dream, please go through it again for our benefit. Our American guests heard the full report at the Lodge, but perhaps will not mind hearing it again."

Nods from the four.

Another careful, bit-by-bit recounting of the dream followed, then a summary of the discussion of the dream that had been held at the Lodge earlier that day. When all felt answered, Luke picked up a 9-by-12-inch envelope containing the message just delivered by courier to his office.

He read its contents slowly.

Monday, 17 June 1985

From: XAOC

To: Lt. Luke Manguson, officer, Royal Navy, and senior consultant, International Security Perspectives, LLC

Luke spelled, rather than attempting to pronounce, the all-caps, four-character name of the originating entity. He then continued.

1. We claim full responsibility for the assaults, on Wednesday and Sunday nights, on Christian ministers who attended the April conference on traditional Christianity in Oxford. There will be more of these assaults as time passes.

2. We claim full responsibility for the destruction of Rebecca Clark's home. We will pursue her, and her family, until they no longer exist.

3. We claim full responsibility for all that is coming: chaos and terror throughout the United Kingdom and beyond, focused next on the Wimbledon Championships, then on Parliament, then on various infrastructure systems throughout the United Kingdom. Eventually, we will spread chaos far beyond the U.K., extending chaos ultimately to all the great democracies of the globe.

You cannot stop us. We will destroy every recognizable aspect of ordinary life, first in the U.K., and then around the world. The people of the democracies will eventually be ruined spiritually, politically, financially, and, in selected cases, physically. To that end, we will destroy Rebekka Yahalomin early in the process.

Luke looked up.

"That's it. Delivered an hour ago.

"Thoughts, anyone?"

No one spoke.

Finally, Sid Belton grumbled.

"Luke, I need t' see this garbage on paper. Can y' make copies fer us before we get goin' on this? I gotta hold this scumbag's memo in my hands."

Smiling at the detective's familiar dialect and unique vocabulary, Luke replied, "Of course, Sid. Give us a moment."

Luke and Kory quickly left the room, to return in minutes with the copies. They distributed the single-page message, and then sat and waited.

The next to speak, after several minutes, was Jaakov Adelman. He made a small movement of his hand in order to request permission from Luke.

"No need for formality here, Jaakov," said Luke. "Any of you … just speak whenever you have something we should hear.

"Jaakov … please go ahead."

"I know a little Russian from my Mossad days," said Adelman. "I'm pretty sure the name of the entity that sent this is, in English, simply 'Chaos,' or something close to that. It sounds to me as though they — whoever 'they' might turn out to be — selected a name for their organization that summarizes their mission: to create chaos.

"If that's the case, I can begin to see how these apparently unrelated events might connect to each other."

"Yes, and not only that," said Kory quickly, "but the fact that the originating entity for this message appears to be Russian suggests that this disruption here in England is connected to the disruption we just faced down in the U.S. Everything that we fought through earlier this month in America was Soviet-Union-originated.

"Perhaps this is, too."

"Yes!" offered Rebecca immediately, agreeing.

"I recall Jaakov speculating," she continued, "while we were still in the U.S., that Artur Volkov and Tatyana Kuznetsova might be condemned in Moscow, when they finally arrived home, for having failed in their mission in the U.S., or … equally plausible … they might be rewarded, promoted, and re-directed … re-commissioned … possibly given yet more resources with which to continue their efforts, but the next time operating in a different country, cloaked in different methods, and using different tools to go about their work."

"Excellent!" said Luke, jumping to his feet in excitement and beginning to pace rapidly around the room. "That would link together everything we have faced and apparently will face."

He continued to stride purposefully, energy bursting from him as he circled the group. He circled the room twice, while the others waited silently, then he stopped and stood behind his chair.

"The Jefferson Bible fraud that we stopped in the United States ... the Russian Mafia's financial dealings in New York and New Jersey ... the KGB's murders and would-be murders ... and here, now, the assaults on C. S. Lewis-styled ministers ... the attempt on my sister and her family and the complete destruction of their home ... and next, according to this message, a widespread terror campaign that will start with the Wimbledon Championships and move on to Parliament and then to infrastructure throughout the United Kingdom.

"All one piece," he concluded.

"And, I suspect," added Rebecca quickly, "all driven by one mind."

CHAPTER FOUR

Monday, afternoon

ARTUR VOLKOV — THE REVEREND FATHER ARTUR VOLKOV — influential Russian Orthodox priest and Soviet political operative, as well as the senior KGB agent in North America, called to order a meeting in London that same afternoon. In attendance were Tatyana Kuznetsova, Volkov's longtime administrative assistant, and a dozen KGB agents.

They met in an austere, unadorned room marked by three enormous gun cabinets along one wall, a single metal desk against the facing wall, and a four-drawer file cabinet situated next to the desk. A single, bare light bulb provided the only illumination for the windowless space, except for that provided by a floor lamp adjacent to the desk. The cold concrete floor held a single folding table in its center and metal folding chairs for each participant. Volkov and Kuznetsova sat at the table, while all others present had arrayed their chairs in a wide semi-circle facing them.

The heavy, locked door was fireproof.

Volkov was a heavy-shouldered man, paunchy in his mid-40s, but exuding bullish strength. His wide, flat face was punctuated by small, black eyes, over which bushy, black-to-graying eyebrows fell like unruly nests. He rested his heavily veined, enormously muscular hands on the edge of the table.

He wore, as usual, a nondescript brown suit with a narrow black tie over an unstarched white shirt, its collars curling upwards unchecked by starch or buttons. This was his usual appearance, since Volkov rarely wore his priestly collar while immersed in KGB-focused work. He spoke passable English and used that language as a matter of policy when operating in the U.S. or in the U.K., even when addressing native speakers of Russian like those before him now. He insisted that all members of his team do the same when operating in English-speaking countries. Thus, English was the language of this, and of all, meetings led by Volkov in the U.S. or England.

Tatyana Kuznetsova, a slight, bespectacled, physically unremarkable woman, also in her 40s, rarely spoke in groups such as this one, given her function as Volkov's assistant and as the only woman present. Consequently, she was often underestimated by those who did not know her, or about her. She, in fact, had family and business and government connections through all layers of Soviet officialdom and beyond. She was far more than Volkov's assistant.

She wore a dark, tailored suit and dark brown, low-heeled shoes. She comprised that unlikeliest combination of ingredients: invisible, indispensable, powerful.

Of the dozen KGB agents arrayed before Volkov, one functioned, both officially and unofficially, as the lead agent. He was Anton Fedorov. He sat facing Volkov on the table's opposite side, his position reflecting his leadership of the other agents, who formed a rough semi-circle behind him.

Fedorov's face was rugged and acutely masculine. Now in his mid-30s, he had a bony, prominent nose and a dramatically jutting forehead, a physical feature emphasized in its prominence by eyebrows that formed a single length of black, neatly trimmed facial hair. Fedorov's wispy hairline was receding, further dramatizing the protruding forehead. His brown eyes were unremarkable when Fedorov was quiescent, as he was at this moment.

He had a distance runner's build. Trim, taut, wiry.

Fedorov was clothed much like the other agents. He wore unremarkable brown shoes, a dark suit, and a plain white shirt. He, like many of the others, wore no tie.

Fedorov was armed, as were they all. The men carried 9mm Makarovs, or the newer 9mm Glocks, under their suit jackets in standard KGB shoulder holsters. Tatyana Kuznetsova carried her recently issued Glock in a specially designed purse. When she was standing, the purse's long shoulder strap allowed her to rest her right hand unobtrusively on, or even inside, the purse whenever danger or opportunity presented itself. The ends of the purse were made of dark-colored silk, allowing her to fire the weapon from inside the purse without the projectile's trajectory or force being affected by the material through which it would necessarily pass.

Fedorov addressed Volkov without obvious deference, despite Volkov's enormous power and reputation for ruthlessness, a characteristic that Volkov displayed as frequently toward those who were under him organizationally as toward those whom he considered enemies. However, as Artur Volkov was soon to realize, Anton Fedorov feared no one.

"Last night's assaults," Fedorov was saying to Volkov, "went perfectly. None of the mistakes that marked our first efforts were evident. As we are all acutely aware, our initial assaults last Wednesday resulted in four of the six planned attacks being aborted, leaving only the successful beatings in Cornwall and Yorkshire. We learned from last week's failures that there is no substitute for research, reconnaissance, and on-the-attack-site flexibility. We now have a formula that we can apply with few, if any, failures, going forward."

Fedorov paused, glancing around him, to see if his colleagues had anything they wished to add to, or subtract from, his statement. None did.

Fedorov continued.

"We shall move forward Wednesday evening with the scheduled church assaults, but our planning will then shift to Wimbledon, just one week away now. We have four All England Tennis Club employees on our payroll at this point. Each of them is a member of the permanent maintenance crew for the All England Club. Their responsibilities include twice-daily cleaning *inside* the players' dressing rooms. Two are women, so we have access to the women players' dressing areas as well as the men's.

"There is no change," Fedorov continued, "to our approach. First, church leaders in the U.K. who were participants at the April conference. All of them have leadership roles beyond their own congregations, each one focused on traditional Christianity and consequently difficult to corrupt … to weaken … to co-opt … for our own purposes. Money will not turn their heads sufficiently to make them truly useful to us.

"They are, in short, actual *believers*.

"Nonetheless, we expect to *intimidate* 100 percent of them.

"Thus, the church attacks come first. Then, second on the strategic agenda, attacks on Rebecca Clark herself … and her family. This meddlesome woman, her family, and her colleagues must be eliminated early on, given their track record for learning of our plans in advance, and then disrupting them.

"Third, Wimbledon athletes, their entourages, the Wimbledon officialdom, the international media, and, in most cases, the spectators. We will disrupt the tournament in ways so varied that the police, MI5, MI6, and even Rebekka Yahalomin … will be unable to anticipate the next day's intrusions. We may be able to bring the whole tournament to its knees … to prevent its even reaching the final rounds at all. The international publicity will be incalculable.

"And, of course, after that, we will move on to Parliament … and beyond."

Fedorov again paused to glance at his colleagues.

Again, no one spoke.

"And," he continued, "our written message to Rebekka Yahalomin — addressed to Lieutenant Luke Manguson, Rebecca Clark's brother — was delivered to him an hour ago at the headquarters of International Security Perspectives. Rebekka Yahalomin has now been warned formally and in advance of what they can expect.

"Having failed to destroy Ms. Clark and her family," concluded Fedorov, "with the firebombing of their home, we now must draw them out. This morning's missive to her brother stands a chance to accomplish that very nicely."

Fedorov nodded to Volkov to indicate the completion of his report.

Artur Volkov leaned back in his chair and folded his arms across his chest. His face was impassive. The silence in the room grew long.

"I am very little impressed, Fedorov," he finally said, his voice flat.

"Beating church people is, or should be, child's play, although, as you note, you failed on two-thirds of your scheduled assaults last Wednesday. So, your track record on the easiest part of your assignment is mixed.

"Your track record on the second objective," continued Volkov, "is that of utter and complete failure. Ms. Clark and her people are unimpaired and, having been alerted to our direct threat to their personal welfare, both by the firebombing of their home and now by letter to Lieutenant Manguson, are on full battle alert.

"You may or may not be correct that the missive will, as you say, 'draw them out.' Whether or not that is the case, they will be much harder to reach at this point, and Ms. Clark, and the rest, are unweakened by anything you have attempted.

"As for your next assignment … generating chaos at the Championships next week … this is a far more complex and delicate task than either of the first two on which you have achieved, in the one case, mixed results, and, on the second, nothing whatsoever. You, Fedorov, as the Americans say, are skating on thin ice."

Fedorov received this reprimand impassively, but then, after several moments, he leaned forward deliberately in his chair, his dark eyes — suddenly no longer unremarkable — boring into those of Artur Volkov. Gradually Fedorov's mouth formed itself into a snarl.

"Thin ice?" he said, his deep voice rough and gravelly.

He stood slowly until he looked down at Volkov from his side of the small table. The snarl on his face drew his lips back, showing teeth much as would those of a wolf preparing to attack and rend a cowering prey.

"And exactly how," said Fedorov carefully, "do you rate your own performance in the U.S. this month? You, Volkov, suffered the full measure of defeat at the hands of Ms. Clark and her minions, assisted by the CIA, the U.S. Navy, and the Royal Navy. Your failure was so complete that you are persona non grata in three countries — the U.S., Israel, and England — to such an extent that special diplomatic arrangements were necessary just to bring you and Tatyana into this country.

"At one point a few days ago on the other side of the Atlantic, you even had Ms. Clark and Lieutenant Manguson captured and secured, then allowed them to escape.

"And now, here they are again.

"How do you rate your performance, Volkov?"

Volkov suddenly rose, now glaring at Fedorov across the table from a distance of perhaps 8 feet. The two men stared menacingly at each other, their mutual contempt and hatred obvious to all in the room. A tense silence descended.

Those present watched, first in puzzlement, then in fear, as Anton Fedorov began to change before their eyes. His thick chest seemed to expand unnaturally with each deep, audible breath. His face flushed bright red. His teeth were fully bared.

Those directly in front of him — Volkov and Kuznetsova — could see that the whites of his eyes were suddenly inflamed, veins standing out starkly red, while the brown orbs darkened into black. His breathing became a prolonged growl, a canine-like sound emanating from savage mouth and distended nostrils.

Fedorov strode forward three steps, grasped the edge of the flimsy table in his right hand, and, in a violent motion, flung the table through the air with such force that it smashed to pieces against the far wall of the room. The barrier between the two men now removed, Fedorov advanced several more steps until his face was inches from Volkov's. Fedorov, slightly taller, raised himself on his toes and, leaning in, expelled a vile, rancid hiss into Volkov's face, a visage that until that moment had struck fear in the hearts of KGB agents, Russian Orthodox bureaucrats, and enemies of the Soviet Union around the globe.

In helpless response, Volkov turned his head, gasping for breath.

He sat down meekly.

Tatyana Kuznetsova, watching the encounter from close range, sagged in her chair, her mouth falling open, uncomprehending. She stared up at Fedorov and then at Volkov, now seated next to her once more. She felt equal parts mystification and a raw, unfamiliar fear, as she considered these two men, one of them her longtime superior, the other a virtual unknown.

She had never seen Artur Volkov defeated until that moment.

And she had never seen Anton Fedorov at all until that morning.

Who was this man, this man who could force Artur Volkov into psychological and physical collapse by mere proximity?

What was this man?

Tuesday, morning

Early on the morning following, now less than one week before the opening day of the Wimbledon Championships, Rebecca Clark collected SallyBelle Jones and Thomas Chambers at their homes and drove them in her Volvo sedan to the site of the Wimbledon qualifying tournament, its courts located in southwest London. The three of them were dressed similarly in the tennis whites traditionally worn by all participants at the Championships.

The two 15-year-olds bubbled and babbled in their nervousness.

"When do you think we'll be issued our outfits for the Championships, Mrs. Clark?" asked SallyBelle.

Then, too excited to wait for Rebecca's answer, SallyBelle continued.

"I wish we could wear our whites next week during the Championships, but I'm sure we'll be in those drab, dark uniforms that the Ball Boys and Girls always wear. Don't you think those are drab, Mrs. Clark?

"And do you think I'll be allowed to wear my hair like this, Mrs. Clark? Or will they not let me wear my ribbons when the time comes?

"And what about my tenners, Mrs. Clark? Do you think they'll let me wear these gold laces next week for the Championships?"

Rebecca realized immediately that the teen was not expecting answers to any of her questions. So, Rebecca simply drove, smiling to herself, enjoying the youthful energy that filled the automobile.

SallyBelle was dazzling in her all-white tennis skirt and top. Her blonde hair was pulled into a high ponytail and tied with a bright purple bow. The bow itself was merely decorative, something she had added to make her outfit more festive.

The one-sided conversation continued in this vein, the teens trembling with excitement, for most of the 20 minutes Rebecca needed to drive from the youngsters' homes, located in adjacent neighborhoods, to the qualifiers' competition venue. As she drove, Rebecca found herself reminiscing about her own teen years, not as a BBG herself, but as an actual participant in the qualifying tournament.

Suddenly, as the Volvo neared the qualifiers' site, Rebecca felt, rather than saw, a looming concrete structure sited a long block from the thoroughfare on which she drove. She tensed.

Then an electric chill ran through her, head to foot.

She did not turn her eyes to look directly at what she sensed was there. Instead, she continued to the qualifiers' site, parked the Volvo, and walked into the venue with the two teens. SallyBelle and Thomas were not screened carefully against the BBG list, simply because Rebecca Clark was known and welcomed on sight by the officials at the gate. She was a revered figure in London tennis circles, still much sought-after for appearances at local events at all levels. She announced her two charges to the officials, who checked them off their lists and smilingly waved them through.

Once inside the grounds, all BBGs were directed to a set of grandstands to await their official welcome and to receive their precise schedules for each day they would be present at the qualifying matches. Rebecca watched only until she was certain that her two youngsters were seated and in receipt of their assignments. She then turned and moved back through the parking area to her car.

Before getting in, she raised her eyes to the massive concrete structure, now a quarter-mile from where she stood, yet still readily visible from that distance. She considered the unadorned mound of gray squareness and consciously pulled into her mind's eye the dream she had been given Sunday night — actually, Monday morning — while still at the Birmingham Lodge. She recalled the dreamed structure and then the dreamed visage that accompanied its image.

She shuddered.

She then moved behind the wheel and started the Volvo. She drove directly to the structure, aware that her pulse was increasing as she neared, aware that her senses were heightened as the ominous mountain of concrete grew larger and more threatening with each block that she traveled. Finally, she stopped in front of the entrance. There was no signage other than the word "Parking" that formed itself in block letters above the vehicle entrance. No attendants were visible.

Rebecca turned the car away, drove two blocks, and parked on a side street. She got out of the Volvo and stood beside it, continuing to study the structure, then moved to the boot and extracted the long, dark-colored raincoat she kept there. She pulled the coat on, over her tennis whites, then lifted her ready-satchel and placed it over her right shoulder by its long strap. She reflexively slipped her right hand inside the satchel, reassuring herself by feel that her three Barringtons Swords throwing knives were there, secure in their individual hard-leather cases.

She did not expect action ... not yet ... but she had learned long before to respect the import of her dreams. If a vision was suggestive of threat, as her Monday morning dream at the Lodge had been, simple prudence demanded that she be prepared.

She spoke the companion prayer to herself — *Father, be present, be present* — then turned and strode toward the looming gray edifice which identified itself as a parking garage. She crossed the side streets and another thoroughfare, and then paused at the garage entrance. She looked for attendants, still saw none, and continued into the dark, cluttered ground floor.

Searching the area, she saw that there appeared to be stairwells in each corner, and another in the center. The center stairwell was sheathed in concrete, concealing the stairs themselves.

She also saw signs pointing toward an elevator, but headed for the center stairwell, knowing that use of the elevator would limit her choices, should a fast escape become necessary. And fast escape seemed to her a real possibility, given the fact that her sense of threat had reached an extreme level.

She was now *inside* her dream.

Rebecca walked to the enclosed stairwell, stepped within, and stopped. She reached into the satchel and removed one of the throwing knives from its sheath. Gripping the knife by its throwing handle, her hand and the weapon still inside the satchel, she began to climb the stairs.

She had rehearsed many times the act of throwing a knife when confronted suddenly by an armed enemy. She had practiced the act of shrugging the satchel from her shoulder, allowing it to fall free to the floor, leaving the knife suddenly unencumbered and ready to be hurled via her violent, windmill delivery. And she knew to aim for an assailant's weapon-bearing shoulder in the expectation that the razor-sharp blade, arriving at devastating speed, would sever the muscles and nerves her attacker would need to use in attempting to fire a handgun, wield a club, or thrust at her with his own knife.

At each floor above ground level, she moved carefully out of the stairwell, quietly circled the stairwell's enclosure, and examined the darkened expanse Only when she reached the fourth floor — the top floor of the structure — did she find anything other than areas filled with automobiles and with the occasional individual walking toward elevator or stairwell, having just parked her or his vehicle.

On reaching the fourth, she hesitated. The sense of danger was now overwhelming. Gripping the knife tightly inside the satchel, Rebecca crept out of the stairwell and crouched beside one of several vehicles parked nearby. Focusing then on her breathing, she quieted herself, closed her eyes, and simply listened.

After a moment, she heard distant footfalls ascending one of the corner stairwells. Heavy footfalls. Two men.

The paired footsteps reached her level and began to cross the expanse of mostly empty space from the corner stairwell toward ... what? Moving in a crouch, her hand still on the knife, she peered around the vehicle and saw the men moving through the dimly lit garage toward a door that appeared to be an entrance to a space — an interior space, a structure within the structure — of moderate size. She estimated the space to encompass perhaps 30 feet by 20 feet, using her at-home target range as a frame of reference for estimating the dimensions.

The space was of concrete construction, as was nearly everything else in the massive building. Its door appeared to be made of steel. The room — she immediately began to imagine the space as a storage room or, perhaps, a meeting room — was nestled in one corner of this, the top-level floor.

The two men, each carrying a long gun of indeterminate caliber, approached the steel door and stopped. One of them pulled a folding metal chair from its place, propped against the wall, unfolded it, and sat down heavily. The two men exchanged a few unintelligible words in low voices, and then one of them strode toward a different corner of the garage, presumably to use the stairwell in that corner.

Rebecca found that, in the full minute during which she had observed the two men moving across the floor, she had become fully calm, even tranquil. And she became aware that her calmness stemmed from a certainty that she was see-ing the critical, but until now unseen, element in her dream. She had dreamed of the garage, certainly, but the core component of the dream was, she was instantly confident, this fourth-floor room that was now being watched by an armed guard.

She was certain that the interior of the room held secrets that would bear on everything Rebekka Yahalomin might be expected to face. And she realized further that she knew two other things of importance.

She knew that the dreamed face would be found, at least at times, within the confines of the room she now studied from a distance of 100 feet. And secondly, she knew that her task now was to extricate herself without being seen by the guards, to report her findings to her brother, her husband, and their colleagues, and then to return as soon as practicable to this, the centerpiece of her Monday morning dream.

She smiled to herself when she imagined Sidney Belton's excitement at the thought of a steel door with its no-doubt "foolproof" lock. It was his favorite kind of challenge. Age and trauma had dimmed some of the renowned detective's physical capacities, but not his lock-picking skill nor his analytical abilities.

Suddenly, Rebecca heard the second guard calling up from the third floor. "Hey Joe… come down. Ya gotta see this Maserati. Unbelievable."

Rebecca waited until the footfalls died away. Then she swiftly moved to the corner stairwell opposite the one just used by the guards, descended silently, reached street level, and was gone.

Once behind the wheel of the Volvo, she bowed her head, spoke aloud a soft prayer of thanksgiving, reflected for several moments on what she had just experienced, and started the engine. There was much to be done before it was time to collect SallyBelle and Thomas from the qualifiers' venue that afternoon.

And *very* much to be done that night.

Tuesday, midmorning

Luke Manguson opened the regularly scheduled meeting of the Wimbledon security unit at ISP with an introduction to the group of a "special guest." He gestured to the conservatively dressed gentleman sitting directly across the conference table from himself. The ISP professionals turned curiously toward the guest, who adjusted his rimless half-glasses and smiled as Luke explained his presence, and the presence of the two individuals — a man and a woman — who sat on either side of him.

"This is Graham Roberts-Holm," Luke was saying, "who chairs a small MI6 unit, one that has considerable interest in what our group is working on, here at ISP. Neither he nor I are free to explain in detail how their interests dovetail with ours, but the fact that Wimbledon attracts enormous international attention, plus the related fact that tensions with the Soviet bloc have never been higher, prompted me to invite him and his two associates to this morning's meeting.

"Welcome, Graham."

Roberts-Holm rose courteously in response and expressed his gratitude to Luke for the invitation. He then began to introduce his two colleagues.

"This," he said, indicating the woman, "is Aarushi Singh. Ms. Singh has been with MI6 for nearly a decade, beginning soon after she immigrated to England to complete her post-graduate studies at Oxford. She has worked with me on several Asia-focused projects during that time. Her background includes …"

Just at that moment, Rebecca Clark quietly entered the room, still wearing the long raincoat over her tennis whites. Despite her attempt to glide to a seat without interrupting, Roberts-Holm stopped mid-sentence and said, "Oh … Mrs. Clark … I didn't realize you'd be attending this session today. I'm delighted to see you."

Luke interrupted to explain his sister's presence.

"As most of you know, I think," he said, "my sister's experience as a Wimbledon competitor gives her certain security-related insights which can be of assistance to us. Our three-person subgroup, the one charged specifically with security for the players themselves, has already held one session with her. I have invited Rebecca to join us this week whenever she can. I didn't know that she would be able to be with us this morning, or I would have mentioned it earlier."

Roberts-Holm, still standing, resumed.

"Well … I say again … I am delighted … absolutely delighted," he responded, somewhat too unctuously for Rebecca's comfort. Luke and Kory caught the trace of a blush on the guest's face, and glanced knowingly at each other, well aware that Roberts-Holm would hardly be the first man in England to have developed a crush on the former international tennis luminary.

With apparent difficulty, Roberts-Holm finally gathered himself and continued. He turned to his other colleague, seemingly oblivious to the fact that he had not completed his introduction of Aarushi Singh.

"This is Declan Murphy," he said, gesturing toward the young man, "one of our Irish refugees at MI6" — polite laughter all round at this — "who is a newcomer to our subcommittee. With Luke's permission, Declan sat in on last week's phone calls between ISP and MI6."

As Roberts-Holm continued, Rebecca looked closely at the three MI6 guests. She was struck by Roberts-Holm's patrician air and his classic Englishman's profile, marked by square chin, long, straight nose, and high forehead. Aarushi Singh, Rebecca noted with interest, wore an exquisitely tailored Englishwoman's business suit, rather than native Indian dress. Her brown skin gave her a glow of robust health, making Roberts-Holm's appear almost sickly in contrast.

Rebecca's gray eyes shifted briefly to Declan Murphy, and her gaze was at once drawn to his shock of remarkably unkempt red hair, giving him the look of someone who had rolled out of bed, thrown on yesterday's brown suit, and left home without looking in the mirror or remembering to brush his hair. His face was strikingly angular and, she noticed when he turned slightly toward her, his eyes were amber and stood out dramatically from his pale skin.

Meanwhile, Luke was moving the session along briskly, summarizing reports from each subgroup and inviting Roberts-Holm to comment at each stage. After an hour, Luke called for a 10-minute break, during which many left the room, while some chose to remain, chatting casually with each other.

Reginald Jones and Horace Chambers, seated near opposite ends of the long conference table, at once turned to Rebecca, seated mid-table.

"Mrs. Clark," said Jones, "how did our two BBGs seem this morning on the way to the qualifiers' venue?"

"They were beside themselves, Reginald," she replied. "I felt privileged to be in their company. Really … they were *so* excited."

"And you'll still be able to collect them this afternoon?" asked Chambers.

"Oh yes," she said. "I'm looking forward to hearing how things have gone."

"And you're still okay with driving them on Friday, too?" asked Jones.

"Of course," she said, smiling. "You know I wouldn't miss the chance."

She turned to Chambers.

"And you can still serve as chauffeur tomorrow and Thursday, Horace?"

He shook his head.

"Actually, Reginald and I have worked things out so that he will handle transport for them on Thursday, but I'll still do tomorrow — Wednesday — as planned.

"In other words, we do have the next two days covered, as we agreed."

Rebecca nodded.

After a moment, Chambers continued.

"And we are so thankful, Mrs. Clark, that you could take them and pick them up today, and again on Friday. They're both thrilled that you were able to help."

At this, Roberts-Holm interjected, "Have your youngsters had this as a goal for very long, or is this a recent interest?"

Jones replied, "Oh, my goodness … SallyBelle has been obsessed with the sport since she was six, Graham. She knows she is unlikely ever to be in Rebecca Clark's league, so to speak, as a player, but she also knows this is a way to dive into the sport's most hallowed event, and to be a part of something that few ever experience."

Declan Murphy, Roberts-Holm's newest subcommittee member, seemingly fascinated by the Wimbledon-focused conversation, spoke up to say, "My daughter is only seven, Reginald, but she's the same way as your SallyBelle. I think I may talk to her about the BBG idea. This will give her something to aim for, if she later finds she is not an elite player. The odds must be astronomical against her ever being good enough actually to *play* Wimbledon."

At this, Rebecca turned to Murphy and said gently, "Declan, I'd suggest you save the BBG idea until your daughter has found out for herself that she is unlikely ever to be invited to play Wimbledon. Let her aspire to *playing* in the Championships. I would encourage you to let her aim high.

"You can introduce the BBG opportunity eventually, when it seems right, although I'd think she might eventually gravitate toward that idea on her own."

Murphy smiled thoughtfully and nodded.

"Thank you, Rebecca," he said. "Absolutely right."

The meeting soon resumed and, in less than a half-hour, Luke drew the session to a close. He thanked the three MI6 guests again for coming and closed the meeting. As participants filed out of the room, Rebecca moved quietly to her brother's side. She whispered to him that she needed "the others" to assemble at once.

He looked into the gray eyes. After a moment, he nodded.

Tuesday, late morning

The available members of the group informally christened Rebekka Yahalomin assembled in a smaller ISP conference room 15 minutes later. The England contingent — Rebecca Clark, Matt Clark, Luke Manguson, and Kory Manguson — was present, along with the U.S. contingent — Sid Belton, Jaakov Adelman, Marie Campbell, and Jack McGriff — to hear Rebecca's report of her early-morning reconnaissance.

The eight regretted the absence of Dr. Eleanor Chapel, Belton's wife, at home in New York with Penelope; the senior Mangusons, still at the Lodge with the children; and Matt Clark's parents, Martha and Paul, now living in Oakham, roughly 100 miles north of London. They knew, however, that Dr. Chapel, the Mangusons, or the Clarks might be called upon for assistance at any point. They often had been in the past.

Rebecca began the session by explaining her having *sensed* a massive concrete structure nearby as she drove two newly selected Wimbledon BBGs — SallyBelle Jones and Thomas Chambers, 15-year-olds to whom she had been giving private tennis lessons — to the qualifiers' venue that morning. She explained her instantaneous certainty that the structure was, in fact, the same structure she had dreamed early Monday morning at the Lodge.

She paused to let her listeners recall details of the dream.

"Everyone?" she asked.

Nods of recollection all around.

Then she talked them through her exploration of the parking garage and its fourth-floor steel-doored enclosure, which, she noted, had already become identified in her own mind as a meeting room — or perhaps a storage space for equipment or weapons — for whatever sinister force had been presented to her in the Monday morning dream. She noted her gathering confidence, as she moved through the garage that morning to a position near the fourth-floor enclosure, that the smallish room might well serve as home base both for the individual featured in her dream, and as point of origin for the missive sent by courier to her brother the previous day.

She went on to suggest that the steel-doored meeting room, or equipment and weapons locker, or some combination of the two, was plausibly the central gathering place, or perhaps the primary resource center, for "Chaos," the self-identified originating organization for the message Luke had received. She then paused to invite questions and observations, but the group remained quiescent, apparently still absorbing this, yet another stunning instance of the dream-to-reality process that had marked Rebekka Yahalomin from its inception.

Rebecca, hearing only thoughtful silence all around her, closed her eyes, and folded her hands together on the table. A full minute of this extended silence passed, and then she looked up.

"We must enter that space tonight," she said forcefully, her gray eyes arrowing around the room.

She paused again, looking first at her brother and then at Sid Belton.

"This will be unlawful, of course," she continued. "This will constitute 'breaking and entering,' at the very least, but there is no alternative I can imagine. Even though there are certain detectives with Scotland Yard and several investigators with MI6 who trust us to know things that they don't — or can't — that does not mean they can *act* on our information, when such action would be unlawful, nor does it mean that they can knowingly permit *us* to act on such information.

"They may believe us, when we say we have learned something from the Source, but they still are bound by the laws of the land.

"We must do this ourselves."

She looked to her brother and then to the detective.

"Do you agree, Luke? Mr. Belton?"

After a moment, both men nodded, Luke thoughtfully, Belton vigorously.

"We hafta know what's in that place," said Belton eagerly, "an' we gotta keep in mind that this garage thing — whatever it is — was at th' heart of Mrs. Clark's dream th' other night … th' other morning …

"We know from experience exactly what that kinda thing means. It means there's somethin' bad gonna happen, and quick. An' we know we can't fool around with somethin' like this, people. It's gonna happen fast, whatever it is.

"We gotta get in an' find out what's in there.

"An' that's all there is to it.

"Know what I mean? Hm?"

The room was momentarily noncommittal.

Rebecca sensed that there was a mixture of apprehension, from some of her colleagues, and of grim determination, from others. Her eyes returned to Sid Belton, who was squirming with energy.

"I got my lock-pick kit with me, Mrs. Clark," he said, "an' Luke carries a pretty good assortment of gadgetry, too. I'd say between th' two of us, we got whatever we'll need t' pop that steel door's locks like it was a can a' sardines.

"Know what I mean, ma'am? Hmm?"

Rebecca smiled her radiant smile, the one that always caused the facial scar to compress slightly. "I do, Mr. Belton," she said. "I certainly do."

Belton, warming to his idea as he considered the task further, added, "An' I also brought two of our firm's little document cameras from New York, Mrs. Clark … an' Jaakov brought the other two … so we got four a' these palm-size cameras we can use t' record whatever docs we might find in there ... or t' photograph weapons, if it turns out t' be some sorta munitions locker ... an' we got plenty of evidence-handlin' rubber gloves for all of us ... an' we'll all wanna wear 'em t' make sure th' dirtbags we're dealin' with won't have any idea we've been in their space ...

"Because ... y' know ... whatever we come out with ... we don't want th' rotten dirtbags t' know we got whatever we got ... we don't want 'em even t' know anybody has been anywhere near th' place ... we want 'em t' just keep sailin' along, thinkin' they got th' world by th' tail ... know what I mean, Mrs. Clark?

"Hm?

"Know what I mean?"

"Oh yes, Mr. Belton ... I do ... I do indeed."

Then, seeing that Belton had apparently wound himself down, Rebecca looked to her brother, at that point silently yielding leadership of the session to him. This transfer of leadership was a seamless process that the others had observed so often that they no longer took notice. This wordless exchange almost always occurred without discussion between the siblings, and rarely with any disagreement regarding which of them should have the leadership role at a given moment.

The session moved forward swiftly from that point, with the others gradually, one by one, accepting the idea of the necessity of a high-risk, completely unlawful incursion into what was likely to be the beating heart of Chaos. Soon they were all focused on the inevitable, and their collective concentration became palpably fierce.

In less than an hour the plan was in place. They would depart the ISP building shortly before midnight and travel in the Rover Five-Door to the southwest area of the city where the parking garage was located, not far from the All England Tennis and Croquet Club itself. Belton, Adelman, Kory, Matt, and McGriff would carry their handguns. Rebecca would carry the three knives, secure in her ready-satchel, that had survived the firebombing of her home. Luke would don his shoulder rig, fitted, as always, with tools, ties, and related accoutrement.

Marie Campbell, the only participant without military or intelligence agency background and training, knew that she would be the only one unequipped to fight, if fighting became necessary. She regarded this merely as a happy fact, but also knew that it placed a burden on the others to protect her.

She had learned earlier that summer to accept this fact of life within the Yahalomin, and to know that the others simply did not think in those terms … terms like "burden" or "liability" … but, rather, in terms of love.

Love for her, the newcomer.

She was, however, much gratified to be chosen to carry one of the four small document cameras. The other three instruments would be transported and operated by Rebecca, Kory, and Sid Belton.

Luke, concluding the session, reiterated the fact, already noted by Rebecca, that the incursion would be unlawful. For that reason, he reminded all, nothing about the plan could be communicated to their possible partners in facing off against the Chaos organization, whether that might eventually include MI6, MI5, Scotland Yard, or local law enforcement. Any information they might extract from the inner sanctum of the parking garage that night might eventually be shared with those others, if deemed necessary, but such sharing would not be accompanied by details regarding how they gained access to their data.

Their occasional partners at MI6 and Scotland Yard had come to understand, long before, that details of Rebekka Yahalomin's periodic revelations would remain shrouded in mystery. Those partners also understood that the ultimate origin of any such revelations would be that to which the Yahalomin referred as "the Source." They knew further that some portions of the data, based on which any of them could be called upon to act, might be obtained by questionable means.

They had come grudgingly to accept all of that.

And, in fact … mostly … they were simply grateful.

Tuesday/Wednesday, midnight

Just before midnight, Luke parked the Rover near the same spot his sister had used earlier that day. He turned off the engine and they sat in silence for several moments, at which point Luke asked Jack McGriff to lead them in prayer.

He did.

"Eternal Father," he prayed, "be present, be present … be present with us this night as we seek to learn more about the evil that threatens our ministers … that threatens Rebecca and Matthew's family … that threatens the athletes and organizers and spectators in the great tournament upcoming … that threatens the members of Parliament … that threatens other citizens of this country and beyond … Father, be present, be present … be present with us this night …

"Amen."

After the prayer, and after another several minutes of silence, which allowed each to formulate her or his own silent prayer, Luke said simply, "Now."

The group, each dressed in dark clothing, unloaded quietly and moved by careful prearrangement toward the parking garage. Once in sight of the entrance, Luke, Matt, and Jaakov crept to one side of the structure, just around a corner from the entrance.

Luke and Jaakov, strong, athletic, and unimpaired physically, scaled the chest-high wall with ease, then turned to assist Matt, hampered by his atrophied left arm, up and over the wall. Not pausing there, they advanced quickly and silently toward the tollbooth at the main entrance.

As expected, no attendants or guards were to be seen.

Luke then turned his flashlight toward the others, waiting on the other side of the street. He signaled them to move forward, using two brief flashes. Luke and his lead unit then turned and moved to the central stairwell, the one Rebecca had used that morning, and climbed to the top floor, pausing briefly at each level to observe and listen for the presence of patrols.

Meanwhile, Rebecca, Kory, Marie, McGriff and Belton ascended by means of one of the corner stairwells, moving slowly in consideration of Belton's physical impairments, his heavy walking cane clacking metronomically on each stair step. At the top, they paused, waiting for the clearance signal from Luke.

At that point, the two groups exchanged places, with Rebecca's unit moving as swiftly as Belton's shuffling, cane-assisted pace would allow, to the mysterious 20-by-30-foot space she had identified that morning. At the same time, Luke's unit descended by way of her corner stairwell to take up observation positions on the ground floor.

Belton, lock-pick kit in hand, went to work immediately on the locking system for the heavy steel door. He had the door open, unmarked and undamaged, in less than two minutes. As the door swung open, Kory and Rebecca entered swiftly.

Rebecca shined her penlight on the alarm system control box while Kory, expertly using her ISP alarm-system deactivation implements, easily disarmed the system in the 30-second interval before it would have signaled their intrusion. Then Belton and Marie joined Rebecca and Kory in the room, while McGriff, Beretta 9mm in hand, stood guard just outside the door.

Once the door was closed behind them, Rebecca used her penlight long enough to find the light switch for the single, bare, overhead bulb. What they then observed was an austere, unadorned room marked by three huge gun cabinets along one wall, a single metal desk against the facing wall, and a four-drawer file cabinet situated next to the desk. Aside from the overhead bulb, light for the windowless room could be provided only by a floor lamp adjacent to the desk. A single, partly broken, folding table held the center of the room, while folding metal chairs were stacked in one corner.

No words were needed to discuss what would be done next.

Belton headed for the gun cabinets with his lock picks while the three women moved immediately to the file cabinet. They removed file folders systematically, placed each stack on the floor, and, using the document cameras supplied by Belton and Adelman, began the task of photographing every page of every file folder.

Once Belton had opened each of the gun cabinets, he photographed its contents with the fourth document camera. This took only a few minutes, and then he joined the women in the work of photographing the documents extracted from the cabinets. They worked silently, focused entirely on capturing every page of every file folder. With four of them working, the task was completed in less than an hour.

Just after 1 a.m., the four of them stood at the door and visually inspected the room a final time, wanting to make sure the space would appear undisturbed to its regular occupants. Rebecca then switched off the overhead light and shined her penlight on the alarm box while Kory used her implements to rearm the system. Then Rebecca turned the doorknob with her gloved hand and opened the door just enough to see what she hoped.

She saw exactly that: McGriff standing quietly, Beretta in hand, just as she had left him an hour before. He turned toward her and nodded. Then he, Belton, and the women crossed the floor to their corner stairwell and were gone.

CHAPTER FIVE

Wednesday, 2 a.m.

WITHIN AN HOUR OF THE ROVER'S DEPARTURE FROM THE PARKING garage neighborhood — now to be referred to as "Chaos Headquarters" — six members of Rebekka Yahalomin had assembled in one of the ISP conference rooms, awaiting Kory and Luke's printing of the four document cameras' photographs. Their wait was short, as the couple began bringing the prints to the conference room piece by piece, as soon as each individual file had been photocopied.

All were still dressed in the dark clothing they had worn on the incursion.

To the group's delighted surprise, the members found that every document had been rendered both in English and in Russian, a circumstance that reduced the amount of material to examine by exactly half. Nonetheless, the line-by-line study of the documents dragged on until daybreak, interrupted only for individually determined stoppages for catnaps, exercise, or snacks, each one making her or his own decision regarding the most effective method for remaining on task.

Oddly, only Sid Belton, by far the oldest person in the group, seemed to need neither sleep nor exercise nor food and drink. The others eventually noticed.

At length, they inquired.

"Well," said Belton in his rasping base voice, "I'm old, see … I get sleepy durin' th' day … so I gotta take a nap or two durin' th' afternoon … then I'm usually good t' go … all night, if I hafta, see … it's 'cuz I'm old … and you're not.

"You're *children.*"

His cackling laugh filled the room.

Then, the inevitable: "Know what I mean?

"Hm?"

When the last files had been reviewed and the last set of notes completed, Luke surveyed the bleary-eyed group. He smiled.

"You all look terrible," he said happily.

Belton made a noise sounding like "hrumph."

"Y' oughta take a look in a mirror, Mr. Big Shot Royal Navy officer," he said, his trademark crooked smile creeping across his weathered face.

"Yer face looks like a tennis shoe that's been left out on th' lawn fer a week."

Laughter all around the room.

Luke resumed.

"Before we find our beds," he said, "I think we need to make several basic decisions. First, we need to decide what to do about the fact that we now know which ministers are targeted for assaults this very evening at their Wednesday services, plus the six listed for Sunday. Second, we need to decide what general approach we ought to take to forestall the devastation Chaos has planned for the Wimbledon Championships, just five days away now.

"And third," he concluded, "as part of each of those decisions, we need to decide which of our cooperating organizations — MI6, MI5, Scotland Yard — we should include, if any, in trying to protect the ministers tonight and Sunday, and the players and spectators next week at the Championships.

"We can wait to think about the rest of the destruction Chaos has planned for the country ... Parliament and the rest ..."

He sighed.

"I know we're tired, but some of this can't wait."

"In our review of the files tonight," asked Luke, "did anyone discover overview material ... big-picture material ... on the Chaos organization itself?"

Jaakov Adelman nodded.

"I had quite a bit of that in my files," he said.

"Anyone else?"

Heads shaking.

"Jaakov … go."

Adelman spoke from his seat, which was next to Sid Belton. As Adelman began, Belton tried to maneuver his chair slightly so that he could look directly at his detective-agency partner. Belton's numerous injuries over his years in the U.S. military and the New York Police Department had left him with stiffness both in his neck and in his spine, those comprising some of the less conspicuous damage.

Adelman, sensing Belton's difficulty, reached over to help him scrape his chair into better position, and then began his report, rearranging the photocopied documents in front of him in order to respond to Luke's request.

"The organization whose name is rendered **XAOC** in Russian," began Adelman, "and which we are translating loosely as 'Chaos,' speaks of itself rather candidly in our documents as 'a brokerage organization for the facilitation of terrorism.'

"For example," he continued, "they seek to put would-be bomb throwers in touch with bomb makers; they seek to put would-be assassins in touch with weapons dealers and experts in the art of clandestine murder; they seek to place bank robbers in touch with experts in safe cracking. Chaos is a multi-faceted, full-service criminal enterprise whose origins appear to have been Middle Eastern, but the organization has developed rapidly into something global in scope.

"The component of Chaos we now face is the United Kingdom branch, and it has developed a mission summarized concisely in the memorandum sent to Luke at noon on Monday.

"You recall its concluding paragraph, everyone?"

Adelman took a moment to shuffle through some of the photocopied material spread on the table in front of him. He soon found the page he sought — a copy of the missive sent to Luke — and read aloud the chilling words of its final paragraph:

> You cannot stop us. We will destroy every recognizable aspect of ordinary life, first in the U.K., and then around the world. The people of the democracies will eventually be ruined spiritually, politically, financially, and, in selected cases, physically. To that end, we will destroy Rebekka Yahalomin early in the process.

Adelman looked up.

"That's the worst of it, Luke," he said, "but there is more. It seems that Chaos collects information and sells it to anyone who will pay. It's hard to determine the size of the organization, because it uses so many part-time people on contract for particular jobs. Those individuals probably know little about the organization's larger purposes, and that means, for example, that the people who are conducting the assaults on ministers may know nothing at all about Chaos, as an organization.

"They just know they are paid to beat up someone … at a certain time … in a certain place … using certain methods. Nothing else.

"The thugs who firebombed Rebecca and Matt's home probably have no idea who lived there, or why they were paid to do that."

Belton lifted his cane and tapped Adelman on the knee.

Adelman turned to face his detective partner.

"Sid," he said, "Eleanor has told you a hundred times to stop whacking people with that cane. As she has noted repeatedly, both to you and to me, it makes you look like an incorrigible lunkhead."

Belton cackled his unique laugh, then tapped Adelman again.

"It's th' only way t' get some people t' stop talkin' long enough t' get in a word or two b'fore th' rest of us forget what we'd wanted to say."

"So," said Adelman, feigning irritation, "you're telling us you want to interrupt my riveting lecture in order to get your two cents in? Is that it?"

"Yeah."

"So? Let's hear your two cents."

"Oh," said Belton, "I got a lot more than two cents."

"Oh, for Pete's sake!" cried Jack McGriff from his end of the table. "Sidney," he said, rolling his eyes, "without your wife in the room we have no one to keep you in line, so I think I'm just going to shoot you."

Belton's laugh once more cackled through the room.

"Father Jack," he replied, "it's Jaakov's fault. If he'd …"

Loud moans from around the room led Belton to shake his head ruefully.

"How'd I ever get mixed up with this bunch, Jaakov?"

"I don't remember, but if you don't say what you want pretty soon, I think we'll all just leave you sitting here."

"Okay … okay …" said Belton.

He cleared his throat noisily, then began.

"Here's th' thing," he said.

"Yer 'overview' is fine, Mr. Big Shot Former Mossad Agent, but we got enough a' that already. Just stop. Makes my brain hurt.

"We oughta be doin' two things right now, an' just two. First, we gotta stop tonight's beatings b'fore they happen. Second, we gotta get yer MI6 buddy t' identify th' dirtbag Mrs. Clark dreamed Monday morning.

"His photo's gotta be in their data bank.

"They can get us straight t' th' main guy — th' one Mrs. Clark dreamed — I'm willin' t' bet. C'mon people ... we got a guy's description straight from th' Source ... straight from Mrs. Clark's dream ... an' we shouldn't be foolin' around with anything except that. We don't have time fer any of this other stuff.

"Know what I mean?

"Hmm?"

Thoughtful silence descended on the room.

At length, Luke spoke.

"Let's decide about tonight, everyone, then discuss Mr. Belton's suggestion about the MI6 data bank."

Kory led off.

"If we make arrangements — arrangements of any sort — to stop tonight's scheduled assaults ... and perhaps Sunday night's, as well ... and those lists are right here in my materials ... do we need to be concerned that action of that sort will let Chaos know we entered their space and photocopied their files?

"Or is that not an issue?"

Marie Campbell responded.

"These Chaos people obviously know about Rebecca's gift, Kory. Would they not assume that she was simply given these schedules in one of her special dreams?"

Rebecca shook her head.

"That would be atypical, Marie," she said. "I don't think I've ever had something like that given me ... a specific list of people, with their locations ... it's hard for me to imagine that *kind* of thing coming to me.

"Wouldn't it be more likely," Rebecca continued, "that they would think that either Scotland Yard had contacted *all* ministers who attended the April conference, and urged them to cancel tonight's worship services, or, alternatively, that they — the Chaos people — had a leak within their own organization?"

Thoughtful silence.

"That's excellent, Mrs. Clark," responded Adelman.

"Sidney has several Scotland Yard contacts — three men, I think, is it not, Sid? — with whom he has worked repeatedly in the past, and who are among those who understand that Rebekka Yahalomin has a Source for 'special communications,' and who would be delighted to be given the lists Kory has in front of her."

"Yeah," agreed Belton, "an' we'll figure out — those boys and I — whether to notify just those six, or … probably better … t' notify about 15 a' those pastors from th' April conference … an' tell 'em either t' cancel tonight's services … and maybe Sunday's, too … or just t' ask a couple a' local police t' go with 'em from th' time they leave home in th' afternoon 'til they get home after th' service."

"Yes," said Adelman, "and that has the advantage of addressing Kory's question of whether or not we want to reveal our infiltration of Chaos headquarters. This will simply look like Scotland Yard doing its due diligence."

"Right," agreed Rebecca. "It's possible, after all, that Scotland Yard is already planning to do something like this, although, without Kory's lists, they'd be faced with covering several hundred attendees from that Oxford conference.

"This will be so much more manageable."

"All agreed, then?" asked Luke.

Heads nodding.

"Mr. Belton," continued Luke, "will you get in touch with your Scotland Yard friends as soon as we finish our session here?"

"Well," said Belton, "it's not even 6 a.m. right now … let's get a little cat nap an' then we can phone those boys a little after eight … right?"

Luke nodded. "Of course. I wasn't thinking of the time."

"Oh …" added Belton, "an' I'll need yer wife's lists … an' a phone."

"You can come to my office downstairs at eight, Mr. Belton," said Kory, "and we'll go through my six-person lists — for tonight and Sunday night — with your Scotland Yard friends, and perhaps select an additional 10, or so, from the comprehensive Oxford conference list to provide cover for our knowing the exact targets."

Belton nodded, satisfied.

Luke resumed.

"That," he said, "brings us to your second priority, Mr. Belton … the individual whose description my sister was given in her early Monday dream. It seems to me that the MI6 subgroup which met with us right here — just yesterday — is the unit which would pursue the identification of the dreamed menace.

"If all agree," he continued, "I will phone Roberts-Holm in a few minutes … I have his home number, and he will not object to being phoned early … and give him the precise description … or, better still … I'll get him on the phone from my office and ask Rebecca herself to provide the description to Graham. After all, the image was given to her, not to me or to anyone else.

"Agreed, Rebecca?"

She nodded.

"Yes," she said, "it would be wonderful if MI6 could actually identify this person, just from hearing my dreamed description. And you really don't think Graham will object to an early call at his home?"

"He'll be excited, Rebecca … thrilled, in fact."

With that, the session drew to a close.

Gratefully, the tired group dispersed, the four Americans to find their beds upstairs on the fifth floor, Matt Clark and Kory Manguson to close their eyes on the sofas in their separate ISP offices downstairs, and Rebecca and Luke to contact Graham Roberts-Holm before he would leave home for his office at MI6.

Minutes later, Marie Campbell and Jack McGriff stood in the fifth-floor hallway, just outside the door to her sleeping room, and chatted, facing each other and holding hands. They were by now, more than two years since their first encounter, deeply in love, and found themselves growing impatient for the quiet wedding they envisioned, an informal ceremony in their downtown Washington church.

If their lives could just settle down for a few days, and if they could find the right pet-friendly, downtown apartment, or affordable downtown house, the wedding would need very little planning time. This was a happy season for them both, despite the ongoing Rebekka Yahalomin crises that had swept them up so unexpectedly.

McGriff looked down at her and squeezed her hands.

"You sleepy?" he asked.

"I think I *am* asleep," she replied, smiling up at him.

She stepped forward and laid her cheek against his chest.

"Let's just sleep like this," she said.

He wrapped his arms around her and pressed his lips into her hair.

"You know," he said mischievously, "we could *sleep* together in your room, or in mine, right now — you know, Marie, literally, *sleep* together, without that word being a euphemism for sex — just *sleep* together. And we'd still be … you know … 'marriage fresh' when the time comes."

She leaned her head back and looked up at him.

"*Marriage fresh,* Jack McGriff?"

"I know," he said. "I made that up. Just now. Spur of the moment.

"Brilliant concept, right?"

She laughed, shaking her head.

He smiled. He loved her laugh.

"Yes," she agreed, "brilliant turn of phrase.

"*Ridiculous* idea … but … yes … brilliant turn of phrase."

She stood on tiptoe, kissed him firmly, and stepped gracefully into her room. Then she turned back toward him and slowly closed the door, her wide brown eyes loving him as she did.

"Patience, Jack McGriff," she whispered sweetly as the door closed.

McGriff sighed, turned, and walked down the hallway to his room.

As he did, he clapped his hands once, laughing softly. What had he done, he wondered, to deserve such a woman.

He had no idea.

Perhaps nothing at all.

It had to be a God thing.

Wednesday, early afternoon

The eight members of Rebekka Yahalomin, having napped briefly and taken time to change clothes, reassembled shortly before 1 p.m. in the small

ISP conference room. Sandwiches had again been prepared by the ISP kitchen staff. McGriff offered a blessing, and they silently began eating, still weary and sleep-deprived after their long night at the Chaos HQ building and the tedious hours laboring over the photocopied documents. Fifteen minutes after they'd begun their lunch, most were finished.

Luke pushed his plate away and began.

"Those still eating," he said, "please continue … but let's start the session."

He turned expectantly toward Sid Belton. "Sid?" he said simply.

Belton chewed, swallowed, and nodded his head.

"Right, Luke," he said. "We had good luck in our conversations with my … um … friends … over at Scotland Yard … an' we asked 'em t' call back t' Kory's office when they'd finished th' work they agreed t' do. She said they called 'er just before noon … just as she was gettin' ready t' leave her office."

Belton looked across the table to Kory and nodded to her.

"Yes," she said. "Mr. Belton's friends called me back, as promised, and reported that they had contacted 34 ministers from the April conference list, including the six we identified as tonight's targets, and the additional six targeted for Sunday. All 34 agreed either to cancel their worship services tonight, or, in two cases — neither of them among the 12 identified targets — to ask their local police to accompany them from home to church, to attend their worship services, and then to accompany them back home again, after their services are completed.

"So," continued Kory, "I think we're set up well for tonight and Sunday, everyone, thanks to Mr. Belton and his Scotland Yard colleagues. Is everyone clear? Tonight's six and Sunday's six have cancelled their worship services, and 22 more from the Oxford lists have taken one action or the other, disguising … for Chaos' benefit … the fact that we know precisely which ones are targeted for tonight and Sunday.

"And," she continued after a moment, "I telephoned one of our church friends — friends of Luke's and mine — at the BBC, here in London, while Mr. Belton was speaking with Scotland Yard, and asked him to announce, both on radio and on television news shows, both at noon and in the evening, that 'at least a dozen' ministers around the country have cancelled their evening services in response to the violence visited on their colleagues last Wednesday and again last Sunday.

"Mr. Belton and I think that those broadcast announcements will complete the misdirection ... Chaos will surely conclude that they have simply frightened a number of ministers into taking these actions."

She stopped and smiled first at Sid Belton, and then at her husband.

Luke smiled back proudly at his wife and said, "Thank you Kory ... and Mr. Belton ... *well done.*"

Vigorous applause ensued, all around the table.

Luke paused and scowled, barely perceptibly, then continued.

"I wish my sister and I," he said, "could report similar success with our efforts to uncover the identity of Rebecca's dreamed individual. But Roberts-Holm and his colleagues were not able to link her word-portrait to anyone in the MI6 database. Graham and his two sub-committee members did willingly make the effort for us but came up dry after several hours of work."

After a moment, McGriff asked, "Did you expect them to succeed, Luke?"

"Yes," he said simply. "I felt that, if this person is important enough in the Chaos organization to be presented to my sister in one of her 'messages,' he would, I thought, be important enough to have found his way into the MI6 database ... and, of course, he may be there somewhere ... as a *named* person of interest ... and yet, just as a *name* ... as a name *only* ... without a file photo or an accompanying description.

"That's certainly possible, but I had hoped ..."

His voice trailed off, but, determined not to let the session be derailed by this disappointment, Luke looked down to his notes, squared his muscular shoulders, and continued with the reports. There followed for several hours a meticulous review of the remaining documents examined during the long night.

One member after another summarized the contents of the material he or she had studied, until at length all had reported in as much detail as possible, and had commented on, or speculated about, the implications of each document.

The primary finding of the afternoon was the most disturbing. Jaakov Adelman reported coming across a dozen clandestine agreements between Chaos and bomb makers scattered about the country. These were bomb makers who specialized in the construction of plastic-based explosives, devices undetectable by the sort of metal-detection equipment common at entry gates to arenas of all types.

In addition, both Adelman and Marie Campbell reported on several related documents that systematically tied the bomb makers, first, to the planned placement of explosives at the All England Club during the Championships, and second, to the planned distribution of yet more explosives in and about the Palace of Westminster, historic site of U.K. Parliament sessions. This revelation — plans for undetectable bombs to be produced, and then planted, first at London's hallowed celebration of sport, and second within the beating heart of the U.K. government — was stunning.

Until this discovery, the group had hoped, somewhat vaguely, that the chaos and terror described in the memo sent earlier to Luke — hand-delivered from the Chaos organization — implied widespread turmoil, but of a sort that would primarily sow confusion, uncertainty, and fear throughout the population. That would have been consistent, after all, with the fact that the assaults thus far on selected ministers had been brutal, but not deadly. It had been clear all along that each of the assaulted ministers could have been killed by their assailants.

They were not.

Bombs, in contrast, were both lethal in their effects and largely indiscriminate in their target selection. In the crush of humanity that would swarm through Wimbledon for the next two weeks, a single well-placed, undetectable explosive could kill or maim hundreds. A *series* of them, day after day, would certainly multiply the effects, and could, within hours, lead to the mass exodus of athletes.

In such a case, the tournament would be forced into cancellation.

Chaos documents further indicated that at least four Wimbledon employees were already on the Chaos payroll. Dozens more would be paid on specific contracts, simply to infiltrate the Championships as spectators, place the explosives, and depart.

As the long Wednesday wore on, and as the magnitude of the threat became evident, a palpable sense of discouragement settled on the ISP conference room. Discussion lagged. Energy seeped from the room.

Rebecca felt the room slowly dying ... emptying itself of hope.

At length ... feeling an internal prompting to reverse the despair overtaking Rebekka Yahalomin — this group that, despite her fervent wishes to the contrary, bore her name — Rebecca sighed deeply, signaled her brother, and rose.

All eyes went to her.

She had changed into a sleeveless white blouse and one of her trademark mid-calf dark skirts. This quiet, soft attire seemed slightly incongruous in view of the obvious athleticism of its wearer, whose exposed biceps were neither quiet nor soft. Rebecca's upper arms were defined, taut, sinewy … and feminine.

Regal in bearing, she smiled lovingly at these, her people.

"Everyone," she said evenly, "we *will* stop this.

"As Mr. Belton, our champion, has often reminded us …" and here she looked down at Belton … "we have available to us resources that our adversary cannot possibly access … and not just the resources of Mr. Belton's selected contacts in law enforcement and in the intelligence services, but, as well, the great Source that led us to the Chaos headquarters, and that has transmitted to me the image of one who is surely one of that terrible organization's major players.

"Do not despair. Have courage. We are not alone."

She smiled again, the facial scar compressing as she did.

"Let's have our evening meal, get some rest, then pray and think. I suggest that in the morning we ask Luke …" and here she looked to her brother, "to assemble his ISP group alongside us, so that we may focus together on next steps. We can inform them that we have learned that explosives are to be planted at Wimbledon during the tournament. We do not need to tell them how we know that. We will simply tell them that we need their help in thinking how to intervene.

"I think we have nothing to fear regarding the ministers who have been targeted for tonight and Sunday. All those listed as targets have canceled their worship services, and I don't want us to rush into our next steps.

"Come to the conference table in the morning prepared to be smart … to be brave … to save those who would be hurt … to defeat those who would destroy.

"We are not alone."

Thursday, 6:30 a.m.

Reginald Jones backed his dark green, right-hand-drive, 1985 Land Rover Defender 90 out of his driveway, daughter SallyBelle in the passenger seat, and headed for Thomas Chambers' house nearby. Traffic would be thick, but the early departure stood to get the teens to the qualifiers' venue well before the 7:30 a.m. start time.

Jones was inordinately proud of his new vehicle, a much-shortened version of Luke Manguson's Five-Door. ISP had purchased a half-dozen of them to use for company business, three of them with the new Nippon Telegraph and Telephone-designed car phones, factory installed at the Land Rover plant as part of the Japanese company's effort to introduce their car phones worldwide.

Jones had driven one of the ISP Defenders enough to know that he "had to" buy one for himself. And so, he had. He had talked himself into not being disappointed that his version did not have the NTT car phone installed. The added cost for the phone would have put the vehicle financially out of reach.

His Defender 90 had bucket seats in front, designed for driver and passenger, and, in the bare-bones configuration deemed affordable by Jones, no other seats at all. The truncated rear area was designed to carry luggage, groceries, the family dog, or, in this case, one teen-age boy. Thomas Chambers would simply fold his angular frame into one side of the luggage compartment, his back against a wheel well.

They arrived at the Chambers' home in minutes. Thomas was waiting out front, and quickly opened the rear door, which opened horizontally, and nestled himself comfortably against the right-side wheel well. Seated thus behind Jones in the right-hand-drive Defender, Thomas could face SallyBelle, who, by turning her head to her right, could look directly at her friend.

Thomas was a friend who was hopeful that this might develop into a boyfriend-girlfriend relationship. Although SallyBelle was aware of her friend's hopes, she was not sure that she wanted the friendship to move in that direction.

But she very much liked being in his company.

This Thursday morning, now only 96 hours before the start of the tournament, was the first day they were dressed in the uniforms they had been issued for the Championships. They both wore the dark blue outfits traditionally worn by BBGs, and, to her mild disappointment, SallyBelle had been informed the day before that she would not be allowed to use her array of colorful ribbons to secure her blonde ponytail. Dark rubber bands, and only dark rubber bands, would keep her hair away from her bright blue eyes during these days of sprinting, stooping, catching, and throwing.

The teens began immediately their usual chatter about what lay before them. Reginald Jones found himself immediately pleased to be left alone with his own thoughts. Luke Manguson had called an 8:15 a.m. meeting at ISP headquarters, and, while Jones did not know details, Luke had said that the session would include members of the Rebekka Yahalomin group.

Jones knew that this could only mean that new data had become available, and that the data would have implications for the direction of their security plans. Ninety-six hours to go, and he felt thoroughly unsettled. His mind raced anxiously through the countless permutations … the nearly infinite number of *types* of threats to the safety and security of the athletes, their support staffs, the spectators…

Thus, distracted from the crush of rush-hour traffic, he was, as he came to a stop behind a line of cars awaiting a traffic signal's change to green, at first startled and then confused by the sudden presence, perhaps two feet from his driver's side door, of a large, white commercial van. The van's side door began to slide open even as the van was still rolling to its stop.

Alarm bells sounded in Jones's brain as he saw the muzzle of a dull-black automatic rifle coming up toward his face from inside the van. Simultaneously, he became aware that the Defender was completely boxed and could move in no direction… not ahead, not to the rear, not to either side. Wide-eyed, Jones saw large, masked men already in rapid motion, one pulling his unlocked door open, two others crossing the front of the vehicle toward the left side where SallyBelle sat.

As Jones was yanked roughly from the vehicle, he heard, rather than saw, the other two doors of the Defender being opened. Then the blow.

Blackness.

SallyBelle, her face turned to the right to talk to Thomas, saw the van before her dad became aware of it. She saw how the driver aggressively maneuvered the vehicle so that it moved up beside the Defender within touching distance. Her left hand went quickly to the inside door latch as the van's side door slid open, some kind of rifle coming up toward her dad's face.

Unlike her dad, SallyBelle always pressed the door-lock button as soon as she entered any vehicle, even before she pulled on her seat belt... something her dad often neglected to do, as well. While her father, unbelted and having not locked his door, was being forcibly taken from the Defender, she was delayed for two precious seconds while she unbuckled herself and popped the door lock.

Nonetheless, SallyBelle was on her feet and sprinting before her two captors could circle the Defender's short hood and get to her. As the pursuit began, the men were no more than three running strides behind the dark-clad BBG.

SallyBelle Jones was lightning fast and could change directions in a flash. She was faster *and* quicker than the men. She reached the sidewalk cleanly and turned, rising into a full sprint, toward the traffic signal that had halted the long line of cars. She reached the corner, wheeled to her left, and, dodging through pedestrian traffic, disappeared from her pursuers' sight.

In seconds, she had reached the next corner, turned again to her left, and, still running hard, weaved her way through automobile traffic to reach the opposite side of the street, one which appeared to have offices of the sort that would give her access to a telephone. But even as she raced past several closed doors — law offices, physicians' offices, real estate firms — she realized that it was not yet 7 a.m. on a Thursday. Nothing would be open.

She slipped around yet another corner, turned to her right, and stopped. The store on that corner, a jewelry store, featured fully glassed-in windows that faced each of the intersecting streets. This allowed her to stand around the corner from her pursuers and yet look through two glassed-in walls, all the way down the street to the corner she had rounded earlier. She saw no one in pursuit.

She was safe, she thought, for the moment, and so tried to focus on next steps. There were no telephone booths in sight, no stores open, no residences available. She needed the police.

Settling into a rapid but sustainable jogging pace, she continued in a direction away from the assault, looking for a traffic-control police officer, but stopping every 50 yards to ask a pedestrian at random if he or she knew where a police or fire station might be located. She continued in this fashion for more than six blocks with no success, now no longer desperate for her own safety, but increasingly desperate on behalf of her father. She stopped again, suddenly overwhelmed.

The magnitude of the disaster fell heavily on her. Tears sprang to her eyes. A sob rose in her throat.

Her father.

Thomas Chambers was sitting behind Reginald Jones, leaning against the right-side wheel well of the Defender, talking happily with SallyBelle, fighting to keep his feelings for her in check, struggling to remain reasonably articulate despite the unwelcome racing of his pulse. Would this ever get better, he wondered? Would he always find his heart pounding when he found himself in proximity to her?

Thus, distracted by the girl, he was as slow as Reginald Jones to see the van. He only saw and heard Jones's door open violently, and saw SallyBelle, in a blur of action, unbuckle herself and spring from the left-side door. He needed no other signals.

He popped the rear-facing door of the Defender and was on his feet and running in less than three seconds from his realization of what was happening. He sprinted between the unmoving lines of automobiles, in the direction opposite that of the traffic. He quickly reached the intersection they had passed two minutes before, and there he stopped, turned, and looked back toward the Defender.

He saw, first, that no one was in pursuit of him. He saw, second, that the white van had moved forward to the traffic signal at which they had stopped and was in the process of turning left. Was SallyBelle's father in the van? Had he been abducted? And where was SallyBelle? Had she, too, been captured?

He stepped to the curb and thought about what he had seen in the seconds before he leaped from the Defender. He had seen Mr. Jones's door being opened by someone and Jones's shoulders being seized by … by whom? And he had seen SallyBelle springing from her side of the vehicle and beginning to run … but with pursuers close behind.

And in which direction had she run? … in the same direction in which they had been travelling, he thought. If so, and if she had not been captured, she had surely turned the nearest corner and sprinted down the same street into which the van had just turned. He guessed, after a few moments of thought, that Mr. Jones had been abducted and that SallyBelle had not.

She was too fast. If they had not grabbed her immediately, before she had launched her sprint, she would have outrun them, whoever they might be.

He needed a phone. He needed the police.

He thought about the time — not yet 7 a.m. — and the unlikelihood of finding a business that would be open at that hour. He looked up and down the streets that intersected where he stood, searching for one of London's ubiquitous red phone booths. He saw none, and realized he had no coins with him in any case.

His best hope, he thought, was to find a traffic-control officer. Or perhaps a pair of bobbies on foot patrol.

He began to run, hard, in the direction away from the kidnapping, looking for police ... perhaps at an intersection ... or on foot patrol ... or in a police vehicle. He ran for what seemed a very long time.

SallyBelle, wiping tears from her cheeks with the palms of her hands, saw a professionally dressed woman approaching, and managed to ask the woman if she knew of a nearby police or fire station.

The woman looked at her closely.

"Are you a Wimbledon BBG?" she asked.

"Yes, ma'am," replied the girl.

"Why do you need police or fire?"

"My dad was pulled from our car five minutes ago by people who, I think, kidnapped him. I've been running, looking for help. I can't find any."

Her statement pulled fresh tears from her eyes ... then, as the utter helplessness of the situation again overcame her ... a fresh round of gasping sobs, her hands covering her face.

The woman moved beside her and placed an arm around the teen's heaving shoulders. Gently, she began to steer SallyBelle toward an office door no more than 15 feet from where they stood.

"Here, dear," she said softly, "is my office. Let's go in and phone for help."

The woman released SallyBelle long enough to rummage in her purse for keys to her office door. SallyBelle, still crying miserably, her hands still covering her face, waited near the curb.

Suddenly she felt a rough, gloved hand covering her mouth and a muscular arm jerking her from her feet, spinning her back into the street and toward the white van. She felt her assailant, holding her to his chest and continuing to cover her mouth with his free hand, driving her roughly through the van's open side door, forcing her to the van's floor with his full weight on top of her.

SallyBelle heard the door slide shut with a bang.

In the split second before the door closed, she heard the woman shouting after her. The words were lost in confusion and terror as her delicate face was thrust viciously onto the van's hard, gritty rubber floor.

The assailant's 200-plus pounds crushed the breath from her lungs. Turning her face to one side, she gasped for air.

"I ... can't ... breathe," she said, her voice straining.

She felt her assailant sit up, pull her wrists roughly behind her back, and secure her wrists to each other with a plastic tie. She sensed him pulling a cloth sack over her head, leaving it loose at the neck. She felt him move away.

Still struggling to breathe, she pressed her forehead into the flooring, moving her mouth and nose as close as possible to the sack's opening at her neck. Satisfied immediately that she would not suffocate, her thoughts turned swiftly to Rebecca Clark's repeated reminders on the tennis court ... and beyond.

Relax. Breathe. Focus. Think. Pray.

CHAPTER SIX

Thursday, 7 a.m.

ANTON FEDOROV PAUSED AS HE WAITED FOR THE CAPTIVES — father and daughter — to be brought to him at his new headquarters. While he waited, he reflected idly on the history of the decaying, two-story house near Cambridge that he had chosen for Chaos Command Central, which he already referenced in his mind as the "CCC." The secure room in a London parking garage had proven adequate, to this point, for the limited scope of the opening sorties, but Fedorov was ready now to expand the operation far beyond those preliminary attacks.

Next … he sought unbridled devastation.

Thus, he would need more. More space. More personnel.

More explosives.

A true Chaos Command Central. A property with ample acreage, sited near, but not too near, a thriving English town. Isolated and difficult to find.

He would, from his CCC, begin the process of bringing the U.K. people to their knees. He would lead them inexorably toward despair. He would drive them ultimately to give up hope, truth, belief.

Why? he asked himself rhetorically … because *that is my nature*, he answered.

He smiled, a smile that was indistinguishable from grimace.

He turned again to examine his newly purchased estate.

The decrepit, vegetation-overgrown structure, located fewer than 10 miles to the west of Cambridge, had once served as a single-family home. More recently, however, the house had been used by a figure with whom Fedorov felt deep kinship, even though that figure had been English, a people toward whom Fedorov and his Russian compatriots felt nothing but contempt. The English were a soft people, muddled in their thinking and confused in their beliefs. They had been easily led by the now-deceased Englishman who had used this house as headquarters.

That Englishman's name had been Meredith Lancaster, a wealthy land-owner who had been prominent in the life of mid-1970s Britain. Lancaster, a Cambridge University theologian and historian whose wealth had, in the main, been inherited, had served for decades as a Member of Parliament. In the 1970s he had become widely known for his scholarly achievements, specifically in the field of historical research into the Church of England's long and complicated past.

Lancaster's telegenic presence had, at one time or another, brought his face into virtually every home in Britain prior to his sudden and unexpected death. His final project had involved the promulgation of something he called the "Creed of St. David," a document ultimately proven to be fraudulent.

Via Lancaster's elaborate scheme — a scheme much admired, then and now, by Anton Fedorov — the document had sought to disseminate a theology devoid of many of traditional Christianity's central tenets, including those embracing heaven … resurrection … eternal life … and more. He called such ideas "imaginative metaphorical constructs," never to be confused with actuality.

Consistent with this approach, he contended that Jesus Christ was merely an outstanding teacher and preacher. Nothing more.

He hoped.

He had been clever enough to retain within his Creed of St. David enough of the more familiar, though subordinate, Christian concepts, as to allow him to claim that the "heart of the faith" had been left intact by the "newly discovered" creed. The new formulation simply introduced a small number of inconsequential changes "around the edges" of the faith, as he put it.

In the present, Fedorov intended to use the nationwide disruption his plans would generate as leverage to eat away the heart and soul of Christianity from the inside, as he thought of it. Rather than introduce disruptive theological ideas, he sought to sap the life out of the faith by disrupting and corrupting the social order on which the church relied for its health and wellbeing.

He sought cultural hopelessness ... a national depression.

Widespread despair. A war zone through which he would march with his hellish message of hopelessness. Ultimately, to dissolve anything that would be recognizable as a culture-wide sense of purpose ... he sought a national loss of direction ... a national loss of the will to persevere.

He wanted the disintegration of U.K. society to serve eventually as a model that would prove replicable in all the great democracies. And this was where his goals diverged from those of his current KGB superior, Artur Volkov, and his powerful assistant, Tatyana Kuznetsova.

They were Soviet nationalists.

Fedorov was a Soviet nihilist.

They — Volkov and Kuznetsova — wanted a disintegrating U.K. society in order that Soviet communism would find fertile ground. Fedorov wanted a disintegrating U.K. society because that was what his sort of Evil always sought. And that was, as always, a condition capable of bringing despair to the individuals who comprised that society. He would employ Volkov and Kuznetsova's talents and connections and influence wherever they might prove useful. They would be among his numerous tools.

A favorite literary warning flitted through his mind.

Abandon hope all ye who enter here.

Dante's warning at Hell's entry gates.

His mind returned to Meredith Lancaster's demise. He knew, as had much of the U.K. at that time, that Lancaster had been the victim of a bolt of lightning — an actual lightning strike — during a mysterious summer storm on the Welsh coast.

At the moment of his execution by the lightning strike, he and his two gunmen had had the as yet unmarried Rebecca Manguson literally in their sights. It was she and the man who would eventually become her husband, Matt Clark, who were that day mere seconds from execution. The strike from heavenward had changed everything in an instant of time.

Fedorov, then in his 20s, had admired Lancaster's accomplishments and his multifaceted approach to achieving societal destruction. And he had grown to understand that Lancaster had been imbued with powers that ordinary human beings did not possess. Fedorov understood, without ever having been in Lancaster's presence, that the man had drawn Evil into himself to such an extent that he could know things and do things that others could not.

He could, it was known, physically disable — and perhaps kill — others, simply by proximity to them. Fedorov knew this, even at the time of Lancaster's death. How he knew this, he could not say. He did not know how he knew.

But he did know. And he knew that he, Anton Fedorov, had gradually come to possess the same kinds of knowledge and the same kinds of power for destruction as had Meredith Lancaster.

He had tested this power just days earlier in the London parking garage headquarters when Volkov had challenged him in front of an array of KGB agents who looked to Fedorov for leadership. Fedorov recalled with satisfaction that he had had only to move his face to within inches of Volkov's, this man who was such a powerful force for *ordinary* evil in his own right, to see the man grow so physically weak as to collapse helplessly onto his chair.

Now, Fedorov looked around the upper-floor room of the ramshackle house in which he stood. He knew — again, he did not know how he knew — that this room had been Meredith Lancaster's inner sanctum, the room in which he planned the masterful and complex St. David's Creed project.

And this was the room, as well, in which Lancaster had planned either to co-opt Rebecca Manguson to his project or, failing that, to kill her. And he had indeed *nearly* won her, prior to realizing that he could never fully accomplish that feat. But he had *nearly* won her … for Fedorov knew that she had been tempted … tempted by Lancaster's invitation to become the face of the project … thereby to achieve worldwide fame … worldwide adulation … worldwide adoration.

But the meddlesome woman had fought the temptation off … an actual physical *fight* against Evil, at length won only by the expenditure of every ounce of strength and will that Rebecca Manguson could summon … and by her desperate plea, in extremis, to God Himself for help.

Failing in the end, Fedorov knew, Meredith Lancaster had then pursued the woman and her suitor, Matt Clark, to St. David's Cathedral along the coast of Wales, thence to the Pembrokeshire Coast Path. And during a wild, confused, storm-filled night, he had pursued her all the way to land's end.

But the end had become his own.

Fedorov thought about all of that and smiled again. Lancaster had been foolish to try to turn Rebecca Manguson … now Rebecca Clark. No, she could only be eliminated, not converted. But even with that prior knowledge, Fedorov reluctantly admitted to himself, he had miscalculated once already. His carefully orchestrated firebombing of the Clarks' home had failed to kill her.

But this … this new plan … could hardly fail.

He moved to the window that overlooked the hilltop venue. By midmorning, the van carrying SallyBelle Jones and her father would arrive. The girl was not, of course, Rebecca Clark's own daughter — her own four-year-old children having been sequestered so presciently at the Birmingham Lodge — but Rebecca Clark certainly loved the teen-aged SallyBelle *like* a daughter.

SallyBelle Jones would do perfectly well for his purposes.

For Anton Fedorov knew about Rebecca Clark's oft-repeated "blueprint of the universe: *my life for yours.*" He'd see whether this Clark woman would commit herself to enact this supposed blueprint of the universe. He'd see whether Rebecca Clark would give her life for SallyBelle Jones. He'd find out the truth about Rebecca Clark.

And so would she. She'd find out the truth about herself.

He smiled again in anticipation.

Thursday, 7:04 a.m.

Horace and Jane Chambers were just saying their every-morning good-byes to each other as they headed for their cars. He wanted some time at his ISP office to prepare for the 8:15 a.m. meeting called by Luke Manguson; she liked to get to the school where she served as assistant head by 7:30 a.m., even during summer hours.

"I'll phone you at school midafternoon, sweetheart, if I'm free, so I can hear about the session with the new parents," Horace was saying to his wife, "and I'll plan to get home long before Reginald drops Thomas off after the BBG sessions."

"Yes, please … I'm not going to be finished until nearly six tonight."

As they stepped onto the front porch, they heard the hallway telephone ring. They both paused, thinking.

"Better pick up," said Jane. "Could be Luke, changing the meeting time."

"Good thought," he said, pushing the door open again.

He picked up.

"Horace Chambers speaking."

"Dad! Dad! Mr. Jones and SallyBelle have been kidnapped."

In seconds, both parents were in Horace Chambers' Audi 100 saloon, headed for the all-night petrol station from which their son had just phoned in desperation. The couple had engaged in a 10-second argument as to which of them should abandon the morning's schedule in order to retrieve Thomas, an argument that ended with both realizing that neither was willing *not* to go to their son immediately.

They had then piled into the Audi and headed for their son's reported location; explanations could be offered to colleagues and clients later, once Thomas had been retrieved and once the Metropolitan Police had been informed of the abduction.

After fewer than 20 minutes of tortured, stop-and-go maneuvering through early-morning London traffic, they saw their dark-blue-clad BBG son waving to them from the corner on which the petrol station was sited. He ran to the Audi, which was stopped once more in the mass of traffic, and jumped into the back seat.

The teen began talking as soon as he closed the door.

"We were stopped for a signal and this white van pulled up and guys in ski masks pulled Mr. Jones out of the car and SallyBelle jumped out of her side of the car and she ran and I don't think they caught her and I jumped out the rear door and ran and when I looked back the van was turning and SallyBelle had disappeared and Mr. Jones was, I think, inside the van and I started running to try to find police and I finally found the petrol station and they let me call you and ..."

Thomas was stopped at that moment as his mother turned and leaned all the way over the front seat and, reaching for her son, pulled him into a tight embrace. He caught his breath and, his face now buried in his mother's shoulder, immediately began to sob. The muffled, angst-laden words spilled out.

"I didn't try to save her, Mum ... I just ran ...

"I just ran as hard as I could."

Horace Chambers flashed his ID at the ISP gate. The guard waved him through, and he pulled the Audi into the parking lot at the rear of the building. He, Jane, and Thomas quickly trotted to the employee entrance at the rear of the building and then raced up the stairs to Luke Manguson's office.

There they found Luke, Kory, Rebecca, and Matt just sitting down after having put on the teakettle. The four of them looked up as the Chamberses, breathless, rushed into the room.

The two men stood immediately.

"Sorry to interrupt, everyone," said Horace, gasping for breath, "but we've got an emergency. Thomas can tell you best … son? Go ahead."

The 15-year-old then recounted his story, this time more coherently and with much more detail, standing in the center of Luke's office with both parents' arms around him. As soon as he finished, Luke said, "You've had no time to phone the Metropolitan Police, Horace? Let me do that before we do anything else."

Luke made the call, giving his police contact the street names of the intersection where the apparent abduction of Reginald Jones took place. He then listened intently for several moments, saying simply, "Oh, really? Yes … yes, I see. Thank you, James. Let's stay in close touch on this."

Luke clicked off, then looked at his small audience.

"The police received an urgent call, apparently just minutes after your encounter, Thomas, from a woman who reported that a 'blonde, blue-eyed, pony-tailed, in-uniform BBG' was kidnapped from just in front of her office and thrown bodily into a white van. No other information on the van … just that it was white."

Color drained from Thomas's face and he sagged in his parents' embrace.

Rebecca stood quickly and strode to the boy, a young man whom she had been coaching, along with SallyBelle, for months now. She knew him well.

She placed both of her strong hands on his shoulders and fixed him with her deep, piercing gray eyes, her entire visage commanding attention. He looked back at her, wide-eyed in confusion and fear.

"Thomas," she said sternly, *"we will handle this.*

"We will get her back, and we will get her back quickly.

"We have information, right now, regarding her whereabouts, and we will handle this as our first priority. We will work on nothing else until we have her and her dad.

"Your job, Thomas Chambers, is to get to your BBG session as quickly as your parents can drive you there. And once you get there, I want you to focus fully and completely on the tasks at hand. You have a once in a lifetime opportunity in front of you, Thomas. Focus on that.

"If you fail to do that, SallyBelle will deliver an overhead volley to your nose as soon as she sees you tomorrow morning."

At this he smiled.

She continued.

"We will take care of SallyBelle. *We will.*

"Now, go."

She stepped back, looked into the eyes of, first, Jane Chambers, and second, Horace Chambers, nodded to each, and said, "Take him now. I will phone my friends at the BBG problem line and explain everything to them. Thomas will not be penalized in any way whatsoever for his lateness today. And SallyBelle will not be penalized in any way whatsoever for what will be her one-day absence.

"Now, *go!"*

The three Chamberses turned immediately, bewildered, relieved, and determined in equal measure, and hurried for the door. As they exited, all three called back to Rebecca, "Thank you, Mrs. Clark. Thank you!"

Rebecca turned to her brother, "Outside line, Luke … please."

As she began to punch in numbers for the BBG problem line, Luke said to Kory and Matt, "You two … please go up and place a note on the conference room door that the 8:15 a.m. will be held later today, and then bring the Americans down from the fifth floor. Tell them we need to meet in my office right now."

Rebecca was already speaking into the phone, saying, "Oh, Janice … this is Rebecca Clark … yes, fine, but I have two problems to report.

"First, Thomas Chambers is on his way, and will be there within the half-hour. His lateness is absolutely not his fault. Please make certain that he is in no way penalized for his lateness. Janice, can you make that clear to all? No penalty for him. None.

"Yes? Good.

"Now, SallyBelle Jones is likely to miss the whole day today, but you should expect her tomorrow morning, on time as usual. This is the result of an emergency that I can't talk to you about yet. I simply need you to understand that she is in no way responsible for today's absence. Can you make this absolutely clear to all?"

Rebecca listened, then smiled.

"Yes," she said, "she is brilliant, isn't she?"

Rebecca listened again.

"No ... she'll be fine. You'll see her in the morning."

She clicked off and looked at her brother.

"Well, Lieutenant Manguson ... I'd say we need to get busy."

Thursday, 8:22 a.m.

The Rebekka Yahalomin members took their seats in Luke's office, most with teacups balanced on their knees or resting on nearby flat surfaces. Taking their cues from the demeanor of the four English, the Americans were on edge.

Something was happening ... now.

Luke began by summarizing the kidnapping reports, first of Reginald Jones, as told by Thomas Chambers, then of SallyBelle Jones, as related first by Thomas and then by Luke's contact at Metropolitan Police headquarters. He answered several questions, then turned to his sister.

"Rebecca?"

She bowed her head in silent prayer. The others followed suit.

Finally, she said her soft, "Amen."

She looked up.

"I dreamed," she said simply.

"About two o'clock," she explained, "the dream came. It was unusual in my dream history, in the sense that it was much more akin to normal dreaming than to 'message dreaming.' I was given a view of a house, one that looked immediately familiar to me, even though it was not one I had seen recently.

"Also, unusually for me, nothing seemed to happen during the dream. Just a house. No movement. No second scene moving into the frame. Just a house.

"The house was old ... two floors that were visible. Vegetation encroaching on its porch and sides. Ill-kept. Possibly vacant.

"But ... here is the critical thing ... after some time, I recognized this house. I realized that it was the house in which Matt's parents, Martha and Paul, were sequestered some years back, when they were abducted from Central Park in New York City and flown across the Atlantic to Cambridge, and then held in that house until Detective Belton and his colleagues from New York tracked them down and freed them from a fantastically evil person named Meredith Lancaster.

"Soon afterward, Luke and Matt and I conducted a raid, of sorts, on that same house, and photographed documents in Meredith Lancaster's office, just as we did here in London with the Chaos files this week, thanks, yet again, to Mr. Belton.

"On the occasion of that original raid, which was successful, Luke was shot in the thigh by one of the gunmen protecting the Lancaster house. The bullet passed all the way through the thigh muscle, and his loss of blood was serious. We got him back to the Birmingham Lodge in time for him to get patched up properly."

Rebecca paused, remembering, then continued.

"In a way, last night's dream seemed to be nothing at all, and, though I awakened after some time, I was not quite sure whether to awaken Matt, because the thing seemed too normal. Too routine.

"And, unlike my other message dreams, I did not feel exhausted ... I was not perspiring ... when I awoke. I was simply thoughtful.

"At length, I decided that the thing ... depicting, as it did, the site of something that was central to our enemies' work in the past ... was *possibly* important, so I did awaken Matt, and I told him what I have just told you.

"Not much to it ... just that."

She looked to her husband.

Matt nodded. "Yes," he said. "Just that. Just a house. But the same house with which we have history."

Rebecca turned to her brother.

"And then," she said, "we arrived here at Luke's office …"

"And," said Luke, "no sooner had we sat down here, about half an hour ago, than Horace and Jane Chambers and their son Thomas burst into the room …"

Luke, Rebecca, Matt, and Kory then took turns recounting for the Americans the astonishing story that the young man had told them. They also described Rebecca's charge to the Chamberses to take Thomas to his BBG session and to leave the rest to her and her colleagues.

Rebecca then told of her phone call to the BBG problem center. And Luke explained his conversation with the Metropolitan Police, including the surprising news that the police had received an emergency call from a woman who described SallyBelle's kidnapping, an abduction involving presumably the same white van that Thomas Chambers had seen kidnapping Reginald Jones.

After several moments of thoughtful silence, Jaakov Adelman said, "So … the dreamed structure takes on new significance, yes, Rebecca?"

"Yes," she said. "The dream seemed ordinary last night, but now …"

"Now," said Marie Campbell excitedly, "we see that it *was* a message dream."

More thoughtful silence.

Then Adelman said, "I wasn't yet part of our unit back then. Where is this house exactly? You mentioned Cambridge, but …"

"Jaakov," answered Belton, "we tracked th' dirtbags t' this place about 10 miles due west of th' town … of Cambridge. It's pretty isolated. Th' house sits on a hilltop … prob'ly 4 acres of cleared land … a ridgeline runs up t' th' acreage … a private road lets ya' drive up t' th' house … but th' trees on th' slopes aren't thick … so there's no problem t' sneak up t' th' clearing at night without usin' th' road.

"That's what me an' some of my NYPD buddies did, back then. See, I don't like it when somebody steals some of my good New York City people. I like t' go an' get 'em back. And I did."

There were smiles around the room as everyone pictured the detective and his "NYPD buddies" rescuing Martha and Paul Clark about seven years previous. Then McGriff spoke.

"Given Rebecca's dream," he asked, "do you think we can assume that the Joneses are going to be taken there … to the house?"

Just then came a knock on Luke's office door.

"Come in," he called.

"A courier just delivered this, sir," said an ISP messenger girl, one of a number of teens hired by the company during the summer months, a job-training program initiated by Kory, Luke, and Matt upon their arrival at ISP.

"Thank you, Jeannie," said Luke, accepting the manila envelope.

He pulled a single-page document from the envelope, looked up, and read.

Thursday, 20 June 1985

From: XAOC

To: Lt. Luke Manguson, officer, Royal Navy, and senior consultant, International Security Perspectives, LLC

1. By the time you are reading this, your colleague Reginald Jones and his daughter SallyBelle Jones will be on their way to our holding cells.

2. We will harm neither of them, provided you give us our adversary Rebecca Clark.

3. You will receive instructions later today regarding how and where the exchange will be made.

4. You cannot stop us. We will destroy every recognizable aspect of ordinary life, first in the U.K., and then around the world. The people of the democracies will eventually be ruined spiritually, politically, financially, and, in selected cases, physically. To that end, we will destroy Rebekka Yahalomin early in the process.

Kory jumped from her seat.

"Let me make copies for everyone, dear," she said to her husband.

She trotted from the room with the document.

"We'll want to wait for Kory," said Rebecca.

They waited.

She returned in minutes with the copies.

"Can we assume the exchange will be set up at the house Rebecca saw in her message dream?" asked McGriff.

Silence. Then, Adelman.

"I don't think so, Jack," he said. "I think Chaos will want to keep the location of what may be their new headquarters secret. I'd guess the instructions for the exchange will designate some specific location, possibly somewhere between London and Cambridge. But I think we can make plans without knowing the exchange spot.

"Agreed?"

Some heads nodded. Others seemed puzzled.

Marie, among the puzzled, spoke.

"But we surely are not actually going to *make* this exchange, right?" she asked a little fearfully. Marie was still somewhat unsure of herself in company with the veteran members of the Yahalomin.

"No, Marie," answered Matt Clark, a mischievous smile on his face. "We're actually going to give them Detective Belton. They'll be none the wiser."

"Listen, kid," said Belton immediately, turning his deep-set black eyes on the younger man, "one more crack like that an' I'm gonna pop ya' one, right in th' schnozz. Know what I mean? Hm?"

The laughter was welcome.

Luke provided a serious answer. "Absolutely not, Marie. Absolutely not."

Within an hour, a skeleton plan was in place. The plan would revolve around the new Nippon Telegraph and Telephone (NTT) equipment. One unit of the Yahalomin would drive one of the car-phone-equipped Defender 90s recently purchased by ISP. That unit would presumably include the three least equipped to engage in running, fighting, or the use of weaponry. Those three would be the combat-untrained Marie Campbell, the physically impaired Sid Belton, and Matt Clark, whose atrophied left arm and hand precluded most of the kinds of action that might be required.

The other unit would include the remaining five, all of whom were athletic and well prepared to use weapons. Kory, the technical expert among them, would carry the new NTT "shoulder phone," as the Nippon instructions labeled the product. This mobile phone prototype was the size, roughly, of a brick, nearly as heavy, and designed to be carried by a shoulder strap.

Kory would, thus, be in continual communication with the NTT car-phone-equipped Defender 90 and its three-person unit. The Japanese manufacturer estimated the maximum range between the two phones to be 10 to 15 miles, but this was uncertain. The distance between the two phones would be kept as short as possible when the actual situation developed.

Rebecca would carry the three throwing knives that she kept always in her ready-satchel. Adelman and McGriff would carry military handguns. Luke would carry his shoulder-holster array of cutting knives, tools, and ties, modified to include his three Barringtons Swords throwing knives.

By midmorning, the group scattered, each individual to attend to her or his own preparations and workouts, and to await the promised exchange-point instructions.

They did not have to wait long.

Thursday, 10:45 a.m.

Rebekka Yahalomin reassembled in Luke's office in response to his summons. Kory had already prepared copies of the instructions from Chaos.

She distributed the copies.

Each individual studied the missive, and then considered it in concentrated and prayerful silence.

Thursday, 20 June 1985

From: XAOC

To: Lt. Luke Manguson, officer, Royal Navy, and senior
          consultant, International Security Perspectives, LLC

1. The exchange will be made on the runway at Duxford
     Royal Air Force Base.

2. You are to bring Mrs. Clark to the main entrance of
     the base at 11:30 p.m. (2330 hours) 20 June. Leave

her there. Instruct her to stand next to the Hawker Hurricane gate guardian. She will be observed there from a distance.

3. Mrs. Clark is then to proceed on foot to the runway, turn to the southwest, and walk to the end of the runway. She is to wait there for a flashing light. When she sees the flashing light, she is then to walk toward the light. She will be met there and transported to her interrogation site.

4. Reginald Jones and his daughter will be released at the opposite end of the runway, once Mrs. Clark has stationed herself at the southwest end. They may be collected there at any time after Mrs. Clark has been transported away from Duxford.

5. If there is any departure from these instructions, Mr. Jones and his daughter will be taken away and the exchange agreement will no longer be available to you.

6. Any evidence of an attempt to circumvent these instructions, by your group, by law enforcement, or by intelligence agencies, will nullify this offer.

7. This agreement is made in good faith, consistent with Mrs. Clark's code: The Blueprint of the Universe: My Life for Yours. This is her opportunity to enact the spirit of her code. We expect her to conduct herself in accordance with this core principle.

8. There will be no further communication.

"Well," said Luke with a smile after several minutes, "I don't see how the framework we set up this morning could fit any better, do you?"

"Seems perfect, Luke," said Jaakov. "Are we all set with the car-phone-equipped Defender 90 for use tonight by Marie, Sid, and Matt?"

"We are," he said. "Kory will be testing the NTT phones this afternoon. Part of her testing will involve experimenting with operating distances. The NTT data suggest a 10- to-15-mile range. She'll see if that holds."

"We'll need to keep in mind," Kory noted, "that mobile-phone communication distances can vary with weather and terrain. In the future, relay stations will be set up to 'jump' the signals to any distance needed.

"For now, no such relay towers exist, and so we'll need to continue to experiment tonight, once we are in the Cambridge-Duxford area. I'm confident, though, that we'll have a workable situation, given the elevation of the Chaos site."

"How about timing, Luke?" asked McGriff.

"The rescue unit will travel in my Rover Five-Door, and we'll want to park at the foot of the Chaos ridgeline by 9 p.m. ... 2100 hours. We'll climb the ridge and circle to the opposite side of the private drive's approach, so that we can observe the house from cover and note the time of departure for Duxford."

"And from there," said Adelman, "we'll also be able to see if the Joneses actually get loaded into that van, or if the whole 'exchange' idea is a ruse."

"Oh, y' can bet it's a ruse, Jaakov," asserted Belton confidently. "They're not gonna do anything with that girl and her dad except keep 'em tied up in that house. No chance they're lettin' 'em go."

"And we should set up at Duxford at the same time you set up at the house, Luke?" asked Matt.

"Yes," said Luke. "We can depart from here together in the Land Rovers. I'd say we should be leaving the lot by seven tonight ... 1900 hours ... agreed, Kory?"

She nodded. "That should give us time to set up and test equipment. The house, which Mr. Belton tracked and found some years ago and which Rebecca has now identified in her dream, is almost exactly 10 miles west of Cambridge. Duxford is 9 miles south of Cambridge. The straight-line distance from the house to Duxford — the hypotenuse of the right triangle — is roughly 13.5 miles. That's within the range cited by the NTT data, and the higher elevation of the house will be to our advantage.

"My NTT shoulder phone should be able to communicate with the NTT car phone easily. I think we'll be fine on that score tonight."

There was a pause, everyone thinking about what they would face, everyone seemingly satisfied. Luke, looking over his notes, suddenly remembered something and said, "Oh ... forgot to say ... no reported problems last night with the midweek church services. Everything seems to have been quiet.

"Well done, all."

The meeting broke up minutes later, with individuals collecting their things and beginning to move toward the door of Luke's office. But Rebecca suddenly stood and called out to the others.

"Everyone!" she called. "Wait."

The others turned to her expectantly. Several resumed their chairs.

Rebecca, still standing, leaned forward, her hands resting on the side of Luke's desk, her dark tresses framing her face.

"I just realized," she said quietly, "that we didn't ask a question we should have asked ourselves in our earlier session this morning ... once the Chambers family had come in to tell us of the abduction of Reginald ... and once Luke's contact at Metro had told us of the kidnapping of SallyBelle ... we didn't ask how the Chaos people knew what route Reginald would be taking this morning ... or how they even knew that Reginald would be driving his vehicle at all ... instead of Horace Chambers or me driving our own vehicles, using our own preferred routes.

"We'd discussed in the conference room and in the hallway yesterday morning how we each preferred different routes to get from the young people's homes to the qualifying venue. We each drive our own vehicles. We go at slightly differing times ... and so, I now ask, *how* did they know?"

"Who was with you yesterday morning during those time-and-route discussions, Rebecca, besides Chambers and Jones?" asked Adelman immediately.

She thought back to the previous day's meetings.

"Ah!" she said suddenly. "The three MI6 guests were standing there with us, Jaakov. Their new subcommittee member ... Declan Murphy, I think, is his name ... even participated a little bit in our conversation, because of his young daughter. But Graham Roberts-Holm and the third member ... Ms. Singh, I think, was her name ... were standing near enough to hear that whole discussion."

Silence.

"Good thing y' phoned Metro Police t' talk about t'day's kidnappins, Luke," said Sid Belton. "Y' knew they'd be th' ones dealin' with city stuff ... not th' intelligence people ... or even Scotland Yard.

"Not that th' kidnappins woulda been news t' MI6 people, if they're th' ones feedin' info t' th' dirtbags at Chaos."

Luke nodded.

"Yes, Detective," he said thoughtfully, "and we'll need things to stay that way. No further communication with Graham Roberts-Holm and his subcommittee at MI6. Going forward, we'll use only my Metro Police contacts and maybe your Scotland Yard contacts, Mr. Belton, if we need something from outside.

"We'll talk to no one else, from this point on. If we need assistance with *anything*, we will not involve MI6. Not after this.

"Good catch, Rebecca," he added, nodding to his sister.

"*Very* good catch."

CHAPTER SEVEN

Thursday, early afternoon

MARIE CAMPBELL AND JACK MCGRIFF RELAXED, COMFORTABLE
with each other, in her fifth-floor ISP guest room. They had removed their shoes,
but were otherwise dressed as they had been for the morning's meetings, in
lightweight slacks and short-sleeved knit shirts. His dark blue shirt was worn
loose, untucked, over his still-too-ample torso; her maroon shirt, fitted to her
trim frame, was tucked neatly into her slacks.

She sat on the bed barefoot, her back against the headboard. In his stocking
feet, he sat on the room's only chair, an uncomfortable, straight-backed chair
placed near the room's one window.

He had moved the chair closer to her … to hand-holding distance.

She was preoccupied.

"Jack," she asked tentatively, "the thing about 'my life for yours' … it didn't
seem to me that Rebecca gave any thought to actually doing the exchange that
was demanded, or to actually 'giving her life' for SallyBelle and her dad.

"Am I wrong?"

"Yes," McGriff responded immediately. "There is no doubt that she *would*
give her life for the two of them … or, indeed … for *anyone* … and she has certainly put her life on the line for others often enough in the past. But … I think
… given her understanding of what she believes to be her calling … I mean, her
calling apart from being a Christian wife and mum … her calling to receive these
'message dreams' and then to act on them … I think she chooses not to give up

her life on earth without first engaging the enemy in ways that are … well … *other* than that … ways that leave her alive and well and ready for the next crisis that may emerge.

"Do you see what I mean, Marie?"

She was thoughtful.

"So," she said, "she probably *was* giving the demand for exchange for the captives her consideration. But she was opting for a different approach because she feels compelled by her calling to *survive* these engagements, and yet to accomplish what needs accomplishing by some means other than giving herself up?"

He nodded.

"Yes," he said, "and often with the assistance of her brother and the rest of us. You know … the Rebekka Yahalomin, as we are called."

She was again thoughtful.

He was watching her carefully.

"What are you thinking, Marie? You're not satisfied."

She laughed.

"Am I that easy to read, Jack McGriff?"

"Yes."

She laughed again, a sound he loved to hear.

"Well," she began, "I would have thought that the *surest* way to retrieve the girl and her father would have been to follow the instructions to the letter and then, once the two of them — father and daughter — were in our hands … then try to rescue *Rebecca,* or to help her rescue herself … whichever seemed more feasible."

He shook his head.

"No," he said. "Rebecca and Luke have come to understand our enemies better than that, Marie. They are certain that Chaos will *not* make the girl and her father available. They are certain that Chaos will retain them in their 'holding cells,' or simply kill them. It's possible that they already have killed them."

Marie, shocked at the thought, dropped her face into her hands. She emitted a small, anguished moan through her hands. McGriff rose immediately and bent over her, cradling her head in his muscular hands.

He kissed her hair and lingered, her delicate scent filling his nostrils.

After a moment, smiling, she pushed him gently away.

"Go back to your chair, Jack McGriff. No sneaking up on me."

He laughed, delighted at her playfulness. He obeyed and moved reluctantly back to his seat. She looked at him, the smile gone, still thinking hard.

She persisted.

"Jack," she said, *"how* can they be certain of something like that ... about people they don't even know?"

"Well, Marie," he said after a moment, "I think Rebecca ... and maybe Luke ... but certainly Rebecca ... would say that she *does* know these people ... even though she doesn't know them by name yet.

"She would say that Evil — with a capital 'E' — is better at destroying individual human beings than it is at destroying systems and cultures and organizations and governments. Evil can't help itself. It drives toward individuals."

"But Jack," she protested, "this Chaos organization wants to destroy whole *cultures ... nations ... democracies ...*"

"True," he said, "but only as a means to get to individuals.

"Evil does not honor agreements with organizations of any kind, as a way to get to individuals. It does not keep commitments to organizations of any kind, as a way to get to individuals. It seeks ultimately to destroy people, usually one at a time."

He was thoughtful for a moment, then continued.

"Evil is drawn irresistibly to big-picture opportunities for creating chaos, but as a means to reach small-picture opportunities to destroy the minds and hearts and souls of individual human beings.

"Just as," he continued, "at the other end of the spectrum, God drives toward ... and cares ultimately about ... individual human beings. Each one of us ... human being by human being ... each single one of us is infinitely valued by God."

She nodded.

"Christ died for us individually," she said thoughtfully.

"Exactly," he replied.

She smiled.

"You just gave me a sermon, Reverend McGriff," she said, teasing.

He found himself blushing. He shook his head.

"Couldn't help myself," he said in a small voice.

She reached over and seized his hand.

"I love it when you do that, Jack. That was wonderful. Really … it was."

He squeezed her small hand in both of his meaty ones.

"Well," he said, "there's a little more."

"Let's hear it," she said, honestly wanting to hear whatever he could tell her about this extraordinary situation, one that was completely novel for her.

"Rebecca," he said, encouraged by his fiancée's response, "knows that *this* particular evil — with a small 'e' — this particular man about whom she has dreamed, but whose identity we do not have … *this* evil individual wants to eliminate *her* … wants to kill Rebecca Clark … and he will violate every agreement and every promise in order to capture … and then torture and kill … this 'message dreamer' who so often has disrupted Evil's plans — Evil with a capital 'E.'

"The Joneses, father and daughter, will be thrown away as soon as he can get at Rebecca Clark. The only puzzling thing to me is why this person — apparently familiar with Rebecca, at least by reputation — seems to think she will actually follow his instructions. I would have thought he would simply go directly for her."

"But he did, Jack … the firebombing was supposed to kill her."

He nodded. "Right … right. That's right.

"And now," he continued, "having failed in that attempt, he's decided to try to appeal to her code of conduct … her blueprint … by actually taunting her with her 'my life for yours' principle.

"He thinks … he hopes … this will work where the other approach did not."

"The blindness of deep Evil," she said.

He smiled.

"Hmmm. *The blindness of deep Evil.* Well said, Marie Campbell."

They were thoughtful, turning the thing over in their minds.

Then McGriff spoke again.

"You know, Marie," he said, "this illustrates how Rebecca can view this particular evil person as 'the same evil' as that of the Meredith Lancaster person … the former occupant of her dreamed house … or as that of all the others she has had to deal with over these years. Every one of them has been driven by forces whom they, each one of them, at some point decided to invite into themselves … as you say, they invited deep Evil into themselves … and so, in a profound sense … they really are all the same … one after another after another after another …

"She *does* know these people."

They were quiet again for minutes, thinking.

Suddenly, Marie started.

"Jack!" she cried.

He looked at her, briefly alarmed.

But she smiled and turned to him.

"You remember yesterday when Luke and Rebecca reported the outcome of their phone request to Graham Roberts-Holm and his subcommittee members, when Rebecca gave Roberts-Holm her 'word portrait' of the man in her dream?

"And when," she continued, "Luke said that the subcommittee members worked for several hours to identify the man, based on Rebecca's dreamed image?"

"Whoa!" said McGriff, eyes bright with his fiancée's realization.

"You're right, Marie. They may not have tried to identify the man at all. They may have known exactly who he is.

"They don't *want* us to know his identity."

They squeezed each other's hands again, gleeful with the new thought.

Then she brightened yet again.

"Who gets to tell Rebecca?" she asked, begging with her eyes.

"Well, Ms. Campbell," he said with exaggerated formality, "I think you have definitely earned the honor.

"It's all yours."

Thursday, early afternoon

SallyBelle sat on the threadbare gray rug, assessing the damage to herself and guessing at the damage to her father. Their kidnappers had driven them a long way, possibly two hours, from the scene of their London abduction. The kidnappers had kept the sack in place, over her head, even after she was removed from the van, a man's hand guiding her roughly by her elbow as she walked.

She had been steered up several steps to a building entrance, then down a hallway and up a long flight of stairs that seemed to include a 180-degree turn about halfway up. A landing, then.

Upon reaching the first level up from the ground floor, she had been maneuvered into a room on her immediate right, and the plastic tie removed from her wrists. The door had shut behind her.

From the other side of the door she had heard a man say, "Toilet is across hall from your room. Your door not locked. Your father on ground floor. He is unharmed. You not be harmed either, unless you make the trouble."

His accent was, she thought, eastern European, but she knew she was no expert on dialects. She just knew the man was not a native speaker of English.

With that, she had heard his footsteps descending the stairs and had heard nothing since. After some time, she had removed the oppressive sack and had tentatively tried the door. She had found it indeed unlocked and had crossed the hallway to the bathroom.

She had been shocked by her image in the mirror. Her face was bruised, her eyes discolored, her nose skinned raw, and her blonde hair in disarray, having pulled itself partially loose from her tight ponytail. But she admitted that she looked worse than she felt. She actually felt strong.

And she felt angry.

She repaired her ponytail, the one aspect of her appearance that was immediately correctible. She splashed water on her face and re-crossed the hall.

Now, minutes later, she sat in her room, an unfurnished space, and, knowing that her bubbling anger was not likely to become productive ... yet ... she tried to relax and to think afresh about the damage to her person. Her facial damage had been visible in the mirror, but nothing seemed broken. Superficial injuries.

However, her rib cage was becoming increasingly painful. Each breath hurt. She wondered if the kidnapper's full weight crashing down onto her small body had fractured one or more of her ribs.

Then she thought of her father, and of what they must have done to him, not only to drag him so quickly from the Rover, but to silence him for the entire trip to this place. She had heard nothing from him at any point.

She decided that, since they had told her that her father was on the ground floor, she would try to go down and pay a visit to him. What could they do, other than to send her back to this room?

Then she thought ... again ... of Rebecca Clark. How would Mrs. Clark view this situation, if she were in it? And she knew.

Mrs. Clark would form an escape plan. And how? She would begin by getting a better sense of the building in which she found herself, and then of the terrain surrounding the building. And what better way to do that than to attempt a visit to her father, sequestered somewhere on the ground floor?

She wanted to find her dad. She had to know that he was going to be okay. She had to know … to see … to comfort him if he were hurting. She had to let him know that she was well … a little damaged, but not much.

She wanted to comfort her father.

But any sort of effort … any attempt to reassure and comfort her father … any sort of reconnaissance of the building and its property … any of this would require courage on her part. She thought of Mrs. Clark's observations on the subject.

"Courage," Rebecca Clark had repeatedly reminded her and Thomas Chambers, "is not something you *have*. Courage is something you do. Don't view yourself as 'courageous' or 'not courageous.' View yourself as someone who can *enact* courage if the situation calls for that.

"And that can be when you are facing match point against you. That can be the day when you are starting a new school. That can be when you are beginning a new relationship. That can be in any context whatever."

And then, she recalled with a smile, Mrs. Clark had quoted C. S. Lewis, the Oxford and Cambridge writer of both scholarly and popular books. "Courage," he had written, "is the name of every virtue at its testing point."

Without further contemplation, SallyBelle stood, stretched, tidied her blue BBG uniform, squared her shoulders, and walked out into the corridor. She looked both ways, saw no one, and, prompted by something she could not clearly identify, turned away from the stairs and walked toward the front of the building.

As she strode down the hallway, she realized that the building was a rundown house, once someone's home. The bathroom fixtures should have suggested that to her, but only now did it become obvious.

At the hallway's end, she stopped and looked out the window. The view overlooked what she took to be the arrival area. The grounds were spacious, but unkempt, in keeping with her sense of the condition of the house.

She saw on her right a doorway which was partially open. She peeked in and saw what was clearly an office space of some kind. A large desk. Other work surfaces. A conference table. A conversation area with several comfortable chairs.

Not making trouble, as I was instructed, she thought to herself, *would mean not investigating this office space.*

She smiled at herself, walked in, and turned on an overhead light. The decor was dark wood, reminding her of old-time headmasters' offices she had seen in photos, something designed to intimidate visitors.

She walked over to a well-worn, red-leather chair, and turned on the reading lamp beside it. There was a file folder on the lamp stand, and she considered examining its contents. She thought to herself again, *not making trouble would mean tiptoeing out of this space and never coming back.*

She smiled again and lifted the file. Her eyes widened.

The thick file appeared to be devoted entirely to Rebecca Manguson Clark. As she thumbed hastily through, she found that it included details about Mrs. Clark's family history, schooling, church commitments, athletic accomplishments, and, especially, about Mrs. Clark's "interference" with various projects mentioned in the text, always without any detailed explanation of the projects themselves. The text assumed that the reader would be thoroughly familiar with those projects.

Turning to the end of the file, she saw the "conclusions" pages, which noted that efforts to co-opt Rebecca Manguson Clark had repeatedly failed over the years, as had numerous efforts to kidnap or kill her. The section emphasized that, at all costs, Rebecca Manguson Clark must simply be eliminated. The final sentence was unequivocal. "No project is likely to reach full and satisfactory completion until this woman — Rebecca Clark — is removed."

The date of the report's release was recent ... the previous month. She returned the file to its place on the lamp stand and turned off the lamp.

And suddenly she saw. She saw that Mrs. Clark, her mentor in tennis and in so many other things, was something much more than that. She had for years apparently stood in opposition to everything this organization — but *was* this an organization? — had tried to accomplish.

She saw that Mrs. Clark was still considered to be *the insuperable obstacle* to every principal goal in the eyes of ... of whom? But she also saw, in a flash of recognition, what her own situation could mean both for herself and for her father. Their kidnappers had no interest in either of them. Not really.

They had taken them in order to lure Mrs. Clark into some sort of trap. SallyBelle didn't know what sort, but it was Mrs. Clark who was the intended victim.

And she saw that this could be good or bad … for herself and her father. They — she and he — could simply be bargaining chips in some unimaginable conflict involving Mrs. Clark and her family. As such, they might simply be discarded like yesterday's newspapers no matter how things went with Mrs. Clark.

But discarded how? Simply released? Or simply murdered?

She took a deep breath and fought off the urge to treat herself, in her mind, as helpless … as a pawn … as a victim. She shook her head, turned, and walked out of the dismal office. She stood again at the window at the corridor's end and studied the acreage fronting the aging house.

Then, a fresh idea emerging, she opened a door on the other side of the corridor and, moving through another empty room to its windows, studied that side of the property. She repeated her surveillance, as she began to think of it, in each direction and then, without pausing, walked down the stairwell to the ground floor. As she made the 180-degree turn at the landing, she saw below her an exceedingly large man sitting in a hallway chair on the ground floor.

He saw her as she made her turn, jumped quickly to his feet, and turned his back to her. He hastily pulled a ski mask over his head. He then turned to face the girl in the BBG uniform, and SallyBelle at once perceived his enormous muscularity. The man's menacing aspect, inherent in his stature and demeanor, was made yet more severe by the mask itself, black with red piping.

She stopped on the last step of the stairwell as he strode toward her. Suddenly she felt even smaller than she was. He stopped three feet from her, towering over her despite her position on the first step of the stairs.

"What you doing?" he said roughly, his deep voice a different one from the one from upstairs, but speaking with the same dialect, she thought.

"I'd like to see my father," she said as assertively as she could, her voice nevertheless sounding weak and tinny to her ears.

He turned his head to look toward the front door of the building, and she realized that there was a second man in the corridor, standing near the door, wearing an identical ski mask. She sensed that her man was asking the other's permission.

"Okay … sure … let her see father for one moment," called the other man who, she thought, was the one who had steered her up the stairs and told her that her father was unharmed and on the ground floor. And, she also thought, he was probably the man who had crushed her onto the floor of the van.

The man in front of her stepped back, gestured for her to follow, and led her down the hallway toward the front door. Halfway there, they stopped, and he reached for a doorknob on his right.

Suddenly she heard a single word thrown in their direction from the front. *"Fedorov!"*

A moment later there was a crashing sound from the direction of the front door … the door swung violently open … and a new figure stood in the doorway. Even though it was not masked, she could not see its features, the figure being backlighted from her perspective. It was just the silhouette of a man.

It breathed a challenge that sounded to SallyBelle as though it came from the depths of the earth. *"Why is the girl on the ground floor?"*

When no answer came from her two captors, the silhouette hissed a command, the words somehow hitting her almost as an actual blow.

"Get the girl out of my sight. I never want to see her again."

She shuddered.

Thursday, midafternoon

Rebecca lay on her back, eyes closed, muscles fully relaxed, on the floor of one of the unused ISP guest rooms, a small pillow under her head. She had explained to the others that she needed to be alone for a while.

Most of the others had decided to do the same.

She had decided that, in the time that remained before their 7 p.m. sortie, she needed to use the hours for rest, concentration, and prayer. She had considered engaging in knife-throwing practice in the ISP basement workout center, but at length concluded that her two practice sessions with her brother in his and Kory's basement would need to be enough. She wanted solitude now.

She smiled at her recollection of Marie Campbell's excited report of her deduction regarding the MI6 contingent's failure to identify the man in Rebecca's word-portrait of the Chaos leader-figure. Rebecca readily agreed that Marie's thinking was probably correct, and that the MI6 group purposely screened Rebekka Yahalomin from learning the identity of the man.

That did not mean, Rebecca had noted to Marie and McGriff, that all three of the MI6 subcommittee members were actively hiding the Chaos figure's identity from the Yahalomin. That was possible, but, Rebecca had said, less likely than that only one of the three was a mole, a subversive within the MI6 subcommittee that had been formed to conduct analyses of "unexplained and unexplainable data."

Her brother's history with Graham Roberts-Holm, subcommittee chairperson, made him less likely than the others, but there was no certainty there. What mattered, she had noted, was simply that they should isolate themselves from MI6, as her brother had said to the group earlier.

Rebecca, eyes still closed, breathing slowly and quietly, next turned her thoughts to the dreamed house which had become, in her mind, the new headquarters of the Chaos operation, and, she further guessed, the likely domicile for the dreamed figure who appeared to have become heir to, and host for, Meredith Lancaster's supercharged evil. Concentrating with her usual intensity, she forced herself to recall those moments, years before, in Lancaster's office ... those tortured moments following her discovery of a file folder devoted entirely to her.

She recalled her shockingly disappointing, yet seemingly irresistible, response to the file's contents ... to its depiction of her future as the face of the enemy project ... as the project's "marketing centerpiece." She shuddered as she remembered the strength of the temptation that had overwhelmed her that day, an actual physical force that had driven her to the floor and had fought to gain her submission, a submission at first physical, but promising to become mental and finally spiritual.

It had been powerfully seductive ... demanding her total surrender.

She recoiled physically at the memory. For she knew, as she had known since that day, that her soul's ongoing health was in a sense partly dependent upon her acknowledgement ... her daily acknowledgement ... that the experience had been real. That she had very nearly succumbed. That she was not then, nor ever would be, impervious to the temptations that ultimate Evil could and would place before her.

No one was, nor ever could be, completely immune.

There could be, she knew with certainty, no complacency against the face of the enemy. Her disciplined prayer life was her first line of defense, and she intended to maintain that line of defense every day of her life.

Now, in her fifth-floor room, Rebecca redirected her mind to focus on that night's plans, the Yahalomin's plans to rescue SallyBelle and her father in a night action. Rebecca expected no further information about what they would face beyond that which she had already been given ... the image of the structure that she, Luke, Matt, and Sid Belton had assaulted successfully all those years before. On this night, they would make their silent approach, would conduct the most comprehensive reconnaissance possible, and then would take whatever action was demanded.

They would pray their companion prayer.

Father, be present ... be present ...

They would then be guided by the Source from moment to moment. No plans beyond that could be formulated. They would present themselves, ready for action, and go forward under God's hand.

Kory would carry the NTT shoulder phone, plus an array of ISP-owned building-entry accoutrement. Adelman and McGriff would carry sidearms, plus two, each, of the detective agency's palm-sized document cameras. Luke would wear his customary shoulder holster.

They would be hurried, she knew. They would need to initiate their rescue steps the moment the Chaos vehicles departed the headquarters structure to move to the proposed Duxford exchange point. Their adversary would not need long, once at Duxford, to see that she ... Rebecca Clark ... was not going to be offered.

Their enemy would return to the hilltop command center as soon as he realized she was not coming to the air base. And he would return with murder on his mind, if indeed murder would not have already been committed.

Marie, Matt, and Sid Belton, with the NTT car phone, would radio them from Duxford at the moment their adversary abandoned Duxford to return to the hilltop headquarters. They would have perhaps 15 minutes to complete the rescue and make their escape.

From that point on, the battle would be joined in earnest.

Rebecca nodded to herself. She was ready. She would pray now, and then sleep. And then finally, before departure, she and Matt would telephone the twins at the Lodge. That done, she would then dress for the incursion.

She would wear black, as would they all. She would carry her satchel with the three Barringtons Swords knives.

She prayed a brief, tightly focused prayer, then rose and moved to the room's single bed. She immediately fell into the sleep of the well prepared.

She did not dream.

CHAPTER EIGHT

Thursday, midafternoon

SALLYBELLE, HAVING HEARD NOTHING FROM HER CAPTORS FOR hours, reached a decision. She was confident that it was something Mrs. Clark would approve of. In any case, she *knew* that Mrs. Clark would endorse the decision to become an *active* captive.

She had learned many things from Rebecca Clark. Some of them were tennis-specific. Many were not. Two came to mind.

Don't wait for life to happen to you, SallyBelle. Move toward it.

Always prayerfully, SallyBelle. Move toward it.

SallyBelle stood, breathed deeply, murmured the companion prayer Mrs. Clark had given her — *Father, be present … be present* — and stepped into the hallway.

Moving silently in her soft-soled BBG shoes, she first crossed to the bathroom and, having closed the door, stood carefully on the toilet seat lid. She reached upward and pressed both hands against the access panel to what she assumed would be an attic. The panel yielded.

She lifted it and pushed it to one side. Standing on tiptoe, she found that she could gain a firm grip on the near edge of the 2-square-foot opening. She placed her hands a few inches apart and, flexing her biceps, pulled herself up — a hands-reversed pull-up — and elevated her head all the way up and into the opening, her chin now resting on the edge of the attic flooring.

The maneuver triggered shooting pains through her damaged rib cage. She screened the pain from her mind as well as she could and focused on what she could see. Turning her head in each direction, she scanned the attic area quickly.

She saw that there were a number of dormer windows all around the attic space, providing ample light from the outside. Satisfied, she lowered herself carefully so that her toes could reach the toilet seat lid. Before stepping down from the toilet lid, she considered whether or not to slide the attic-access panel back into place. Thinking of what she expected to do next, she left it open.

She carefully stepped down from the toilet, conscious of how easily upper-floor footfalls could be heard on the ground floor in an old house. She then flushed the toilet in case someone on the ground floor was tracking the sounds of her movements. She opened the bathroom door and moved across the hallway. Still standing in the corridor, she closed the door to her room.

She closed the door more noisily than necessary, and then stood, listening. She could hear faintly from the ground floor the sound of her captors talking, though their words were indistinct. Satisfied, she crept swiftly down the length of her hallway.

In her earlier exploration, she had not opened several of the doors on her floor. She had looked out hastily on each side of the building, just enough to get a sense of the extent of the surrounding property. That had left five of the long hallway doors unopened. She hoped to find a storage closet behind one of them, but was dimly aware that such old-house features might be found only on the ground floor.

She moved down the corridor, quietly looking in each space. The final door — the fifth — yielded what she hoped … an upper-floor storage closet containing, carelessly entangled with cleaning supplies, unopened paint cans, and a pair of toolboxes, a folding step ladder, and two coils of 1-inch-diameter rope.

Perfect, she thought.

She quickly slipped the two coils over one shoulder and carefully lifted the stepladder from its place, pain again shooting through her ribs. She closed the door quietly behind her and, thus encumbered, moved as swiftly and silently as she could back down the corridor to the bathroom. She opened its door again and moved inside, closing the door softly behind her.

Without hesitating, she tied one end of one of the ropes around the top rung of the ladder, then spread the ladder's legs so that it stood solidly on the floor, its legs straddling the toilet. Holding the rope's end in her teeth, she climbed to the top rung, which allowed her head and shoulders to rise cleanly through the opening.

She tossed the second coil of rope onto the attic's surface, then maneuvered herself onto the same surface. She immediately stood and, bracing herself firmly and gritting her teeth against the pain in her ribs, she pulled the rope up, the ladder following, its legs folding together of their own weight as it rose.

She placed the ladder on its side near the access-panel opening, and, treading as quietly as possible, moved to a dormer window that, she thought, was situated directly over the ground-floor room in which her father was being held. She secured one end of the second rope to one of the main pillars supporting the roof itself, then examined the dormer window. She flipped the lock release, then raised the window two feet for quick egress when the time would finally come for her to leave her cell.

Then she returned to the attic-access panel, freed the first rope from the ladder, made sure the ladder was within two feet of the opening, and tied one end of the rope around the roof support closest to the panel. She dropped the rope down into the bathroom. Then she tested the rope, found it secure, and confidently lowered herself down into the small space, her tennis-strong hands and arms easily handling her own weight during the short descent.

Once standing firmly on the floor, she again climbed onto the toilet seat lid, coiled the rope she had just used for her descent, and, holding its free end firmly in her left hand, tossed the coil up and into the attic with her right.

Standing on tiptoe once more, she then pushed the rope's free end up, until only a few inches were visible from below. She slid the access panel back into place and stepped down to examine her work.

Satisfied that a visitor to the bathroom would be unlikely to notice a few inches of exposed rope protruding from the closed attic-access panel, she opened the bathroom door and stepped into the hallway. Not 6 feet away from her stood one of the guards, ski mask in place.

"Girl!" he said roughly.

"What you doing? Why you in toilet room so long?

"What you *doing*, girl?"

An athlete well trained to relax under duress, she took a single, measured breath, and fixed her blue eyes on the masked face.

"I'm using the bathroom mirror to try to repair my face where you or your friend smashed me into the floor of that van this morning," she said. "You hurt me. I think you're a terrible person. I think you are a bully."

He laughed behind the mask.

"I'm a terrible person?" he said. "You lucky Anton Fedorov has not got his hands on you, girl. I'm nicest person you going to see here."

She thought about the man's response and saw a chance.

"Well," she said, "if you're the nicest person I'm going to see, then you'll want to take me downstairs to visit my father, right? You'll want to escort me to my dad's room so I can see that he's okay, right? And so he can see I'm okay, right?"

He shook his head.

"You come to ground floor again and Fedorov see you …"

He shook his head again.

"You watch yourself, girl. You watch yourself."

"You in danger, girl. You in very big danger."

Thursday, 9:30 p.m.

The five-person Rebekka Yahalomin rescue unit settled into place on the ridge, just inside a tree line on the north side of the aging structure presumed by them to be the new headquarters. They had estimated 10:30 p.m. as the earliest time Chaos would depart in order to arrive at the Duxford rendezvous a full half-hour prior to the 11:30 p.m. time given the Yahalomin to present Rebecca Clark at the entrance gate. The Yahalomin had timed their departure from ISP headquarters so as to give them a full hour to reconnoiter and to test the NTT communications equipment.

Kory had immediately activated her NTT shoulder phone and prepared to punch in the contact number for the reciprocating car phone monitored by Marie Campbell. The ISP-owned Defender had been in position at Duxford for 30 minutes.

Matt Clark was the Defender's driver. Despite his useless left arm and hand, which made shifting the right-hand drive manual transmission vehicle impossible, he was the only one of the three with experience driving on the left-hand side of English roadways. Marie, sitting to his left, handled the floor-mounted shift lever for him.

The arrangement had proven clumsy, but decently workable, on the drive from London to the Duxford area. Sid Belton sat just behind them, injecting his inimitable humor into the tense situation. His favorite barb had to do with speed.

"Ya' drive this thing like my great-grandma, kid," he noted repeatedly, poking Matt in the shoulder for emphasis. "I could go faster on a tricycle."

"Know what I mean? Hm?"

His two colleagues in the front seat had decided early on, by unspoken mutual consent, that they'd simply ignore the detective until he provided substantive observations, something that they knew he would eventually begin to do.

At 9:38 p.m. the car phone chirped. Marie lifted the receiver immediately and switched on the phone's speaker to allow her colleagues to participate.

"This is Marie," she said.

"Oh!" responded Kory, almost 15 miles away, "I can hear you perfectly, Marie. How is my transmission to you?"

"Excellent," said Marie. "It's as if you're here in the car with us, Kory. I didn't expect this to work so well."

"Neither did I," said Kory, "but this is wonderfully clear. And, since there are no weather changes expected tonight, I think we can count on the communications to remain just like this.

"Now," Kory continued without pause, "ask Mr. Belton to tell my husband and Jaakov here exactly how you are positioned and what you can see."

"Turns out," said Belton, shouting comically at the NTT car phone from a distance of 12 inches, "there's a nice little hill about half-mile from th' southwest end of th' airstrip where Mrs. Clark's supposed t' stand at midnight. We got th' Defender hidden in trees an' bushes, but with a good visual through our binocs of th' end of th' airstrip an' of any place around there where th' dirtbags might set up."

"Sounds good, Sid," replied his detective-agency partner. "We will let you know as soon as the Chaos people leave here for Duxford. We think probably 10:45 p.m., right?"

"Well ... maybe ten-thirty, Jaakov," said Belton. "Just let us know."

"We're good here."

Having established the communications link, Adelman and Luke, the two best-trained at infiltration, moved out separately to examine the Chaos setup from much closer range. Creeping forward in severe crouches, staying away from any light cast from the house's windows, they approached the building from opposite sides. Luke moved toward the front, the east side of the building; Adelman, toward the back — the west side — and, continuing, on around to the south side.

Twenty minutes later, at 10:15 p.m., they returned to the observation post north of the structure. All five then moved 30 feet back from the tree line and turned their faces away from the building. They spoke in low voices, not whispers, all of them aware that the human whisper carries further than a quiet voice.

"No outside sentry at the rear or on the far side of the building," reported Adelman, "and only two rooms on the far side show lights, one on the ground floor and one just above it. The light on the upper floor was extinguished during the several minutes I was on that side of the building. I'm guessing that the captives are in one of those two rooms, or, equally plausible, one in each."

"How about access to those rooms, Jaakov?" asked Kory.

"If we have to go in fast and loud," he replied, "the ground-floor room can be penetrated by breaking its window and going in hard. But there is no outdoor fire escape that would lead to fast entry into that upper-floor room. And we *know* someone is using that room. Someone turned off the light up there."

Rebecca, Kory, and McGriff turned to Luke.

"No sentry at the front," he said. "I eventually moved up and onto the porch and was able to see along the ground-floor's main hallway, through the small window in the door. There is one sentry standing beside what I'd guess is the ground-floor room where Jaakov reported a light. That reinforces your thought, Jaakov, that that room holds at least one of the captives … maybe both."

Jaakov nodded.

"I stayed on the porch," Luke continued, "and moved to the right of the door, and was able to see into what appears to be the main sitting room of the house … maybe a parlor. There were four men in the room, seated at a low table, all looking at a map. One of them appeared to be explaining something he understood … or that he had planned. He was the only one to speak while I watched.

"But the most interesting thing to me was that the man doing the speaking looked to me exactly like the person in Rebecca's earlier dream."

"Ah!" Rebecca exclaimed. "I felt sure we'd come upon him soon, Luke. We're getting so close to Chaos that he just *had* to materialize."

Luke nodded. "I felt the same, Rebecca."

"Tell me how he looked," she said.

"He was sitting down," Luke began, "and I saw him only in profile, but I could see that he had a prominent nose and an oddly protruding forehead. I could see, too, that his hairline was receding, which made the forehead seem even more ... odd. He was a strange-looking person.

"Rebecca, you saw only his face in your dream, and you saw him from head-on, as I remember your word-picture, so I couldn't match up every aspect of your image, such as eye color, or color and characteristics of his eyebrows. I did note that, since I could see him in his entirety, he appeared trim, taut, athletic.

"I'd guess him to be mid-30s."

Rebecca nodded. "That *has* to be the man, Luke."

"That's the Chaos leader."

Moments of silence passed while the group processed this.

Then Luke turned to the task at hand.

"Given what you and I have seen, Jaakov, 'Plan A' is still best?"

Adelman nodded. "Yes, I think so, Luke."

There was no further conversation.

Seeing this, Rebecca placed her hand on the ground, and the others immediately placed their hands on top of hers. Five hands together as one. Without the need for words, they bowed their heads and closed their eyes.

Each was praying silently: *Father, be present ... be present ...*

Thursday, 10:08 p.m.

SallyBelle Jones, having lain on her side on the thin rug for more than an hour, trying unsuccessfully to sleep, suddenly sat up. She sensed someone was on the grounds just outside the building. She didn't know how she sensed that, since she could not say with certainty that she had heard anything, but she was sure.

Without showing herself in the window, she crept across the room to turn off the overhead light. That done, she returned to the window and looked down.

The ground was illuminated dimly by light from the room beneath hers on the ground floor. She could see no one.

But she was sure.

I don't know what is happening, she thought, *but it's something.*

She again recalled Rebecca Clark's words.

"Don't wait for life to happen to you, SallyBelle. Move toward it.

"Always prayerfully, SallyBelle. Move toward it."

She knelt by the window and repeated the companion prayer to herself.

Father, be present … be present …

She rose quickly, moved to the door, listened, and turned the knob as quietly as possible. She opened the door and crossed the hallway to the bathroom. Once in the room, she closed the door behind her and, without pausing, stood on the toilet seat lid and reached up to move the attic-access panel aside and to pull the end of the rope so as to allow the full coil to fall to the bathroom floor. She stepped down from the toilet seat, grasped the rope firmly, and tested it. It felt solid.

Entwining her legs with the rope, she began to pull herself up, one arm-length at a time, using her legs to secure her position after each pull. Five determined pulls placed her face even with the attic opening, and she used her legs a final time to push herself up far enough for one hand to reach the ladder, lying flat and within easy reach of the access panel. With her right hand on the ladder to increase her leverage, she pulled her legs up, one at a time, through the opening.

She quickly stood, turned back to the opening, and pulled the rope up to herself. She slid the access panel back into place and pressed it firmly into its slots.

She did not expect to return.

In near-complete darkness, she moved across the attic to the raised dormer window she had prepared earlier. She moved her head out the window and listened. Faintly, she could hear men conversing at the front of the house. She strained to decipher their words, but could understand nothing.

She closed her eyes and recited the companion prayer once more, then turned and tested the second rope. Gripping the rope tightly with both hands and without further pause, she pushed herself out the window. She swung her body around so as to face the building, her damaged ribs protesting the twisting motion. She placed both feet against the outside wall and began her descent to the ground.

Her feet touched the grass and she moved, gliding softly, toward the sound of the voices. She reached the corner and moved her face far enough forward so that one eye could see the men. She saw that one man was clearly in charge, and guessed that he must be the "Fedorov" person her guards feared so much.

She watched and listened.

Fedorov did all the talking.

"Dimitri will drive …

"Bogdan and Lev will seize the woman on the airstrip …

"Da … da … shoot her *before* she runs … lower leg …

"She must not escape …

"Of course … and kill both captives as soon as we leave the house …"

SallyBelle shuddered.

"Kill both of them immediately and bury the bodies down on the north slope …

"You have your orders. Kill them now."

She watched as the 'Fedorov' person turned, his face well lit by the front porch light, and moved to a vehicle. She thought to herself that he was a strange-looking man. There was something about his forehead and his eyebrows — no, it was a single eyebrow — and his hairline …

A very strange-looking person.

She moved away from her corner and, as she glided back toward the one window that was lighted, she heard a vehicle's engine start. After a little more conversation that she could not decipher, she heard, and then actually saw, the indistinct shape of a vehicle moving off toward the perimeter. It quickly disappeared, and soon there was just the silence of the night.

She had no clear plan other than to find her father and rescue him. If she had been asked, she would have acknowledged that her chances were poor. But she knew precisely where her responsibility lay, and so she knew precisely what she must try to do. She crept to the lighted ground-floor window where she assumed her father was most likely to be. She took a deep breath and, pushing herself up on tiptoes, pressed her face to the window.

Mrs. Clark's words resonated in her mind yet again: *the blueprint of the universe ... my life for yours ...*

Thursday, 10:30 p.m.

By the time the Chaos van's engine sprang to life, Kory and Jaakov were already looking into a darkened ground-floor window on the north side of the building, the side opposite the one where SallyBelle now stood on tiptoe, also looking in a window. Kory, using one of her ISP-issued building-entry tools, twice tapped the hitting surface on a circular glass-cutting device, using the rubber hammer that formed part of the kit.

She felt the glass yield immediately. And she felt the attached suction cup holding the glass section firmly to itself.

She tugged the 12-inch-diameter glass circle smoothly back to herself, turned, and placed it on the ground beside her. She then reached carefully through the aperture and slipped the window lock to its open position.

Adelman stepped forward and, using another of Kory's tools, a small crowbar, levered the window up from its sill and pushed the window wide open. Adelman, a lanky athlete well over 6 feet in height, pulled himself up and through the window, then turned and helped the much smaller Kory up and into the room.

The entire process took less than 30 seconds.

Without pausing, they moved swiftly to the central hallway and, peering out from the room through which they had just moved, looked both ways. They saw that the hallway toward the rear of the building was now empty of guards.

But the front door stood open, with two sentries easily visible, both standing on the building's front porch, apparently watching the Chaos vehicle's departure. Adelman and Kory could see through the open door that one of the men held a long-barreled handgun; the other, an automatic rifle, doubtless the ever-present Kalashnikov.

As they watched, the two guards turned toward them to move into the hallway, presumably to carry out the just-ordered executions of the two captives.

Adelman, his service 9mm in hand and held down against his leg, stepped fully into the brightly lit hallway and faced the guards.

The two men stopped, incredulous.

"Good evening, my good friends," called Adelman loudly in English.

As he said this, he held his 9mm out to the side, the muzzle of the weapon pointing to the wall, a movement that further confused the already baffled guards. The guards looked at each other, mystified. Then they raised their weapons.

As the weapons came up toward him, Adelman could see past them to the front doorway, and so was able to see exactly what he expected. He saw two black-clad figures, a man and a woman, glide swiftly through the doorway and, in a stunning blur of athleticism, launch in unison a pair of Barringtons Swords throwing knives.

The knives were released by his two colleagues using their unique under-hand, no-spin technique, a method learned in the Royal Navy by Luke Manguson and eventually taught to his sister, whose rangy, long-limbed build had allowed her quickly to surpass her brother in both accuracy and power. But at this range — less than 20 feet — he was as accurate and as effective as she.

In a fraction of one second, Adelman heard the unique sounds — thudding and tearing sounds — of two razor-sharp knife points ripping into the right-side trapezius muscles of each guard. The men staggered forward, weapons clattering to the floor.

Adelman was on them in a flash, as was Luke. They threw the wounded men to the floor, face down, and bound their hands behind them with two pairs of Luke's plastic handcuffs. And, even as the guards' hands were being handcuffed behind them, Rebecca and Kory pulled the knives free, each knife buried deep in the men's trapezius muscles, and tore open their shirts. They swiftly applied antiseptic from Kory's kit and staunched the bleeding, which, since the damage was from puncture wounds, was not profuse. Without pause, they slapped strips of duct tape over the men's eyes.

In the nearly 60 seconds that had elapsed from the moment Adelman had stepped into the hallway, both guards had been disabled and handcuffed, blind-folded with duct tape, and superficially treated for their wounds. Meanwhile, Jack McGriff, having first reported the van's departure, using the shoulder phone, to the Duxford unit, sprinted past the scene of the hallway action and raced up the stairs, his 9mm in hand. In less than 30 seconds, McGriff returned and called down from the landing.

"No one present on the upper floor."

Suddenly a ground-floor hallway door opened not 10 feet from where Rebecca, Luke, Adelman and Kory were finishing their work. They spun to face the threat, Adelman's 9mm coming up as he did.

SallyBelle Jones stood in the doorway, her mouth open in astonishment.

After a heartbeat consumed equally by her amazement and her delight, Rebecca rose from tending to her patient — who was also her victim — and raced to the girl. The resulting embrace lifted the teen off the floor.

Rebecca laughed from the sheer joy of finding the child safe and alive. Simultaneously, SallyBelle squealed in pain as her damaged ribs protested.

Rebecca quickly released the teen, who then, once again on her own feet, resumed the embrace, throwing her arms around Rebecca and finding herself gasping, laughing and crying, all at once. After long moments, SallyBelle managed a halting sentence, her face buried in Rebecca's shoulder.

"Mrs. Clark ... my dad ... he's hurt."

Thursday, 11:30 p.m.

Settling into one of the rear seats of her husband's Land Rover Five-Door, Kory Manguson placed the shoulder phone on the floorboard. She lifted the receiver and punched in the number for the ISP car phone, simultaneously switching to speaker mode. Marie Campbell, monitoring the car phone, picked up on the first ring.

"Yes?" she said, switching the car phone also to its 'speaker' mode.

"Marie," said Kory, "everything has gone swimmingly here. We are in the Five-Door and starting home. Luke says you three can leave Duxford whenever you think you should. Have you been able to get a visual fix on the Chaos van?"

"Yes," Marie replied. "But it never moved to the southwest end of the airstrip, as we assumed it would ... since that's where they instructed Rebecca to wait. We saw through our binoculars that the van stopped at the extreme opposite end of the airstrip ... but we don't know where the occupants went, or if they left the van at all.

"We have not seen them, but Mr. Belton thinks they may have placed themselves behind one of the original RAF buildings. He thinks it likely they have hidden there to wait for Rebecca to walk from the entrance gate to the airstrip. He thinks they expected us to wait at the southwest end of the strip, as we have indeed done, and so they planned to attack her somewhere else on the air base.

"So ... we aren't sure where they are, Kory, but you're saying it doesn't matter, right? We should just go ahead and start for home?"

"Right, Marie," replied Kory. "We're all finished here.

"Rebecca and Luke downed the guards," Kory continued expansively, knowing that Marie had the car phone on 'speaker,' and that Sid Belton and Matt Clark would be eager to hear, "as soon as we entered the building. They stepped in behind the guards and put them out of commission with those terrifying knife throws. The guards went down almost instantly, with a little help from Jaakov and Luke.

"And Marie," Kory continued, "SallyBelle was right there.

"She had escaped her 'cell,' as she called it, all on her own, through the building's attic, and had lowered herself by rope down the south wall of the structure while we were moving in from the north side. Her dad is badly concussed, though, and we have him lying down, here in the back of the Five-Door.

"Our first stop will be at an emergency room on the northeast outskirts of the city. Then we'll head for the ISP building. Luke estimates 1:45 a.m. to 2:00 a.m., Marie."

Marie took a few seconds to process the torrent of information, then asked, "Kory, if your rescue work went so fast, why has it been nearly an hour before you've reached Luke's vehicle?"

"After we dealt with the guards," Kory replied, "we spent most of our time in the upper-floor Chaos office, Marie. We discovered several files that apparently had not been kept at the London garage site at all.

"We needed to photograph some of those pages, and then, of course, we needed to resist the temptation to rush out of there. We wanted to get Reginald to an ER without delay, but we also needed to leave everything undisturbed.

"We left no trace. They will assume we rescued the Joneses and left the area as fast as we could, without exploring the building or even finding the office."

Sid Belton leaned forward in the ISP vehicle and shouted toward the car phone, again from a distance of barely 1 foot.

"What about those two guards?" he bellowed in his rumbling base. "Won't they be able t' tell th' Chaos bosses that you were upstairs for a half-hour or so?

"Hm?

"Won't they?"

Adelman leaned toward the shoulder phone's speaker-receiver and spoke to his New York City partner in his carefully modulated, Israeli-accented English.

"Sid," he said, "after we handcuffed and blindfolded those two, Jack and I walked them into the north-side woods, took them down the hill about 50 yards, and used some of Luke's clothesline cord to tie them to a couple of sturdy trees. They're far enough down the hill and into the woods that they can't hear anything.

"And, of course, we parked the Five-Door earlier tonight all the way down the hill on the opposite side — the south side — of the ridge. They won't even be able to hear the car start. They'll have no idea we were in the Chaos office.

"Our only concern was whether or not their leaders would bother to look for the two guards at all. They're probably not such bad fellows, you know … just caught up in something they can't escape … anyway, that's why we didn't tape their mouths. They'll be able to shout, and presumably be heard, when the time comes."

Belton thought this over. "Yeah … alright," he finally shouted in response. "I guess ya' did okay, Jaakov. About time ya' did somethin' half-smart.

"Know what I mean?

"Hm?"

Smiles flooded both vehicles at the affectionate banter between the long-time colleagues. But some of the smiles in the Five-Door were also smiles of relief. Gaining Sid Belton's approval after any completed operation was never a given.

Seeing that Adelman had finished speaking to his partner, Kory prepared to sign off, but stopped when she saw SallyBelle suddenly turn around from the front passenger seat and gesture to Kory, obviously a request to speak.

"SallyBelle?" she said to the girl.

"I just remembered something I should have told you way before now," said the teen, "but I was too caught up in all the excitement. Sorry."

"It's okay, SallyBelle," said Kory reassuringly. "What did you remember?"

"I just remembered that, in the afternoon, a man arrived at the ... prison house ... a man who actually *frightened* my guards ... a man whose name my guards later used to try to frighten me.

"And then tonight, after I escaped, I crept to the corner at the front of the prison house and watched that same man giving orders to the guards. He ordered them to kill us ... my dad and me ... as soon as he had gone.

"He said those words to them more than once: *kill the two captives*.

"He was a horrible person ... and a very strange-looking person, too ... something about his forehead ... and his eyebrows ... eyebrow ... very odd ...

"I'm sorry I forgot to tell you until now."

Silence. Then ...

"You said the guards told you this man's *name*, SallyBelle?" asked Rebecca.

"Yes," replied the girl. "They said his name is ... um ... Anton ... um ... Fedorov ... not sure of the spelling.

"I really think he's in charge back there, but he left the building in the van just before all of you stormed the prison house. I think he's really important."

Silence again.

Then Rebecca spoke once more.

"Thank you, SallyBelle," she said. "I can't tell you how useful that piece of information is going to be. We finally have a name to go with a face.

"We have needed this name for some time.

"Thank you, SallyBelle. *Well done.*"

There was a burst of applause from the occupants of both vehicles. SallyBelle turned toward the front and smilingly covered her face with her hands. She was grateful for the darkness. Her blushing would not be visible.

More thoughtful silence ensued, and then Kory also seemed to remember something ... in this case, something she had not yet reported to her colleagues in the other vehicle.

"Oh ... Marie," she said, "there is something else ... we noticed as we handled those files that there was a repeated reference to 'information from MI6' and to someone designated 'Cobra.'

"Those two references — to MI6 and Cobra — seemed to be used interchangeably in the memos we saw. We're going to need to talk about this in the morning."

Matt took this as his cue, and started the Defender's engine, anxious to head for London. But before asking Marie to move the gear shift lever for him, he turned his head and saw Sid Belton again leaning forward.

He waited.

Belton yelled immediately.

"Hey! You're tellin' us that th' Chaos dirtbags actually *wrote stuff down* about gettin' intel from th' other dirtbags over at MI6? How stupid can those meatheads be?

"Let's meet at ISP as soon as we can get there ... Luke, you just drop Mr. Jones at th' ER an' head for th' ISP office ... we gotta sort this stuff out ... right now. We don't hafta *speculate* any more about a mole over at MI6. The Chaos dummies actually *wrote it down*.

"An' now th' kid has come up with th' name we been lookin' for.

"We gotta sort this stuff out. Right now.

"Know what I mean? Hm?"

After a long moment, Rebecca leaned past Kory and spoke gently to the "dear detective" in her low, measured voice.

"Mr. Belton," she said in her exquisite Oxford dialect, the contrast stark to Belton's shouted Brooklynese, "all of us should try to rest during the hours that remain in this long night. I'm going to stay at the emergency room with SallyBelle until her Mum arrives to be with Reginald. Then, if her Mum approves, SallyBelle and I are going to take a cab to Luke and Kory's house, where my car is parked.

"She and I will get whatever sleep we can, and then I will drive her and Thomas Chambers to the qualifiers' venue in time for BBG practice. That way, she will have missed only one day.

"And I can make sure everyone supervising the BBGs understands that her absence was unavoidable. I can do that and get back to the ISP offices in time for the morning meeting, if my brother agrees.

"And so, Mr. Belton ... I'll just need everyone to be patient until then."

Rebecca paused, then placed a period on her statement, her words heard by all Rebekka Yahalomin members as both authoritative and final.

"Come to the meeting fresh, everyone. We'll need to do our best thinking.

"Does that sound alright to you, Mr. Belton?" she asked courteously.

"Yes, ma'am," replied Belton quietly, chastened.

"We can do that, ma'am. Absolutely."

Friday, 12:15 a.m.

Anton Fedorov looked irritably at his watch for the dozenth time in the fore-going half-hour. He ground his teeth together. A snarl formed on his lips.

"She is not coming," he said, more to himself than to his associates.

"She may just be late, Fedorov," said one.

Fedorov shook his head. "Nyet … nyet … she is not late.

"She is not coming."

"But …" began the associate.

"Silence!" shouted Fedorov.

And silence descended upon the three men — the driver waited in the van with the engine running — as they crouched in the shadows of one of the original Duxford RAF buildings. Fedorov's plan had been to seize Rebecca Clark as she walked, following his instructions, from the main gate to the runway.

Knowing the former tennis champion's legendary speed of foot, his plan was to have one of his colleagues — a sharpshooter with deadly accuracy up to a half-mile distance — fire one small-caliber round into Rebecca's lower leg from a distance of less than 50 yards … a precision pass-through wound at comfortable distance from her upper thigh's femoral artery … one shot expected to result in a "designer wound" which would not in itself be fatal, but which would make escape impossible.

Fedorov planned then to have the van brought onto the runway, where the woman would be thrown into its cargo space. He would then have his men staunch and wrap the leg wound so that she would not bleed out. With a pass-through wound to the calf muscle, nothing else should be required to keep the woman incapacitated, yet alive and alert, for the relatively short period of time he would require.

The sharpshooter, Bogdan Baranov, had asked, "Why do I not just shoot her in the head … or in the heart … why not kill her now?"

Fedorov had replied, "Because I wish to interrogate her … and I wish to see her suffer … and I wish to see her weep and beg for mercy … and I wish to punish her for all she has done to our cause … and I wish then to kill her slowly."

But now, realizing that the woman would not be coming, Fedorov seethed.

He was genuinely surprised. He had been fully confident that Rebecca Clark would do as he had ordered. He had been certain that she would follow to the letter her own strict code of conduct: *My life for yours.*

Now, hidden in the Duxford shadows, a new thought began to form itself. This novel awareness crept upon him gradually … an awareness that this "blueprint of the universe" nonsense might contain subtleties that had never before occurred to him. He tried to dismiss the idea peremptorily.

But the idea gained traction in his brain, bit by bit, until it solidified with a strength that nearly took his breath away. He saw finally that the concept … *My life for yours* … could mean something altogether different from the simple, straightforward, sacrificial concept he had always attached to the idea.

This new thought was radically different … and profoundly disturbing.

Anton Fedorov was not accustomed to being disturbed. He found he did not care for the sensation. He shook his head, as if this might be something he could throw off like an ill-fitting cap.

But the thought stubbornly remained in place.

Could the concept … *My life for yours* … under these conditions, be turned on its head so as to become a threat to *him*? Could the idea be twisted in such a way as to suggest, in this exigency, not that the Clark woman would sacrifice herself in exchange for the Jones girl, but that Rebecca Clark would seek to procure *his* life in exchange for that of SallyBelle Jones, this 15-year-old nonentity?

Had this ridiculous sacrificial idea become some sort of boomerang in which *he* would become the sacrifice? Could this actually mean that the child would be saved, but it would be *he* who would be placed at risk?

Could *My life for yours* really mean, on this night, in this situation, that the two captives — the Jones girl and her father — were being rescued from Chaos Command Central at that very moment, while he, Anton Fedorov, waited helplessly and foolishly for Rebecca Clark to appear at Duxford?

Could it mean somehow that the Rebekka Yahalomin motley would actually be coming for *him*? And if so … coming for him *how*?

Coming for him to take his life? … no, that would be impossible for the Yahalomin … they would not plan a murder … they would not commit murder … but perhaps coming for him in some other sense … coming for him to take away his purpose? Coming for him to take away his reason for being?

Coming for him to take away his reason for being?

So… Rebecca Clark and her people think they can take away Anton Fedorov's *reason for being*. Well … he would demonstrate how ludicrous that idea was.

Did this woman not know who he was? Did she not know *what* he was? Did she not understand what forces he long ago invited to live inside him?

Did she not understand that those forces comprised *his very existence?*

Breathing heavily in his fury, he turned to agent Baranov … the KGB sharpshooter who carried a sniper rifle and who could shatter a teacup at 800 meters…

Through clenched teeth Fedorov hissed, "She thinks she is rescuing the girl tonight, Bogdan, and that she and the girl will now be safe …

"But we know from our MI6 source … from Cobra … that the woman will be driving the teens to the qualifiers' venue tomorrow … this morning. And so, tomorrow afternoon you will activate the sniper's nest on the roof of our former headquarters … the nest we prepared for exactly this eventuality … and you will kill them as they exit the training facility … the first round into Mrs. Clark's heart … the second round into the girl's."

The agent smiled and nodded.

"Yes, Fedorov," said Baranov. "One round into each. I will kill them.

"Two seconds … two dead."

CHAPTER NINE

Friday, 6:30 a.m., three days before the Wimbledon Championships

REBECCA, NOW DRIVING THE FAMILY VOLVO, APPROACHED THE Chambers' home with SallyBelle bouncing excitedly on the front passenger seat beside her. Thomas was waiting at the curb and began waving as the Volvo came into sight. Although he was excited to see SallyBelle, he was nonetheless beset with a sense of dread … a sense that his failure to try to save her from their attackers would prove unforgivable in her eyes, just as it threatened to be in his own.

As the car stopped, SallyBelle leaped out, took three running steps, and jumped into Thomas' outstretched arms, her arms around his neck. Rebecca watched, amused, as the young man's face changed from amazement to concern.

"SallyBelle?" he managed, "What's wrong?

"Why are you …"

But she just squeezed him tighter and planted a noisy kiss on his cheek.

Quick to adjust to this unexpected circumstance, Thomas promptly kissed her back … on the cheek … deciding quickly that, although he understood nothing, his role was to enjoy every second of something he'd hoped for, but doubted would ever happen. SallyBelle Jones was hugging and kissing *him!*

His dread vanished.

When she stepped back, he looked closely at her face.

"You're hurt," he said, his face clouding. "What did they do to you?"

She began her reply, but the teens' concentration on each other was broken by the sound of their mentor's voice.

"Young people," Rebecca called cheerily, "talk in the car.

"We need to get moving."

They quickly piled into the back seat of the Volvo.

Rebecca smiled, thinking she was again in her proper role … serving as chauffeur for two excited BBGs who, on this morning, were seeing each other for the first time since they had been forced to run for their lives 24 hours earlier.

The car pulled away, and SallyBelle, facing Thomas on the back seat, resumed her effort to tell him *everything* … to cover 24 hours of danger, action, and rescue in the 30 minutes she would have before arriving at the courts.

"My face is a mess," she said, words tumbling out, "because a huge man grabbed me off the street and threw me in a van. He landed on top of me and smashed my face into the floor and cracked some of my ribs and pulled a sack over my head and took me to a prison house near Cambridge and put me in a prison cell and …"

Thus, she continued, her rapt audience hanging on her every word. She told him of her desperate efforts to escape her prison-house cell and of her descent from an upper floor by means of a rope she had found in a storage closet. She told him how she had broken into the room where her father was being held and how she found him semi-conscious and how she had heard violent noises from the corridor.

She told him how, when she looked into the hallway, she found that Mrs. Clark and her brother and their friends had broken into the prison house from the side opposite the one down which she had descended, and how they had disabled the guards with throwing knives, and how the guards had been hand-cuffed, and how the guards had been taken somewhere in the woods and tied to trees, and how Mrs. Clark and the others had then gone upstairs to make photographs of documents, and how they had then walked down a long hill, through the trees, helping her unsteady father to walk, eventually to reach Mrs. Clark's brother's Land Rover Five-Door, and how they had helped her dad into the Five-Door and had taken him to an emergency room.

She told him how she had been X-rayed, how the X-rays showed several cracked ribs, how her rib cage had been expertly taped, and how her father had been treated for concussion. She told him how her Mum had arrived at the hospital, and how SallyBelle and Mrs. Clark had taken a cab to Mrs. Clark's brother's home.

She told him of waking after a short sleep and of Mrs. Clark's repairing her messy hair and damaged face to make her more presentable for that day's work at the BBG venue. She talked and she talked and she talked …

Meanwhile, Rebecca drove.

Her route to the qualifiers' venue was circuitous, following neither her own regular route nor those used by Reginald Jones and Horace Chambers.

Rebecca knew that Anton Fedorov … that name SallyBelle had reported and, Rebecca was certain, the name that identified the dreamed face … would by no means be finished with his plans to destroy the great tournament and, according to the documents they had studied from the Chaos garage files, thence to destroy Parliament and eventually to destroy the very spirit of the British people. Fedorov, she was sure, was the Evil she had known for years … the Evil she had been called upon to face repeatedly … the Evil that would persist until it won … or until it was defeated.

Her route took her a full mile past the venue, allowing her to approach from the side opposite the one normally used by BBGs and guests, a side hidden from the Chaos parking garage that loomed only one-quarter mile away. She parked and walked with the two BBGs to the VIP entrance. The security guard recognized Rebecca and quickly unlocked and opened the door for them.

Rebecca located the two BBG directors, reinforced her phone message of the previous morning, and, satisfied that her teens were in the proper hands, hurried back to the Volvo. She intended to be on time for Luke's 8:45 a.m. session at ISP.

If Rebecca could have seen what her protégés were doing as she left the qualifiers' venue, she would have rolled her eyes at the happy stubbornness of the irrepressible SallyBelle Jones. For she had promptly led Thomas into one of the ladies' dressing rooms, squeezed with him into one of the bathroom stalls, lifted her BBG shirt high enough to expose the taping around her lower midriff, and ordered him to strip off the tape that had been affixed by an ER physician overnight.

Thomas did not respond immediately to this stunning development.

He stood, thoroughly nonplussed, looking determinedly at the ceiling.

"Thomas!" she said with some asperity, "I've tried to stoop, the way we'll have to do all day today, and I can't bend over with all this tape around my middle. We'll be bending over a million times; every time a ball is sent our way and every time we have to sprint onto the court to retrieve balls that have gone into the net.

"I can't reach the ends of this tape … I need help …"

"But …"

"Thomas!"

Squinting to avoid seeing her exposed midriff clearly, he began pulling the tape off, his mind a complete muddle. When he had removed several layers of tape and was finally removing tape that adhered to her skin, she winced… he paused … she looked at him impatiently … he continued … and in just 90 seconds, she was completely free of the tape. She pulled her BBG shirt down, looked up at him, rewarded him with her radiant smile, and, yet again, planted a noisy kiss on his cheek.

Surely, thought Thomas, *this is heaven.*

Friday, 8:50 a.m.

Rebecca arrived at the small ISP conference room just five minutes after the meeting had begun. The meeting comprised Rebekka Yahalomin only.

"Rebecca," said Luke to his sister as she entered, "we were just discussing Reginald Jones's condition. His wife phoned Kory this morning to say that the concussion was determined to be severe enough that the hospital plans to keep him overnight. But the physicians expect to allow him to go home tomorrow morning. It sounds as though Reginald might be here at work on Monday."

"Wonderful," she replied. "That's everything we could have hoped."

Luke wanted to begin the session with an overview, and so he summarized what had been learned from all sources … the courier-delivered memoranda, the parking garage files, and the newly photographed files from the Chaos office. He reminded everyone that the Chaos organization, which, according to its own documents, existed to spread confusion, alarm, and terror nationwide, focused first on the series of coordinated attacks on ministers who had attended the Oxford conference the previous April. Then he reviewed the evidence that the Wimbledon Championships, starting in just three days, would be next, then Parliament, then a variety of infrastructure systems throughout the United Kingdom.

He emphasized that the organization's self-proclaimed larger mission was "to destroy every recognizable aspect of ordinary life, first in the U.K., and then around the world." Continuing to read from a memorandum, Luke reminded the group that Chaos intended ultimately "to ruin the U.K. — and then the other democracies — spiritually, politically, financially, and, in selected cases, physically." And, to that end, they intended to destroy Rebekka Yahalomin "early in the process."

He looked up at the group. Heads nodded solemnly.

"We now have hard evidence also," he continued, "that Chaos is being fed information by MI6, presumably by one of the members of Graham Roberts-Holm's three-person subcommittee. That person is code-named 'Cobra' in some of the documents. We had inferred that that was the case when it became apparent that Reginald's attackers knew his exact route on Thursday morning.

"Now we see it in writing.

"And finally," said Luke, "thanks to young Miss Jones, we have a name to go with Rebecca's dreamed face of the enemy ... that of Anton Fedorov. We assume that it was he who was in command of the van that arrived at Duxford last night for the purpose of taking my sister into their custody. And, since I do not wish to gloss over anything here, let me note that Fedorov's purpose in capturing Rebecca would unquestionably have been first to torture and then to murder her."

Again, he stopped and looked around the conference table. Several were shaking their heads in dismay at the horrifying thought. Luke saw that Jack McGriff wished to speak.

He nodded toward McGriff.

"As I was handling the documents that we photographed last night," began McGriff, "I tried to get a sense of the content as I went along, even though I couldn't stop and read anything carefully. I 'saw' much of the material without it truly registering on my consciousness. But this morning, thinking about all that again, I suddenly remembered something that may be relevant.

"I remembered a passage in one memorandum that mentioned, just in passing, that what it called 'New York City money' had been funneled to Chaos to 'purchase the cooperation' of an employee of MI6. And the more I considered that … the more I turned it over in my mind … the more I wondered if that reference to 'Cobra' might not link to the New York Russian Mafia."

A lengthy silence followed.

After several minutes of studied concentration, Jaakov Adelman rose and began to pace around the room, unconsciously mirroring one of Rebecca's own habits.

"Maybe we've been wrong," offered Adelman as he circled the table, "to assume that the Russian Mafia in New York was fully destroyed by our actions — and, of course, the actions of the FBI and other agencies — in seizing the Mafia leaders and their funds … just two weeks ago, was it?

"Maybe one or more of those leaders escaped the net, perhaps taking at least one funding source with him, and …"

"Hey!" cried Belton, interrupting his detective agency partner, "D' y' think this Fedorov guy is a refugee from New York? … a dirtbag who managed t' get outta there, crossed th' pond, and landed on his feet right here in London?"

Matt Clark jumped into the discussion.

"And *bought* Graham Roberts-Holm's traitorous cooperation?" he asked incredulously, "so that Chaos would have inside information on anything our group … and Rebecca specifically … might be thinking and planning?"

Adelman, still pacing, said, "Yes. That would explain how this Fedorov person could, from what we can guess, gather to himself enough money, influence, and person-power to launch coordinated attacks on ministers throughout the country, firebomb Rebecca and Matt's home, abduct the Joneses in broad daylight, establish contracts with bomb makers who specialize in plastic-based explosives designed to be undetectable by metal-sensitive equipment at the All England Club and at Parliament, accumulate and deliver tons of explosives to target sites …"

"That's *gotta* be th' story," interrupted Belton yet again. "Fedorov must a' come here from New York with a ton a' Mafia money an' he jumped in right here with both feet … collected a bunch a' KGB scumbags around 'im an' got busy throwin' monkey wrenches everywhere he can find somethin' t' throw at …"

There was a thoughtful pause before Luke broke in to say, "Before we go any further down this road, let me inform everyone that my sister told us … Matt, Kory, and me … at breakfast this morning, before she left to pick up the Chambers youngster … that she *dreamed* … at 4 a.m. today. We don't have details, because Rebecca was literally running out the door with SallyBelle Jones in tow, but now …"

He turned his eyes to Rebecca.

Her eyes were down, praying.

All waited patiently.

She looked up and smiled.

"We seem always to get help when it is most needed," she said. "Let me give you what I was sent at four this morning.

"I did not awaken Matt or SallyBelle, who was sleeping on a cot in Kory and Luke's guest bedroom — our temporary quarters — because Matt and SallyBelle had just gotten to sleep a few minutes before. So, I didn't repeat this dream to anyone … until now. I hope this will be accurate and complete.

"The dream was, as once before, a stationary vision. No movement. No changes. Just a picture, presented in the usual way … the vision consuming the whole of the dreamed field … obviously, from the start, not a 'regular' dream …

"The vision was … as before … of the house we are calling Chaos' new headquarters — this aging structure that was first found by Mr. Belton and his NYPD associates years ago … the building to which the Joneses were taken yesterday morning after they were abducted from the streets of London …

"But this vision, unlike the previous, was of the *underground* of the Chaos headquarters. The above-ground portion of the house was visible, but only at the upper edge of my dreamed field. Most of what was presented to me was underground, and it seemed to run the full length of the ground floor above it …

"The 'message' that was carried wordlessly in my dream was this … we must get inside that basement … and quickly … because it is filled … absolutely filled … with electronic and, I assume, telephonic equipment. *Filled*, from one end to the other, with switchboard-style machines …

"This Chaos underground facility didn't appear to be staffed. It appeared as a complex of highly automated machines that operate without moment-to-moment human direction. No doubt, there are technicians, but there was no hint of any need to *operate* the machines from moment to moment and hour to hour.

"After perhaps half a minute, the vision faded. I awoke … as before … *not* perspiring … *not* enervated … just clear on what I'd been given. I replayed the vision in my mind, thanked God for helping us yet again, and fell asleep immediately.

"That was all."

She turned her eyes to her brother, but then had another thought.

"Oh …" she said, "I should mention that my quick overview of that dream was offered this morning at breakfast, as Luke said, but not to SallyBelle. I took some breakfast to her in our guest room, explaining to her that we needed a short business meeting over breakfast. She seemed unconcerned … just hungry."

She turned her eyes to her brother again and nodded.

He returned her nod and looked around the table.

"Thoughts, anyone?" he said.

"Luke," said Rebecca after a moment, "let me suggest a few minutes of silence. I'd like everyone to spend several minutes thinking about the fact that the entire underground of a large structure is filled with electronic and telephonic equipment, and is apparently unstaffed, and thus, presumably, automated.

"In silence, new thoughts may emerge.

"I have, as yet, had no time at all to think about what this vision means … and I, for one, badly need a few thinking-minutes …"

There was no need for comment. The thinking-minutes began.

The silence grew much longer than Rebecca expected; for more than 15 minutes, no one stirred. But finally … there was a throat-clearing sound from Jaakov Adelman, who had taken his seat when Rebecca had begun.

Luke nodded in his direction.

"Jaakov?" he said.

Adelman straightened in his chair and began.

"I've spent my thinking-minutes," he said haltingly, looking down at the table surface in intense concentration, "focused on … um … on the … ah … the *brokerage* function … um … the *brokerage* function of Chaos."

He looked up to see if others were following.

He thought not.

"Do you remember," he explained, "that in our Wednesday early-morning meeting ... when we got back here from our photo session of the files on the garage's fourth floor ... I noted that X-A-O-C" — he spelled the letters — "speaks of itself as a 'brokerage organization for the facilitation of terrorism?'

"Remember that?"

Nods of assent.

"I noted," Adelman continued, "that they seek to put bomb throwers in touch with bomb makers, assassins in touch with weapons dealers and experts in clandestine murder, bank robbers in touch with safe crackers ... that sort of thing?"

More nods around the room.

"Chaos appears, I said then, to be a multi-faceted, full-service criminal enterprise that has Middle Eastern origins, but has developed into something global. And we seem to be facing the United Kingdom branch, which may, in fact, be the spearhead."

Adelman looked around the table again.

"You remember?" he asked.

Nods from some. Some murmured "Yes."

"I also said then," Adelman continued, "that Chaos collects information and sells it to anyone who will pay. And I said that it was hard to determine the size of the organization, because so many of the involved personnel are simply carrying out a particular contract ... often a one-time service contract."

He paused again.

"Given all that," he said, "the only conclusion I can draw from Rebecca's newest message is that her dreamed underground ... her dreamed automated and telephonic equipment ... all of that must comprise the physical mechanism by which the brokerage functions are to be carried out."

He paused again to allow his statement to be processed.

"In my years with Mossad," continued Adelman, "we sought to automate *everything* that could be automated.

"And I've been thinking that the Chaos brokerage function and its attendant equipage would have to be *more* extensive and *more* sophisticated than anything we were able to develop in Israel back then ... more than a decade ago.

"Something this complex ... something this necessarily *fast*... something this elaborate ...cannot be carried out by means of a handful of employees answering

telephones and then telephoning other people, and then laboriously beginning
to put the action components together in ways that can work smoothly."

"And then working out billing arrangements by hand," interjected Kory.

"Right. That, too," agreed Adelman.

"Their system," he continued, "for matching weapons of terror … explosives, in this case … with targets of terror … absolutely *must* be automated.

"With Mossad, back then, we never imagined anything like this," he concluded, "but Rebecca's new report makes it clear. She has seen the *fact* of the
automation, and she has seen the *location* of the automation. It is our responsibility now to destroy the mechanism … to make it impossible for the terrorism
to be carried out, starting with the Championships on Monday … just three days
from now.

"We have 72 hours."

After several moments of stunned silence, Luke spoke.

"That was brilliant, Jaakov," he said. "Absolutely brilliant.

"Has anyone formulated an idea," he continued, "or a set of ideas, that either
contradicts what Jaakov just offered … or surpasses it … or renders it moot?"

"Y' gotta be kiddin' me, Luke," said Belton immediately. "When I invited
Jaakov t' partner with me in th' New York agency, I knew I'd picked th' smartest
guy on th' planet. He just showed ya' how quick he is. Nobody coulda come up
with that in 15 minutes except my big-brain partner here …

"Know what I mean?

"Hm?"

Adelman demurred.

"Actually, Sidney," he said, "I'm guessing several people in this room formed
a similar set of ideas during those thinking-minutes, including Rebecca herself,
but now … thanks to your big mouth … none of them is going to admit they did,
because you've turned me into something *weird* … and they don't want to place
themselves in this special category of *weirdness* you've invented for me.

"You're a terrible person, Sidney Belton … something your wife has been
pointing out to me since the moment I got mixed up with you."

Smiles. Heads bobbing.

Then Matt Clark.

"Okay, everyone," he began. "We agree, do we not, that Jaakov has 'nailed it' — another Sidney Belton phrase — and I've started to think, even while Jaakov was giving us his conclusions, that we've got to get Kory into that basement *tonight* ...

"This is Friday morning," Matt continued, "and the Championships start on Monday. It seems to me that the Chaos automated systems are going to be rolling at top speed this weekend, organizing the delivery of undetectable plastic explosives to the individuals that Chaos has on contract ..."

He looked smilingly at Kory.

"If we can get our techno-wizard ... Mrs. Manguson here ... into that basement tonight for an extended period of time ... along with some of ISP's state-of-the-art diagnostic instruments ..."

"But Matt," interrupted Kory quickly, "don't you think that the explosives are likely to be in the hands of dozens of contract people already? Don't you think deliveries have already been made, probably over the last several weeks?"

More silence. Then Adelman again.

"Kory," he said, "if you and I can both gain access to that basement tonight, I'm thinking we might be able to address even that issue effectively. Even if the explosives are going to be placed, or perhaps are already placed, all around the Tournament site — you know, in the dressing rooms and in the spectator venues and, let's say, even under the elevated chairs of some of the umpires for the matches — someone will need to trigger the explosions remotely."

"But Jaakov," Kory objected immediately, "why could the explosives not be set on timing devices? Why would they require any further human action at all?

"If the entire network is automated, as you suggest, why would anyone need to trigger the explosives remotely?"

Rebecca broke in.

"Kory," she said softly, "I need to remind you ... and everyone ... of a feature of my dreamed face ... the original dream-message I was given ... the dreamed face we now think must be that of Anton Fedorov. In that first vision, as I watched, you may recall that a hand gradually materialized.

"That hand was holding an implement ... and although the image was not sharp ... not detailed ... that implement was almost certainly a handset ... but not just a telephone ... it was a phone that somehow, in my dreaming state, presented itself also as a weapon ... a weapon of huge destructive power."

"Oh," said Kory, "I do remember, Rebecca."

"This Anton Fedorov," Rebecca continued, "a man who, I am convinced, embodies the same force that has presented itself to the Yahalomin over and over through the years, will be compelled to *control* the outcomes ... for this level of Evil, we know from experience, requires *control* ... this level of Evil cannot tolerate the uncertainty of, as you reasonably suggest, reliance on timing devices for the explosives. With timing devices, the explosives could be set off at a time when a given dressing room was empty, or when a particular match had been halted because of weather, or ... please think about this ... when the royal box was completely unoccupied.

"The uncertainties of timing devices would be unacceptable to this man."

Rebecca paused, thinking.

"Furthermore," she continued after a moment, "Mr. Fedorov will assume that we do not know him ... that neither we nor law enforcement nor the intelligence agencies will recognize him if he enters the All England Club on Monday morning as the tournament gets underway. And so, I've little doubt, when the time looks right to him, or to the people working for him, he will move to one of the phone booths somewhere on the grounds and dial a particular number.

"That number ... I feel certain ... but this will be something for Kory to try and confirm ... will connect to the telephonic equipment that was shown me in my early morning vision. When the number connects, the automated equipment will trigger explosions all over the grounds of the All England Club.

"A completely automated response.

"And people will die.

"The explosives that Mr. Fedorov's contracted associates and employees will have planted," she concluded, "will kill athletes — some of them internationally known — their trainers, their coaches, their family members, the spectators, members of the media ... and, assuredly, if he waits until the royal box is occupied, members of the royal family and their invited guests."

She paused and closed her eyes.

The room was silent.

She looked up.

"We do not yet know," Rebecca finally added, "exactly who … or what … Anton Fedorov is. I say 'who or what' to acknowledge that our chief enemies in the past have at times been so consumed by Evil … having invited ultimate Evil into themselves … that they were able to inflict weakness, pain, and suffering simply by proximity.

"I think that eventually this man will want to get physically close to us … almost certainly physically close *to me* … but for now, on Monday, in order to inflict maximum damage, confusion, and terror … he will operate remotely.

"He intends, you know, to devastate the *soul* of the country," added Rebecca, her words placing an exclamation point on her monologue. "He intends to confuse and corrupt the heart, first, of *this* country … and then, eventually … to confuse and corrupt the hearts of democracies far beyond this one.

"He intends to spread his unique terror throughout the entire world."

After a moment, Reverend Jack McGriff added the postscript.

"As the greatest Evil has sought to do … always … from the beginning."

At the conclusion of the early-morning Yahalomin session, and following a short break, a four-person action-plan unit assembled in Luke's office. The group comprised Kory, the tech expert; Luke and Jaakov, veteran spearheads of the expected Friday night action; and Sid, the senior strategic and tactical planning expert.

Luke began.

"Before we get into details regarding tonight's raid on the Chaos underground," he said, "I need to hear your thoughts on Graham Roberts-Holm and his MI6 subcommittee. He has left four voice mails on my office phone since yesterday morning, and another two on Kory's and my home phone.

"I need to tell him *something.*"

Belton responded immediately.

"Tell 'im y' don't trust 'im … an' tell 'im why, Luke. He's either a mole fer Chaos, or one of his people is a mole fer Chaos … tell 'im th' Chaos dirtbags knew exactly where Jones an' his daughter were gonna be yesterday mornin', an' that that intel had t' come from him or from somebody in his unit.

"Tell 'im he's th' *enemy* … just as much as th' Chaos dirtbags are th' enemy. No need t' tiptoe around it.

"Know what I mean?

"Hm?"

Luke nodded thoughtfully.

Then shook his head.

"Sid," he said, looking the detective in the eye, "it's not Graham himself."

Luke dropped his eyes, thinking of how to explain.

"My sister and my wife have taught me," he continued, "how to trust the *feel* of a person. And when I think of how Graham and I have come to know each other … and to know each other's families … over the years …"

He shook his head again.

"That just doesn't work for me … the notion that Graham himself would betray us … would betray me … would betray Rebecca … no … he's not the traitor here.

"The mole has to be one of the two people he introduced to us … one of the two people on his MI6 subcommittee."

Kory quickly inserted herself into the discussion.

"Mr. Belton," she said carefully, "I know I'm speaking about my husband, and so my thoughts are suspect on this point …"

Belton interrupted.

"You've got a better head on yer shoulders than anybody else in th' room, ma'am … an' yer husband knows it. Just say it … whatever ya' got.

"Just say."

She smiled.

"But you just told us, Mr. Belton, that Jaakov is the smartest person in the *world*. How did I become the smartest person in the room?"

"I meant he's th' smartest *male* person. Compared t' you, he's a dim bulb."

Belton cackled at his own humor. Then he turned his intent black eyes back to Kory, his lopsided grin still in place.

"So … ma'am … just say."

"Well," she said finally, "I suggest that we allow Luke to speak with Mr. Roberts-Holm and, in that conversation, to make the decision on our behalf."

She looked searchingly at Luke, then back to Belton.

"I agree with you, Mr. Belton," she continued, "that Luke should confront this longtime friend of his by challenging him regarding that vile kidnapping of Reginald and his 15-year-old daughter … but once Luke issues the challenge and hears the response from Mr. Roberts-Holm … let's let Luke decide.

"He may decide to tell Mr. Roberts-Holm that we will need to go forward without involvement from MI6, simply because he does not find MI6 worthy of our trust any longer … or he may decide to urge Mr. Roberts-Holm to ferret out the … um … mole … and then to handle the situation as he sees fit.

"We may *need* MI6, Mr. Belton.

"You know … we have needed intelligence agencies before.

"Let's allow Luke to work on it."

Belton, a willing listener, quickly acceded, and from there the discussion turned to that evening's raid on the Chaos building and its underground complex, as revealed in Rebecca's dream. Adelman provided the key tactical observation.

"As Kory and I approached the building at midnight," he said, "we noticed, near the window we entered, one of those long-defunct coal chutes … remember those? Those structures the coal trucks used to dump coal into basements? The thing had a small padlock, but Luke's bolt cutters will make short work of that.

"That's our access point tonight."

Adelman paused, thinking, then continued.

"If we find guards outside the building, we'll deal with them first, but once we have incapacitated them, we can get into the basement in seconds through the coal chute. Once down there with the equipment, Kory can get started on her tasks."

After that, the plan shaped itself quickly.

Belton emphasized to Kory the importance of her using her electronic analytical devices not only to identify the automated signals connecting deliveries of explosives to individual terrorists, but to redirect the final "go" signal — presumably to be sent by Anton Fedorov — in such a way that the whole system would be disabled permanently. She agreed with his suggestion immediately, and, over the next two hours, Kory, with input from the others, gradually developed on paper a set of schematics that she, assisted by Luke and Jaakov, would implement that night in stepwise fashion.

At length, Kory summarized the resulting program and sequence for the others' evaluation. She looked up at each of them.

"Alright, then?" she said.

They nodded.

Luke smiled broadly at his wife.

"Well then, Mrs. Manguson," he said proudly, "it will be in your hands."

As Luke then began to discuss details regarding his wife's checkout of an assortment of ISP electronic devices that afternoon, Belton waved his hand to indicate that he had yet another issue.

"Yes, Sid?" said Luke.

"Somethin' else, people," said the detective. "I've been thinkin' about th' distance from th' Chaos parkin' garage t' th' qualifiers' venue where Mrs. Clark is gonna pick up th' kids this afternoon … it might be a quarter-mile or so … right, Luke?"

Luke nodded.

"Yes … I'd say so."

"An' this is th' last day of th' qualifiers' tournament, right?"

Luke nodded again.

"An' this'll be th' last time Mrs. Clark will be pickin' up th' kids there, right?"

Luke and Adelman looked at each other and their eyes widened.

"Uh oh," said Luke.

"Indeed," echoed Adelman.

"What?" said Kory.

"That's *easy* sniper-rifle distance, dear," said Luke.

The four sat silent for several moments.

Then Adelman sat up sharply in his chair.

"And I know the sniper."

"You mean they may try to shoot Rebecca and the kids this afternoon," said Kory, "in full view of everybody there for the final BBG practice?"

"Exactly," said Luke and Adelman at the same time.

Decisions on action to counter *that* issue came quickly, each regarding the solution as obvious, and the foursome dispersed.

As Kory was entering the stairwell to climb one floor from her husband's office level to her own, she encountered Marie Campbell and Jack McGriff descending the steps, headed for a stroll around the block. They stopped for a moment.

"Did you decide anything we ought to know, Kory?" said McGriff.

"Well … no … nothing about tonight's raid on the Chaos headquarters," replied Kory, "but of interest … to us all … was Mr. Belton's pointing out that the Wimbledon qualifiers' venue is just a quarter mile, or so, from the parking garage where Chaos has had its HQ up until now. Jaakov immediately connected that fact to his knowledge of a sharpshooter — a sniper — a man whom he actually knows … apparently one of the KGB agents.

"He and Luke are thinking that, since this is Rebecca's last afternoon to pick up the two BBGs from the venue, Anton Fedorov might order this sniper guy to kill Rebecca, and probably SallyBelle Jones, too, since Fedorov probably resents her having escaped what she called the 'prison house,' and since he ordered her to be executed when he left the Chaos headquarters for Duxford."

"What are Jaakov and Luke going to do?" asked Marie.

"They're going to handle it," said Kory.

Marie and Jack continued to street level and began a leisurely stroll around the long block on which the ISP office building and parking lots were situated. This was not "exercise" for them; this was time alone to talk about where they now found themselves … as a couple … as members of the Yahalomin … as foreign participants in extra-legal activities they could neither control nor fully understand.

"Jack," Marie began, "what do you think Jaakov and Luke are going to do about the possibility of this sniper person … a gunman trying to kill Rebecca and the girl this afternoon? Why not just get in touch with the Metro Police or Scotland Yard or any of the others who are equipped to handle such a thing?

"After all," she continued, "Mr. Belton seems to have contacts with *everybody*, in both countries, who could help in that way."

McGriff laughed softly.

"Actually, Marie," he said, "Mr. Belton has contacts with everybody in a *dozen* countries who could handle such a thing … not just the U.S. and England."

They walked together in thoughtful silence for several moments, then McGriff attempted an answer to his fiancée's question.

"I would think, Marie, that there are several ingredients in their reluctance to ask anyone outside the Yahalomin to handle *any* of this. First, there is the uncertainty regarding Mr. Roberts-Holm and his MI6 people ... but beyond that, there is the issue of dream-based data ... you know ... Rebecca's original identification of that parking garage as temporary headquarters for the Chaos group ... then the thoroughly illegal search and photographing of all those files in that HQ ... and now her dreamed focus on the basement of the permanent Chaos headquarters near Cambridge ...

"But entirely aside from the visions-as-data-source problem, I just think that Luke and Jaakov trust themselves more than any outside unit to stop this ... this presumed sniper ... even though they have no power to arrest him."

He looked down at her as they continued to walk slowly around the three-quarter-mile perimeter of the ISP grounds, waiting for her response. After a moment, she looked up at him, her sad brown eyes belying the happiness she felt in being alone with the man she loved and would marry, and, almost as powerful, her joy in having been swept up in the godly mission of Rebekka Yahalomin.

"That has really been the story from the first, hasn't it, Jack?" she said. "From what I gather, each year of the Yahalomin's existence has been marked by dreamed threats ... dreamed by Rebecca ...

"And then those were always followed by the realization that there would be no workable way to involve law enforcement, given the Source of the information. No realistic way to engage outside organizations.

"Right?"

He thought for a moment, then answered.

"Mostly right ... occasional exceptions," said McGriff.

"But there is also the fact," he continued, "that the intelligence agencies ... CIA, MI6, Mossad ... and now, even the Soviet KGB ... have eventually become aware that Rebekka Yahalomin, as Mossad originally named them ... named us ... had a Source for information that was at times better than anything they could develop using their own approaches. So, we have this small subcommittee at MI6 devoted entirely to the study of 'unexplained and unexplainable data,' and there are, it seems, comparable units at CIA and, no doubt, at Mossad ..."

"And now at KBG," added Marie.

"Yes," he agreed again.

They resumed their thoughtful stroll, McGriff now taking Marie's small hand in his oversized one, a public gesture that the two had quickly come to regard as right and natural and comfortable. They turned the first corner of their perimeter walk and entered a tree-lined residential area, the homes across the street from ISP property marked by tidy, flower-filled yards and well-tended, white-painted wooden fences.

Marie soon looked up again and asked, "Are you worried, Jack, about the magnitude of all this? ... about the ... the *reach* of the Chaos organization ... you know ... its involvement with KGB and maybe with MI6 somehow ... and with all these explosives makers and ... and with their explosives-distribution agents ... and with their sophisticated, automated equipment that apparently can transmit instructions and ... um ... well ... *triggers* for those explosives ... and ..."

"Wait, Marie," he interrupted. "I know exactly what you mean, but it won't do us any good to think like that. Our people ... our Rebekka Yahalomin people ... have been in far worse situations than this, as I understand their history ... and you see how they are ... you see how they respond.

"They don't really seem to worry about what they face. And they certainly don't obsess about it. They just deal with it all as it comes."

He paused, thinking, then continued.

"It seems that they just pray ... then they act ... then they move on.

"To them, it's straightforward. Do you know what I mean?"

"Yes, I do ... I really do ... but I can't help but think about the fact that they have all been wounded, Jack ... including some serious injuries. Some of those wounds could have been fatal. They just weren't.

"Jaakov and Luke have both been shot ... Mr. Belton was once beaten nearly to death and still walks with a cane ... Rebecca has that awful facial scar ..."

McGriff turned, grasped Marie by her small shoulders, and pulled her into him. He enveloped her in his long, muscular arms, pressed her into his still-too-generous belly, and kissed the top of her head, his lips lingering in her clean-smelling brown hair. He felt her nod against his chest. And faintly, he heard her muffled reply.

"I know, Jack ... I know.

"I'll stop."

He smiled.

CHAPTER TEN

THE EMBRACE CONTINUED FOR LONG MOMENTS. BUT FINALLY, McGriff felt a stirring from her and he relaxed his arms. Marie looked up, inviting a kiss.

They kissed.

They smiled their shared understanding to each other, each lost in the other's eyes. Then they turned reluctantly and resumed.

The second corner of the rectangular block was some 80 yards away, marking a minor intersection. Some 20 yards from that corner stood a small bus shelter, several people standing in its shade as they awaited the next conveyance. Even at that distance, McGriff quickly alerted to a disheveled figure that stepped purposefully from the shelter and onto the walkway. The figure immediately faced the two of them and began striding in their direction.

McGriff could see that the figure was stooped, yet not apparently from age. The man appeared, as the distance between them rapidly diminished, to be in his late 30s, but possibly older. He wore a light brown sport coat with patched elbows, wrinkled corduroy trousers despite the warmth of the midsummer London day, and a pair of brown loafers of a sort that McGriff saw often in the U.S., though rarely in England. The man's dark hair was shoulder length, tangled, and possibly dirty. He appeared not to have shaved in several days.

McGriff automatically touched his chest, feeling through his black "priestly sport coat" for the Beretta 9mm he still carried as a part-time CIA employee, his carry permit for England having been arranged by Sid Belton for the six members of the Yahalomin contingent who had served in their nation's military and/

or intelligence agencies. He squeezed Marie's elbow to indicate he wanted her to stop.

She did, only then noticing the man, who continued his brisk pace toward them. He was now only 30 yards away. And closing.

McGriff stepped in front of Marie and waited, his eyes fixed on the intent, brooding face of the unkempt stranger. The stranger, for his part, locked eyes with McGriff. Both men appeared expressionless to the other.

When the stranger's distance shrank to 15 feet, he stopped and reached toward the inside of his sport coat. In an eyeblink, McGriff drew the 9mm, causing the stranger to freeze, his hand inches from his sport coat's chest-level opening.

After a moment of chilled silence, the muzzle of the Beretta staring him in the face, the man spoke.

"Monsieur McGriff," he said in a raspy, French-accented voice, "please rest assured that I mean no harm to you … nor to Madame Campbell."

As he spoke Marie's name, he bowed to her from the waist. The gesture was both graceful and practiced, unexpected characteristics in one whose bearing was so slouched, whose attire was so slovenly, and whose personal hygiene appeared to be so lacking. From the 15-foot distance, the days-old beard appeared to McGriff to be patchy, the result of neglect, rather than a misguided effort to enhance the masculinity of his appearance.

The man's hand had not moved from the position that had led McGriff to draw his weapon, even during his deep bow to Marie. Now he opened his hand toward McGriff in a gesture that asked silently for permission to continue the movement.

McGriff nodded.

"Carefully," said McGriff, not lowering the weapon.

The man slowly drew from an interior coat pocket a small identification folder. He allowed the folder to drop open, displaying a photo ID. From 15 feet, McGriff could not read the name, nor could he see the photo clearly.

"My name is Louis Bois," the man said carefully.

He then moved slowly toward McGriff, still holding his ID in front of him.

"I am," he continued, "an investigative journalist with *The New York Times'* London Bureau," he said, "and I am hoping that you and Madame Campbell will allow me to speak with you, just for five minutes."

McGriff gestured for the man to step closer and patted the self-described journalist down with his left hand, still holding the 9mm in his right, although lowering its muzzle to his side. Satisfied, McGriff returned the weapon to its CIA-issued shoulder holster and said, "Why, exactly, would we allow that?"

Bois returned the ID to its interior coat pocket and began his response.

"Monsieur," he said, "I fear this will sound to you somewhat rude, but my answer is this. We are going to publish a story about you ... both of you ... and about the Rebekka Yahalomin ... and would like the story to be as accurate as possible.

"We fear that, unless you permit us to give you the outline of the story, and to ask you to comment and correct the facts, the story will contain inaccuracies. Given the dangerous situation in which you ... and the Wimbledon contestants and spectators ... and members of the royal family ... all find themselves ... we fear the consequences of the slightest inaccuracy.

"As we are all aware, the tournament begins just three days from today. Our story must run tomorrow ... or Sunday... at the latest."

McGriff stepped aside, no longer shielding Marie from the stranger, and turned his head to look down at her. He raised his eyebrows in question.

She first looked up at her fiancé, **but then turned immediately to Bois.**

"How is it," she said, "that you know anything at all about us? Where does your information come from? And why would you want to speak with Jack and me, rather than with the principals in the group? Why not Rebecca herself? Or her brother?

"Explain, *s'il vous plait.*"

Bois smiled at her use of the French phrase, spoken perfectly.

"The *Times* has many sources worldwide, Madame Campbell," he said, "and I cannot reveal most of them to you.

"But I can say," he continued, "that some of your ... activities ... are public knowledge ... at least 'public' for those of us who want ... or need ... to know.

"*Par exemple,*" he said, "the FBI raid on the New York City Russian Mafia, only days ago, was not secret in the least, nor was the FBI's confiscation of a great deal of the Mafia's illegally obtained money. And I had only to speak with two of my closest ... um ... *confidantes* ... within the FBI to learn of the critical role played by Rebekka Yahalomin in that astonishing takedown of the seemingly all-powerful New York City Mafia and its numerous allies and co-conspirators.

"Further," he continued, "we have developed evidence that the FBI did not succeed in confiscating *all* of the Russian money. We know that at least some of that money has been used to pay someone within MI6 to *inform your adversaries* about Yahalomin plans and activities. We are almost certain, for example, that that money induced an MI6 operative to disclose exactly where Monsieur Reginald Jones and his daughter were likely to be, on the morning on which they were kidnapped, an incident that was reported in all the local newspapers.

"And still further," he said, not pausing, "we know that certain Christian ministers have been attacked and beaten in their own churches …

"And we know that Rebecca and Matthew Clark's home here in London was firebombed … a fact presumably related to Rebekka Yahalomin's culpability, in the eyes of leaders in the Russian Mafia, the Soviet KGB, and others of influence, in taking down the New York City operation.

"And still further, if I may," he said, now speaking rapidly as he brought forward fact after fact to bolster his response to Marie's question, "we know that Monsieur Jones is now in hospital … no longer a hostage … and that his daughter is, even as we speak, participating in BBG practice at the qualifiers' venue here in the city."

Turning his face now to McGriff, Bois said, smiling again at his own investigative efficiency, "And we know, Monsieur McGriff, that you have been in the employ of the CIA for several years now, helping to recruit … ah … I believe 'talent' is the word … for that organization's clandestine operations around the globe.

"Thus, your possession of the 9mm firearm with which you have just chosen, somewhat rudely, to threaten me."

McGriff and Marie stood silent. They were genuinely impressed by the extent of Bois' knowledge and apparent understanding of the facts he had recited. One of those facts — the suggestion that Russian Mafia money had been used to bribe an MI6 employee to inform on Yahalomin members and their associates — was, though it was something that their colleagues had suspected, an interesting confirmation of their speculation on that subject.

After several moments of silence, McGriff probed.

"Monsieur Bois," he said carefully, "given all that you have just said, what more could you possibly need to know in order to print your story?"

Bois opened his mouth to reply, but Marie held up her hand.

"And please, monsieur," she said, "answer my original question: why would you wish to speak to Jack and me, rather than to the principals in our group?"

Bois smiled again, nodding his appreciation to her for her persistence.

"As to your question, madame," replied Bois, "the principals in your group will not speak to us. We have tried many times. They do not deign to reply at all. They simply ignore us. They seem to regard themselves as … um … separate … separate from the world of media and popular understanding of what they do and how they conduct their operations … especially … how they manage to conduct successful incursions, time after time, into the danger-filled world of crime and corruption.

"We would be delighted to speak with them. They will not allow it."

Bois paused to consider the other question.

He turned his face again to McGriff.

"And as to your question, monsieur," he continued, "in addition to my earlier explanation … that we wish to be certain that we have the facts … and to know whether or not you have other facts to add … the truth is that we do *not* know enough to print the story and to have it generate anything other than more questions … many of which we cannot possibly answer…

"We fear that an incomplete story, of the sort we would presently be able to publish, would accomplish nothing."

He paused, thinking, then added, "We fear the present story would accomplish nothing other than, perhaps, to generate a sense of widespread panic in the U.K. Our present story, we must admit, can do nothing to stop the perpetrators … *whom we cannot identify.* We do not know who they are.

"In its present form, our story would be an indulgence on our part.

"Nothing more. An exercise in futility."

There was a pause.

McGriff then asked, knowing the question would strike Bois as cynical.

"Are we to conclude that you *actually* care, monsieur," he said, "and that your news organization cares … one way or another … whether your story is accurate and complete, and, beyond that, whether the story generates, as you say, a sense of panic in the population?

"Are you and your organization truly concerned, one way or the other, about reportorial accuracy … or do not sensationalist stories and newspaper sales comprise one of your primary goals ... and, if that is the case, is not 'panic in the U.K.' an outcome that would simply boost your sales still further?

"I find it hard to take seriously your high-minded words about a story that would be incomplete ... that cannot identify organizations or individuals who have been behind the beatings, kidnappings, or destruction of the Clarks' home ..."

McGriff paused, searching for his main point.

And then finding it.

"You've said, monsieur, that your story needs to be published prior to Wimbledon to avert danger to athletes, spectators, the royal family, and others. What danger are you talking about? And where does information about such danger come from, Monsieur Bois? How is *that* information, as you say, 'public knowledge'?"

Bois smiled sheepishly, his eyes skidding away from McGriff's.

"Ah ... you have caught me, monsieur ... the fact is that I have sources within the Soviet embassy here in London, some of whom are on close terms with certain KGB operatives. There is a strong rumor that a KGB-affiliated organization will attempt an attack during the tournament. We do not know what such an organization might be, and we do not have information regarding the nature of such an attack.

"We do not know if this is to be a gunman ... or many gunmen ... or someone with a knife ... or someone with a hand grenade ... we do not know.

"But, monsieur and madame ... if you *do* have such information ... about the nature of such an organization ... and about the nature of such an attack ... and if we can publish ... just think of the lives we could save.

"After all," Bois concluded, "if the rumor is true, there is nothing you can do to stop such an attack, regardless of its nature. You will require the assistance of Scotland Yard, or of MI6, or of MI5, or perhaps of the Metropolitan Police.

"Our story, if it is a *complete* story, will alert those who can take effective action. Our story will save lives. Our story will accomplish what you cannot.

"You see this, yes?"

The couple shook their heads in tandem.

"No," they both said at the same time.

"*Non?*" said Bois, incredulous.

"No," repeated McGriff, while Marie continued to shake her head.

"The fact is, monsieur," said McGriff, "that only Rebekka Yahalomin is equipped to assess whatever violence may be intended, either at Wimbledon or beyond Wimbledon… and perhaps far beyond Wimbledon. Rebekka Yahalomin is uniquely positioned … uniquely *chosen* … to understand these forces, to *anticipate* the steps these forces intend to take, and to take action to stop them … or, in some cases, to *arrange* the actions that are needed to stop them — as was the case recently in America, with the FBI, something you just noted.

"We are not allowed to explain this to you … but those are the facts.

"Now," concluded McGriff, "if you will excuse us, Monsieur Bois, Marie and I need to return to our people. We will summarize your observations and requests. If they see a need to communicate with you, they will no doubt be in touch."

"May we, in that case, have your business card?"

The journalist's shoulders slumped.

He shook his head in disappointment as he dug out one of his cards.

"*Oui,*" he said unhappily.

As he passed the card to McGriff, Bois looked him earnestly in the eye.

"*Va avec Dieu,*" he said sadly. "*Va avec Dieu.*"

"Thank you, Louis," replied McGriff. "That's exactly what we intend to do."

The Yahalomin assembled in the small conference room immediately upon the couple's return to the ISP building. The session was brief.

After listening quietly to Marie and McGriff's report, the group agreed, and with very little discussion, that, first, if Louis Bois and his London Bureau went ahead with their story, either Saturday or Sunday, it would be MI6 which would face scrutiny and exposure, not the Yahalomin. Bois' disclosure of a New York City Russian Mafia connection with MI6 would be ruinous to that organization's reputation.

Graham Roberts-Holm would likely lose his job, dismissed in disgrace by the Prime Minister or her designee. The Yahalomin's only action would be, therefore, a phone call from Luke to Roberts-Holm, something already agreed upon in the earlier meeting that morning in Luke's office, but now given added urgency by the intrusion of Louis Bois and his impressively lengthy journalistic tentacles.

Informed by Luke of the new situation, Roberts-Holm could be trusted, in Luke's view, to clean up his own subcommittee by ridding it of whichever member was being bribed, and then to deal with news media as he saw fit.

Given the apparent fact that Bois knew nothing whatever about Chaos, or about the Chaos HQ locations, or about Anton Fedorov, or about the impending placement of explosives at the All England Club … to say nothing of the Chaos group's plans subsequently to attack Parliament and beyond … eventually to attack the heart and soul of the U.K. and of the other great democracies … the published story would, as Bois feared, appear to the newspaper's readers as transparent sensationalism.

And if that night's Cambridge incursion — by Kory, Luke, and Jaakov — proved as successful as they expected, the story's investigative weaknesses, if Bois chose to go forward with publication, would become glaringly apparent. Accordingly, Luke drew the session to a close after less than a half-hour's discussion.

He immediately dialed Graham Roberts-Holm.

Friday, 3:30 p.m.

At the qualifiers' venue, late afternoon on the final day of BBG preparation, SallyBelle Jones and Thomas Chambers joined other BBGs in the stands, their practice sessions completed, to watch the final match of the qualifying tournament. The two had been working on different courts throughout the day, and, as they took their seats, Thomas saw her grimace.

"You're in pain, aren't you, SallyBelle?" he asked, although it was not really a question, but an observation.

She nodded.

"My ribs hurt more," she said, "now that I've stopped running and stooping and throwing … or maybe it's just that I have time to think about the pain, and so it seems to hurt more. I should have brought some aspirin with me."

He shook his head at her reproachfully.

"You just didn't want Mrs. Clark to think you're a wimp, is that it?"

She smiled at him.

"Can you even imagine Mrs. Clark taking an aspirin for a cracked rib or two?"

He laughed.

"No ... but there are a lot of things that I can't imagine Mrs. Clark doing."

SallyBelle raised her blonde eyebrows.

"Like what, other than taking an aspirin?"

"Well," he said, "like... I don't know... just getting tired, the way ordinary people do ... you know ... getting discouraged ... getting overwhelmed..."

It was her turn to laugh.

"Oh, that's ridiculous. Mrs. Clark would whack you with a forehand if she heard you say that about her. She's a regular person, Thomas.

"I'll bet that, when she was our age, she was just like we are ... not quite sure of what she was doing ... discouraged by things ... disappointed by things ...

"It's just that she's in her 30s now. She just *seems* beyond us."

Thomas thought about that for a long moment, then said, "Nope. She's not ordinary, SallyBelle. I can't imagine she ever was, in her whole life."

After another short silence, SallyBelle conceded, "Well ... I admit ... I *try* to think of her as someone I could someday be like. You know ... I want someday to be that poised and that confident and that assertive ... and yet that compassionate ...

"Sometimes I admire her so much I feel ... well ... discouraged ..."

She paused, then shifted gears.

"Last night in her brother's Five-Door," she said, "bringing my dad back from the prison house ... during the conversation I was part of ... I found out that this Fedorov person who seemed in charge of my prison guards ... I found out that he wanted to kidnap and maybe torture and maybe even *murder* Mrs. Clark."

She shuddered.

"This man and his group are focused on *her*, Thomas ... focused on ... on eliminating ... actually *killing* ... Mrs. Clark. She's no ordinary person ... you're right. There is something about her that leads certain people to want to *destroy* her."

They were quiet for several moments. Thinking.

Finally, SallyBelle asked, "Do you think these people will try to get at Mrs. Clark when she picks us up today? Is that why she took us to the other entrance and told us she'd collect us at that same gate this afternoon?"

"I don't know," he replied.

"I just know that you and I … and your dad … got attacked only *yesterday* on our way here, SallyBelle. I don't know what to think about any of this.

"I guess I just trust Mrs. Clark to take care of us somehow."

She nodded.

"Me, too."

Friday, 4:40 p.m.

Kneeling behind the parking garage's rooftop parapet, KGB sharpshooter Bogdan Baranov turned to his young associate.

"Lev," he said, speaking in English, even privately, as Artur Volkov's and Anton Fedorov's policies required, "set up the nest while I prepare the weapon."

Volkov and Fedorov had had the foresight, months earlier, to select a location for the Chaos organization's temporary headquarters nicely positioned to support a sniper's nest within range of the qualifiers' venue. While they could not then have known anything regarding the two young people's selection as BBGs, nor would they have been at all interested even if they had known, they knew for certain that Rebecca Clark would be a sought-after presence during the qualifying tournament.

Killing her with a rifle bullet had never been their first choice as a means of eliminating her — that method was not nearly "personal" enough — but the Yahalomin's history suggested the importance of not just one, but several fall-back plans.

After setting up their temporary headquarters on the fourth floor of the parking garage, Fedorov had ordered a half-dozen 40-pound sandbags to be stashed under a tarpaulin on the parking garage roof. And he insisted that a custom-built sniper rifle, complete with detachable tripod and adjustable long-range scope, should be among the weapons to be stored in the gun cabinets located in their headquarters,

Now, months afterwards, struggling through the disappointment of the previous night's abortive attack on Rebecca at the Duxford air base, Fedorov had instructed Baranov to be in position well before the BBGs finished practice for the day at 5 p.m.

Fedorov made sure that Baranov and his associate had been given descriptions not only of Rebecca's Volvo, but also of the aging Vauxhall driven by her husband, and of the Land Rover Five-Door driven by her brother, any of which Rebecca might use to pick up the Jones girl and the Chambers boy at the conclusion of practice.

Baranov was to wait for the primary target, Rebecca Clark, to find a parking place, walk to the athletes' gate, and escort the teens to her vehicle. Then, as they approached the vehicle, Baranov was to fire his first round into Rebecca's chest and, without pause, his second into the girl's.

At exactly 4:45 p.m., as expected, Rebeca's Volvo pulled into the parking lot.

"There she is, Bogdan," said Lev, peering toward the qualifiers' venue through his image-stabilized field glasses.

"She's driving the Volvo."

Baranov raised the rifle and placed the barrel on the stack of sandbags. He manipulated the scope while adjusting the position of the weapon itself.

"Will you want the tripod, Bogdan?"

"No, the sandbags will be better."

At that moment, the two KGB agents heard a voice from behind them.

"Stand up and step back from the weapon, Bogdan. You'll not be killing anyone this afternoon. Besides ... that's Matt Clark driving his wife's Volvo ... Rebecca is collecting the teens in her brother's vehicle ... from the other side of the complex."

Neither KGB agent moved.

After several tense moments, Baranov said, without turning his head, "Is that you Jaakov?"

"It is, and I have my Glock trained on your spine. We try not to take the lives of our adversaries, but, if I must shoot, you'll never walk again."

There was another pause, then Adelman continued.

"Lieutenant Manguson is 15 feet from you, his throwing knife at the ready. So ... I say again ... stand up and step back."

Baranov sighed and nodded to his associate. The two of them stood slowly and turned to face their adversaries. Baranov smiled.

"I did not expect to see you again," he said, "after our last venture, Jaakov, but I am not surprised that you have been recruited by Mrs. Clark."

Holding the Glock steady, the muzzle now trained on Baranov's right knee, Adelman replied, "I find this more … palatable … than my work with Mossad, Bogdan. I appreciate the precision of … um … the Yahalomin's moral compass."

Baranov nodded.

"I always felt you were a little … reluctant … in your Mossad work, Jaakov," said Baranov. "I can see how this might suit you better."

There was a pause.

"Well," said Baranov after several moments, "what now?"

Luke Manguson replied to the question.

"We have no authority to arrest you or your associate, Baranov," he said, "as I'm sure you know, and no authorization from my sister to harm you. I will check you and your associate for handheld weapons, and, once we are satisfied that you are clean of weaponry, you may go.

"We will keep the rifle and whatever handguns the two of you are carrying, but you will otherwise be free to rejoin your organization."

As Luke, sheathing his knife, moved to the two agents, Adelman spoke.

"I think you might inform Anton Fedorov, when next you see him," he said, "that he will not be allowed to succeed with any portion of his plans. The lot of you, I suggest, should simply pack up and go back to Moscow.

"And you should go there now … before any of you get … um … *injured.*"

At the mention of Fedorov's name, Baranov visibly flinched.

He recovered quickly. Yet he made no reply.

As Luke completed his pat-down, removing a handgun from each man, Baranov said, "It was good to see you again, Jaakov, but the next time, I expect I shall be the one who holds the weapon and you who will be disarmed."

Adelman smiled.

"I really think," he said, "that you should reconsider your career choices, Bogdan. There may be forces arrayed against you that you cannot defeat. This is not KGB versus Mossad and CIA and MI6, you understand.

"This is altogether different."

Baranov returned the smile.

"We shall see, Jaakov," he said. "We shall see."

Saturday, midmorning, ISP basement gymnasium

Rebecca, breathing deeply but evenly as she neared the midway point of her 30-minute treadmill run, called to her brother as he entered the room, "Luke, how did everything go last night at the Chaos HQ? All smooth?"

Luke nodded. "Yes. All smooth, Rebecca.

"The guards were inside the building, and never had an inkling that we had entered the basement area. We simply ignored them.

"Our bolt cutters got us into the old coal chute in 10 seconds flat. And Kory handled all that equipment like she was born to it."

"No issues, then?" Rebecca asked.

"None," he replied.

"Kory finished," Luke continued, "in less than two hours. We were out of there and on the road by 0300 hours this morning. Jaakov and I were of no use whatsoever. With no guards to deal with, Kory could have done the whole thing solo."

Kory entered the room just as her husband said this about her.

She rolled her eyes.

Rebecca laughed, and then spoke without breaking stride.

"It's nice to have a husband who is president of your fan club, isn't it?"

"It's horrible," Kory said, shaking her head at Luke.

"I couldn't have done *anything* with that equipment," she said, "if Luke and Jaakov hadn't been there to help sort everything out. It would have taken me at least twice as long, and without their help, it's likely I would have missed something."

"But you didn't miss anything, you think?" asked Rebecca, still maintaining her comfortable 7-minute-mile pace on the treadmill.

"We went through our checklist three times," said Kory. "Before starting, and then, after completion, two more times, just to be certain."

"What will happen Monday morning?"

Luke answered.

"We will drive up there again," said Luke, "to be in position to handle any unexpected problems that might arise. Kory has said she doesn't expect to need to do anything further with the equipment, but, whatever the case, we'll need to clear the place by 0800.

"That may mean, at some point, going inside the building and once more disarming and disabling a couple of guards."

"And possibly escorting a couple of technicians out of there, too," added Kory. "We doubt any technicians present will be armed, and we hope they will simply leave the place on their own, once we explain everything to them."

Luke nodded.

"That's what we hope, Rebecca."

Just then Matt Clark walked into the gymnasium.

He looked over at Rebecca, who was still running smoothly, and blew her a kiss.

"How much further, Rebecca?" he asked.

She glanced down at the treadmill's timer.

"Just four more minutes," she said.

"We'll phone the twins as soon as you finish, shall we?" he asked.

She laughed, still not missing a stride.

"Listen to you," she said, "using that British sentence structure as if you'd spent your whole life right here … I'm so impressed."

He beamed. "I'm getting better, huh?"

"Well," she replied, "not exactly 'better,' sweetheart … just a trifle more … um … you know … a little more *naturally* artificially British."

"And you think that's a *good* thing?" said Jaakov Adelman, just finishing another set on the nearby bench press.

Ignoring his playful question, Kory turned to him and asked, "Jaakov, you heard us saying just now that things went smoothly last night. Do you agree?"

Busily adding weight to the bench press bar, he nodded.

"Yes, Kory, but that doesn't mean there won't be problems Monday morning, you know. I'm still concerned that the Chaos technicians might go into the equipment today or tomorrow and somehow figure out what you have changed. If they're really good, they might find any number of places where you have rerouted the circuitry. And that means …"

"Right," said Kory, "if they actually inspect their equipment array, they could uncover quite a bit of what I did last night.

"I'm truly hopeful, though, that they won't see any need to do that kind of examination of equipment which, they'll assume, is still set up exactly as it was when they left it yesterday afternoon.

"That's what I think," she added.

"And that's what we hope," said Rebecca, starting her cooldown, now slowing her pace and lifting a hand towel to her face, neck, and hair.

"And that's what we'll pray," she added, almost to herself.

Saturday, midmorning, MI6 offices

"Yes? MI6 here."

"Is this Graham Roberts-Holm?" said the voice.

"It is. Who is calling, please?"

"My name is Louis Bois. I am an investigative reporter with *The New York Times*' London Bureau. I'm calling to ask if you'd like to comment on a story that we'll be running in tomorrow's editions."

"Yes?"

"The story will focus on several electronic transfers of funds from the New York City Russian Mafia to an account labeled 'MI6 source' and drawn upon on three specific dates and times that I can read to you."

"You can stop there, Mr. Bois," said Roberts-Holm. "I am painfully familiar with the facts you just cited, and have been since yesterday at about this time, when I got a call from Royal Navy Lieutenant Luke Manguson, now with Independent Security Perspectives here in London.

"Luke phoned me yesterday and I wasted no time in ferreting out the mole. He has been summarily dismissed from the service. And that is my comment for your story, sir."

"Since you used the masculine pronoun, I infer that it was Declan Murphy?"

"I won't elaborate, Mr. Bois. I've nothing to add."

"Not even to comment on the upcoming Wimbledon ..."

The line went dead.

Sunday, midmorning, ISP conference room, one day before Wimbledon

"Thank you, Father Jack," said Luke. "We're grateful."

Jack McGriff had just concluded a Sunday morning worship service in the small ISP conference room for the eight members of Rebekka Yahalomin, including Jaakov Adelman, their Jewish member. Adelman had attended services at a nearby temple on his Sabbath, but asked to be present for the Christian service on Sunday. His colleagues were, as always, delighted to have him present.

"Shall we turn now to a review of tomorrow morning's plans?" asked Luke of the group. Several heads nodded their ascent.

Rebecca shook her head.

"No, Luke," she said to her twin.

Faces turned to her.

"The worship service is still fresh in our minds and hearts," she said. "I suggest we wait a half-hour … or more.

"Some of us might want to walk outside during that time," she added, "and I have discovered a lovely copse just on the far side of the parking lot in back. That's where I'd like to spend some prayer time now.

"My heart resists going immediately from worship to business."

She was rising from her seat as she said these words, and the others all took this as their cue to follow.

Luke smiled to himself as he did the same. *It's nice that my sister lets me pretend to be in charge of things … up to a point …*

He chuckled softly, and his wife overheard the small noise.

"It's alright, dear," said Kory, placing a hand on his rock-hard bicep. "We'll be glad to let you be in charge when we come back to the room."

Rebecca heard her brother's loud laughter halfway down the hallway, as she entered the stairwell. She smiled, picturing in her mind the exact scenario that had just taken place back in the conference room.

Thank you, Father, she prayed as she descended the stairway, *for giving me such a wonderful brother and such a marvelous sister-in-law. They're far more than I could ever have deserved.*

CHAPTER ELEVEN

"Okay," said Luke to the group. "I think we're good to go."

He had just led a detailed review of the planned five-person movement, the next morning, onto the site of the Chaos headquarters.

He, Jaakov, Matt, Jack, and Kory would conduct the incursion, the latter four armed with their military or intelligence-service sidearms, and Luke himself with his array of knives, tools, and bindings. Kory would handle the NTT shoulder phone, and Sid and Marie, in one of the car-phone-equipped Defender 90s, would monitor Kory's transmissions. That ISP vehicle, driven by Jaakov, would follow Luke in his Five-Door Rover to a preselected position just 2 miles from the Chaos property.

At that point, Jaakov, having parked the Defender, would ride to the Chaos site with the others.

The review complete, Luke turned to his sister.

"Rebecca," he said, "what are your plans for tomorrow morning? Is there anything we can do, now or tomorrow, to be of assistance to you?"

"No, Luke," she replied. "I'm going to drive SallyBelle and Thomas to Wimbledon in the Volvo, and then I'll just be available throughout the day to the BBG staff. It may be that they'll need nothing from me at all, and that I'll be able to watch SallyBelle and Thomas as they're working the matches to which they're assigned.

"There is also the likelihood that the tournament staff will ask me to warm up one or more of the qualifiers. None of the qualifiers has an on-site coach, to say nothing of an entourage, and so I'll be ready to serve as their warm-up, if needed. To that end, I'll be wearing my tennis whites throughout the day."

"I hope to have a lovely day at the tournament."

Seeing that her response had produced several perplexed looks, Rebecca continued, "Does that sound … um … a trifle callous? Or frivolous? That I intend to have a lovely day, while the seven of you conduct a mission that will include considerable danger? Does it seem that I'm going to be unconcerned about you seven, and about your safety, and about the success of our mission?

"Is that why your faces seem … um … puzzled?"

One of the faces — it was Marie Campbell's — changed quickly from perplexity to a kind of shy embarrassment.

"Well … I confess, Rebecca," said Marie, "that I'd imagined you in more or less continuous prayer, from our pre-dawn departure until our return. But that suddenly strikes me as … well … silly … but honestly … that's what I'd imagined."

"And what do you imagine now?" asked Rebecca, smiling sweetly.

"Well," answered Marie, "I think I'm now going to imagine you offering prayers for us almost continuously from now until our return.

"But," she continued, "at the same time, I'm going to imagine you going about your business and welcoming your responsibilities. And those will include, I think, helping the BBG staff, if you're needed to do that, and then shepherding your young charges through what surely will be an unsettled time for them … their first day as Wimbledon BBGs …

"You know … international TV networks … throngs of tennis afficionados … and, above all, internationally famous athletes expecting perfection from each and every BBG throughout the tournament. I'm going to imagine that you'll be doing what you do, Rebecca … tomorrow's version of the 'blueprint of the universe.'

"Your prayers will certainly carry us," Marie concluded, "but meanwhile you'll attend to the BBG staff members and to your two teens and to the qualifiers. After all, you can certainly do more than one thing at a time."

And Marie laughed her infectious laugh, causing relieved smiles to spread around the conference room.

But Sid Belton, not smiling, cleared his throat.

Faces turned to him.

"I gotta say, ma'am," he said, looking toward Rebecca, "that I still got my wife's words right up front in my brain. Remember what Eleanor said in our New York conference room, just what? ... maybe 10 days ago? ... hm? ... remember?"

"Which words were those, Mr. Belton?" asked Rebecca.

"Eleanor said that th' stuff we were focused on was ... er ... just a red herring ... th' dirtbags tryin' t' get us t' look at one thing while they worked at somethin' else.

"Remember?"

Several heads nodded.

Marie shook her head.

"I need help, Mr. Belton," she said. "Please."

"My smart-as-a-whip wife said th' *main* thing th' dirtbags wanted was t' eliminate Rebekka Yahalomin from th' face a' th' earth ... because until they did *that*, their plans were gonna be messed up every time they started on some new project ... until they did *that*, they'd never get anything *completely* done ...

"An' that meant they had t' get their hands on Mrs. Clark so they could ... well ... try t' convert 'er t' their side ... ridiculous idea ... and, if they couldn't do that ... t' torture 'er an' then ... an' then ..."

"And then kill me," said Rebecca. "And yes, Mr. Belton," she added, "I do recall Dr. Chapel's words. And she was proven correct, was she not?"

"Yes, ma'am," Belton said, "she was."

"And so?" asked Rebecca.

"An' so ..." Belton responded, "an' so ... y' can't just go traipsin' around th' All England Club tomorrow like there was nothin' t' worry about.

"This Fedorov guy doesn't believe yer data source is th' *actual* data Source ... if y' know what I mean ... he doesn't believe in anything at all, I'd guess ... but he an' Volkov an' th' Kuznetsova woman ... they know you've always had *some* kind a' data source ... an' they've always known that they can't get their hands on it ... whatever 'it' might actually be ... an' they've always known that y' keep ruinin' their plans ... an' they figure they gotta ... like Eleanor said ... they gotta eliminate you ... an' maybe us ... before they can get anything really big *completely* done.

"Know what I mean?

"Hm?

"Know what I mean?"

"Yes, yes, Sid," replied Jaakov, shaking his head at his detective agency partner, "but the tournament starts in just hours now, and the seven of us intend to make sure, tomorrow morning, that Kory's work Friday-Saturday overnight will remain in place. So … won't Rebecca be free to … well … to have a nice day?"

Belton looked at Adelman as though he were a third grader struggling to grasp the fact that two plus two was four.

"So, Jaakov," he said, "didja take a stupid pill this mornin' when y' got outta bed? If Mrs. Clark lollygags aroun' th' tennis courts all day just thinkin' about th' kids and th' BBG staff … Fedorov's boys can just grab her an' … y' know …

"Have y' just *forgotten* th' other point Eleanor made in New York when she helped us see what th' bad guys were really doin'?

"Have y' just *forgotten* that she made th' point that, when God calls th' Rebekka Yahalomin t' action, God *never* guarantees our safety?

"I mean, just look at us … look at Mrs. Clark's face … look at Matt's left arm … look at Luke's face and neck … watch me try t' walk …

"*Come on,* people!" concluded Belton, nearly shouting in his urgency to make them understand the danger, "we coulda' been killed every time we stepped into these fights … we just weren't … not yet …"

Rebecca raised her hand to interrupt the detective in his struggles to make plain the depth of his concern on her behalf.

Belton stopped and looked hopefully to her.

"Yes," said Rebecca, "I do know what you want us to understand, Mr. Belton. And so, let me assure you that I'll not be 'traipsing around' unmindful of danger. I'll carry my shoulder satchel throughout the day. My throwing knives will be within inches of my right hand every minute.

"Beyond that, I'm aware, as are we all, that we *can* be … eliminated … if our adversary is crafty enough, or if we become careless enough. Why, on Friday, just two days ago, if you, Sidney, had not pointed out the fact that the garage was 'sniper distance,' as you put it, from the qualifiers' venue …

"Who knows, in that case, what would have happened?

"The safest approach," Rebecca concluded, "would always be for me … and you … and all of us … to stay in our rooms and not come out until each crisis has fully passed us by … if, indeed, any of these crises *could* pass us by.

"But we're not going to do that."

The room fell silent for long moments.

Then Belton spoke again, seemingly chastened.

"I know, ma'am," he said, crestfallen.

"I just wanted t' say that … y' know … I'm really worried about tomorrow … especially about you, ma'am … I'm just … y' know …"

He stopped suddenly because Rebecca had sprung from her chair, circled behind her brother and her husband, and enveloped the detective in a bear hug, leaning down over his head and shoulders, her thick black tresses falling down over his chest. She held him thus for long moments, the room silent and somber.

During this dramatic display of deeply felt love, tenderness and gratitude, Matt Clark and Luke Manguson, husband and brother, respectively, of the woman after whom their group had been named, looked searchingly into each other's eyes.

Neither appeared any less worried than was Sid Belton.

Simultaneously, each shook his head grimly.

Monday, 3 a.m., opening day of Wimbledon

Jack McGriff knocked quietly on Marie Campbell's door on the fifth floor of the ISP building.

"Marie," he whispered, "it's me."

She opened the door immediately, dressed and ready to go, even though scheduled departure from the ISP lot was still an hour away.

McGriff entered, leaned down, cupped her face in his hands, and gave her a tender good-morning kiss.

"Did you sleep?" he asked.

"Off and on," she replied. "My mind kept bouncing back and forth between this morning's work at the Chaos headquarters, and the conversation we had after yesterday's worship service. Mr. Belton was just so worried about Rebecca …"

"Yes," agreed McGriff, "and I noticed Rebecca's husband and brother seemed no less so, given how grim they were during that discussion."

They drifted over to the only seating available in the ISP dorm rooms, Marie taking a seat on her bed, leaning against the headboard, and McGriff arranging himself on the uncomfortable wooden chair near the window, facing her.

After moments of thoughtful silence, Marie continued.

"Every time I start drowning in the swamp of possibilities, Jack, I try to pull my mind back to the fact that Rebekka Yahalomin has so obviously been 'called' into action … repeatedly *enlisted* by God to accomplish some particular thing …

"Do you know what I mean?"

McGriff smiled.

"You know, Marie, you can't use that phrase without calling to mind the detective … 'Know what I mean? Hm? Know what I mean?'"

She laughed her happy laugh.

"Isn't he the most interesting person *ever?*" she asked rhetorically.

They smiled, picturing the gnome-like Belton's endearing and yet desperate concern for Rebecca Clark.

"He is indeed unique," agreed McGriff. "And I truly love how she cares for him. That bear hug she put on him …"

They smiled again, picturing the brief concluding scene of their post-Sunday-worship discussion and debate.

Then Marie returned to her question.

"Jack," she said seriously, "what do you think? Do you think Mr. Belton … and Matt and Luke … need to be as worried as they appeared to be … those three, in particular … even though it's undeniably true that God's hand has always been so strongly present in our midst?"

"Well," replied McGriff, "there is the point Sidney tried to make about the extent of the woundings they have experienced over the years … Rebecca's face, Matt's arm, Luke's neck and face, the detective's whole body … and he could have also mentioned Jaakov's near-death experience with gunfire …"

"And Kory's permanently damaged left hand," added Marie.

"Yes, that, too," he agreed.

She was thoughtful for several moments, then shook her head definitively.

"No," she said, "I just don't accept it, Jack. I just don't accept the notion that the Lord will allow Rebecca Clark to be … eliminated … that awful euphemism … when He has so clearly continued to thrust her into one crisis after another …

"When He has repeatedly *depended* upon her willingness to be … what was the term she used in New York? Oh, a *strategic instrument* on His behalf."

McGriff thought for a moment, then said, "I think it was you, Marie, who said, during that same New York City conversation, that it seemed to you that our adversaries, having succeeded in engaging Rebecca, were 'pulling the ceiling down on their own heads' … or words to that effect … yes?"

"My goodness," she said, "you really do pay attention to me … sometimes … don't you, Jack? I think that is the exact phrase I used then.

"But," she continued after a moment, "Dr. Chapel did not agree with me, you recall. She just emphasized that nearly every Yahalomin member has been seriously wounded at some point, and that some of those injuries could easily have been fatal … that God, as her husband noted just yesterday in our post-worship conversation, has never guaranteed our members' safety."

McGriff nodded.

"And yet," he said, "if I remember, Marie, it was Sid Belton who had the *very* last word in that New York City discussion. I'm pretty sure he looked his beloved Eleanor in the eye and said … um … let's see … he said *Rebecca isn't going back to England until she has 'whipped 'em like scrambled eggs'* …"

Delighted laughter then bubbled from them both, as they remembered the detective's novel way of saying what needed to be said.

Then, after still more moments of thoughtful silence, Marie offered a complementary thought to the detective's "scrambled eggs" observation.

"You know what scripture passage this brings to my mind, *Reverend McGriff?*" she said teasingly. "That passage in which Jesus physically attacks the moneychangers in the temple. You know … when He made 'a whip of cords' and drove them out."

McGriff nodded thoughtfully.

"Yes, Marie … that certainly does fit."

"Where is that," she asked, "in the New Testament?"

"John's Gospel," replied McGriff. "The 'whip of cords' passage is in the second chapter. The passage starts with verse 13, I believe. Jesus is outraged that the temple has been turned into a marketplace. He not only drives out the moneychangers, but the livestock, too … He even turns over the moneychangers' tables …

"He really cleaned house, Marie."

Then he smiled and nodded to himself.

"Interesting to think of Rebecca 'cleaning house' like that …"

Marie smiled, pleased that he liked her scriptural allusion.

"Hm …" he mused. "Like 'a whip of cords' …

"I like it, Marie," he said.

He nodded and murmured the phrase once more to himself…

"Yes … 'a whip of cords' indeed."

Monday 6:00 a.m., Chaos Command Center, near Cambridge

Luke, having again hidden his Five-Door Rover in deep foliage at the base of the ridge, led the contingent uphill carefully, picking his way through the loosely spaced trees and sporadically dense underbrush that covered much of the hillside. Although the sun had risen earlier, low overcast seemed to trap the darkness near the ground, making the going slower than he had expected.

Although his four colleagues were armed, only his wife was encumbered with anything more than a sidearm. Kory carried the NTT shoulder phone in one hand, having found that its shoulder strap pinched the skin near her neck. The leather carrying handle proved easier for her.

There was no talking among the five. Each was alone with private thoughts and, frequently, with silent prayers, Father Jack McGriff's companion prayer prominent among the latter. As they reached the crest, which also marked the edge of the grassy parking area, they stopped and crouched or knelt in light underbrush.

After several long moments of watching and listening, the five concluded that the guards were not yet stirring, or, if they were, they were simply starting the teakettle in the kitchen. Without discussion, Luke and Jaakov started forward across the 75 yards of clear space between the tree line and the house, knowing from their previous reconnaissance that the kitchen faced away from them.

The other three — Kory, Matt, and McGriff — watched as this pair of expe-rienced infiltrators closed on the structure and systematically crept from one window to the next, eventually circling the entire building and then returning to the group's observation spot. They crouched close to their colleagues and spoke quietly.

"It looks just as we expected," said Luke. "Just the same two guards … both of them armed with Glocks … moving around in the kitchen and putting something together for breakfast. They're not expecting action this morning."

"So," said Kory after a moment, "we'll just stay here, in position to intervene if the technicians … or anyone else … arrive later?"

"Yes," replied Luke. "But let's retreat about 20 yards further back, so we can converse more easily, and so you, Kory, can communicate with Marie and Sid — his being the loudest voice — without our being heard in the house."

"You think they're KGB, Jaakov?" Matt asked of the former Mossad agent.

"Yes," he replied. "I think everybody engaged with Chaos is either KGB or USSR embassy security … or both."

"Well, Luke," Jaakov added, "since there's nothing we need to do unless others arrive here, I suggest we leave two here on watch while the other three go back to the vehicle and get comfortable. If there are any arrivals, the three can easily get back up here in time to take whatever action might be needed."

"Good," agreed Luke. "You and I take the first watch, Jaakov?"

By 7 a.m., full daylight had arrived at the Chaos headquarters, although overcast skies prevented the sun's rays from helpfully brightening the scene that faced Luke and Jaakov. The two did not need daylight to hear, however, just after 7:15 a.m., two vehicles climbing the ridge toward the plateau on which the Chaos building stood.

Looking through numerous gaps in the foliage, the men watched as, first, a black Mercedes 500-Class sedan quietly purred to the crest and then across the parking area, coming to a stop on the near side of the structure's broad front porch. Seconds later, a dark green Mini Cooper struggled to the summit and bumped noisily to a spot some 50 yards from the Mercedes, both vehicles now parked on the side nearest the watchers.

Luke and Jaakov then observed two men, both wearing shoulder holsters, as they emerged from the Mercedes, pulled sport coats over their white dress shirts and ties, and strode into the building. The watchers' eyes then turned to the

Mini Cooper, where they saw two 20-something women exit the tiny car. Both women wore jeans, long-sleeved khaki-colored work shirts, and running shoes.

Luke and Jaakov watched the Mini's driver as she turned to lift a small tool-box from the coupe's back seat, while the other collected her purse from the floorboard. The women then walked briskly, side-by-side, across the grassy parking area and, pausing to tap lightly on the front door, entered without waiting for a response.

The two men rose immediately from their observation post, intending to descend the ridge to consult with their colleagues, but paused when they heard those same colleagues climbing toward them through the undergrowth. Matt Clark led the way with his sister-in-law following close behind. Jack McGriff brought up the rear, Kory's shoulder phone slung over one burly shoulder by its long strap.

The five immediately crouched together in a small clearing, encircled by the close-knit curtain of vegetation that muffled the sound of their voices and simultaneously shielded them visually from any watchful eyes.

"We heard the vehicles start up the hill," said Matt to Luke and Jaakov, "so we got moving immediately. What do you think?"

"There were two agents — we assume they're agents — in the Mercedes," said Luke, "but we don't need to do anything about them. There were two youngish women in the second car, both wearing jeans, work shirts, and running shoes. One carried a toolbox with her into the building."

Luke looked from one face to the other, seeing the concern on each.

"You've got to go get them," said Kory to her husband.

Luke nodded.

"Confirm with Sid, dear?"

But she was already punching the ISP car phone number into the shoulder phone. In seconds, she heard Marie Campbell's response, followed by Sid Belton's rumbling voice. Kory switched to speaker-phone setting.

The voice demanded, "What d'ya find up there, people?"

Informed of the situation that had materialized, Belton's response was unhesitating. "Ya' gotta get those women outta there … Luke … Jaakov … Do it fast. Go get 'em now!"

As Kory began her response, Luke and Jaakov were already moving at a run, Luke's hands searching his shoulder holster for the largest of the serrated knives he always carried there. He would use that knife to cut through the tape Jaakov had applied to the coal chute padlock's severed clasp during the Friday-Saturday overnight raid. At their departure then, Jaakov had carefully restored the padlock's appearance with light-colored duct tape.

Ten seconds after their arrival at the coal chute, the two men had dropped down the chute and, as they were moving through the equipment-filled basement, they heard the interior door from the ground floor above them open and close, followed by the soft sound of running-shoe-clad feet descending the stairs. Crouching to remain hidden by the masses of cabinet-housed equipment, Luke and Jaakov quickly placed themselves in position to stop the women as they moved through the central corridor formed by the array of 6-foot-tall, electronics-filled metal cabinets.

As the women reached them, the two men sprang at them from opposite sides. The women's toolbox dropped to the concrete floor, a metallic crashing sound that, Luke and Jaakov knew, might alert the four men upstairs.

As one, Luke and Jaakov had clamped powerful hands over each woman's mouth. Each man had lifted his lightweight captive off the floor with his free arm, wheeling the women around to face each other, inches apart. They then held the silence, waiting to hear if inquiries were called down from the ground floor.

Hearing none, Luke then spoke, his voice barely audible.

"No noise, ladies … *none*. We will *not* harm you … but no noise."

He looked at the woman held by Adelman, then turned his face so that his mouth was almost in his own captive's ear.

"Do you both understand me? No noise. We will *not* harm you."

He felt his captive nod her head and saw Jaakov's do the same.

Neither Luke nor Jaakov removed his hand from his captive's mouth, but softened somewhat his free arm's hold around her waist. Luke felt his captive relax slightly and sensed that Jaakov's had done the same.

Luke continued.

"You probably don't know anything about these men who've hired you, but I will tell you … they are Soviet KGB agents. You doubtless know nothing about the actual purpose of the circuitry you have set up here, but you'll want to know now that the explosives you've arranged to detonate elsewhere are *not* for the purpose you've been told. You're under the impression that you have set up automated systems that will detonate, by design, in the midst of road-building and bridge-building construction projects around the London and Cambridge areas.

"Those explosives are actually set to detonate in specified locations throughout the All England Club grounds, where the Wimbledon Championships are scheduled to begin just hours from now. People will die."

He paused to allow his message to be processed by the helpless women, whose eyes had just widened in horror. Then he continued, his free arm and, he knew, Jaakov's, as well, loosened still further around his captive's waist.

"We assume you know nothing about that. We assume that you are highly skilled women who have been hired to do what you regard as interesting and challenging work ... and you have done exactly that.

"Yes?"

He felt his captive nod. He saw Jaakov's do the same.

He looked Jaakov in the eye, and they simultaneously nodded to each other.

"We are going to take our hands away from your mouths now, ladies," Luke said, "and we are going to trust you to remain silent when we do. If you call out to the KGB agents upstairs, they will no doubt come crashing down those stairs with their guns drawn. You will then be in the midst of a gun and knife fight, because we will not allow them to capture us ... or you.

"Understood?"

The women nodded.

"Now," Luke said, "one more thing."

He let go of his captive's waist and swiftly removed his military ID from his hip pocket, raising the identification folder to the women's eye level.

"I am Royal Navy Lieutenant Luke Manguson, now on active reserve. I, Mr. Adelman here, and others with whom we work, intend to prevent the tragedy that these KGB agents have planned and readied.

"You are ... right now ... in good hands ... safe hands.

"You'll want to remain that way."

He nodded at Jaakov again.

The men removed their hands from their captives' mouths.

Then Adelman mirrored Luke's action in removing his arm from his captive's waist. Both women were now unrestrained.

The men then turned to face the women, who now stood side-by-side.

"Ladies," continued Luke, "it is essential to your safety that we get you out of here … now … without the upstairs gentlemen knowing that you have departed. That will entail climbing up through the coal chute that we just came down. The chute has wooden rungs usable for climbing up and out."

He paused again while the two women thought about this unexpected and previously unimaginable set of circumstances.

The women looked at each other and, after several moments of what seemed to the men silent … but somehow real … communication, they nodded to each other.

Recognizing something familiar in this unspoken dialogue between the two, Luke asked, "Are you sisters?"

"Yes," they whispered simultaneously, smiles now playing across their lips.

Luke smiled in return.

"My sister and I can do that."

The smiles broadened.

"Now," he concluded …

"Your hands and jeans are going to get filthy as you climb through the chute… but you're going to be safe."

Each woman spontaneously clasped her sister's hand. As one, they nodded their readiness to proceed.

"Mr. Adelman will lead," said Luke, "and I'll come behind you. I'll bring your toolbox with me as I come."

Jaakov immediately turned and moved toward the coal chute.

The sisters paused, exchanged looks, then turned quickly to follow.

As Luke fell in behind the women, the thought ran through his mind: *how does God always seem to provide us with such astonishing people as these sisters?*

Monday, 9:45 a.m., the All England Club

Anton Fedorov was heavily disguised in a bushy black beard and a pair of thick-framed sunglasses, also black, which were more like glare-protection goggles than glasses. The goggles covered his eyebrows — his single eyebrow — and, in their thickness, made his oddly jutting forehead seem almost normal.

Almost.

He wore a loose-fitting, long-sleeved, dark-colored knit shirt and a pair of khaki trousers that were 2 inches too long, both garments taking the eye away from his taut, distance-runner's build. His receding hairline was covered by a broad-brimmed hat that further camouflaged his unique features.

Now, satisfied that he was fully unrecognizable, even though he knew his beard and clothing made him conspicuous among the throngs of short-sleeved and clean-shaven men, he strode confidently through the All England Club's spacious grounds. It did not occur to him that a blonde teen-age girl, unencumbered by such adult social conventions as those that discourage staring at unusual-looking people, might see through the disguise without difficulty.

In his left hand, concealed within his closed fist, a coiled garrote, its 8-inch length wound tightly into itself, awaited an unsuspecting victim, should she happen to appear under opportune circumstances. Fedorov, appearing to stroll aimlessly through the grounds, was, in fact, purposefully orbiting All England's Centre Court, glancing repeatedly through the gates toward the royal box.

He wanted at least some members of the royal family present before he moved to one of the always at-hand red phone booths placed around the facility. There, he would dial the number that would, thanks to three weeks of exhaustive work by the two female technicians, trigger 14 explosive devices, each placed strategically around the facility by his contracted hirelings.

Two of the most powerful of those devices had been hidden, following his exacting instructions, within the royal seating area.

That morning, however, Fedorov had seen that the royal box was still unoccupied as 10 a.m. approached, the scheduled start time for many first-round matches. He reminded himself that he was in no great hurry. Everything was in readiness. All that remained was his decision regarding the exact moment.

He would wait until the explosions were likely to be as devastating and as attention-getting as possible. In the context of the overall Chaos design, the Wimbledon bombings would constitute the true opening salvo.

While the church-focused ministerial beatings had certainly been anxiety-producing among church leaders and their followers in the U.K., the momentarily impending, mostly indiscriminate killing of dozens — possibly hundreds — of athletes, media personnel, spectators, and, if he could time the explosions perfectly, members of the royal family, would constitute the *de facto* announcement of his terror campaign. With the world's attention now focused on the Championships, the coordinated eruptions would launch the real beginning of the Chaos scheme, a scheme designed to destroy the spirit of this uniquely English democracy ... and then, one-by-one, systematically, each of the world's other great democracies.

And, as each nation fell into a kind of national despair, Christians by the millions would feel themselves betrayed by the One in whom they had trusted. Fedorov was sure of it.

And so, he found himself smiling quietly at the inevitability of triumph ... the triumph of Evil ... the triumph of Anton Fedorov ... *his* name to be the name to be known ... to be honored ... to be feared ... *his* name above all other names.

His name synonymous with Evil.

Meanwhile, garrote in hand, his eyes scanned the crowd continuously, alert for the willowy height and glistening black hair of his prey.

Anticipation of these events consumed him fully, giving him a renewed sense of purpose, a certainty that this comprised his reason-for-being. In these exquisite moments, he experienced something akin to happiness. Yet it was a happiness so profoundly saturated with Evil that only a handful of human beings who had ever lived could have understood it. He gloried in the fact that he was one of the few.

One of the very few in history ... to achieve total *saturation* with Evil.

11:45 a.m., the All England Club

SallyBelle Jones and Thomas Chambers, their opening-round matches involving high-seeded players against unseeded qualifiers having been completed in less than an hour each, found each other immediately, and excitedly bubbled out the news of how they thought they had done. Both were thrilled.

"I was so nervous," said SallyBelle, "the first time I had to run onto the court to retrieve a service fault I stumbled and nearly fell before I even got to the ball."

"Oh, me too," said Thomas, "except that when I got to the ball I actually fumbled the thing off the court ... kinda dribbling the ball along ... so awful."

They shook their heads in unison at their mutual embarrassment.

"But, you know," she said, "once I'd looked so foolish right at the start, I got really calm. That stumble seemed to put everything in focus. I was fine after that."

Thomas thought about that for several moments.

He shook his head.

"Not me," he said finally. "It took me longer. I don't think I calmed down until the first set ended … 6-love, of course … and then I started feeling badly for the qualifier guy and stopped thinking about myself so much."

She mulled that observation and nodded.

"Yes," she said.

"You know," she continued, "that may be how things always turn out … we don't start doing really well at something until we stop thinking so much about how we look to other people. Maybe that's what we need to learn."

Thomas smiled.

"Yes," he agreed.

"And fast, too."

They both heard Rebecca's voice at the same instant.

They turned and saw her jogging easily toward them through the crowd. They smiled and ran to meet her. Rebecca was dressed in the traditional all-white attire for women competitors at Wimbledon … short skirt, sleeveless cotton blouse … tennis shoes … her long, glistening black hair caught up in a tight ponytail.

The whiteness of the short skirt and sleeveless blouse contrasted with Rebecca's healthy skin color, a hint of bronze brought about by hours in the sun. And the brevity of the skirt and blouse gave emphasis to the length of Rebecca's sinewy legs and the obvious strength in her upper arms, biceps that were muscular and yet somehow feminine at the same time. Both teens were, at first, surprised to see her dressed as a competitor, but then both recalled her having mentioned that tournament officials had asked her to be prepared to serve as warm-up partner for some of the qualifiers, none of whom brought the sort of entourage that accompanied the seeded players of both genders. Rebecca had dressed accordingly.

Slung from her right shoulder was her leather ready-satchel. The teens gave no thought to the bag, but, had they been told that it contained three Barringtons

Swords competition throwing knives, and had they been told that Rebecca's right hand was always positioned near those knives, they would not have been surprised. They had both been personally confronted with the kind of danger she faced.

"You were both so *good*," said Rebecca, opening her arms to embrace them both at once. "I looked in at each of you several times during your matches. You both seemed so confident and knowledgeable.

"I was proud."

The teens smiled.

"We hoped you saw us," said SallyBelle, "but we also hoped you weren't watching at the very start. We were a little nervous."

"More than a little," said Thomas with a small laugh.

"Well, that's certainly to be expected," said Rebecca.

She looked closely at SallyBelle.

"I couldn't see that your ribs were bothering you, SallyBelle," added Rebecca. "Were you in pain?"

"Well … I can feel the ribs now," she said, "but while I was at work, on the court, the ribs never spoke to me at all. I was fine, Mrs. Clark."

The three fell into step, moving together in the general direction of Centre Court, where one of the top seeds would be playing at noon. Their progress was interrupted several times by teenage girls who stopped the easily recognizable Rebecca Clark to ask that she autograph their Wimbledon programs. She cheerfully obliged, in each case asking permission to add a Bible verse below her signature.

As they approached the Centre Court stands, SallyBelle suddenly stopped, turned, and looked hard at a strange-looking person who had just turned to walk in the direction opposite theirs. As she stared after him, she saw him turn and glance over his shoulder at her.

And she knew.

"Mrs. Clark," she said in alarm, running several steps to overtake Rebecca and Thomas. "That man that just passed us, going the other way … I'm sure that was that Fedorov man … the man who wants to …"

She did not finish her sentence, concentrating instead on pointing in the man's direction. The three looked hard in the direction indicated.

But they saw only an anonymous mass of humanity.

Fedorov spotted the two objects of his continual searching at almost the same time. He had just glimpsed some of the Centre Court spectators beginning to stand at the sudden appearance of several members of the royal family. That had been his top priority from the moment he had entered the grounds that morning.

Seconds later, he saw, from behind, the short blonde ponytail of SallyBelle Jones and, a full head higher than the girl, the long black ponytail of Rebecca Clark.

He pivoted away, just as the girl turned her head and saw him.

He strode quickly in the direction opposite. But seconds later, he found that he could not stop himself from turning to look back. And in that fleeting moment, he locked eyes with the girl. He saw instantly that she knew him.

He turned away again, ducked into the sea of moving bodies, and, once clear of the tightly packed mass that moved toward Centre Court, broke into a sprint down a long corridor that ran between the secondary courts. Reaching the end of the corridor, he turned again and ran hard in the direction of a phone booth that his earlier reconnaissance had shown to be the booth furthest from Centre Court.

That booth was located in a short, obscure cul-de-sac with almost no foot traffic of any kind. He stepped into the booth, breathing hard from his sprint, and fumbled in his trousers pocket for the correct change. His hands now beginning to shake from the adrenaline rush that had driven his sprint away from Rebecca Clark and her young charges, he nonetheless managed to insert the necessary coins into the slot.

After taking a moment to get his breathing under control, he dialed the number that would trigger the automated explosions, his right index finger struggling to manipulate the rotary dial. He stopped with one number remaining to be dialed.

In that moment, he acknowledged, to his surprise, a sense of anticlimax.

This was the moment toward which his efforts had built for months … years, really … and yet his grand triumph was reduced to this solitary act of placing coins in a slot while standing in a dusty phone booth in an obscure corner of a sports venue.

Where was the happiness he had experienced moments earlier?

Where was the expected exhilaration?

Where were the crowds of admirers he had imagined?

Where were the imagined trumpets sounding his triumph?

He shook his head to clear it of the nonsense.

Stop this. Focus. Dial the number.

He dialed the final number. Pressing the receiver hard against one ear, he waited impatiently for the telephonic connections to be completed. For one panicked instant, he thought that the automation had failed.

But then he heard the final connecting clicks, followed by the dispassionate ring-sounds indicating, he knew, that the system was delivering its electronic prompts to the equipment in the basement of the Chaos Command Center.

He opened the folding door of the booth, listening for the riot of muffled explosions and terrified cries that he knew would ensue.

Then he heard the decisive click … the final connection had been made. The automated trigger mechanism had been activated. The explosions would follow quickly … in 5 to 10 seconds.

The seconds ticked by … 5 … 10 … 15 …

He stared toward the moving crowd in the distance.

People continued to move purposefully, each individual and each group striding calmly toward the noon matches of their choice. Where were the cacophonous sounds of destruction, the cries of agony, the screams for help, the moans of slow death?

He uttered an oath and dropped the telephone receiver, leaving it swinging loosely from its metallic cord. He started to move toward the crowd. He found himself striding more and more rapidly as he approached the throng.

Then he found himself running … and running … and running …

CHAPTER TWELVE

Monday, 11:55 a.m., Chaos Command Center grounds, near Cambridge

FOR KORY MANGUSON, THE TENSION WAS BECOMING unbearable.

She thought, but did not *know*, that she had succeeded in redirecting the complex circuitry installed by the two sisters. She thought, but did not *know*, that Anton Fedorov's automated trigger mechanisms would no longer devastate the All England Club and slaughter hundreds of unsuspecting human beings.

She reflected that Luke and Jaakov, nearly five hours before, having persuaded the sisters to accompany them out of the Chaos basement, had huddled with everyone in the same surveillance spot they had occupied since their arrival on the ridgeline. The group had decided on their next steps with very little discussion.

First, Luke, accompanied by Jaakov and Matt Clark, would proceed to his Range Rover Five-Door and drive back to London, arriving there by 9 a.m., a full hour before the opening matches of the Championships. There they would wait in the ISP offices for Rebecca's expected phone call from Wimbledon.

Luke had spoken the evening before with Graham Roberts-Holm. As a result of that conversation, Roberts-Holm had agreed to order two MI6 agents, next morning, to be on standby in case Rebecca requested them. The agents, as bodyguards commissioned by the U.K. government, would be given access to the All England grounds, even with their holstered firearms setting off metal detectors, whereas Luke, Jaakov, and the others would not.

Roberts-Holm had seemed to Luke altogether delighted to be included once again in Yahalomin plans. He had emphasized to Luke that Declan Murphy had been excised from the organization, and that he was "beyond 100 percent confident" in the two agents whom he had chosen to add to the small MI6 unit devoted to dealing with "unexplained and unexplainable" data sources.

Meanwhile, Kory, Jack McGriff, and the two sisters had volunteered to remain on site at the Chaos headquarters, waiting to report, using Kory's shoulder phone, on whatever outcomes might be apparent, once Fedorov decided to dial the trigger number. They assumed that he might reach that decision at any time from midmorning on.

They also knew that innumerable unanticipated events might occur at the Chaos site, and that someone's eyes and ears needed to be in position to report to Marie Campbell and Sid Belton via the NTT equipment.

Marie and Belton had volunteered to remain in their car-phone-equipped Defender throughout the morning, waiting to hear from Kory. Once they had heard, they, knowing the shoulder phone's limited range, would serve as a relay station to forward her report to Luke, Jaakov, and Matt in the ISP offices.

Now, minutes before noon, Kory, McGriff, and the sisters suddenly heard a muffled explosion from the equipment-filled basement. At the same time, they saw the wooden door of the coal chute explode, its pieces propelled high in the air and landing, after perhaps five seconds of erratic flight, all over the parking area on the coal chute's side of the old structure.

The spectacular detonation of the coal chute itself was followed instantaneously by smoke-laden components of file cabinets and related detritus from the underground equipment center. Impressively, however, the basement structure itself, constructed of reinforced concrete and native stone, appeared to maintain its integrity, having ejected its contents in a thousand metal, plastic, and wood fragments.

The two vehicles — the agents' black Mercedes and the sisters' green Mini — remained unscathed, having been parked beside the building, and thereby not directly exposed to the coal chute's explosion. Survival of the four KGB agents remained, for the moment, in doubt, since the ground floor on which they presumably sat or stood rested on a latticework of wooden beams and layered planking and might be expected to experience the same fate as the basement equipment.

Kory began dialing the number of the Defender's car phone while fragments were still fluttering through the air. Marie answered anxiously.

"Yes, Kory?"

"The basement just blew, Marie," she said. "Pieces of Chaos equipment are still raining down all around the parking area.

"We'll wait a few minutes," Kory continued, "to see if the agents ... well ... first, to see if they're still alive, and, if they are, to see if they leave in the Mercedes."

"My goodness!" exclaimed Marie. "You actually did it, Kory?

"My goodness!"

Kory smiled.

"Yes," she said, glancing at the sisters, both of whom seemed incredulous at what they had just witnessed, "*We* actually did it, Marie.

"Oh," she added, *sotto voce*, "by the way, the sisters, who seem a little stunned at the moment, do actually have names ... they are Catherine and Nicole, and they live together in Oxford ... although they've been placed in a Cambridge hotel while they've been working here.

"They're non-identical twins, Marie, just like Rebecca and Luke. They seem very ... um ... sweet."

Silence then fell over the on-site observers and, as well, over the two off-site participants, Marie and Sid, several miles away. They all — including Kory herself — were trying to comprehend the success of her work, a success fully expected, and yet ... somehow ... not truly expected at all.

Finally, Marie asked her long-distance colleague a question.

"So, Kory," she said into the car phone, "if it seems safe there, Catherine and Nicole will retrieve their little car and just go home?"

Sid Belton leaned in the direction of the phone.

"No!" he quickly and loudly shouted.

"Those two ladies need t' get in their Mini an' then follow us back t' ISP in London. We need t' figure out how safe they're gonna be. We need t' talk t' 'em about how much they know, an' how much they think th' dirtbags know about *them* ...

"Of course," he continued, "th' scumbags may think th' two ladies just got blown t' smithereens in th' basement explosion ... but ...

"We need t' talk t' 'em, Kory."

He paused, then added, "Oh … an' we need t' get an estimate from them about how much lost wages we just cost 'em. We need t' reimburse 'em fer lost wages, an' … y' know … we need t' give 'em some hazardous duty pay.

"They didn't sign up fer what just happened.

"Know what I mean?

"Hm?"

After several moments during which it seemed that Kory was ignoring the detective's question, she spoke again into her shoulder phone.

"Mr. Belton," she said quietly, "we just watched the four KGB agents scramble out of the house, glance toward the Mini-Cooper, and leap into their vehicle. Their Mercedes is just now starting down the hill.

"The agents appeared to be a trifle … shaken."

Belton cackled happily into the car phone.

"Those dirtbags won't be able t' hear fer a month, ma'am.

"They're gonna be deaf as doorknobs …"

The detective's cackling continued until Marie, her own musical laughter ringing in Kory's ears a few miles away, shoved him away from the phone.

"Bye, Kory," Marie said, still laughing. "Catherine and Nicole will need explicit directions, so they can find us, and so they can follow us back to the city. Phone me when they're ready to take some notes."

"Roberts-Holm speaking."

"Graham? Luke Manguson again."

"Luke! I was hoping to hear. What can you tell me?"

"I can tell you that our group — well, my wife Kory — was able to reroute the circuitry at the Chaos headquarters in such a way that their basement facility just blew itself up. Kory stayed to see it happen. No explosions at Wimbledon, we assume, although those explosive devices are still in place there.

"My next call, after this, is to the Metro police to ask them to get their bomb squads over to the All England Club, posthaste.

"And I'll add, Graham, that we're in agreement here," Luke continued, "that, with Kory's having routed all the circuitry away from the All England, Chaos is finished, so far as their Wimbledon terror attack is concerned."

Roberts-Holm took a moment to absorb Luke's news and to think about the implications for MI6.

"Well … this is marvelous, Luke. Please give your wife my heartfelt congratulations. That's an extraordinary technical accomplishment.

"You must be very proud of her, Luke."

"Well … I'd say I'm more in awe of her, Graham."

"Yes," Roberts-Holm said, thinking it over. "Much better said, but, big picture," he continued, "we've still got the Chaos organization intact and thinking about their next targets, yes?"

"No," Luke answered without hesitation, "not at all.

"Once the Metro bomb squads find and disarm the explosives at the All England, Graham, the U.K. government will shift into high gear and get Fedorov and his accomplices deported. They may, in fact, shut down the USSR's entire London embassy and send everybody back to Moscow."

"Oh … yes … right … of course," agreed Roberts-Holm. "I wasn't thinking, Luke. *This* Prime Minister is not going to stand for this. She'll demand the USSR get Anton Fedorov and his group of thugs on their way home by this time tomorrow. She'll turn it into an international embarrassment for the Kremlin.

"You're quite right, Luke. Chaos is finished … at least on our turf."

There was a pause, both pondering Chaos's future.

Then Luke continued.

"But speaking of Fedorov, Graham, I talked minutes ago with my sister. She phoned from the All England to say that Fedorov was on the grounds, no doubt for the purpose of triggering the explosives. But now, if he is *still* there, his target may shift to Rebecca herself … or possibly … to the teens who are often with her.

"He's reportedly in disguise, but the girl who was kidnapped earlier by Fedorov and his people saw him … saw through the disguise.

"There's no question in her mind that it was him.

"As soon as Fedorov and the Jones girl recognized each other, he fled on foot, apparently to make the phone call that, to his eternal humiliation, actually blew up his own outfit, but I'm betting he's still there."

There was a pause while both men considered this.

Then Luke continued.

"He's dangerous, Graham, and perhaps even more so, now that he'll have realized that his automated destruction arrangements have been defeated. He may not know *how* those arrangements were defeated, and he can hardly know, as yet, that the circuits were rerouted so as to blow up his own headquarters, but he has tried to kill Rebecca several times before.

"If he is there on the grounds with her ... and young Miss Jones is certain that he was, just minutes ago ... then Rebecca is in harm's way ... again."

The MI6 leader's response was decisive.

"I'll have my two men on their way immediately, Luke. They'll be allowed to carry their sidearms onto the grounds. They can act as your sister's bodyguards for the rest of the day, and beyond, if you want.

"Tonight, after Rebecca is safe at your house with you and Kory and Matt, you and I can talk by phone about how to protect her, going forward. I don't know her well, but I know her enough, by reputation, to know she's not going to hide in your and Kory's house. It seems obvious to me that she's irrepressible.

"I mean," Roberts-Holm continued, "she's been at All England all morning, despite knowing that explosives could go off at any time. She's not deterred by anything, it seems to me ... right, Luke?"

Luke nodded to himself.

"My sister had complete confidence in my wife's technological acumen, Graham," he replied. "Once Kory reported, on Saturday morning, her success with the circuitry, I doubt if Rebecca gave the danger any more thought."

He hesitated, then continued.

"Rebecca also maintains a healthy confidence that she is in God's hands, for as long as He wants her to serve Him here on earth. She doesn't think He is likely to be finished using her yet, if you can see what I mean.

"God may allow her to be treated roughly ... you've seen the scar that runs across her face ... but she doubts He is finished with her."

Roberts-Holm considered this for a moment, then commented, "Well, Luke, as you're aware, my Christian faith holds to the same perspective ... but ..."

"I know ... I know," said Luke. "*Acting* on that faith in all circumstances, including walking around the All England, knowing explosives have been planted ..."

Another pause, then Roberts-Holm.

"She'll be at Wimbledon tomorrow morning, Luke?"

"Yes," Luke replied. "She will. And your offer of the two agents to act as bodyguards right now … today … is exactly what I was going to ask of you."

"Good then. They'll be on their way in five minutes. Tell me how they can locate Rebecca once they get there, and how she is dressed today, if you know that."

"She'll probably be near Centre Court, and she's wearing the traditional all-white skirt and blouse for women competitors, since she's warming up some of the qualifiers today. And she'll probably have a gaggle of teens around her, Graham.

"You know … autographs."

"Got it, Luke. My agents will be with her in 15."

Monday, 1 p.m., the All England Club

SallyBelle and Thomas jogged away from Rebecca, going in slightly differing directions. She watched them disappear, then saw two men approaching.

Each was dressed in casual attire, like that of most male spectators. Rebecca noted, however, the looseness of their collared short-sleeved shirts, suggesting they were armed. She instantly began plotting an escape route in her mind, although something in their demeanor suggested friend, not foe.

As she gathered herself to turn and sprint toward a security checkpoint, she saw both men pull from their hip pockets an identification folder. She relaxed.

"Ma'am," said one, holding his ID at her eye level, "we were sent by Graham Roberts-Holm to serve as your bodyguards for as long as you might need us. We were also informed by Mr. Roberts-Holm, as we left our HQ, that your brother has requested that you join him and his team at his office.

"It seems the Prime Minister has requested recommendations from your team regarding her response to the threats posed by Anton Fedorov, Artur Volkov, Tatyana Kuznetsova, and others in their 'terrorist cell,' as she put it. She has been made aware of the explosives that were planted here, and of your team's success in turning those terror devices against themselves.

"The Minister, respectfully, requests your recommendations within the hour."

The men waited courteously while Rebecca processed this.

After several moments, the MI6 spokesman continued.

"We're available to you right now to drive you to the ISP building, ma'am, or to follow you to ISP in your car, if you'd prefer to drive yourself."

Rebecca turned this over in her mind, then replied.

"You're very thoughtful to offer, gentlemen," she said in her low contralto, her gray eyes moving from one to the other, "but I'd like to ask you, instead, to make Miss SallyBelle Jones and Master Thomas Chambers the objects of your protection this afternoon. Mr. Fedorov and his colleagues have already successfully kidnapped SallyBelle once and attempted to kidnap Thomas.

"Mr. Fedorov knows they are here … knows they are both serving as BBGs … and can easily find each of them at any time, since the BBG assignments are posted and available for anyone to see.

"I'll drive myself to ISP, given the fact that the Minister has specifically requested our team's advice and counsel … and within the hour."

She consulted her watch.

"I can be back here in time to warm up my next qualifier … at four. So, I'm going to run, gentlemen. Please attend to my BBGs for me.

"They're precious to me … and they're vulnerable."

The men looked at each other.

"Ma'am," said the spokesman, "we'll need to check with Mr. Roberts-Holm on that. We've been ordered to provide *you* with protection, and we've got to do that, unless he releases us from that order.

"Please give me a moment to run to the nearest phone to ask him if your request is okay with him."

Rebecca smiled and said, "I understand. Please tell Mr. Roberts-Holm that the only way you could have stopped me would have been to shoot me."

Without further conversation, she laughed, spun, and ran in the direction of the VIP lot, where she had parked the family Volvo that morning.

The two MI6 agents looked at each other, shrugged unhappily, and moved off at a jog to find a phone and then to study the BBG assignment list.

As Rebecca neared her car in her graceful run, she gradually slowed to a walk and then, 20 feet from her vehicle, stopped. There in the center of the VIP parking area, unconcerned about others' eyes on her, she bowed her head.

She breathed deeply once, and prayed.

Father … be present … be present …

Be present with us as we seek to give counsel to our government leaders …

Be present with me, please, as I travel to my brother's side …

Be present with SallyBelle … Thomas … and me … to keep us from harm …

Father … be present … be present …

She opened her eyes, looked up, breathed deeply once more, and jogged to her vehicle. She unlocked the driver's side door to her right-hand-drive Volvo, tossed the ready-satchel across the front seat, and slipped gracefully behind the wheel.

Almost immediately, as she prepared to insert the key in the ignition, she felt a familiar, long-ago-experienced sensation of physical weakness. A debilitating weakness that swiftly, inexorably, turned her muscles to water. She recognized the sudden incapacity from a years-past experience on an upper floor of what had since become Anton Fedorov's Chaos headquarters, and yet again, two years after that experience, in a San Francisco apartment building.

And she knew, as she slumped forward into the steering wheel, her keys falling noisily to the floorboard, that Anton Fedorov himself was present, perhaps close enough to touch her.

She felt a searing, acidic breath on the back of her neck.

Her eyes closed.

Moments earlier, Fedorov crouched on the back-seat floorboard of Rebecca's sedan, the garrote coiled in his left hand, confident that finally he could bring an end to the troublesome woman's earthly career. This time, the killing would be close, swift, and personal. Nothing indirect.

No firebombing of her home in *hopes* she would be there.

No kidnapping arrangements in *hopes* she would appear.

This would be certain death ... right now ... at his hand.

He had hardly settled into his position, flattened against the seatback of the driver's seat, when he heard the soft footfall of her tennis shoes. Then the key in the lock. Then the opening door. Then the sound of the woman slipping athletically into her vehicle. Then the closing of the door.

Then the sound of keys being readied for the ignition switch.

He rose from his kneeling position and, his left hand holding one grip-handle of the garrote, he raised that end of the implement over the helpless woman's left shoulder, while his right hand simultaneously reached over her right. There, in perfect position to snatch both grip-handles and to pull the wire, with an upward, left-to-right slicing movement, Fedorov's muscles tensed.

He *willed* this final act with all his mental strength.

Rebecca, her upper body collapsed against the steering wheel, all her considerable muscular capacity gone, sensed the satanic hands positioned over each of her shoulders ... knew what was going to happen ... and *willed* her mind, her sole internal resource, into action.

Silently, she cried out.

Father ... help me ...

Father ... help me ...

Please ... help me now ...

She sensed the strong hands tensing ... hands powerfully gripping the garrote handles ... the deadly wire inches from her throat ... sensed the murderer's biceps and forearms bulging in preparation ... then ... then sensed the hands somehow hesitating ... hesitating just millimeters from the slicing movement of wire into flesh.

Time seemed to stop.

She was aware that seconds were passing with no further movement from her assailant, yet still with no muscular response available to her. Suddenly, her driver's side door opened and someone else's rough, muscular hands seized her around the waist, dragged her forcefully from the car, lifted her clear of the vehicle, and moved her to the just-opened rear door of the Volvo.

These hands and arms flung her unresponsive body across the back seat. There, she felt Anton Fedorov seize her shoulders, grab her wrists, and rip them up and behind her back. She felt him then bind her wrists with what felt and sounded like strapping tape. Finally, she saw Fedorov's hands pull a strip of black cloth across her eyes and felt him tie the strip tightly behind her head.

At the same time, Rebecca felt the assailant who had thrown her into the back seat binding her ankles together. She then heard both men moving to the front seat, heard the Volvo's engine start, and felt the car move carefully, so as, she knew, not to attract attention, out of the VIP lot. She realized the second attacker must be driving, since, as they moved into the flow of traffic, the man ordered Fedorov to consult a street map and determine "the most efficient route to the van."

She heard the map rustling, heard Fedorov suggesting the route, and then decided she actually knew the driver's voice. The fact that the man had *ordered* Fedorov to consult the map, and the tone he used as their conversation continued, made clear to her that the voice could only be that of the Reverend Father Artur Volkov. Technically, she knew, Volkov outranked Fedorov in the USSR's various hierarchies, but somehow, she sensed also, Fedorov's level of satanic power introduced a certain ambiguity into the relationship.

"What happened back there, Fedorov?" demanded Volkov after several minutes of travel. "You froze. You had the woman's death in your hands … and you froze.

"*What happened?*"

"I … I don't know," came the halting reply, Fedorov's voice strangely small and submissive, in contrast to Volkov's. "I had the implement positioned perfectly, and the woman was helpless … but something stopped me.

"I don't know what happened.

"Something made it impossible for me to complete the motion.

"Something stopped me."

There followed a full minute of silence, as the car continued to maneuver through London's afternoon traffic. Then Volkov spoke again.

"What do you mean 'something' stopped you?" said Volkov. "What kind of 'something' could possibly have interfered with your completing the kill?"

Another silence followed, then Fedorov attempted an answer.

"Something … Supernatural … stopped me," he managed to say.

This answer produced a still longer silence.

"There is no God, Fedorov. There is no Supernature. There is nothing that stopped your kill motion of this woman except your own cowardice," said Volkov, his anger building as he delivered his short sermon. "Coward!" he shouted.

Fedorov did not reply, but he knew better. He knew from long personal experience that Supernature existed.

It was perhaps not the same Supernature that had brought his killing motion to a halt, moments earlier … but it was Supernature, nonetheless … *his* Supernature, the Supernature that had inhabited his own body and mind and soul since the time, not so long in his past, when he invited Ultimate Evil into himself.

He *knew.*

Supernature existed.

CHAPTER THIRTEEN

Monday, 1:30 p.m., the ISP offices

"WE CAN'T AFFORD TO WAIT ANY LONGER FOR REBECCA," SAID her brother. "Let's go ahead and formulate something for the Prime Minister. I want to phone her office by two, at the latest."

Kory Manguson, well read from childhood in the fields of U.K. history and government — in addition to her technological wizardry — was first to speak.

"I suggest the Minister communicate directly with her opposite number in Moscow. She wants to rectify this situation quickly. Any route she chooses other than one that goes to the very top of the Soviet government will be time-wasting. To that end … the end of immediacy … I suggest also that she inform the Kremlin that she will, this very afternoon, go to the British news outlets.

"She should tell Moscow that she will speak directly with ownership of all high-profile U.K. media outlets. She will describe to them — media ownership — a Soviet plot to slaughter hundreds of athletes, their families, members of the media, members of the royal family, and others in attendance at the Championships. She should say that she will insist that the media outlets photograph the results of the Metro police bomb searches … that they show the actual explosives that have been planted all over the grounds at Wimbledon.

"She should say that she will urge the media outlets to interview members of the bomb squads, to have them explain in detail what explosives they found, and where they found them.

"She should say that she insists that the Kremlin recall to Moscow every leader engaged in the plot, starting with Anton Fedorov, Artur Volkov, and Tatyana Kuznetsova, and, as well, other high-level administrators in the Soviet embassy in London. She should insist that every ranking individual involved be recalled from British soil and placed on flights to Moscow by noon tomorrow."

Before Luke could respond to his wife's wide-ranging set of recommendations, there was a knock on the conference-room door.

"Yes?" called Luke.

A young intern opened the door far enough for her face to appear.

"Sir," she said, "a shop owner near the All England Club just phoned Metro to report seeing two men carry a woman, wearing all-white tennis gear, bound and blindfolded, from a Volvo sedan to a light-colored van. He had just come out his shop's rear door, into an alleyway, and thought he should report what he saw.

"He wrote down the license number of the Volvo before he called Metro.

"Sir, it's your sister's car."

The room fell absolutely silent.

The intern nervously spoke again.

"Sir," she said, "he emphasized that the woman was wearing tennis whites."

Luke nodded his thanks and the intern disappeared.

After another half-minute of quiet, Sid Belton spoke.

"Luke," he said, "here's what we gotta do.

"First, authorize Kory t' phone th' PM's office an' say everything she just said t' us right here. We could sit here fer a week an' not improve on anything she just said.

"Second, you and Matt gotta stay outta this until there's a clear target you two can go after. She's yer sister an' she's Matt's wife an' there's no way in th' world either one of you are gonna be able t' think straight about what t' do about her bein' taken like that ... you two gotta stay outta th' detective part of this.

"Third, y' gotta turn this over t' me and Jaakov. We're detectives. This is what we do. Th' rest of you are smart people ... but this is what we do. Leave it t' us. We'll get t' th' bottom a' this ... an' prob'ly before anything else can happen t' 'er."

Belton looked around the table. The faces were blank, stunned.

He looked at Luke.

"Luke?"

Luke nodded. "Go."

Belton looked at Matt.

Matt nodded. "Go."

Monday, 2:30 p.m., the ISP offices

Detectives Belton and Adelman remained alone in the small conference room, having been furnished with two telephones, both set up with direct lines to the outside. They had also been supplied with two of Luke's young interns, to serve as runners, if needed. Belton, ending a lengthy call, hung up his phone.

He turned to Adelman.

"My guy at Metro says there was a young couple who happened t' be crossin' th' VIP parkin' area when Ms. Clark was taken …

"Says th' couple saw a woman fittin' Ms. Clark's description — wearin' tennis whites — get in a Volvo, then get jerked outta th' car by a big, heavy-set guy … big, broad shoulders … maybe in his 40s … dressed in suit an' tie … not dressed like a typical guy who'd be hired t' do a snatch n' grab …"

"Artur Volkov," said Adelman.

"Right," agreed Belton.

"My Metro guy says th' guy in th' suit an' tie threw th' woman in th' back seat … says th' woman seemed limp … like maybe she was unconscious … says they saw another guy in th' back seat … says th' guy was funny lookin'… somethin' odd about his face … or his forehead …"

"Anton Fedorov," said Adelman.

"Right," agreed Belton.

"My Metro guy says th' couple said th' two guys started strappin' th' woman's wrists and ankles together, an' that's when th' couple got scared an' started runnin' fer th' gates t' try t' get t' a phone booth … couldn't find one … finally did. Th' booth was occupied, with a line waitin' … but they talked their way t' th' head a' th' line."

Belton took a moment to look at his notes, then continued.

"My guy says th' couple finally phoned Metro with th' report, but th' on-duty phone guy at th' desk was still bogged down with th' Prime Minister's office callin' 'im with questions … didn't get t' listen t' th' report from th' Wimbledon parkin' lot … from th' young couple … 'til 10 minutes ago …

"Says that's it … that's what they got … apologized fer not gettin' that info t' us faster … says they're still tryin' t' get more info on th' van, but there may not be any more t' get … it's just a light-colored van … says there are maybe 100 a' those in th' city an' maybe 1,000 a' those in th' country …"

He paused for a moment, then continued.

"One more thing, Jaakov," Belton said. "My guy at Metro also said they checked on th' Volvo … said it was definitely Ms. Clark's car … said th' license plates were hers … an' said there was a leather satchel on th' floorboard … had her passport an' three Barringtons Swords competition throwin' knives in it."

Belton took a long, deep breath.

"That's what I got, Jaakov.

"Ya' got anything from Roberts-Holm at MI6?"

Adelman shook his head.

"Nothing helpful, but I'm troubled by something else … not just by Rebecca's abduction … I'm troubled by something else, as well, Sid.

"Roberts-Holm," Adelman continued, "went over the sequence for me… twice. He said that Luke phoned him … they agreed that two agents would rush to Wimbledon to serve as bodyguards … he said those two found Rebecca and explained about the PM's request for recommendations within the hour … he said she declined their offer to drive her, or to follow her, back here to meet with us … and he said that she turned and sprinted toward the VIP lot where her Volvo was parked.

"That was Roberts-Holm's summary.

"And now," Adelman continued, "this young couple reports to the police seeing two men — Fedorov and Volkov, almost certainly — abduct Rebecca, and that she appeared to be unconscious.

"And this, after she *sprinted* to her car."

Adelman shook his head again.

"That doesn't make sense, Sidney."

Belton nodded.

"An' I know why, Jaakov."

They nodded to each other, each reading the other's mind.

They started to speak at the same time. Adelman deferred.

He gestured to his partner to go ahead.

Belton did.

"How'd they know," he said, "she'd be goin' t' her car at that moment?"

3 p.m., Graham Roberts-Holm's office, MI6 Headquarters

"How'd they know, Graham," said Belton, sitting with Adelman in the MI6 office, "that Ms. Clark would be told, right then, about th' PM's demand fer recommendations? How'd they know that Ms. Clark'd be goin' t' 'er car? How'd they know t' be waitin' fer her just at that minute, just as she got there after talkin' t' yer two agents?

"How'd they know, Graham?"

Adelman leaned forward in his chair.

"The only way Volkov and Fedorov — and they've got to be the two men the couple saw carry off the abduction — could possibly have known," he said, "that Rebecca would be given the information about the Prime Minister's demand for recommendations would be if you, Graham, or your agents … told them.

"They were told, Graham. Volkov and Fedorov were *told.* And, once they knew Rebecca would be informed, they knew she would be sprinting to her Volvo at that moment. No one else had the information about the PM's demand … just we, you, and your two agents.

"How could Fedorov and Volkov have known to be waiting for her, and positioned perfectly to assault and kidnap her, at that moment?

"Rebecca was not expected back at her brother's house, where she and Matt have been staying, until late tonight, after the evening matches finished. She expected to be driving her two BBGs to their homes about then. She was not due at her car until … roughly … 11 p.m. tonight, at the earliest … maybe much later than that, depending on how long those late matches ran.

"How did they know, Graham?"

Roberts-Holm flushed crimson.

"You're actually accusing *me* of informing Fedorov and Volkov of the PM's demand, and then sending my agents to talk to Mrs. Clark about that, so that she would race to her car? Are you mad? How can you even form that thought?

"And," he continued after a moment's reflection, "even if that preposterous idea were true, how would I … and my agents … and Volkov and Fedorov … how would any of us know that Rebecca would decline my agents' offer to drive her to the ISP building, and, instead, would send my agents off to guard the two young people?

"You're clutching at straws here."

He slammed his fist down on his desk.

"*Nothing* of what you're implying makes sense!

"Absolutely *nothing!*"

Belton and Adelman were unmoved.

They stared into the flushed face of Roberts-Holm and shook their heads.

"I'll start with your second point," said Adelman, having received a nod from his partner. "Anyone who knows Rebecca would also know that declining your agents' offer for protection and, instead, sending those agents off to protect her two teens, would be *exactly* what her response would be.

"That's *exactly* who she is, and that's exactly what she'd *always* do."

"Yeah," added Belton, "*you* know Ms. Clark that well, Mr. Big Shot MI6 guy, at least from reputation, and *we* know Ms. Clark that well, an' … I can promise ya' this … Artur Volkov an' Anton Fedorov know 'er that well, too … they know *about* 'er, at least … they know *about* 'er in almost as much detail as any of us …

"So … we'll ask ya' again, sir … how'd those dirtbags know she'd be told about th' PM's demand fer recommendations? Once she knew that, *of course* she'd be runnin' t' her car at that minute.

"So … how'd they know, sir?

"Huh?

"How'd they know?"

Adelman spoke again.

"*Mister Roberts-Holm,*" he said, suddenly standing, his looming, angular frame towering over the seated MI6 official, "you know as well as we do that the first hours of a kidnapping are critical. Furthermore, the police report from the young couple suggested Rebecca may have been unconscious.

"We don't have time to sit here in your office and listen to your manufactured outrage. If you didn't tip off Fedorov and Volkov, then who did?"

Adelman's face was red with fury.

"Who, in this sieve-like organization," he shouted, "would have had that information, and then would have tipped off the Russians?

"Who, Graham?"

Roberts-Holm stood to face Adelman, the width of his desk keeping the two men from being chest-to-chest. He was breathing heavily.

"No one ... no one, I tell you!"

And then, in a flash, his face changed. His eyes slid away from Adelman's. He turned his head to one side, then stepped back from his desk, pushing his swivel chair out of the way. He turned slowly to face the window.

The silence grew long.

Finally, Roberts-Holm spoke, almost in a whisper.

"There might be one other," he said softly.

Monday, 4:15 p.m., the west London suburb of Ealing

Jaakov Adelman and Graham Roberts-Holm stood on the front porch of an aging frame home in a working-class neighborhood, waiting for Sid Belton to climb the four steps. Belton slowly negotiated the stairs, using his cane carefully and, as always, declining assistance from his colleagues.

Belton joined the two at the front door and, not hesitating, reached up and pounded on the lion's head door knocker.

"Law enforcement!" he shouted, knowing he could not accurately claim to be police, and knowing that shouting "detectives" or "MI6" would produce only confusion from the home's occupants. After several moments, the three men heard movement from within the house, and, after another delay, heard someone manipulating the door latches on the inside. The door opened hesitantly, and a woman's face appeared in the opening. Her countenance asked wordlessly for an explanation.

Roberts-Holm held his MI6 ID near her face.

"Ma'am," said Roberts-Holm, whose native London dialect would, the men had agreed, be less alarming than Belton's harsh Brooklynese or Adelman's clear, but Hebrew-tinged, English, "we need to come in, please. There are some questions we need to ask of your house guest."

"I have no house guest."

"No," said Roberts-Holm, "but you do have a tenant."

The woman hesitated further, then backed away from the door and pulled it open as she did. The men entered, then looked at her inquiringly. But the woman turned and walked timidly away, leaving the men standing uncertainly in the front hallway. Belton looked up at Roberts-Holm.

"Shout," he said.

Roberts-Holm did.

"ANYONE HOME?"

Roberts-Holm's rich baritone echoed through the house.

Silence greeted the two-word inquiry.

"We've no search warrant," Roberts-Holm said to the two Americans. "We really can't go looking through the house."

"Ms. Clark was taken at about one o'clock, which is about three hours ago now," said Belton. "She appeared t' th' witness who saw 'er transferred from 'er Volvo t' a van t' be unconscious. Jaakov an' I are foreigners here. We don't know anything about English search warrants."

With that, Adelman started up the stairs, taking the steps two at a time. Belton clumped off to examine the ground-floor rooms. Roberts-Holm stood at the front door, helplessly watching, feeling guilty.

Then, shaking his head unhappily, he started off after Sid Belton.

Five minutes later, Adelman stood at the top of the stairs, as Belton and Roberts-Holm arrived at the foot. They shook their heads at each other.

But then Adelman, looking down at the others, said, "There's a locked room just off the top of the stairs behind me. It's not a closet. Unless you're planning to arrest me, or something, Graham, I'm going to go in."

A pause … then, from Roberts-Holm and Belton, in unison, "Wait for us."

Belton, moving at his top speed, arrived at the locked door only seconds after Roberts-Holm. He nodded for the Englishman to speak.

"Law enforcement here," Roberts-Holm called through the door.

"Open, please. We need to speak to you."

There was no response.

Belton turned his head and looked up at his partner.

Adelman moved in front of the other two and stood 3 feet from the door-knob. He raised his right foot high, coiled his body, and crashed his military-style, lace-up shoe into the flimsy door latch. The wood around the latch splintered.

The door now stood ajar. Adelman shoved the door with his open hand.

It swung open.

There, seated at a small card table, not looking up at the men, but down at her lap, sat Aarushi Singh, third member of the original MI6 subcommittee on "unexplained and unexplainable data and their sources."

The tableau remained frozen for nearly 10 seconds, the three men staring at the small woman, the woman continuing to look down at her lap, where her hands were folded and still.

Finally, Roberts-Holm crossed the room, pulled out a chair across the small table from the woman, sat, and indicated with a gesture that Belton and Adelman might sit at the tattered sofa near the door where they stood.

"Aarushi," said Roberts-Holm calmly, "what did you tell, and to whom did you tell it? We need to know quickly, since Mrs. Clark was taken forcibly more than three hours ago. She may be …

"We need to find her. Now, Aarushi.

"What did you tell, and to whom did you tell it?"

In response, Aarushi Singh simply tucked her chin down further, her gaze locked on her own hands, which remained still and folded in her lap. This barely perceptible movement heightened Sidney Belton's frustration.

He raised his voice, a voice formidable even when he was calm. A voice much deeper in pitch than the detective's diminutive size would suggest.

Now, in this emergency, his voice was not calm.

"Yer boss here is gonna be nice t' ya', but we're not, ma'am," he said loudly in the small space, "an' we're gonna have answers from ya' … an' right now …

"We're not goin' anywhere without knowin' what ya' told somebody … an' who the somebody was … so ya' might as well …"

Belton was interrupted by the woman, who spoke with an Indian accent in a carefully modulated and surprisingly clear voice.

"They threatened my family back home … in New Delhi. They know my parents and my siblings. They know their names. They know where they live."

She looked up at Roberts-Holm.

"I'm so sorry, sir," she said, tears starting down her cheeks.

"I'm just so very sorry."

Roberts-Holm nodded. "I know, Aarushi," he said.

"And I understand the terrible pressure you've faced. Once these Chaos people get to a person, they will threaten that person with unspeakable things, and you and I understand them well enough to know that they are perfectly capable of doing exactly what they threaten.

"That's past now, Aarushi. Let that go.

"Tell us what we must know in order to find Mrs. Clark."

The woman took a deep, ragged breath, and began.

"Ms. Kuznetsova came to me … to this house … a little before one today … and said that, if I wanted to save my parents and my siblings and their children … my family in India … if I wanted to keep them from being *tortured* … and then *killed* … then I would tell her what I knew … tell her how Mr. Volkov and Mr. Fedorov … how they could 'lay hands on' Mrs. Clark … immediately."

She began to sob, her small body wracked with the agony of betrayal.

Roberts-Holm rose, moved to her side, placed his hands gently on her shoulders, bent close to her ear, and said softly, "Aarushi, what did you tell Tatyana?

"We just need to know what you said. Then you and I can talk, tomorrow, about next steps for you and your family. Just tell us what you said to her, Aarushi."

Her voice was so low and soft that only Roberts-Holm could hear her complete answer, though Belton and Adelman strained to hear as well.

"I told Ms. Kuznetsova about the Prime Minister's wanting Mrs. Clark's group's recommendations immediately … I knew that would lead Ms. Kuznetsova … and Mr. Volkov and Mr. Fedorov … to realize you'd send our agents to Mrs. Clark … to tell her about the Minister's demand … and then Mr. Volkov and Mr. Fedorov would know that she … Mrs. Clark … would run as fast as she could to her car … as soon as she was given the information …

"I knew … and … I think … so did they … the Chaos people …that Mrs. Clark would tell our MI6 agents to guard the teens, not her…

"Because that's who she is …

"She'd go to her car alone … without protection … as fast as she could run …

"That's all …

"That's all I said …

"I'm just so sorry."

Roberts-Holm gave the woman's shoulders a gentle squeeze, stood, and looked to Sid Belton. Roberts-Holm raised his eyebrows.

Belton shook his head.

"What else did ya' tell th' Kuznetsova woman, ma'am?" he said more gently. "That info would … like ya' just said … get Volkov and Fedorov t' Ms. Clark's car, but what else did ya' tell 'er? An' what did she say t' *you?*

"We need t' know *where* they've taken 'er, ma'am. She's been gone fer more than three hours …

"We need t' know … right now … where'd they take 'er?"

Aarushi Singh shook her head in despair.

"I don't know …

"I just don't know."

The three men slipped into Roberts-Holm's silver Audi Quattro, and collectively sighed their disappointment. As the car pulled away, Belton spoke first.

"Y' think she really didn't know where they've gone?" he asked.

Roberts-Holm shook his head.

"I can't imagine she knew any more than she told us," he said sadly. "And I can't imagine why Tatyana would have given Aarushi information about their destination, even if Tatyana had that information … and she may not have. She just wanted to know what she could tell Volkov and Fedorov about how to get to Rebecca … fast.

"Nothing else."

They rode in silence back toward the MI6 office where Adelman had parked the ISP Defender he and Belton had used to get to Roberts-Holm. At length, Adelman turned to face Belton, who sat alone on the back seat.

"What's next, Sid?" he asked.

Belton fixed his partner with his deep-set black eyes and asked, "What was th' name a' that newspaper guy that stopped Marie an' Jack on th' sidewalk near th' ISP building th' other day? Some French-soundin' thing, wasn't it?"

Adelman nodded.

"Yes … give me a minute."

He sorted through his mind for a moment, then found it.

"Louis Bois ... said he was with the London bureau of *The New York Times*. Knew quite a bit about us, it seemed.

"Why do you ask, Sid?"

"He told Marie an' Jack he had contacts at th' Soviet embassy, remember?"

Monday, 5:15 p.m., MI6 offices

Graham Roberts-Holm dialed a number given him by his assistant, who was staying late in the emergency. He was passed through two people at the *Times'* London Bureau before reaching Louis Bois.

"Monsieur Bois, this is Graham Roberts-Holm at MI6. You and I spoke several days ago. You wanted my comments about New York City Russian Mafia money for a story you planned to run, over the weekend. I was not forthcoming. You and your editors have thus far held back on that story, I think."

"Oui, monsieur ... that is correct ... we have held back on the story, pending further developments. What can I do for you today?"

Roberts-Holm "explained Sid Belton" to the journalist, and turned the conversation over to Belton, who without preamble asked Bois how good his contacts were at the Soviet embassy. Told by Bois that he had two contacts that were completely reliable, the detective went on to describe the desperate situation with Rebecca Clark, Artur Volkov, and Anton Fedorov.

"What'r th' chances ya' can get yer friends at th' embassy t' tell ya' somethin' about where these dirtbags have taken Ms. Clark, Mr. Bois?

"Good chance? No chance? Fifty-percent chance?"

Bois was silent, considering the request.

Then he said, "Oui, monsieur ... the chance is ... good.

"You may know," Bois continued, "or perhaps not ... that the Prime Minister's office has ordered the Soviet embassy's key officials and KGB operatives to leave the country, and, as we understand it, by noon tomorrow. I have already been in communication with my sources there. They are *beyond* furious with Volkov, Fedorov, and Tatyana Kuznetsova, the three whom they hold primarily responsible for the PM's expulsion order of this afternoon.

"I'd think my friends at the embassy would strongly consider giving me any information whatever that might punish these ... ah ... what was your turn of phrase, detective? Ah, yes, these *dirtbags* ... your excellent technical term for them.

"And so, I must say ... the chance is ... good.

"*Non* ... better than that, detective ... *tres* good."

Monday, 5:45 p.m., MI6 offices

"Roberts-Holm speaking."

"Louis Bois again, monsieur. Is Detective Belton still there with you in your office, and, if so, may I speak with him, s'il vous plait?"

"We've been counting the minutes, Louis ... may I place you on speaker?"

"Oui, of course.

"I have your information, sir," said Bois to Belton.

"Great. Lemme hear it."

"My embassy contacts say that Volkov and Fedorov have taken your Mrs. Clark in a commercial van, that they have placed stolen license plates on the van to preclude identification, and that they're driving her to Scotland ... to Glasgow."

"Scotland!" exclaimed the detective.

"Oui, monsieur. I am told the KGB has leased a small, unused airstrip east of the city ... toward Edinburgh. My embassy contacts say the KGB owns a twin-prop, American-built Cessna, with a range of over 1,000 miles. The aircraft is housed at that rural airport, and no other aircraft are present there. I am told further that Anton Fedorov is a licensed pilot and is fully qualified to fly that aircraft at night.

"My contacts understand that Fedorov ... probably without Volkov or Kuznetsova ... plans to fly Mrs. Clark to Moscow, presumably, given the Cessna's range, flying Glasgow to Oslo, Norway, thence to Tromso, in the extreme north of that country, thence east to Archangel, in Russia.

"The final leg would be Archangel to Moscow.

"Once they have her at the Kremlin, they can … ah … deal with her … however they like … and at their leisure, so to say."

Roberts-Holm looked at Belton and Adelman. All three were staggered by the information. And they each had the same thought. Could the information be trusted? Could they act on what they had just heard?

Bois continued, as though reading their minds.

"I imagine that you and your colleagues are wondering, monsieur, whether my information is reliable. Well … I have two questions for you.

"First, why would I … or my contacts … invent such a tale?

"And second, what other information, conflicting or otherwise, do you have, regarding Mrs. Clark's whereabouts?"

All three of Bois's listeners found themselves nodding to each other in apparent agreement with the obvious answers to both questions.

"Those questions are unanswerable, Louis," said Roberts-Holm.

"We can only express our gratitude to you. But, knowing media professionals as I do, I want to ask you this.

"What will you want from us in return?"

Bois's cheerful laughter came clearly through the MI6 speakerphone.

"Shrewd, Monsieur Roberts-Holm. Quite shrewd."

"And your response?"

"An exclusive, monsieur … once this is all over. An exclusive interview with you, at least some of which I can actually use … in print."

Roberts-Holm laughed.

"Done, sir …

"Done."

Monday evening, 7:45 p.m., a private airport north of London

Jaakov Adelman ran through the checklist for the Beechcraft Model 50 Twin Bonanza, a four-seat, twin-engine prop plane on emergency loan from the U.S. embassy in London. Luke Manguson, seated beside him in the cockpit, read slowly through the bullet points in the checklist. Adelman followed each checklist item with his eyes and hands.

Standing on the port wing, one of the two U.S. embassy staff members who had been directed to assist helped Adelman find and interpret the Beechcraft's instrument array. The whole flight would be done on instruments, the most difficult kind of flying, especially in an unfamiliar aircraft.

Meanwhile, Matt Clark, his 6-foot, 4-inch frame folded uncomfortably into one of the two cramped seats behind the pilot and co-pilot's seats, studied the route data given him by the embassy's staff members.

The route information suggested a flight plan that would take them directly from the small London-area airport where the Beechcraft was housed to the even smaller airstrip outside Glasgow. Flight time was estimated at two hours.

The checklist completed, Adelman saluted the two embassy men, turned the ignition switch, and cranked the engines to full power while he stood on the left-wheel brake. The aircraft spun responsively to its left, Adelman released the left-wheel brake, and the agile Beechcraft sprang forward toward the main taxiway.

Matt Clark had not been the obvious choice to accompany Adelman and Luke on this desperate flight to Scotland. His useless left arm and hand always made his utility questionable on any venture likely to include physical conflict, with or without weapons. But Matt made clear he would be on the flight, and anyone trying to stop him would have a fight on his hands.

"This is my wife we're talking about," he had said firmly.

"I'm going to be on that airplane, people.

"And furthermore … there is nothing wrong with my shooting hand."

No one said, or even thought, anything to the contrary, once his position had been made clear with such impressive finality.

Louis Bois had learned from his Soviet contacts that the Cessna 421, waiting near Glasgow to carry Fedorov to Moscow, was normally configured to seat six passengers, although the one leased and modified by the Soviets was set up to seat only a pilot and co-pilot.

Aft the two pilots' seats, this Cessna was set up for cargo only. In this instance, the cargo would comprise just one person, a woman bound hand and foot and lying prone in the cargo space. If Louis Bois's embassy staff sources were correct, the Cessna could easily handle the distances involved — Glasgow, Oslo, Tromso, Archangel, Moscow — and could readily be flown by a single pilot.

Belton and Adelman had estimated that the KGB van, with Rebecca inside its cargo hold, would reach the Glasgow area by about 10 p.m. Their Beechcraft, flying at 180 mph, would reach the area at about the same time.

It would be a close-run thing.

CHAPTER FOURTEEN

Monday, 8:30 p.m., Glasgow, Scotland

FIONA BRUCE, 37, WHEELED THE CANADIAN-BUILT, RIGHT-HAND-drive F-150 out of her long, dirt-and-gravel driveway, and mentally began to wrestle with the peremptory order she had received a half-hour earlier from London. On the one hand, the money she received for serving as caretaker for the tiny airstrip east of Glasgow had certainly been a welcome addition to her personal finances over the last year.

On the other hand, orders to drive to the airstrip to prepare the Cessna for travel never came at a time convenient to her. On this occasion, she was told that the Cessna's regular maintenance crew had completed all their checks earlier that afternoon. What remained was for her to prepare a half-dozen sandwiches, pack the cooler, tidy the interior of the aircraft, and mop the floor of the kitchen.

That would meet this evening's requirements, but, on most weekends, she was paid to keep the building itself in ship shape. And the building comprised not merely a small hangar with attached kitchen. It also housed an out-of-use armory. The facility had been constructed in the 1930s, with World War II on the horizon. The rifles and pistols in the armory would now be unusable without significant investment in cleaning and repairing those firearms, which were obsolescent even when they were manufactured.

Ammunition in the armory had long since passed its safe-to-use date.

As Fiona reached the last grocery store she would see on her way, she pulled her Ford into the parking lot and spent 10 minutes picking up fresh bread and non-alcoholic drinks for two people. She had not been told who would be flying, but she understood there would be only the pilot and one passenger.

Fewer than 15 minutes after leaving the grocer, she pulled the F-150 onto the grassy parking area beside the hangar and carried her provisions to the back door of the building. Using her key, she undid the heavy padlock, entered, and turned on the lights. The Cessna stood gleaming under the brilliant overhead lights, looking eager to take to the skies.

It was an impressive airplane, thought Fiona. She had a pilot's license herself, though she was not qualified to fly twin-engine aircraft, nor to fly even single-engine planes at night. She crossed to the kitchen-and-armory side of the hangar, undid yet another padlock, and entered the kitchen.

She immediately set about preparing the food, drinks, and cooler. Once finished with those tasks, she mopped the floor and moved to the lavatory, which was housed just off the passageway connecting the kitchen to the armory.

She knew the pilot and passenger would be likely to use the toilet, knowing the Cessna was not large enough to house its own. She gave the toilet and sink a quick scrub, left the light on and the door open, and returned to the kitchen where she checked the wall clock. It read 9:55 p.m.

Exactly on time, two vehicles came bumping across the lot. Fiona walked into the hangar and toward the rear door to greet the arrivals and to ask if there were other tasks she might undertake. As she neared the door, she noted an unfamiliar level of anxiety rising through her.

She did not actually know any of the people for whom she worked, only that it was the Soviet embassy in London that leased both the facility and the aircraft. She was not a "political person," in contrast to some members of her family and church, but she viewed the Soviet Union as a monolith both hostile and fearsome. In fact, if she were to allow herself at that moment, she could become truly frightened.

But Fiona Bruce was not easily frightened. Not normally. She was physically formidable herself, standing nearly 6 feet tall and weighing 180 pounds, much of it muscle. She lived on her family's modest farm and worked hard maintaining the small tractors and power implements essential to working farms.

She was also expert with pistols and single-shot rifles, having served, years before, in the Royal Army's construction corps. When she was younger, she had often hunted small game on the acreage on and around her farm. She had once been a fine shot with one of the .22 rifles her family kept in a small gun safe in their barn.

Now, she neared the hangar's rear door and heard footsteps approaching the building. She quickly pushed the door open and stood aside while two men carried a woman, bound hand and foot and blindfolded, past her and into the hangar. Following the men came a woman whom she recognized from earlier occasions. She even recalled her name: Tatyana Kuznetsova.

The two men ignored Fiona as they carried their inert burden into the hangar. Tatyana Kuznetsova nodded curtly, but passed into the building without speaking. As Tatyana passed, Fiona saw that she carried in her left hand a leather shoulder holster, and she saw, as well, nestled securely in the holster, the standard Glock 9mm sidearm used by Soviet military officers and KGB agents.

She assumed the shoulder rig and pistol belonged to one of the men, and that one of them would don the holster as soon as he finished doing his part to carry the prisoner to the aircraft. Fiona knew that she was expected to do her work at the airstrip without questions of any kind, but this was the first time she had observed anything violent: a person being carried to the aircraft as an obviously unwilling captive.

Trailing the arrivals, Fiona realized that she would not be able, in good conscience, to continue her employment with these people, not if they were capable of doing this sort of thing. It also occurred to her that she might actually attempt to do something about what she was seeing.

And in that moment her fear suddenly left her. It was replaced by anger.

All this just made her mad.

As Rebecca was being carried into the hangar facility east of Glasgow, Jaakov Adelman, having descended to 1,500 feet, peered down unhappily from the cockpit of the Beechcraft. He had hoped for a moonlit night, but a low overcast made the night, in effect, moonless. The landscape below him was featureless except for vehicle lights marking the major highways and thoroughfares. Knowing he would be unable to fly straight to the Soviet's leased airstrip under these conditions, his mind shifted to the backup plan he had developed before departure from London.

He would find the intersection of the M73 and the M8 on the eastern edge of the city, an easily recognizable confluence of roadways. He would then fly low and slow along the M8 as it stretched east, away from Glasgow.

His calculations suggested that, once he slowed the aircraft to something just above stall speed, it would take six to seven minutes from that intersection to a point at which, after making a 45-degree turn to the right, he should pass directly over the airstrip and hangar about 30 seconds later. He turned his head and spoke loudly to his colleagues in order to be heard over the sound of the engines.

"I'm going to circle round to the Glasgow intersection we talked about, which is going to delay us by maybe five minutes … then I'll fly low along the M8. Matt, if you'll track the time, let me know after six minutes from the moment we cross over the intersection. At the six-minute point, we should be over the second interchange that leads off the M8. That's when I'll make the right turn.

"That should put us over the strip about half-minute later."

"Got it, Jaakov," said Matt.

But all three men, Luke included, were thinking: *Our chances of finding this airstrip are poor. We might not see it even if we manage to fly directly over it.*

Forty-five minutes later, circling endlessly over the black, featureless countryside, Adelman watched as the Beechcraft's fuel gauge neared empty. He shook his head in the darkened cabin and said, "We'll need to head for Glasgow International. We can rent a car and drive to this airstrip. That's our only chance."

Silence greeted Adelman's grim announcement.

"One more loop near that second intersection off the M8, Jaakov," said Matt, a touch of urgency in his voice. "Just one more pass … maybe that van is going to arrive a little later than we figured. Maybe we'll see some kind of light from the hangar."

"The fuel gauge …"

"One more pass," said Luke. "We can do one more, Jaakov."

Adelman banked left and headed back toward the interchange they had used as a point of departure nearly three-quarters of an hour before. He lined up the Beechcraft's nose with the intersection, and, when he estimated the aircraft to be less than a mile from that spot, he banked sharply to the left again, and followed his original estimate of 45 degrees from the interchange.

Sixty seconds into what would have to be the final pass, they saw it.

A powerful set of landing lights suddenly punched a bright beam through the darkness, about 15 degrees off to their right. They saw immediately that the landing lights were being used as a takeoff beam for what could only be Fedorov's Cessna 421. As the Beechcraft arrowed toward the tiny airstrip, they saw the Cessna begin to roll forward and, no more than 30 seconds from the moment the Beechcraft would have touched down, they saw the Cessna rise into the air.

The Beechcraft passed fewer than 200 feet from the other aircraft, the two on near-opposite courses, one ascending and the other descending. Adelman pulled up sharply and circled back toward the Cessna, mindlessly in pursuit of Fedorov and his precious cargo of one.

All three men were picturing Rebecca, bound hand and foot, lying in the cargo hold of the Cessna as it arrowed up into the black sky. All three desperately wanted to be able somehow to intercept the aircraft and effect a rescue … *now.*

But one man's mind forced itself to confront the reality of their situation, and he spoke forcefully to the pilot.

"No," said Luke. "Go back, Jaakov."

"We can't even get to the Scottish coast with the fuel we've got left," Luke said insistently. "Put the plane down on that little strip Fedorov accidentally showed us just now. We'll get fuel for the Beechcraft, figure out the bearing to Oslo, and get back in the air. We'll probably be no more than 20 minutes behind them. They'll be on the ground in Oslo longer than that. We can still get this done.

"Put the plane down, Jaakov."

As Adelman moved into his approach and studied the narrow airstrip, now illuminated by his plane's own lights, he realized how small the strip was.

And he saw that he would never have found it, had not the Cessna's lights come on at the last moment before he would have been forced to turn away and head for the Glasgow Airport. He touched down skillfully on the two main wheels, allowed the nose to drop gradually onto the nose wheel, and reversed the blades to apply braking force to the aircraft. He found he needed to apply moderate main-wheel brakes, in addition, to stop the plane before it reached the grass at the end of the strip.

Once achieving full stop, he spun the Beechcraft back toward the fuel pump, which sat just outside the still-open hangar door. Near the pump, Adelman again turned to the left to bring the fuel spout close to the pump. He cut the engines and set the brakes. And he breathed in deeply.

As often had been the case in his life, he had not realized just how tense he had been until the action stopped. Flying the unfamiliar airplane on instruments and putting it down safely on the too-small landing strip had taken every ounce of concentration and skill at his command.

He bowed his head and spoke the Jewish prayer to be said "after hazard."

Blessed are You, LORD our God, King of the Universe, Who bestows good things upon the unworthy, and has bestowed upon me every goodness.

Luke and Matt simultaneously murmured *Amen.*

The men clambered down from the plane, stretched, and, conscious of the need to get the Beechcraft back in the air as quickly as possible for their pursuit of the Cessna, Jaakov and Luke began the process of coaxing fuel from the ancient pump and into the fuel tanks.

Matt paced nearby, his mind churning with images of his wife.

In his mind's eye, he saw her, clad only in tennis skirt and blouse, wrists and ankles bound, now being taken across frigid waters to … here his mind recoiled, yet again, at the prospect of Rebecca's finding herself at the mercy of Anton Fedorov and his like-minded comrades in Moscow.

He groaned the companion prayer, nearly despairing.

Father, be present … be present …

Help us, please …

Help her, please …

Father, be present … be present …

Suddenly, as he strode miserably through the darkened hangar, he heard a metallic, pounding noise from somewhere inside the cavernous space.

Rebecca? Could it be?

Matt turned and ran back to his colleagues as they worked to prepare the Beechcraft for pursuit of the Cessna.

"Luke!" he cried, "I can hear somebody pounding on a door in there. Let me have your flashlight."

Luke, focused on the refueling process, reached absently into one of the innumerable compartments in his specially made shoulder harness, pulled a small flashlight from its niche, and handed it to his excited brother-in-law.

Matt raced back into the hangar and followed the noise of the pounding. Finding a padlocked door, he shouted over the pounding noise, "Rebecca? Are you there? Rebecca? Is that you?"

The pounding stopped.

"Rebecca!"

Nothing.

Matt turned and sprinted back to his companions.

"Luke, she might be here! Bring your bolt cutters."

Luke, now alert to what Matt was saying, let go of the fuel pump handle, leaving it inserted in the Beechcraft's fuel spout, as all three men ran back through the hangar to the padlocked door. As Luke produced his bolt cutters and reached for the padlock with the implement, Adelman said, "Wait, Luke … wait."

Jaakov then pulled his Beretta 9mm from his clip-on belt holster, racked a round into the chamber, and stood off to one side of the door, prepared to aim through the doorway as soon as it began to open.

"We don't know who's in there, Matt," he said quietly. "Both of you stand back away from the door as soon as the padlock is off. This could be KGB on the other side, and, if so, they're armed."

Once all three were positioned, Luke snapped the padlock in two and carefully removed the device. He stepped as far back from the door as he could.

Leaning forward, he reached for the handle and, glancing once more at Jaakov, who held the 9mm steady with two hands, pulled the door open.

Nearly an hour earlier, Fedorov and Volkov carried their prisoner into the airstrip's kitchen. They placed Rebecca, still bound and blindfolded, on a metal food-preparation table in the center of the kitchen, as if she were nothing more than a 130-pound slab of material to be worked on with kitchen implements.

Fiona Bruce, the facility's principal caretaker, winced at the sight of this woman, helpless and dressed in an all-white tennis outfit, being handled as though she were nothing of value. To Fiona, all creatures had God-given value, human beings above all others. And this woman, whoever she was, and whatever these men thought she had done, deserved better.

Fiona got even madder.

She watched the men stand back while Kuznetsova, first, handed the shoulder holster holding the Glock 9mm to one of the men, who immediately donned the rig, pulled out the Glock, and checked the seating of its magazine. While he did this, the Russian woman pulled from her shoulder bag a strange-appearing device, which, at first, Fiona could not identify. But then she realized the device comprised a pair of metal shackles connected not by a chain, but by a very thin, adjustable-length leather belt, one with a separate locking buckle where the ends of the connector belt came together.

The belt, as a connector for the metal shackles, appeared to allow a prisoner's captors to adjust the captive's length of stride from just a few inches to as long as two feet … something approaching a normal stride … but not enough to permit a captive to run. Captors could select any length of stride they wished the prisoner to have.

Fiona watched as Kuznetsova snapped the shackles into place around the captive's bare ankles, adjusted the connecting belt to something approaching 10 inches in length, and fixed the connector's length at 10 inches by inserting one belt end into a metal buckle attached to the other end.

The buckle appeared to have, as did each of the shackles, a keyhole for unlocking the device. Presumably a single key would unlock the connector belt and, separately, each of the shackles.

Having secured the prisoner's ankles to the locked shackles and the locking connector belt, Kuznetsova lifted one of the kitchen knives housed in a wooden knife block and cut the tape that had until then bound the prisoner's ankles together.

Fiona saw that the captive would now be able to walk on her own, though each step would be restricted to no more than 10 inches of connector belt length. For the captive, Fiona saw, walking — very slow walking — would be possible.

But not running.

Fiona then watched Kuznetsova place the key to the shackles and the connector belt in one of the pockets of the dark slacks she had worn each time Fiona had seen her. When the captor finally removed the blindfold from the captive, Fiona's jaw sagged in disbelief. She realized immediately that she was looking at a face well known to the nation's sports fans, even casual ones like herself.

The tennis player and captive was none other than Rebecca Clark.

The dramatic scar along the right side of the regal face confirmed Fiona's initial impression. These Soviet criminals were actually kidnapping a woman who was not only an English citizen, but one easily recognized, widely known, and universally respected for her athletic accomplishments and, as well, for her commitments to church and to early-childhood education in the U.K.

Fiona happened to know, also, that Rebecca Clark was a married mother of two. Most of the readers of sports pages and viewers of television sports in the U.K. knew at least the outlines of this woman's life.

Fiona Bruce grew madder still.

Her anger now bubbling dangerously close to the surface, Fiona breathed deeply, endeavoring to calm herself. She knew that aggressive action on her part, in these circumstances, had no chance of success. These Soviet men looked very strong. And one of the men was now armed.

The men turned and walked in the direction of the passageway that led to the armory, both knowing that the toilet lay to one side of the passageway. Suddenly Fiona realized that Kuznetsova was speaking to her. She tried to attend.

"When the men return, take the woman to the loo. Do not remove the strapping tape from her wrists. Let her fend for herself in the toilet.

"And don't worry about her trying to escape. She can't take steps of more than 10 inches. After she uses the toilet, walk her out to the aircraft."

"Yes, ma'am," replied Fiona meekly.

Having used the toilet, the two men strode briskly through the kitchen and into the hangar. As they passed a control panel outside the kitchen door, they stopped and turned a switch activating the hangar door. The enormous overhead door cranked itself noisily into the fully open position while the men were still walking to the aircraft. There, they opened a large map, placed it on a small table near the Cessna's port wing, and began to discuss the flight plan.

They focused especially on the initial headings Fedorov would use as the Cessna began its short flight toward the east coast of Scotland, there to begin the longer overwater flight across the frigid North Sea.

Meanwhile, in the kitchen, Tatyana and Fiona together helped Rebecca down from the table on which she had been placed. Tatyana then stood back and watched the two women move, their pace limited by Rebecca's 10-inch steps, in the direction of the passageway to the armory. Satisfied, Tatyana left the kitchen and joined the men as they continued their discussion of headings and altitudes.

In the kitchen, Rebecca, finally unblindfolded, saw, as she and her escort passed alongside the kitchen counters, Fiona's keys, wallet, and, next to the wallet, a pocket testament — the New Testament, plus Psalms and Proverbs.

Rebecca stopped. She looked at the woman.

"You're Christian," she said, not asking, but declaring.

Fiona was struck by the penetration of the woman's deeply gray eyes, as they searched for the faith implied by the presence of the small book. Fiona was also struck by the voice, low for a woman, and its quality of gentleness and … love.

She found herself smiling as she said, "Yes. And you're Rebecca Clark. I'm Fiona Bruce, ma'am. I'm honored to meet you."

Fiona glanced back toward the kitchen's open door to the hangar. She gestured with her eyes that they should continue to move toward the loo. As Rebecca resumed her slow progress in that direction, Fiona looked back again.

She wheeled, took three quick steps back toward the preparation table, seized the kitchen knife Tatyana had used to cut the strapping tape from Rebecca's ankles, and rejoined Rebecca in the hallway.

She put her hand on Rebecca's arm to stop her.

Then she knelt and skillfully cut through the thin leather belt connecting the metal shackles to each other, a cutting action clearly indicative, thought Rebecca as she watched, of a woman with strong hands and forearms who uses tools and implements daily. Fiona quickly rose and stepped around behind Rebecca, then carefully cut through the strapping tape that secured her wrists.

Fiona then stepped in front of Rebecca as she stood rubbing the feeling back into her hands, and the two women smiled at each other. Rebecca stepped forward and hugged her Christian sister gratefully. Then she turned and entered the loo, her ankles now unrestricted even though the metal shackles remained firmly in place, with the severed connector ends, including the metal buckle, scraping across the floor behind her as she moved. When Rebecca closed the door behind her, Fiona walked further down the passageway to the World War II-era armory.

Minutes later, as Rebecca exited the toilet, Fiona gestured for her to come into the musty, metallic-smelling room, one filled with old firearms, ammunition boxes, and, on the walls, faded photos of men and women in WWII uniforms.

"I don't know what those Russians are planning to do with you, Mrs. Clark," said Fiona, "but you mustn't get on that airplane. None of us will ever see you again."

The Scotch woman gestured to the array of rifles and pistols stored in racks and on sectional tables around the armory. Rebecca's eyes swiftly scanned the room.

"I don't know if any of the ammunition is usable," said Fiona, "but we can try to bluff our way past those people. They'll probably believe the guns will work."

But Rebecca was already moving to a table that displayed not guns, but bayonets and knives. She turned back to her new friend and said, "Fiona, we'll use no firearms … just knives and … um … the rolling pin I saw in the kitchen."

Fiona laughed … a deep, loud noise befitting her considerable size and bulk. "We're going to fight them with knives and a rolling pin?"

Rebecca was already examining a pair of Ka-Bar knives, 12-inch military weapons used, she knew, by the United States Marine Corps and, she also knew, by her brother when he was a Royal Navy boarding party combat specialist.

She hefted one of the knives, testing its balance and weight, gripping its handle as she would her Barringtons Swords throwing knives. Suddenly, to Fiona's astonishment, Rebecca wheeled and, in one practiced, fluid movement, windmilled the Ka-Bar into an underhand, no-spin throw.

The Ka-Bar flew fast and straight into a wooden ammunition cabinet positioned along the wall opposite. She then turned, lifted the second Ka-Bar, and repeated the throw with the same outcome.

She turned to Fiona.

"The Ka-Bars will do," she said. "They're a little heavier than my competition throwing knives, but they're the same length. And their balance is excellent.

"Pick up the rolling pin as we pass through the kitchen, Fiona."

They walked fast through the connecting passageway, then through the kitchen to the door from kitchen to hangar. Fiona collected her keys, wallet, and pocket testament as they did. At the door they paused, the two Ka-Bars in Rebecca's left hand, and the slender, heavy, wooden rolling pin in Fiona's right. Rebecca reached for her new friend's hand, squeezed it, bowed her head, and prayed softly.

Father, be present … be present … help us please to escape our adversaries … help us please to escape them without destroying them … we pray this to You in the name of our Lord Jesus…

Father, be present … be present …

She opened her eyes and said, "Please call Ms. Kuznetsova to the kitchen, Fiona. After she enters, step aside and close the door behind her."

Rebecca moved behind the door, then stood with her back against the wall. She held her ankles together as though her shackles, which were still in place, remained fastened to each other by the leather connector belt which Fiona had severed. Rebecca held her wrists behind her as though they were still bound by the tape.

Her objective was to appear to Tatyana, if Tatyana were to look directly at her, as though she were still physically helpless, unable to move either her hands or her feet. But, moments later, when Tatyana entered the kitchen, she looked not at Rebecca, but at Fiona, asking, "Is everything okay here?"

Without waiting for a response, Tatyana turned to face Rebecca just in time to receive the full force of a heavy metal shackle as it was driven up and into her jaw by a powerful right leg kick from Rebecca Clark. The crack of the weighted kick snapped the woman's head back with such violence that she was rendered unconscious almost instantly, toppling backward in an uncontrolled fall that threatened to become a fatal one, had her head been allowed to hit the concrete floor unrestrained.

But Fiona sprang forward and caught the Russian's head inches before its impact with the rock-hard surface. Without pausing, Fiona lowered the woman's head gently to the floor, retrieved the key to the shackles and connector belt from one of Tatyana's pockets, then turned to unlock each device from Rebecca's ankles.

"Well done *you!*" said Rebecca.

"Now, Fiona," she continued confidently, "let's finish this."

Fiona inwardly thought:

How? ... How will we 'finish this' when those men are physically formidable and one of them is armed with a pistol? We are but two women ... two women with two knives and a rolling pin.

Her doubts were quelled by Rebecca's certainty, a certainty that pulled Fiona forward until suddenly she found that she had stepped through the door and into the hangar itself. The women's soft footfalls had not attracted the men's attention, fully consumed as they were with the map and their murmured calculations.

The two Russians, backs to the women, were 40 to 45 feet away from the women, both men leaning on the table that displayed their 60-by-36-inch map of the North Sea and its contiguous land masses.

Rebecca, having moved one of the two Ka-Bars from left hand to right, gestured silently with the left-hand Ka-Bar, indicating she wanted Fiona to creep forward, nearer the men, but well out of Rebecca's line of fire. Fiona, wide-eyed, moved forward perhaps 15 feet, stopped, and turned to watch Rebecca as this world-class athlete raised the right-hand knife to a position over, and forward of, her head, planted her right foot solidly on the concrete floor, strode forward with her left, and, in a movement so swift and strong Fiona could hardly follow it, wind-milled the weapon through nearly 270 degrees to propel the Ka-Bar in a straight line from Rebecca's hand into the back of Anton Fedorov's right thigh, nearly 45 feet away.

The Chaos chieftain's hamstring muscle — the body's longest — was instantly severed longitudinally by the blade's high-velocity, ripping penetration into his unsuspecting flesh.

Screaming in surprise and pain, Fedorov crumpled to the concrete, the Ka-Bar buried nearly to its hilt in the back of his thigh. Volkov, standing close, spun and leaped back, backpedaling away from the women, his face uncomprehending.

Both women started forward at a run. Fiona, quick for her size, arrived at the stricken Fedorov within four seconds of the Ka-Bar's ferocious impact. She found the victim, having sunk to the floor, twisting his body to reach in desperation for the Ka-Bar in an attempt to extract it.

But as his hand touched the Ka-Bar's handle, Fiona's rolling pin, wielded with tremendous force by her 180 pounds of farmer strength, smashed down onto his wrist, shattering the grouping of small bones connecting wrist to hand, and producing yet another howl of anguish from the congenitally stoic KGB leader.

Fedorov, now groaning in pain, tried next to pull the Glock from its holster, a futile maneuver that his horribly damaged right hand could no longer execute. But even if the wrist and hand had been functional, there was no time for him to use the pistol. For Fiona swung the heavy wooden implement a second time, this time directly into the center of Fedorov's face. The blow crushed the nasal cartilage and simultaneously concussed the victim, his head falling back onto the concrete and his broken nose streaming blood down one side of his face and onto the floor.

The Chaos leader now lay unconscious and bleeding, his intricately planned Wimbledon project undone, his physical being in shreds and shards. Fiona, without pause, reached to his shoulder holster and pulled the Glock 9mm from its leather sheath. Her work completed in mere seconds, she then stood and watched as Rebecca faced off against Artur Volkov.

During the brief time consumed by Fiona's attack against the knife-wounded Fedorov, Rebecca had run straight toward Volkov.

As she had closed on him, she had raised the second Ka-Bar to its over-head-and-forward position in preparation for another windmill throw. This throw would be aimed at her enemy's abdomen, where it would do crippling damage to the core muscles, certain to render him immediately *hors de combat*.

Fiona watched now as Volkov, eyes wide in fear, raised his hands toward Rebecca, palms toward her, shouting, "*Nyet … nyet … nyet …*" all the while backpedaling as fast as possible. Rebecca now paused in her run, the second Ka-Bar still overhead-and-forward in throwing position and gestured toward the kitchen.

"Walk to the kitchen," she commanded.

Still wide-eyed, Volkov turned toward the kitchen, and, looking back nervously over his shoulder, did as he was ordered.

Twenty feet behind him, still poised to throw, Rebecca followed.

As Volkov neared the kitchen door, Rebecca heard Fiona call out to her. She kept her eyes on Volkov and called back to her partner.

"Yes, Fiona?"

"This man's gun, ma'am?"

Rebecca called back unhesitatingly.

"Run outside the hangar and throw the gun into the tall grass. Then run back to me, Fiona … quickly, please."

Fiona ran out the open hangar door, tossed the Glock into the tall weeds, as directed, and returned, still at a run, as Volkov moved into the kitchen, Rebecca now just 10 feet behind him.

Fiona arrived in time to hear Rebecca say, "Tatyana needs your attention, sir. She may have a broken jaw. She is certainly concussed, although we did not allow her head to strike the floor."

Only then did Volkov realize that his friend and colleague lay unconscious nearly at his feet. He knelt beside her and looked up at the women, who now stood together just outside the kitchen door. Seeing he was going to be allowed to live, and to live undamaged, he recovered his natural ferocity and bluster.

His lip curled in a sneer, he said, hatred in his voice, "You've won this round, Mrs. Clark … there will be others."

Fiona slammed the kitchen door in his face.

Volkov listened grimly as the padlock clicked into place on the hangar side of the door. Looking down at the unconscious Tatyana, he said to her unhearing ears, "She will regret allowing us to live, Tat. I promise you that."

While Volkov nursed his colleague and his own anger, the women returned to the still-unconscious Anton Fedorov. They knelt beside him and turned him more fully onto his stomach. Rebecca then carefully pulled the Ka-Bar from the bleeding muscle. She used the blade to slice the trouser fabric laterally to expose the wound, nodding to herself with satisfaction.

"The wound is not pulsing, Fiona," she said. "The femoral artery has not been touched. He will not bleed out, but we do need to staunch the wound.

"Is there a first-aid kit on this aircraft?"

"Yes," said Fiona, rising to climb the three-step stairway into the Cessna. She returned in seconds with the kit.

"We need antiseptic and sterile gauze, Fiona."

Working efficiently, the women cleansed the wound, applied the gauze, and secured the dressing with first-aid tape from the kit. When they had finished, they realized that Fedorov was beginning to stir.

"Shall I hit him again, ma'am?" asked Fiona, reaching for the rolling pin she had placed beside her on the floor.

Rebecca smiled.

"We don't need to fear him, Fiona. His gun lies somewhere in tall grass, his leg wound will make it impossible for him to walk normally for quite some time, to say nothing of running, and his broken nose will place him in an agony of pain for days.

"And we have disabled his organization, back in London and Cambridge, so that he now has no resources and no followers."

Rebecca paused for a moment, thinking.

"Do you have a car here?" she asked.

"Yes, ma'am … actually, a truck."

"Well, could you drive me to your home, so that I might use a telephone? I'll need to get in touch with my husband and my brother.

"They'll be terribly worried."

"Yes, ma'am … but there is a pay phone on the other side of the hangar. You could use that, but I hope you'll consider letting me drive you to my home anyway. You could use our phone more comfortably … and you could get some rest.

"You're tired, ma'am … I can see it."

Rebecca smiled gratefully.

"Yes. I certainly am … I'd love to lie down for a while in your house."

The women rose and, as they did, heard Fedorov mumble something.

They looked down at him.

Fiona shook her head and said, "Won't this man, even with his wounds, be able to fly this plane somewhere, Mrs. Clark? Won't he be able to get out of the U.K. without being punished?"

Rebecca nodded.

"Yes," she agreed, "he may.

"But he is a Soviet national, protected by his status with the Soviet embassy, and punishing him through our court system would be messy ... maybe impossible ... and, besides, Fiona, we have punished him enough.

"Even if he does manage to fly this plane home ... to Moscow ... via Norway, I should think ... his humiliation when he arrives there is likely to be worse, actually, than anything English courts might do.

"His career is as broken as his hand and his nose."

Fiona laughed.

Then, thoughtfully serious again, she asked a deeper question.

"If he takes this airplane somewhere and recovers, isn't there the chance he will return to try to ... to ... um ... hurt you ... or your family ... even a year from now ... or even 10 years from now?"

"Yes," replied Rebecca, "there is that chance. But we have learned over the years that, if not Anton Fedorov or Artur Volkov or Tatyana Kuznetsova, there will always be Evil, in some form, embodied in someone, that we will be called upon to face ... and defeat ... if God wills it...

"Evil will still exist ... but so will good people ... like you."

Fiona smiled shyly, simultaneously embarrassed and honored that this woman whom she had long admired would say this to her. She did not know what to say in response, but sensed a reply was not expected.

Together they walked toward the doorway at the rear of the hangar. As they passed out of the building, they paused and looked back. Anton Fedorov was crawling, using his knees and his left hand, toward the steps to the Cessna. Blood was still running from his nose onto the concrete, and he held his right hand up as he crawled, the shattered bones in his right wrist and hand preventing his use of either.

The pitiful sight of her enemy led Rebecca to stop again, take Fiona's hand, and bow her head. She prayed softly.

Father, thank You for helping us to escape our adversaries ... thank You for helping us to escape them without destroying them ... thank You, Father, for Your presence with us ... thank You in the name of Your Son ...

Father ... please continue to be present ... be present ...

They looked up, watched Fedorov struggling up the steps into the Cessna, then turned and walked to Fiona's truck. Seeing the F-150, Rebecca brightened.

"Fiona," she said, "Do you think there's enough room on the floor behind that seat for me to lie down? I could get some rest while you drive."

Fiona quickly pushed the seat forward on its hinges and arranged the blankets she always carried in the truck so that Rebecca could lie down on a cushion of softness while Fiona drove to her farm. Rebecca crawled into the narrow space, lay down, and accepted Fiona's help in wrapping the top blanket around her, covering her bare legs and arms against the nighttime chill.

"Thank you, Fiona. I'm going to try to sleep.

"I'm just so very tired."

Rebecca's eyes closed as sleep began to envelop her. But as she faded, the thought ran through her mind: *How does God always seem to provide us with such astonishing people as this woman?*

As Fiona closed the passenger-side door to walk around to the driver's side of the Ford, she heard the drone of an aircraft in the distance, flying low.

She opened her door and said, more to herself than to Rebecca, "I hope that pilot's not in trouble.

"There's really no place to land over there.

"This is the only airstrip between Glasgow and Edinburgh, and that pilot doesn't seem to know where he is."

CHAPTER FIFTEEN

ANTON FEDOROV CRAWLED PAINFULLY UP AND INTO THE PILOT'S seat of the Cessna. He sat for a moment, mentally assessing the damage to his body. The greatest pain came from the throbbing in his crushed nose, a pain that at times almost blinded him. But he knew the fractured right hand and wrist would become his top problem in flying the complex twin-engine aircraft through the darkness, using instruments only, over the North Sea and into Oslo Gardermoen Airport.

The deep Ka-Bar wound in the back of his right thigh was painful, too, but it hurt mainly when he tried to move the leg. Now that he was seated in the cockpit, the knife wound was the least painful of the three injuries. And inexplicably to him, the leg wound seemed to be rather expertly bandaged.

Who would have done that, he wondered. And why?

He tried to focus on the task at hand: flying the Cessna to Norway. But his mind kept returning to the disaster that had befallen his Chaos organization at the hands of the witch who had just humiliated him …

He continued to puzzle endlessly over his failure to execute her when his garrote was perfectly positioned to do exactly that. Something had blocked him, and he knew that the killing movement had *not* been stopped by his own cowardice. He feared *nothing* in this world. And yet he had not, with the opportunity literally in his hands, executed the simple violence that would have led to victory.

Not victory in the immediate context of Chaos's planned disruption of the Championships … that chance had been lost in ways he still did not understand. No, Rebecca Clark's death would have increased the chance for victory in the larger battle … the effort to corrupt the souls of the great democracies. *That* battle would have become infinitely simpler if only he had …

Now he shook his head, trying to clear his brain of the fog that seemed to consume him. He *must* focus on his next steps. He would fly this aircraft across the North Sea to Oslo, thence to Tromso, thence to Archangel, finally to Moscow.

That much was settled. He would fly this airplane all the way to Moscow.

He next forced himself to imagine his reception there. Volkov and Kuznetsova might be in Moscow, too, by the time he arrived, if they and other embassy personnel had been expelled, because of the Wimbledon failure, and then sent direct from London to Moscow by commercial jet.

But, even if they were not yet in Moscow, their report of his failures would certainly have arrived before he could. He would then doubtless be called upon to appear before the KGB hierarchy.

There he would be expected to account for the failure of his plans to wreak havoc at the tournament, thereupon to launch his U.K. terror campaign. He pictured himself entering a room at the Kremlin, two days hence, his nose smashed, his eyes blackened from internal nasal bleeding, his right wrist in some sort of cast or wrap, his right leg dragging behind him. He imagined himself trying to explain everything that had conspired to defeat his plans.

And his imagination immediately revolted.

He could not do this. He *would* not do this.

He *would not* appear before his authorities as the beaten, humiliated leader of a movement that, for the moment, appeared stillborn. Evil lived in him … still.

And now, perhaps, more than ever before.

He looked this ridiculous existential crisis full in the face. Had he lost his reason-for-being? *No.* Was there meaning remaining in his life? *Yes.*

The answer, ultimately, was action. Evil lived in him, and Evil always did unflinchingly whatever came next … except … except less than 12 hours earlier in Rebecca Clark's Volvo. The shame of that failure flooded his mind once more.

He shook his head violently.

Something stopped me. It was NOT my fault.

He shook his head again.

Not my fault … not my fault … not my fault …

He took a deep, ragged breath and forced himself to concentrate.

He did not need to know answers to questions he could not answer ... nor answers to questions of longer range than the immediate one. For the answer to that question was simple. *fly this airplane to Moscow.*

Life's meaning at this moment lay in an action he understood.

Fly this airplane to Moscow, or ... perhaps ... he suddenly thought for the first time ... to a destination other than his home. After all, this aircraft could, fully fueled as it was, reach Copenhagen ... Hamburg ... Amsterdam ... Dublin ... or ... London.

But he shook his head yet again.

No ... I must go to Moscow ... I must explain how events have conspired against me ... how it was not my fault ... not my fault ...

He tried to smile. That effort sent acute pain firing into his nasal cavities. He spoke a silent oath and sent it winging in the direction of Rebecca Clark and her friends, and returned once more to his task.

Using his good left hand, he turned the ignition switch and listened while the Cessna's twin engines coughed to life, a deafening noise inside the hangar, even though the hangar door was open. Manipulating the throttles by stretching his left hand across his body, he ran up the power to the two engines and, using his good left leg and foot, released the brake pedals.

The aircraft responded immediately, rolling swiftly out of the hangar and into the darkness of the Scottish night. He turned the wheel to take the Cessna to the south end of the airstrip and bumped along the runway until the nose wheel was almost on the grass. He then jammed on the left-wheel brake and spun the plane counterclockwise until the nose faced north.

He then switched on the landing lights, which, in this case, would serve as takeoff lights, pushed the throttles all the way forward, and steered the Cessna straight down the runway until takeoff speed was reached. He pulled back gently on the steering column and the craft became airborne.

Evil lived ... it lived within him.

Fifteen minutes after Jaakov Adelman, Matt, and Luke had watched Anton Fedorov lift off in the Cessna, they stood at the padlocked door to the hangar's kitchen, the door at which Matt Clark had heard such vigorous pounding noises minutes before. Adelman had stopped Luke from immediately cutting the door's padlock with his bolt cutters, cautioning him that armed KGB agents could well be on the other side of the door. Adelman had pulled his Beretta 9mm from his clip-on belt holster, racked a round into the chamber, and stood off to one side of the door, prepared to fire through the doorway as soon as it began to open.

Luke snapped the padlock in two and carefully removed the device. Stepping as far back from the door as he could, he reached for the handle and, glancing once more at Jaakov, pulled the door open. Light from the kitchen flooded through the open door and Artur Volkov stood, his brow clouded with anticipatory anger, staring into the muzzle of Adelman's Beretta.

Adelman slowly lowered the firearm, and Luke and Matt stepped forward.

Electricity snapped between Lieutenant Luke Manguson and Father Artur Volkov, antagonists who had last seen each other, only weeks before, on a speeding 94-foot Hatteras motor yacht off the coast of North Carolina. The yacht had been intercepted by a Royal Navy destroyer, which had demanded of Volkov the release of the Royal Navy lieutenant it held captive, the demand backed by .50 caliber machine guns from the deck of the destroyer.

Volkov had wisely relented, Luke had been freed, and Volkov had returned the leased yacht, via the Chesapeake Bay and the Potomac River, to its marina in Washington. Volkov had then been recalled to Moscow, but had been there only for hours before being ordered to travel to England.

It seemed he had been urgently needed in London.

"Volkov," said Luke evenly.

"Lieutenant," replied Volkov.

"Where is my sister?" said Luke, moving toward his enemy.

Volkov shrugged.

"Where is my wife?" said Matt, advancing to Luke's side.

"Wait, gentlemen," said Adelman, moving quickly toward the three men, the 9mm still in his hand, but now held down at his side.

"Let me check this space before we take this scumbag apart."

"Scumbag?" cried Volkov, a high-ranking Russian priest unaccustomed to vulgarities, especially vulgarities directed at him.

"*Da … pridurok!*" replied Adelman in his good Russian, tossing the insult while striding up to Volkov. Adelman had cleared the kitchen at a glance, seeing only Tatyana Kuznetsova, now seated on the floor and holding her head in her hands.

Suddenly, as Adelman arrived within reach of Volkov, he jammed the muzzle of the Beretta into the Soviet's throat so forcefully that the burly Volkov staggered back, coughing and gasping.

Adelman followed Volkov close enough to swing the gun barrel viciously across Volkov's face, the muzzle opening a ragged cut across the big man's cheek and lip. Adelman flipped the muzzle again into Volkov's throat, at the same time slamming him up against a bulkhead with his open left hand.

Then, his face inches from his adversary's, he hissed, "You are my enemy. I am Mossad. I will kill you without hesitation.

"You will tell me where Rebecca Clark has gone. You have five seconds."

Volkov believed him.

Once Tatyana Kuznetsova, her head clearing gradually, had explained that she had been rendered unconscious by a karate-style kick from Rebecca Clark, and once Artur Volkov had explained that Mrs. Clark had incapacitated Anton Fedorov with a knife thrown into his thigh from 40 to 50 feet, and once Volkov had further noted that Fedorov had been struck repeatedly by what appeared to be a large club wielded by a very large kitchen employee, the men began to relax.

Given the explanations, it seemed obvious that Rebecca had not only survived, but she had also managed to turn the tables on her tormentors. Further, it seemed that she must have been driven to the home of the kitchen staff member who had helped her. Finally, it seemed obvious that Fedorov, though terribly wounded, had retained enough strength and mental acuity to pilot the Cessna ... at least to get the airplane off the ground.

Adelman, still glaring at Volkov murderously, looked toward Rebecca's husband and brother and said, "So ... I can kill this *pridurok* now?"

Matt and Luke knew this was Belton-style verbiage, now being used by Belton's detective agency partner entirely for effect. Adelman's Mossad days were behind him, and he had fully embraced the Yahalomin's ethic: no killing, unless absolutely no alternatives existed, and no actual use of firearms, unless ...

Luke turned to Volkov.

"You are every bit the 'scumbag' our friend suggests, but we have no authority over you or Ms. Kuznetsova. I assume you have a vehicle outside the hangar. You're free to drive back to London, but you're going to find, once you arrive, that the Prime Minister has ordered you and many of your colleagues out of the country. She has given you until noon tomorrow."

Volkov and Kuznetsova, seething, left the hangar silently and drove away in their two vehicles — the van and her leased BMW — presumably headed for London, where they would arrive in the early morning just in time to pack their things.

Luke quickly found the pay phone on the other side of the hangar and phoned his wife. He summarized the events of the evening for Kory and added that, since it appeared that Rebecca had gone home with a kitchen staff member, he planned to wait there at the airstrip on the assumption that Rebecca would phone Kory as soon as she arrived at the staff member's home.

Rebecca would then discover that "her men" were at the airstrip and return as quickly as she could.

As Luke and Kory finished their conversation, Fiona Bruce pulled her F-150 into the farmhouse's gravel parking area. She switched off the engine and said softly, "Ma'am? You awake, ma'am?"

Hearing no response from her exhausted passenger, she quietly opened and closed the truck's driver-side door and crossed to the other side. She opened the passenger-side door, leaned in, and touched the sleeping woman on the shoulder. There was still no response … just continued sleep-breathing.

"Mrs. Clark," Fiona said quietly, "you said you wanted to phone your family in London, and we're at my house now."

Rebecca stirred and opened her eyes.

"Yes," she said, waking quickly. "Thank you. I'll come in."

Rebecca, keeping one of the truck's blankets wrapped around her shoulders, walked beside her new friend up to the farmhouse porch. Fiona unlocked the front door, whispering to Rebecca that her parents might be sleeping, and the two entered. They found a plump and graying 70-ish couple seated comfortably in front of an ancient black-and-white television set. Both looked up curiously.

"Fiona?" said the woman.

"Mum ... Dad ..." said Fiona, "this is Mrs. Clark ... Rebecca Clark, you know, the women's tennis champion? ... She needs to use our phone to call home."

The couple, suddenly wide awake, jumped to their feet at the mention of Rebecca's name.

"Please come sit down, Mrs. Clark," said the one.

"Let me warm up something for you to eat, dear," said the other.

"You're very kind," said Rebecca, "but let me phone London, please, before I do anything else."

Within minutes, Rebecca had phoned Kory, learned that "the boys" had flown a leased airplane to Glasgow to find and rescue her, and had just phoned from the airstrip to which Rebecca had been taken. They had given Kory the phone number of the pay phone in the hangar, knowing Kory would phone them once Rebecca had gotten in touch. Kory assured Rebecca that she would phone them immediately.

Rebecca was instantly rejuvenated.

She hung up the phone, a wall phone mounted in the farmhouse kitchen, and returned to the living room where Fiona and her parents waited.

"Fiona!" said Rebecca excitedly, "Matt is waiting for me at the airstrip, along with my brother and a friend who's a pilot! Can we go back?"

Mrs. Bruce would not let them leave without preparing a "nice, big sandwich" for Rebecca, along with a bowl of chips for her daughter.

Soon the women were back in the truck, Rebecca with a sandwich in her hands. As they retraced their route to the airstrip, Fiona asked if she might be trusted with "a few bits" of the kidnapping story.

Between bites of the enormous sandwich — Rebecca had not realized how famished she had become — she sketched the main events of the last several days, starting with the firebombing of her home and including both kidnappings ... SallyBelle's and her own.

She also summarized her years of receiving visions, trying to be clear about her perspective, that these "special messages" were simply more elaborate and detailed versions of everyday prayer ... sending and receiving messages from God. Rebecca felt, when she finished, that she had probably included more than she should have, since there was so much, and since so much of it was ... strange.

Fiona did not, however, appear surprised or confused by anything she had heard, nor did she appear to find the lengthy overview as interesting as Rebecca had assumed she might.

She was quiet for a while, processing the high and low points of Rebecca's recent history as best she could. When she finally ventured a question, it was not focused on the aspects of the story that Rebecca would have thought most puzzling and intriguing. Instead, Fiona seemed to be more focused on the parts of the story that she had actually experienced.

"Mrs. Clark," she said finally, "how did you learn to kick like that? I've never seen anyone kick so hard and so high. Where did you learn that?"

Rebecca took the last bite of Mrs. Bruce's sandwich, chewed, swallowed, and dabbed at her lips with a paper napkin.

"My brother Luke," she began, "taught me everything I know about fighting and knife-throwing, Fiona. He was a Royal Navy officer — he still is, as a reservist — whose job was to lead boarding parties onto hostile decks at sea. Firearms were rarely practicable. He and his men fought with hands and feet.

"Luke knew that I do not have anything remotely approaching his upperbody strength, but that I have long limbs — legs and arms — and, consequently, great potential leverage for kicking and throwing."

"Oh ..." Fiona interrupted, "that was my next question ... the knife throwing."

"Luke taught me the underhand, no-spin throw that you saw, saying it was the surest way to disable an adversary at distances up to 50, or even 60 feet. Since he taught me, I have practiced my throws almost every day in the basement throwing range we had set up, before our house burned.

"Matt and I have been staying with Luke and his wife Kory, and they have their own basement throwing range. I've practiced in their basement most days since the firebombing. I've also done regular workouts — treadmill and light weights — in the small gym in my husband's office building. Those workouts include several dozen karate-style kicks against the heavy bag they have.

"Oh ... and I should add, Fiona, that I don't really know karate. I've never studied that, or any other, form of martial arts. I just know these few things Luke taught me."

More thoughtful silence, while Fiona, a skillful driver of the big F-150, negotiated the small backroads that led from the M8 to the airstrip.

"Ma'am," she said finally, "did you mean to throw that Ka-Bar into the back of the man's thigh? Or were you trying to hit him somewhere else?"

"He and Mr. Volkov," Rebecca replied, "were bent over that little table, studying their map, Fiona. I would have preferred to strike him near the right shoulder blade, just at the point that would have disabled his right arm. That would have made it impossible for him to reach his pistol, holstered on the left side of his chest.

"Since his position at the table took away that option, I chose the hamstring muscle, hoping that would cause him to crumple onto the concrete, giving you an excellent chance to use your rolling pin to prevent his reaching the Glock.

"And you were the perfect person to wield that rolling pin, Fiona. My goodness, you looked as if you'd practiced those strokes all your life.

"The poor man had no chance.

"Nor did we want him to have one."

By the time refueling of the Beechcraft had been completed and the men had scrounged a few pieces of bread, butter, and fruit from the suddenly available kitchen, the F-150 was thumping across the parking area next to the hangar. The men, hearing the truck, ran out the rear door to meet the two women.

Rebecca stepped from the Ford and was immediately caught up in the strong right arm of Matt Clark. She threw her arms around his neck and they held each other long, the wife's and the husband's tears mixing together on their faces.

Luke and Jaakov, respecting the privacy of the couple's reunion, walked around to the driver's side door of the truck and introduced themselves to Fiona Bruce, who was suddenly uncomfortable to find herself the center of attention.

"Fiona," said Luke, "can you tell us in a couple of sentences what has happened here tonight? We can get the full story later from my sister."

"Mrs. Clark threw a knife into a man and then I hit him with a rolling pin."

The men burst out laughing.

"A rolling pin?" said Luke. "Really?"

She nodded, more than a little irritated that these ignorant men did not seem to be giving her weapon its proper respect.

Her face suddenly red, she said, "How'd you like a face full of rolling pin? I'm bettin' your nose'd break just as good as his did."

Abashed, Luke backtracked.

"I apologize, Ms. Bruce. I'm sure my nose would indeed break just as good as Anton Fedorov's did. A rolling pin is a fearsome weapon, when swung by someone who knows how to use it."

"Better believe it, mister," she said, only slightly mollified.

Rebecca and Matt arrived at that moment.

Rebecca ran to Fiona and hugged her long and hard. The men saw that the Scottish woman returned the embrace with equal vigor.

Rebecca finally relaxed her hold on her new friend and stepped back. Taking both Fiona's hands in her own and fixing the burly farm woman with her steady, strong gaze, Rebecca said, "Fiona Bruce, you saved my life tonight. Had you not freed me from my bindings, helped me to find the knives, and used that rolling pin with such effect, I would never …"

Her voice trailed off, choked by the emotion of the moment, something the men had rarely seen, if ever. Tears coming now to her eyes, Fiona said, "God put me here just for that, ma'am. I've no doubt that's why I was here. Just to help you.

"It was my privilege, ma'am. I'll never forget it … or you."

Rebecca rewarded Fiona with her radiant smile, the one that forced the long facial scar to contract. As she released Fiona's hands, she said, "Please give your mailing address to Mr. Adelman here. He's a detective and always has a little notebook and pen with him. I'll want to write to your mum to thank her for the delicious sandwich, and to you for everything else."

Five minutes later, Adelman cranked the Beechcraft's engines, having completed his final checks, Luke using his flashlight to confirm that the list was fully covered. Rebecca and Matt had managed to squeeze their long frames into the compact second row and were now quite uncomfortable but extremely happy.

Two minutes later the plane lifted off.

Two minutes after that, Rebecca slept.

Friday, June 28, noon, Moscow, the Kremlin

Anton Fedorov slowly walked into a KGB conference room in the Kremlin. An armed guard closed the door behind him and remained stationed outside the room. Five KGB senior officials sat facing Fedorov across the table.

He was acutely aware of how he appeared to these unsmiling men.

His nose was covered by a white bandage that obscured not only his nose but also much of the blackened, yellowing skin under each eye. His right wrist was encased in a heavy plaster cast. He limped badly, his right leg unable to move normally. He sat down gingerly on the hard-backed wooden chair.

The chairman, speaking Russian, clicked on a tape recorder that sat in the center of the long, rectangular table. He looked up at Fedorov.

"State your name for the recording, comrade."

"Anton Fedorov."

"Give the name of the project you have overseen."

"XAOC"

"Summarize the results of the project."

Fedorov stirred unhappily in the chair. His eyes slid away from the chairman's, drifting toward a large, framed, black-and-white photo of the current Soviet Premier mounted on the wall to his right.

He stared at the stoic image in the photo until the chairman's voice called him back to the interrogation he had dreaded from the moment he had realized that his intricately orchestrated series of Wimbledon explosions had failed. In that moment of clarity, only four days before, he had glimpsed his future.

It was this.

His one chance, following the failure of the explosives, was to bring the principal player in the cast of Rebekka Yahalomin into this very room as a prize: to present a captive Rebecca Clark to these officials. Had he brought her, bound and shackled, into this room, it would have been she who would be the focus of the interrogation, and she who would ultimately endure punishment.

Had events developed in that way, then he, Anton Fedorov, might have been forgiven. And forgiveness might have meant mere demotion in rank. But he had failed at everything, and he knew that these men would not even bother to mention demotion in rank. No ... he was to be sentenced, not demoted.

"Fedorov!" said the chairman yet again. "Speak!"

Fedorov cleared his throat and began, speaking in his native Russian.

"The project's first stage was a complete success. We attacked and disabled Christian ministers all over the United Kingdom, leading to panicked speculation in the media and among the Christian population ... we saw the widespread confusion ... we saw the creeping despair."

The chairman cut him off.

"So," said the chairman, "your small-scale preliminaries were successful. Enough of that. Move to the first high-profile project ... the Wimbledon Championships. Summarize your project's outcomes to date."

"We have been ... ah ... somewhat less successful," responded Fedorov, "with the Wimbledon project, in that our adversaries re-routed the automated signals designed to detonate explosives planted successfully around the All England Club ... so that it was, in fact, our own headquarters equipment that was ... um ... damaged."

"You blew up your own equipment."

"I do not know how the re-routing was done, though I know at whose bidding it must have been."

"You blew up your own equipment, and none of the explosives planted at the All England Club were detonated. No explosions at all occurred at the tournament. No one at all was injured there. No damage was done at all, except to our own, highly expensive equipment."

"Da."

"And you say you know at whose bidding this was done."

"Da ... Rebecca Clark ... Rebekka Yahalomin."

"And what has been done to her?"

"We ... Artur Volkov and Tatyana Kuznetsova and I ... we captured her and drove her to our private, leased airstrip near Glasgow, in Scotland."

"And?"

"We were betrayed by the Scottish woman we employed to maintain the facility. She helped the Clark woman to escape."

"And?"

"The Clark woman is a skilled knife thrower. She threw a military knife into my leg from some 50 feet distance, and the traitorous employee then took advantage of my incapacity ... of my leg wound ... and struck me with a heavy rod ... breaking my wrist ... and my nose."

"You were defeated by two women, neither of them armed."

"Volkov and I were focused on our flight plan."

"Your failure has been total."

Fedorov dropped his eyes and sat silent.

"Is there any reason we should retain your services in our organization, Fedorov, or should we do the obvious and cut you out of government service entirely?"

Fedorov looked up.

"No one … NO ONE … can match the extent to which I can access the ultimate strength on which I can draw … and no one understands our enemy … Rebekka Yahalomin … in as much depth as I.

"I request a new assignment, but with the same primary enemy. I can obtain victory. I *will* obtain victory. I alone have full access to ultimate strength."

The five men exchanged glances, then the chairman turned again to Fedorov, rising to his feet as he did. The other four men followed, all now standing.

Fedorov struggled to his feet to receive the verdict.

"Anton Fedorov," said the chairman, "we have listened to you, and we hear you, but we also see the results of your efforts. And what we see is disaster. That being the case, we do not find our verdict to be difficult. A clear decision."

The verdict was a single word.

"*Siberia.*"

Saturday, July 6, New York City, the Belton-Adelman Detective Agency

"So, Jaakov," said Sid Belton as he clumped into the agency's sixth-floor conference room on an early Saturday afternoon in July, "didja' watch th' women's final t'day from Wimbledon?"

Adelman shook his head.

"I went to temple this morning, Sid.

"When was it on?"

"Started midmornin' our time … two o'clock, London time. Martina beat Chrissie in three sets. Eleanor watched th' whole thing.

"She was pretty mad. She wanted Chrissie t' win."

"Why?"

"I don't know. How would I know what my wife wants?"

"Well … you're married to her."

"Well … that doesn't mean I know anything. If you'd ever decided t' marry somebody, you'd know that.

"Know what I mean?

"Hm?"

Belton took a seat across the conference table from his friend and colleague, and opened a file folder detailing the next case the pair had accepted. After a moment, he looked up, remembering.

"Oh," he said, "I forgot. Eleanor saw SallyBelle runnin' around the court, all through that match. She was workin' th' women's final.

"That's a big deal fer a first-time BBG."

Jaakov smiled.

"Excellent, Sidney. Rebecca must be so proud of that kid."

"Yeah … she really invested in that girl … an' in that boy, too."

Belton absently leafed through the file, then looked up again.

"What time ya' wanna leave tomorrow mornin' fer Washington, Jaakov? Th' wedding is supposed t' be at three, I think."

"I was thinking we ought to catch the 10:05 a.m. from Penn Station. That would get us there a little after 1:30 p.m. … plenty of time to get a taxi over to the church."

Belton considered this.

"Yeah, but I'm guessin' Eleanor is gonna wanna go earlier than that. She's gonna wanna spend time with Marie … y'know… helpin' 'er get dressed an' all.

"An' not just that … just *talkin'* t' 'er. She's gonna wanna *talk.*"

Adelman nodded.

"You're right. We should probably take the nine-fifteen, then?"

Belton shook his head sadly.

"We're talkin' about Eleanor Chapel, Jaakov. Y'know … th' woman I've been married to fer … however long it's been. She's gonna wanna get t' D.C. 'way before noon. She's gonna wanna get t' *Marie's house,* in fact, before noon."

Adelman thought this over.

"So," he said morosely, "the 7:10 a.m., from Penn?"

Belton nodded.

"Sounds right."

CHAPTER SIXTEEN

Sunday, July 7, Marie Campbell and the Reverend Jack McGriff's soon-to-be home, Washington D.C.

MARIE CAMPBELL, STANDING AT HER LIVING ROOM WINDOW JUST before noon on this July Sunday, watched the taxi arrive with the New York City contingent. She ran to the door and flung it open wide, then ran down the short sidewalk to the street.

As Eleanor Chapel stepped from the taxi, Marie opened her arms and enveloped the tiny woman in a warm hug.

"Oh, Eleanor," she said, "thank you so much for coming. I've explained to Penelope that you'd be here early enough to spend plenty of time with her. She was absolutely delighted to know that."

"Well, I should think so, Marie.

"She and I have much to catch up on, you know. You and Jack picked her up from me in New York more than a week ago.

"That's more than eight weeks in cat time," she added mischievously.

"It is?"

"Anyone knows that, Marie," declared the Old Testament professor authoritatively, her blue-green eyes twinkling.

"I'm so glad to learn that, Eleanor. My cat-time education was lacking."

Eleanor looked up at the house, an old, but apparently well-kept two-story structure situated on a tree-lined street within a 15-minute walk, Marie had said on the phone, from the White House. And, as well, she had added, within a

15-minute walk in another direction to the Episcopal church where Marie and Jack had met, and where their ceremony would be conducted that afternoon.

As the taxi pulled away, Sid Belton and Jaakov Adelman started up the side-walk behind the women, Jaakov carrying both overnight bags.

Suddenly Marie turned.

"Oh, I'm so sorry," she said to the men. "I was so excited to see Dr. Chapel that I forgot she'd brought you two along with her."

"We're usta that," said Belton. "We don't expect t' be noticed when Eleanor is around. Y'know… these divas gotta have center stage …"

Eleanor Chapel rolled her eyes and kept walking.

Once the group was seated in the tidy living room and Marie had brought iced tea for all, Belton asked, "So, where's Jack, Marie?"

"Oh, he doesn't live here yet, Mr. Belton. We're not married yet, you know. He's been staying in a hotel not far from here, but we won't see him until the wedding … at least, I won't.

"You may, though," she added. "I know he'd like to see you."

Marie passed the sweetener to Sid, then continued.

"I'll phone him after we've talked for a while, and maybe you and Jaakov can go over to his hotel. Then Eleanor and I … and Penelope, of course … can have some time to ourselves without the men around."

At that moment Jaakov heard the squeak of automobile brakes and stood in time to see another taxi pull to the curb in front of the house.

"More arrivals?" he said, wondering.

All four went to the window in time to see, to their amazement, Rebecca, Matt, Kory, and Luke emerging from the cab. Marie squealed and ran out the front door to meet them while the others moved to the porch and waited for the new arrivals to come into the house.

Eight adults quickly overwhelmed the small living room, but Jaakov and Luke brought more chairs in from the dining room, and everyone squeezed together, Marie bringing more glasses of tea to the small coffee table around which the chairs were arrayed. As she did, Eleanor and Rebecca noticed tears in the hostess's eyes.

In the midst of a comical three-person embrace — Rebecca, 6 feet tall, bending down to embrace Eleanor Chapel, 2 inches under 5 feet, and Marie, one arm up to reach Rebecca's shoulders and the other down to reach Eleanor's

— Marie managed to say, "I'm just so astonished that you've come all the way across the ocean just to be with us at our little ceremony. I never dreamed.

"I'm just so happy."

Tiny rivulets of tears spilled onto her cheeks.

Once everyone settled in, Luke explained that, as was routinely the case, he was able to arrange accommodations on a Royal Air Force flight from Brize Norton RAF Base in Oxfordshire to Andrews Air Force Base southeast of Washington. Their early morning flight had arrived, with the five-hour time difference, at 1100 hours.

Luke, well known by the senior officers at Andrews, had asked them to have a city taxi waiting. The cab had whisked them to Marie and Jack's downtown Washington address as soon as they had stepped down from the huge cargo plane.

"Luke," said Sid Belton, "y' got any news fer us ... anything we might not have heard about since we got back?"

Luke nodded.

"I've spoken several times with Graham Roberts-Holm at MI6, Sid. He's been in regular contact with his opposite number in Norway. Apparently, Anton Fedorov did pass through the Oslo airport in the Cessna ... arrived there early morning on that Tuesday ... which was ... what? ... about 12 days ago?

"Fedorov checked himself into an Oslo hospital for about 24 hours, then filed a flight plan that would take him to extreme northern Norway, then east to Archangel, then on into Moscow.

"Graham knows about Fedorov's arrival in Moscow, because he runs a mole out of the Kremlin."

Here Luke paused to look around the room.

"You understand, everyone, that you can't know this ... about an MI6 mole inside the Kremlin? The agent would be executed if he were discovered."

Heads nodded.

"Graham received a couple of reports from the mole, both reports saying that Fedorov has been ... um ... kicked out of the KGB ... and — this is possibly not accurate — sent off to Siberia.

"As you know, people who are 'sent to Siberia' are usually never heard from again. They just disappear.

"That's all we have on Fedorov."

The group was thoughtful, imagining their enemy's fate with mixed feelings. No one in the room was celebratory.

"How about Volkov and Kuznetsova?" asked Belton after several moments.

"Graham hadn't heard anything about those two, from his Kremlin mole or from any other source."

"Except," Kory interjected, "to confirm that the Soviets followed our Prime Minister's orders. They were indeed out of the U.K. by noon on that Tuesday."

"Right," agreed Luke, "which suggests that they may not have been greeted with open arms in Moscow. That's consecutive failures for Volkov and Kuznetsova: their Jefferson Bible project in the U.S. got thoroughly derailed, as did their effort to ship my sister and me to Cuba, and, now, their Wimbledon-directed extravaganza got redirected by my genius wife so that they blew up their own HQ.

"Granted, that was more Fedorov's project than Volkov and Kuznetsova's, but ... still ... that project was certainly blessed by the Reverend Father Volkov. He backed that project from the start.

"And he ... and she ... were *directly* involved with the attempt to get Rebecca flown back to Moscow for what was surely to be interrogation and torture ... and, I would guess ... eventual ..."

"Murder," offered Rebecca.

That word stopped the discussion for several moments.

"Sorry," said Rebecca, "but we might as well use the right word. And it's worth reminding ourselves that God stepped in quite forcefully at several points to keep me alive. He was *extremely* active and *extremely* forceful on my behalf during those interminable hours in England and Scotland.

"I am so very grateful."

After another half-hour of "catching up" conversation, the London and New York people, sans Eleanor Chapel, called taxis to take them to their downtown hotel rooms for check-in and freshening prior to the 3 p.m. wedding. Eleanor stayed with Marie and Penelope, the latter who, after several days' exploration of the old house's extensive array of nooks and crannies, had proclaimed the structure a satisfactory one for herself, Marie, and the newcomer to her life, the Reverend Jack McGriff.

Dr. Eleanor Chapel had dressed for the wedding that morning in her West Side New York City apartment, even though she knew that that would mean she would be wearing her "wedding clothes" for many hours prior to the wedding, with much of her day to be spent sitting in taxis and on trains. Somehow, thought Marie, this tiny woman can look fresh and crisp under conditions no one else could have managed.

"Dressed for the wedding," however, meant that Eleanor Chapel was dressed as she always dressed. She wore a two-piece gray suit and mid-calf skirt combination with an off-white blouse accentuated by her trademark iridescent red scarf. She wore a single piece of jewelry other than her wedding ring, a gold cross pendant.

The startling red of the scarf and the bright gold of the pendant tended to draw the eye away from the scuffed, once-white tennis shoes, the only footwear Marie had ever seen on Eleanor Chapel's small feet.

Her lengthy gray hair was caught up in a tight bun. Her blue-green eyes shined brightly, eyes which, though of a different color than Rebecca's, were reminiscent of Rebecca's in their deep penetration into and through a listener's or speaker's privacy settings. She and Rebecca both seemed to search their conversationalist's face in the expectation of seeing into that person's soul. Neither woman's gaze had the potential to prove unnerving to the other person, because the two women's usual demeanor was both warm and affectionate.

"Tell me, Marie," said the older woman, her pixie-like face alive with excitement, "how are you viewing your new adventure?"

"Which do you mean, Eleanor … marriage to Jack, or the hoped-for startup of a branch of Sidney and Jaakov's detective agency?

"Oh, never mind," she added, "I know which one you mean."

Both laughed at this.

"Yes … you do," said Eleanor.

"Well," began Marie, "Rebecca and I talked about this during her time in the U.S. last month, and again when we arrived in England last week. She noted that, even though Jack and I have been 'an item' for just a few weeks now, we'd been in a counseling relationship for two years. We're not 'new' to each other.

"And I especially liked Rebecca's emphasis on the facts that, not only is he a believer ... an in-depth believer ... but he is a 'grown-up' who will not need to be *mothered* by me, as his wife. We've had a grown-up relationship from the first, and we should expect that to continue."

Eleanor nodded thoughtfully, but Marie sensed a hesitation.

"What?" she asked.

"Oh, I was just remembering," said Eleanor, "that Sidney, like Jack, had lived his whole life as a bachelor until marriage to me. Granted, Sidney was almost 15 years older then than Jack is now, but that's a striking similarity in your wedding and mine ... and, Marie ... like you ... I had been a widow for years before meeting the man who became my second husband."

"You know," said Marie, "I had completely forgotten that your first husband was killed in the war. So, both our first husbands died in the military."

"Yes," agreed Eleanor, "and, given the similarities, I want to issue this word of caution. Bachelors grow terribly set in their ways ... their daily habits ... their daily expectations of how each hour will unfold.

"Marriage *surprises* them, Marie.

"Marriage proves *disconcerting* to them.

"Marriage *bewilders* them.

"Marriage turns their worlds upside down in ways they hadn't thought of, and hadn't counted on. You'll need to prepare yourself to be ... well ... flabbergasted almost every day at the things your husband will say and do without the slightest awareness that he is saying and doing things you'll regard as ... um ... strange ... no, more than strange ... positively *weird.*"

Both women burst into laughter at this, even though Eleanor knew, and Marie sensed, that this description of transition from a life of settled bachelorhood to one of novice husbandhood was only slightly exaggerated.

"But," added Eleanor when their laughter subsided, "one of the great things about both these men, Marie, is that each has a wonderful sense of humor ... and that includes the happy willingness to laugh at themselves. They *know* they're quirky. So, just help Jack laugh at himself, and you two will be fine."

She thought for a moment, then added, "It's worth remembering, too, that you and I lived alone for a number of years, and we, too, have developed living-alone habits that our husbands might view as strange. Be ready to laugh at yourself, Marie."

Marie pretended not to understand this.

"But Eleanor," she said, "neither you nor I have a single trait that could be considered quirky."

Both dissolved in laughter at the happy nonsense.

When they recovered, Eleanor turned serious again and asked, "Marie, it's obvious to me that Jack is 'in love' with you. Are you 'in love' with Jack?"

"Oh, yes," she answered without hesitation. "It's not the same sort of 'in love' that I remember with my first husband, Eleanor, but it's even better. My heart does a little flip when I see him, and a little bit bigger flip when he touches my hand. I know that won't always be the case, but I know this ... I love him deeply, Eleanor ... more deeply than I've ever loved anyone before."

Three o'clock came and all were assembled in the tiny chapel of the church that had served as the first meeting ground for the bride and groom. The presiding priest was Jack's longtime friend and colleague, and had known Marie, as well, almost from the first day she attended worship there. The little chapel had no organ, but the church organist, another good friend of both the bride and the groom, played softly on the chapel's aging upright piano.

Jack, dressed in his best suit, stood nervously but handsomely near the altar. Sid Belton, best man, stood near him.

Jack had known Belton for only a few years.

But Jack's regular visits to New York on CIA recruiting business had swiftly led the two to form a close bond. Belton now stood leaning lightly on his cane, dressed in his only suit, one that Eleanor had taken to the dry cleaners earlier that week.

Despite the dry cleaning, the suit seemed, much like Sid Belton's other clothes, to become wrinkled the instant it came in contact with his wizened, gnome-like frame. Unconcerned with any of that, Belton beamed with anticipation. He had decided somehow that he and Eleanor were to fill the role of parents to all the others who formed Rebekka Yahalomin.

He poked McGriff in the knee with the tip of his cane.

"Loosen up, kid," he said loudly enough for the others to hear easily in the small space. "You're punchin' above yer weight, but you're gonna be okay. Eleanor says Marie thinks you're th' cat's pajamas. High praise, that.

"Know what I mean?

"Hm?"

Eleanor Chapel hissed at her husband from the side door where she stood, waiting for the bride.

"Sidney Belton, if you don't behave, I'm going to walk over there and throttle you with my bare hands."

This produced delighted laughter from the half-dozen witnesses and served to "loosen up" the groom, as Belton had directed.

At that moment, in response to some unseen signal, the piano prelude was abruptly paused, and, after five seconds of anticipatory silence, the wedding march began. Marie Campbell, looking radiant in her new gown, entered from the side door — the little chapel had no center aisle — and was escorted to the altar by Eleanor Chapel. Tears of joy welled in the bride's eyes ... and in the groom's.

The service began with the priest's familiar words:

"Dearly beloved: We have come together in the presence of God to witness and bless the joining together of this man and this woman in Holy Matrimony ...

"The union of husband and wife in heart, body, and mind is intended by God for their mutual joy; for the help and comfort given one another in prosperity and adversity; and, when it is God's will, for the procreation of children and their nurture in the knowledge and love of the Lord."

After more paragraphs of exquisite language from the Episcopal Book of Common Prayer, the priest came to the prescribed questions:

"Marie, will you have this man to be your husband; to live together in the covenant of marriage? Will you love him, comfort him, honor and keep him, in sickness and in health, and, forsaking all others, be faithful to him as long as you both shall live?"

"I will."

"Jack, will you have this woman to be your wife; to live together in the covenant of marriage? Will you love her, comfort her, honor and keep her, in sickness and in health, and, forsaking all others, be faithful to her as long as you both shall live?"

"I will."

"Will all of you witnessing these promises do all in your power to uphold these two persons in their marriage?"

"We will!" exclaimed Rebecca, Matt, Kory, Luke, Eleanor, Sid, and Jaakov.

The brief ceremony continued through the reading of scripture, the passing of the peace among those present — all of them members of Rebekka Yahalomin — and, finally, the celebration of Holy Eucharist, the couple kneeling at the altar and taking the bread and wine before the others.

All participated in accepting the bread and wine except for the unbaptized participant, the observant Jewish member, Jaakov Adelman.

Adelman did, however, come smilingly forward to the altar, escorted by Rebecca and Kory, to receive the heartfelt blessing of the presiding minister.

And it was over.

Marie and Jack, wife and husband, blissfully held hands while they thanked the priest and the musician. When all hands had been shaken and all hugs delivered, Sid Belton cleared his throat noisily, and all turned to him in response to this by-now familiar signal. He turned to the newlyweds, excitement in his demeanor and in his voice.

"Marie and Jack," he said, offering his most lopsided grin, "Jaakov and I have got a little weddin' gift for ya'. It's a two-minute walk from here, but you'll wanna see what we got for ya'. You're gonna like it … we promise."

Mystified, bride and groom willingly followed Sid and Jaakov out through the church's side entrance. On the sidewalk, the group turned away from the National Mall, several blocks to the south, and began the short walk to view their wedding gift.

The walk took longer than the two minutes Belton had forecast, given his own hobbled gait, but the afternoon was sunny and the temperature mild for a July day in Washington. Consequently, the slow-paced stroll was something all could enjoy in the lingering sense of having been part of a memorable and blessed event. Other than the two gift-givers, only Eleanor Chapel knew the purpose behind the short walk, although others were beginning to have their suspicions.

At length, the detectives stopped in front of an empty storefront, and Sid Belton, grinning proudly, pointed to a hand-lettered sign his wife had made before leaving New York, the sign having been taped to the storefront window by Jaakov Adelman:

Belton and Adelman Detective Agency, New York City
Campbell and McGriff, D.C. Agents

The couple stared at the sign, stupefied.

"We've paid the lease for a full year," announced Adelman, "and we've applied for all the licenses you'll need. We've also employed an experienced administrative assistant who'll be here every day, Monday through Friday. We've set up a payroll account for her, with funds for her salary and benefits in the bank and ready for distribution on the first of each month, also for a full year. In 12 months, we'll take a look at income and expenses to see if you're ready to be self-supporting."

"We don't expect ya' t' have that much business so quick," said Belton, "so we're all set t' give y' whatever financial help y' might need fer at least three years."

He paused and glanced at his wife.

"Oh," he added, "Eleanor wants me t' say that ya' shouldn't think this is just us bein' generous. We're not generous. We've wanted a presence in D.C. fer a long time. We jus' needed t' find a couple a' people that we could trust t' get things goin' here, an' t' do everything th' right way.

"An' we found 'em."

Eleanor Chapel stepped forward. She handed a packet to Marie.

"Here is all the paperwork we've completed for you," she said. "There are still a few things for you to do ... that we couldn't do for you ... but your assistant will be here tomorrow morning, and she has experience in all this.

"She's good. You'll like her."

With that, she handed a set of keys to Jack McGriff.

"Why don't you and Marie ask Jaakov to take you and everyone through your office spaces?" she suggested. "I know our England contingent will want to be able to picture you at work in your agency.

"We don't know when they'll be back here."

With that, McGriff turned and unlocked the door and, with an uncharacter-istic flourish, scooped his bride up in his arms and carried her over the thresh-old. Amid the joyous laughter, the members of Rebekka Yahalomin entered the office and were escorted through its rooms by Jaakov, while Sid and Eleanor, the Yahalomin "parents," relaxed on the comfortable sofa they had selected for the reception area.

When the group returned after their tour, Eleanor stood and said, "Marie and Jack, we've taken up enough of your post-wedding time.

"We're going to go back to the hotel and get out of our formal attire — although my own formal attire is almost the same as my casual attire — while you two go to your new home ... as a *family* ... for the first time. Penelope will be waiting."

She turned to Rebecca.

"Rebecca?" she said.

Rebecca, understanding immediately, bowed her head and prayed softly.

"Father, be present ... be present ...

"We ask that you place Yourself at the center, not only of this marriage, but of this business enterprise, as well... be present, please, in all that Marie and Jack undertake, both in their marriage and in their business, here in this office, here in this community, here in this city... please hold them in Your hands every hour... every day... every year of their lives together, joined as one in Your service.

"And now, Father, please go forth with us all to serve You and Your people... this we pray in the name of Your Son, Jesus Christ.

"Amen."

In the comfortable silence that followed Rebecca's benediction, no one seemed anxious to leave, all lingering in the warmth of the ceremony and of Sid and Jaakov's extraordinary wedding gift to the couple. But after several minutes, there was a murmured "Oh" from the groom.

Eyes turned to him.

"I just noticed that this phone's voicemail light is blinking. I didn't realize you'd gone so far as to set up phone service for us, detectives," he said.

"You're not gonna get much done ... or get much business," said Belton, "if ya' don't have phones that work. So, yeah ... we got yer phones set up.

"An' I'd say y' oughta see what that message is, Jack."

McGriff hesitated. His eyes shifted to his bride's.

She smiled and nodded.

"Just press the speaker-phone button, sweetheart," she suggested, "so we can all hear our first voicemail message in our office."

McGriff blushed crimson at the endearment — the word *sweetheart* — offered so naturally that it barely registered on most of those present. He sensed that no one else was giving the word the slightest notice.

I have a long way to go, he thought to himself.

He smiled, shook his head at his own awkwardness about such things, then pressed the "retrieve" and "speaker" buttons.

A deep male voice filled the room. It was a voice familiar to some.

"Jack and Marie ... this is Chief Horace Johnstone, D.C. police. You may remember ... I'm one of Sid Belton's many protégés ... worked under Sid when we were both with the NYPD. And you'll remember that I've also worked recently with you both, right here in D.C.

"I'm calling because we've got an unusually messy set of crimes we're trying to deal with, and I'm looking to get a private detective's take on all this ... I'm thinking we're not having much luck with our efforts to think outside the box ... and fresh eyes from outside might move us off square one. Our own detectives weren't exactly happy about the idea of going outside, but when I said it would be Sid Belton and his people, they said, 'Well ... okay ... we can live with that ...'

"Don't really want to say more than that over the phone.

"I'm leaving this message on Saturday, and Sid told me that Monday will be your first day in the office.

"So, if you can get organized quick enough, I'd like to ask one of you — Marie or Jack — to come over to my office midmorning Monday. If you both could come, that would be even better. And if Monday morning won't work, get in touch with my assistant and give us a better day and time for you. Thanks very much.

"Oh ... I understand you two are getting married tomorrow ... Sunday.

"My sincerest condolences to you, Marie."

Johnstone's hearty laughter at his own joke came through the speakerphone just as he clicked off.

"Hey," said Belton. "Y' got new business before you're even open. That's gotta be a new record."

McGriff looked at Marie.

"Marie," he said uncertainly, "should we sit down for a few minutes and get organized for our meeting tomorrow morning with Captain Johnstone?"

Marie stepped to her husband's side, took his hand, and looked up into his eyes. She smiled her beatific smile and shook her head.

"Husband," she said sweetly, "we're going to get up early tomorrow morning and talk about that. We're going to talk about that *tomorrow*.

"Tomorrow."

And then she turned and, pulling the groom behind her, walked out of their new office and onto the sidewalk. The last the group glimpsed of the couple was the image of Jack turning his head, grinning with newlywedded embarrassment, and waving happily at the wedding party.

The wedding party waved back.

And it was done.

~ End ~